THE ADVENTURES OF VIVIAN SHARPE VEGAN SUPERHERO

MARLA ROSE

ISBN: 1475084366
ISBN-13: 978-1475084368

Follow the Adventures of Vivian Sharpe, Vegan Superhero
at viviansharpe.com

DEDICATED TO
TRUE SUPERHEROES EVERYWHERE

ACKNOWLEDGEMENTS

I would like to thank John Beske, my husband, for everything. Just everything.

I would like to thank Justice Beske, my son, for inspiring me daily with his kindness, creativity, and unique vision.

I would like to thank Sandra Rose, my mom, for her sweet soul.

I would like to thank everyone who read early drafts of Vivian Sharpe and *still* encouraged me: Jane Zawadowski, Lisa Joy Rosing and Oryna Hrushetsky-Schiffman.

I would like to thank Rae Sikora for being one of Vivian Sharpe's first champions and for believing in this book and for being just about the best person I know.

I would like to thank Martin Rowe for letting me know how I could do it.

I would like to thank Alexandra Jones for finding what you found and still not thinking that I'm an idiot. Your generosity is so deeply appreciated.

I would like to thank Lorraine Murray for all of her dedicated editing skills and for caring as much as she does. I cannot thank you enough, friend.

I would like to thank my Chicago community of amazing activists and friends. Thank you for all you do.

Last, thank you to every one of you who are working to build a more compassionate world. You give me hope beyond what I can express.

A BOLD AWAKENING

The pig, a male, six-months-old and thus of age, identified as 4716, instinctively locked his legs, but was easily pushed through the chute into the building by the force of the ones behind him. Once there, he was forced into the opening of the building, then farther inside, where he was strapped by two quick, rough hands into metal cuffs that jerked him upside-down with the abruptness of a thunderclap. The sharp clanking of gears, the shrieks and the mechanical buzz of the motor pulsed in his already inflamed ears, and he twisted on the line, his body feeling like it was being pulled from his hooves, the bulk of his weight hanging below, swinging. He was moved down the assembly line, a pig in front of him and a pig behind him, and dozens more in front and behind them, all struggling against the cuffs, all in silhouettes, screaming. Steam rose from the floor and vapors from the stench burned the pig's eyes. He caught a silhouette of a standing two-legged figure as he swung side-to-side and the pig knew that this meant he was near the end of the line. Though he didn't know what that meant, it was at once terrifying and came as a small measure of relief.

Fewer than 100 miles away was a town called Center City, and in that town lived a 15-year-old girl named Vivian Sharpe. Vivian was a regular, normal girl, unremarkable by most measures except for the coppery red hair that set her apart. And for the fact that in May of her fifteenth year, she developed powers previously unknown to her overnight.

Vivian lived in the town where she was born, Center City, USA, the capital in the middle of a state that grows a lot of corn and wheat near the middle of the country. It was also frequently described as being "in the middle of nowhere." Although Center City was not an urban mecca, it did occasionally bustle, usually around Pioneer Days every fall, where one could learn how to make apple cider and cornhusk dolls, and the town was the only thing approaching urbanity for hours in each direction, in that it occasionally had traffic jams, graffiti-sprayed underpasses and random groups of teenagers eating French fries out of cups in the food court of Woodcreek Mall. The town also did have an independent and dingy coffee shop where one could sip espressos (not "expressos", the proprietor insisted) and read about the Surrealists if he or she were so inclined. Vivian did not set foot into this particular coffee shop until her fifteenth year.

Things were very quiet in this town, which the parents universally professed to love and their children, once they became teenagers at least, usually compensated with an equal measure of loathing. The main excitement Center City generated was due to its status as a state capital. If one were craving a more urban experience, that person would have to go four hours away to New Dublin, a dynamic city of four million, which was originally little more than a murky wetland and prairie landscape originally settled by Irish laborers.

Vivian's family was more esteemed and well known than most in town because her mother, Sally Sharpe, owned a popular beauty salon, *Look Sharpe!* It was considered the only place in Center City for an upscale salon treatment, and anyone who could afford it, from teenage girls who'd been scrupulously saving their babysitting earnings to Governor Driscoll's wife, had their hair, nails and eyebrows done at *Look Sharpe!* Mrs. Sharpe prided herself on hiring only the most respected stylists available and kept herself knowledgeable of the latest hair trends in New York, Los Angeles and New Dublin. Sally Sharpe was the first female president of the Center City Merchant Association, and while some considered her a little blunt and aloof, many townspeople also had a lot of admiration for her confidence and style. Sally Sharpe, formerly Wheeler, was raised by a single mother, Alma Wheeler, in Center City, abandoned by her father shortly after her fifth birthday at a time when single parent households were very uncommon, so any lack of personal warmth on her part was usually attributed to that. As she grew up, Sally Sharpe rarely heard her father mentioned, except occasionally through a hushed voice as the teachers whispered at school or people gossiped a few pews behind her at church, but over time, her father receded until he virtually disappeared from the collective memory. Alma Wheeler worked two jobs and died of a heart attack while mopping at the hospital when her daughter was still in college. Alma instilled in her daughter an independent spirit, one that insisted that if anything important was to get done, the only one she could trust to do it was herself.

Vivian's father, Roosevelt Sharpe, was a respected state historian, whose work emphasized Center City and its mother county of Good Earth. He wrote heavily footnoted, dry books very few people read (tomes such as *And The Earth Turned To Dust: A 19ᵗʰ Century Drought in Good Earth County Told Through Correspondences* and *From Sod to Wood: Building Materials of a Prairie Town's Earliest Settlers*) and spent a lot of time poring over old documents in the Center City Historical Society, of which he was director. Mr. Sharpe was tall and reedy, favored tweed suits and, for as long as Vivian could remember, had had prematurely silver hair, exploding in wild tufts all over his head like the clichéd absent-minded professor; her mother, a marked contrast with her smooth chestnut hair and manicured nails, had long since given up on trying to tame it.

Rounding out the family was Vivian's little sister, Millie, who was named after an early Center City settler, Mildred Gooch, a woman famous for the moonshine she made in her bathtub and for the husband who died under strange circumstances, drowned in six inches of Mrs. Gooch's whiskey in her notorious bathtub. Millie was six years old, nine years younger than Vivian, free-spirited and whimsical where Vivian had always had a more serious, cautious nature. Vivian was very grateful throughout her life that her father's obsession with local lore didn't influence her name, or she might have been named after Miss Hortense Doostrich, a contemporary of Mrs. Gooch, who ran a popular brothel visited by Jesse James and his gang. Instead, she was named after Vivien Leigh, her mother's favorite actress.

Vivian maintained a 3.7 grade point average with the occasional blip in either direction, had a dozen or so people she considered friends, fewer with whom she was close. She was of medium height with greenish-grey eyes and a dimple on her left cheek that she was always rather proud of despite her vague feeling that vanity was wrong.

In her fifteenth year, just a month or two before everything happened, Vivian's life couldn't have been more normal. She could usually be found in bed no later than 10 o'clock each evening, reading a book or watching black-and-white episodes of *The Twilight Zone* or *Alfred Hitchcock Presents* on the little television across from her bed. Aside from Bobby Hendrickson, her endearingly clumsy paramour of three weeks in the fifth grade with the bucked teeth she adored, Vivian had never had a boyfriend, but that only fueled her naïvely romantic spirit. She liked to read about Sir

Lancelot, imagining herself as Guinevere, and, when she wasn't doing her schoolwork or helping care for her sister, Vivian wanted nothing more than to just lock herself away in her bedroom, one still filled with the comforting soft pastel yellows and pinks and the starched off-white curtains of her childhood, lying on her stomach on her soft bed, legs bent at the knees, ankles crossed, daydreaming about knights and castles and dragons and being freed from a tower. Mrs. Sharpe occasionally characterized her daughter as being "an escapist" while her father described Vivian more charitably as being "a dreamy child." Several years ago, Vivian overheard her mother laughingly remark on a telephone conversation that all the fire in her daughter went straight to her hair, the copper-red that set her apart, and that, temperamentally, she was the opposite of the stereotype of a redhead: quiet, demure, introverted. This deeply hurt Vivian's feelings at the time, but she had to agree. She was happiest tucked away in her room with a book and her thoughts, quietness around her, locked away as if in a tower herself.

Everything changed one May day in 1995, when Vivian's life was plunged into chaos and shaken like a snow globe in an earthquake, all because of a sandwich. Nothing seemed too out of the ordinary on that day, the first Saturday of the month, except that it was a beautiful day after a typically long and brutal winter. The first mild, sunny day in months, it drew people out of their homes and gave the townspeople a little uncharacteristic festiveness as they rolled down their car windows and turned up the music a little louder than was typically considered polite. That afternoon, there was a party at Vivian's friend's house and she ate a ham sandwich on rye bread with lettuce, American cheese, a little mustard and mayonnaise. Nothing noteworthy occurred except that Jed and Allison had an argument and broke up for the fourth or fifth time, and most people there didn't consider that to be too noteworthy, not even Jed or Allison.

When she got home that night, Vivian felt kind of woozy and lurchy, like how she'd felt after a particularly nauseating ride on a Tilt-A-Whirl at the state fair. She took a couple of aspirin and gulped down a cup of water, falling asleep as soon as she went to bed, which was unusual for her as she'd usually have to read for an hour before she got sleepy. She had so many haunting and peculiar fragments of dreams, though, that it felt as if she weren't sleeping at all. It was closer to being trapped in a horror movie that she

10

couldn't escape. There was a lot of noise in these dreams and Vivian could hear the sounds of cries and shrieks and people shouting, their voices all around her at times and distant at others. There were gates slamming shut, loud motors, the jaw-clenching sound of metal against metal, chainsaws, clanking gears, terrified shrieks. She felt chilled to the bone and alone, yet claustrophobic, clammy and surrounded all at the same time.

There was one vision, though, that stuck with Vivian and returned throughout the dream: a pair of the softest brown eyes with thick pale pink lashes curled down, unblinking, brimming with an immeasurable sadness and incomprehension that seared through her. At the same time, she recognized them as hers, even though those eyes weren't quite human, even though she knew that her own eyes were different.

Twisting in a dream that seemed to stretch on for days, Vivian woke finally, her heart racing but her limbs leaden. Lying still and breathing hard, trying to shake off the last fleeting fragments of the dream that moments ago had held her captive, she opened her eyes, adjusting them to the darkened but familiar shapes of her bedroom. She easily identified her dresser, closet door, her desk and chair, but she also noticed something else: a large form in her chair, a kind of a lumpy mass glinting off the moonlight, something she couldn't decipher. Sitting up, squinting at what she was sure was some trick of light – it might be a laundry bag, she reasoned – she leaned over, switching on her bedside lamp. Light flooded her room, momentarily blinding her, but as she blinked, her eyes adjusted. Now Vivian could plainly see that in front of her was a large cross-legged pale pink pig, gently levitating over her desk chair as though that were perfectly normal.

Blinking once, twice, a dozen times, Vivian stared dumbly with mouth agape as the pig smiled sweetly at her, as if waiting politely for her to speak. The most she could muster under the circumstances was a choking cough.

When it became unavoidably clear that he would have to initiate the conversation, the pig chuckled and spoke to her with a hearty, melodic voice. "Well, I'll take that as a hello. Hello back to you, Vivian Sharpe. Nice to meet you – do you think I could call you Viv? It seems so much less formal."

Vivian was unresponsive as the gift of speech presented a whole new issue to process, but the pig continued, unfazed.

"Yes, I think that unless you indicate otherwise, I shall call you Viv. My name is Tolstoy. I rather like my name; it came to me very recently, but it feels quite natural. *Tol*-stoy. Tol-*stoy*. Tolstoy."

Vivian realized that as he spoke, his mouth did not move. She heard his words inside her head as though they were her own thoughts, amplified. The pig looked at Vivian, waiting patiently for a response, and then looked around the room, as though searching for an ice-breaker. Finding none, he smiled and spoke again.

"I'm not exactly an expert yet in the art of conversation, so some guidance from you would be most appreciated if you feel so inclined. I understand that when two humans meet, you often shake hands, so perhaps we should have started that way, but it would have been an empty gesture. You wouldn't be able to feel my hoof as I have no actual form. Maybe I'll just float over to you so you can see me better and you won't have to strain your eyes so much." He glided over to where Vivian remained utterly still in her bed, immobilized not so much with fear but complete shock. Vivian stared wide-eyed at the pig, unsure of what else one should do in this situation.

"Ah, there, this is nice... Now we're getting somewhere," Tolstoy continued, crossing his thick legs rather daintily as he hovered over the edge of her bed, looking at her. "Oh, yes, I knew we'd be fast friends. I knew the moment I saw you, well, I said to myself − because I was the only one around − yes, that Vivian Sharpe and you are really going to get on well. I believe that you can feel this, too."

Now sitting fully upright, Vivian nodded at him, mute though she was. As absurd as it seemed at the time, it did seem like she could accept the presence of this hovering pig. Something about him struck a familiar chord with her.

"Don't be concerned. It's been quite a confusing few minutes, I would imagine, so I certainly don't mind if you don't feel like talking much. I'll just be sitting here − if you can call it sitting, I guess floating is more technically accurate − entertaining myself with my own thoughts, so whenever you can think of something you want to say, feel free to say it. Yesiree, any time you're ready, here I am." He gazed out the window, arms folded across his belly. "I'm not in a hurry."

Vivian remained sitting upright, still blinking at him, as though if she blinked hard enough, he'd disappear, this pig with the hearty voice. Thinking of her situation, having a conversation with a pig in the middle of the night, Vivian had to let out a trickling laugh. Tolstoy, who had begun to look a little concerned, momentarily startled at the sound of her laugh and his face lit up.

"I'm glad that you can see the humor in this, Viv. I know that my visit has been abrupt and even shocking, but you've been such a good sport about it. I knew you would be."

Something about the way that he said that, and the fact that she knew somehow that she had nothing to fear, helped her ease out of her state of shock, and thoughts began shuffling back in.

"So..." Vivian spoke for the first time, her voice barely a croak, "so, you're a pig, right?"

Most would consider this to be a not very impressive start, but Tolstoy responded as though she'd just made a very astute observation.

"Oh, quite right." Then Tolstoy paused, furrowing his brow, hoof to his head. "Well, though, now that I think about it, I'm not quite sure. It's complex. I mean, I was once a pig biologically speaking, though my life as one was pretty narrow. Very constrained. Now I think I'm more of a..."

"Ghost? Are you a pig ghost? Oh, please, don't say yes," Vivian said, eyes wide.

"Ghost? Oh no, that's not it. I'm quite certain I'm not a ghost. Definitely not. Let's see – spirit. Yes, spirit... that feels right. I know the difference may seem like I'm quibbling, but, really, 'ghost' has such a negative connotation. Ghosts creep up on people but are actually sort of vaporous and inconsequential. That's not me," he said, stretching his front legs over his head casually. "If others not of the physical realm want to spend their days and nights wailing and rattling chains in musty old boarded up houses, that's their business, but it's certainly not how I choose to spend my time. Then again, I think that all of that business is mostly imaginary. I have no proof of this yet, though."

"So you're a pig spirit?" Vivian asked, no less confused.

"If I must be labeled, then, yes, one could say spirit. 'Spirit' meaning what's left once we depart the mortal plane, as you humans say. One's essence: the specific, unique parts that make up one's being. Yes, that's the closest to what I am. I'm a pig spirit."

"Oh."

"Or..." he started thoughtfully.

"Yes?"

"I could be thought of as simply a spirit like any other spirit."

13

Vivian coughed a little. "Simply a spirit," she repeated in a murmur.

"Yes. Or, if you want to be even more generous and expansive, I am just a manifestation of one aspect of the whole spirit we embody. Regardless, you can just call me Tolstoy and not care too much as to whether I'm a pig or a ghost or a spirit or a leprechaun."

"But you're not a leprechaun, right?"

"A pig leprechaun?" he said incredulously. "Whoever heard of that? No, I'm not."

She squinted at him in a way she hoped wasn't impolite but seemed unavoidable. "And, how – why – are you here? I'm sorry," Vivian said, flustered, "this has never happened to me before."

"I'm quite sure of that, Viv. No need to apologize. This is a quite unusual situation to be sure. As to why I'm here, well, it's really anyone's guess. I suppose you can say that I'm here because I am needed. Yes," he said, smiling warmly and hugging his front legs across his pink chest, "I'm quite satisfied with that answer."

"Okay..." she said, her grasp on understanding still tentative, but deepening. "But who needs you? Do I need you?"

"Oh, yes, you need me, and I need you," he said, gesturing toward her. "What's more, the world needs *us*, together. That's the point of this, Viv. We're partners, you see, one without the other would be like a needle without a thread. A bicycle without wheels. It's that we..." Tolstoy stopped abruptly, noticing the sheer bewilderment creep back onto Vivian's face. "Well, I see that I'm getting ahead of myself again. Forgive me for this, but it's just because I'm so hopeful, and I've never felt that way before."

A flash of déjà vu washed over Vivian as he spoke his last few words, his eyes finally taking on a familiar quality she recognized with a jolt.

"You..." she found herself gasping, shaking off the last vestiges of sleep as she leaned forward and pointed at Tolstoy, "you were in my dream. In that awful dream with all the shrieking and machines...I saw you there. That was you; I know it was. I saw your eyes."

The memory of what Vivian felt in the dream poured back into her mind, swirling around her body like a sandstorm.

"Was that you?" she whispered as Tolstoy looked away for the first time, gazing out her bedroom window with a distant look. "Was that *you*?"

Quite a few moments passed before Tolstoy spoke, his voice quiet now. "Yes, that was me. It could have been any of us, though. In front of me. Behind me. Everywhere I looked. There was no escape from the noise, the smell, the panic, despair. And we were all alone, struggling to survive, struggling to even breathe. So the eyes you saw could have been any of ours."

Vivian was speechless, tears filling her eyes, stinging from the physical memory of the dream.

Tolstoy turned to look at her. "We knew we weren't born for that life, that no one would be born for that life, but it was all we knew."

"I don't understand," she sobbed, heat filling her chest, her throat.

"I know. I didn't understand either. None of us did. Every day there'd be screaming and pushing all around me but there was nowhere to go. Most of us had pneumonia from the stench; we had swollen, aching joints from living on concrete day and night. But worse than anything was that it was unending: every moment of every day was the same degree of torture as the next until the day the men came and packed us in the truck. Then," he said quietly, "it became terrifying."

"But how? How could this happen?" was all she could manage, hot tears streaming down her face. "Who did this?"

"It is horrible, isn't it," Tolstoy said, the familiar softness filling his eyes.

"But I don't understand," Vivian nearly shouted, getting angry. "Who is doing this? Why are they doing it? How can they get away with it?"

Tolstoy took a deep breath and was silent for a few moments, composing himself. Calmly, he said, "Think for a moment about what you did this afternoon."

"What?"

"What did you do earlier this afternoon before you arrived back at your home?

Vivian shrugged. "My friend had a party. A bunch of us hung out. What does that…"

"Did you eat anything?"

She nodded slowly. "Yes."

"What did you eat?"

"I don't know…I had a pop and a sandwich and some potato chips. Why do you ask?"

"And what kind of sandwich did you eat?"

"Well," Vivian said, thinking, "um, roast beef. No, wait, it wasn't roast beef..." She struggled with trying to remember.

"I believe it is called a 'ham' sandwich," he said, gently.

"Oh, my gosh, yes! How did you..." she began to ask when the appalling realization washed over her, settling into a burning coal in the pit of her stomach. "Oh, my God – that – it – was *you*, wasn't it?"

She looked at Tolstoy and he looked back at her with a calm, peaceful look upon his face. There was no need to affirm or say a word; the little hairs on Vivian's arms stood up, poking painfully against her pajama sleeves. They stared at each other wordlessly until Vivian finally collapsed forward in a heap.

"But – I – no one told me. Oh, god, I feel sick. I feel sick," she gasped, feeling like she was moments away from throwing up. "Oh, my god." She darted from her room and ran to the bathroom, her hand over her mouth, making it just in time. She brushed her teeth shakily, wondering if he'd be gone now. He was still waiting for her as she'd left him, a sympathetic look on his face.

"So you're still here," she said as she crawled back into bed.

"I'm still here."

"I thought maybe throwing up would..."

"Right. Nope. I'm not going anywhere."

"This is awkward."

The pig cocked his head at her.

Vivian tore at the stray tissue she'd grabbed, not remember when or where. "But I didn't know a thing, Tolstoy. I – I didn't know," she trailed off, clenching her blanket. She couldn't meet his eyes. "I never thought about it."

"I know you didn't, Viv. I don't blame you. But now you know."

Vivian sighed, wiping at her tears. "Oh, I wish I didn't know, Tolstoy." He didn't say a word, just looked at Vivian with that same steady, calm gaze until she finally looked back at him. "I wish I'd never felt this way inside," she moaned.

"What do you mean?"

"I mean how horrible I feel. I'll never be able to forget this feeling. I know it."

They sat silently for some time, the weight of everything seeming to push the air out of the room. Vivian's bedroom, its girlish yellow walls and ruffled lampshades, suddenly felt extremely quaint and frilly, a parody of adolescent innocence.

"I know I'll never go back to who I was," she uttered finally, as though to herself, "I wish I could not know. I wish I could go back to before I went to sleep."

Tolstoy sat quietly as Vivian spoke, looking at her with a tenderness that cut through her. "Do you really?" he asked.

"Yes," she said, arms still clenched around her stomach. "No. Oh, I'm not sure. I don't know anything, that's one thing that's clear to me. Who am I if I'm not who I was before I went to bed?"

"Why, you're Vivian Sharpe." Tolstoy said this as though it were the most obvious thing to see.

"Yes, I know that, but, no, I'm not."

"How are you not Vivian Sharpe anymore?"

Vivian was silent as she thought. "Because I feel different."

"How so?"

"I just don't really recognize myself right now. I just feel so weird in my body, like I'm a stranger or something."

"How do you mean?"

"It's weird. I mean, it's like there's a giant hole blown through me. Like there used to be something in this," she said, pointing to her chest, "that I woke up to every day, that was familiar, that was me. Sitting here, I could just as well be a complete stranger. I guess I'm just saying that I don't feel like me anymore."

"Who do you feel like if not yourself?" Tolstoy asked.

"I have no idea. Maybe this is what it feels like to be a new me."

Tolstoy thought to himself and blinked at her a few times. "I think that you're on the right track. You see, here's my analogy: do you think a butterfly remembers what it felt like to be a caterpillar?"

Vivian considered this for a moment, forgetting once again the strangeness of the situation. "I would think that some part of her would always be a caterpillar, because that's where she began. She's still a caterpillar, but now she's got wings. Then again, having wings will have to have changed her, at least her perspective."

Tolstoy nodded. "That's an apt analogy for you, I think. You're Viv with wings."

"I am?" she asked, half-tempted to look back at her shoulders. It wouldn't have shocked Vivian if she had indeed sprouted wings with how this evening was going.

Tolstoy smiled, reading her thoughts. "Don't worry, I'm speaking metaphorically, but, yes, I believe you *do* have wings. You'll always be Vivian Sharpe because that's your essence, but as you grow and evolve, new dimensions will be refined and unnecessary parts will be stripped away. Sort of like a sculpture being carved from a slab of marble. A work in progress, as we should all be."

Something about Tolstoy and the way she felt around him that made Vivian feel like he was an old friend. His eyes sparkled in a way that reminded her of laughter. She found herself strangely encouraged by what he had to say, though much of it confused her. "So why did you come to me?" she asked.

"I come to you? No, Viv, we met halfway. I could only meet you because you invited me in. There was a little window inside you that must have opened a crack, even though you didn't recognize it yourself. Some little seedling of awareness. I couldn't come in unless you invited me – and this awareness – to float inside. As to *why* I'm here, well, that will come for both of us when the time is right." Tolstoy sat for a moment, looking at Vivian, his warm eyes glistening. "Well, it's probably been quite a night for you. How are you feeling now, Viv?"

She was silent for a moment. "Gosh, I don't know. I feel lots of things. Scared. Angry. Kind of sick. Sad. I guess a little lost. Confused. A little excited."

"Well," said Tolstoy, winking at her, "that's a good place to start. I'll see you soon, Viv. It was so nice to meet you."

He looked as if he wanted to hug her. She leaned away from him forcefully.

"That's it?" Vivian asked incredulously.

"What do you mean?"

"You come in here, turn my life upside-down and leave? That's so unfair. What am I supposed to do from here?"

An enigmatic smile crept upon his face as he began fading out in wavy thin lines, some sparks glinting around him as he faded.

"Observe," he said peacefully, before he finally disappeared from sight.

"Observe? Observe? What am I supposed to observe? Tolstoy!" she reached into the empty space where he once floated, fingers raking through the air.

At once there was a quick knocking on her door. Her heart lifted – was it Tolstoy again, coming through the door this time?

18

"Vivian – it's 2:30 in the morning...Get off the phone right now or I'm taking away your privileges," spoke her mother's tired, irritated voice through the door.

"I wasn't – oh, never mind. Goodnight, mother."

"Goodnight."

Vivian settled down into her bed, completely spent.

"Oh, and I saw the state of your bedroom earlier today. I want that room cleaned up tomorrow morning. It looks like a pigsty in there."

A GIRL NAMED WREN

The morning after Tolstoy's visit, Vivian woke questioning if it had really happened. Lying in bed, everything from the night before still quite vivid, she grasped for a suitable explanation other than the one she kept arriving at, the one that reasoned that she had simply lost her mind. How *could* it have been real? But Tolstoy's visit was so shockingly real that even after she'd resigned with herself that she had in fact dreamed the whole thing, Vivian found herself feeling that her explanation – that this was all just a dream – was less believable than her having been visited by a pig spirit. How could her dreams, not normally very vivid, have created a being like Tolstoy, have inspired emotions she'd never felt before? Vivian remembered every word of her conversation with Tolstoy, every gesture and feeling without any loss of detail or effect, and though it was certainly unusual, it wasn't dream-like.

In addition bringing her sanity into question, Vivian's time with Tolstoy revealed another unexpected result the next morning. As Vivian sat down to breakfast, still in a fog from the night before, her sister Millie humming a grating song from a kid's television show on the chair next to her, Mr. Sharpe set down what was known as his Sunday Morning Special in front of her: scrambled eggs and bacon, and two slices of toast with melting butter, staring up at her from the plate below. Vivian let out a gasp and clasped her hand to her mouth. Her throat clamped shut. Her pulse quickened. She looked at her father in horror, looked back at the plate, and let out a small shriek as she pushed out from the table and ran to her room as fast as she could, slamming the door behind her. Vivian lay on her unmade bed, curled in a ball, her heart beating fast and loud against her chest.

"Honey," Mr. Sharpe said breathlessly moments later as he knocked quickly on her door, "are you okay? Can I come in?" Vivian could hear her mother's voice in the background, alarmed and confused.

"All right. I'm okay. Come on in." Vivian took in a deep breath to try to sound normal.

Mrs. Sharpe pushed past Mr. Sharpe as the door opened.

"Are you sick?" she asked as she rushed past him to Vivian, the back of her hand coming to rest on her daughter's forehead. "I heard that the flu was going around."

"No. I'm not sick. I just don't feel like eating, I guess."

Mrs. Sharpe narrowed her eyes at Vivian, the way she did when she didn't trust what someone was telling her.

"Well, you don't feel warm. You'd better stay in bed just to make sure, though. I don't want to nurse this whole family through the flu. I don't have that kind of time."

Vivian rolled her eyes. "I'm not sick, Mom."

Mrs. Sharpe turned over her shoulder and shot a look at her husband that made him leave the room in a hurry. Vivian's mother excelled at that sort of thing, getting what she wanted with just a small glance or gesture.

"Shut the door, please, Roosevelt," she said as Millie could be heard running up the steps.

As soon as the door shut behind him, Mrs. Sharpe sat down on the bed, lowered her voice, looked Vivian square in the eye and asked solemnly, in a this-is-just-between-you-and-me kind of way, "Vivian, is it that time of, you know..." her voice trailing off.

Vivian's cheeks burned bright and hot as she looked away, "No," she said, rather sharply. "I just don't feel like eating this morning."

Mrs. Sharpe continued cheerily. "Because if it is, it's all right to tell me. That's the sort of thing mothers and daughters can talk about. There's nothing to be embarrassed about, you know."

"Mom..."

"Every girl goes through this, Vivian. It's perfectly normal. If you don't feel well, I have some painkillers I could give you."

"No, Mom, it's not *that*, okay?" Vivian whined, sighing as she slumped down. "Can I be left alone for a while? Maybe I will go back to bed."

Mrs. Sharpe looked at Vivian again, still unconvinced and a little suspicious, it seemed.

"Well," she said, drawing out the word for effect, "you do look a little pale. I'll have your father put your breakfast in the refrigerator if you want to eat it later. Okay?"

"All right, Mom," Vivian said as sweetly as she could manage so her mother would finally leave. The thought of it made her stomach lurch again, but she kept smiling wanly, which was the best she could manage.

"And you're sure nothing's the matter?" Mrs. Sharpe asked as she stood.

"Yeah. I'm just tired or something. I slept funny last night."

Mrs. Sharpe kissed Vivian's forehead and stood to leave.

"I'm surprised you slept at all. You shouldn't have stayed up so late on the phone. We're going to have to nip that one in the bud, dear heart, or those phone privileges will be reconsidered."

Vivian nodded her head dutifully, her eyes cast down. Mrs. Sharpe took a long look at her again and, finally satisfied, smoothed her skirt as she turned to leave. Vivian felt a little sick with the confirmation that she hadn't dreamed everything.

"Get some sleep," Mrs. Sharpe said as she shut the door behind her. Vivian didn't eat the breakfast her father prepared that morning, or any other day. In fact, the smell or even mention of meat completely sickened her. Other things, like milk and eggs, had a similar effect; she didn't know why for certain, but she sensed that it had something to do with Tolstoy's. Just seeing someone eat an ice cream cone, something she had done just days before without a second thought, made her stomach take an unpleasant little dive.

But Vivian went on as though nothing were different, eating lots of peanut butter and jelly sandwiches while enduring the withering glances of her mother and confusion of her father, as though she were an alien with bizarre habits who had suddenly assumed the body of their daughter.

Vivian couldn't blame them, because she felt like an alien herself. Not only did Tolstoy leave her wondering whether he'd actually visited or if she'd merely been responding to a particularly vivid dream, but Vivian had a new sense of awareness she had no idea how to live with. She worried about the squirrels who darted across the street as cars raced past. She wondered why the people couldn't drive a little more carefully. She worried if the cats she saw on the construction site on her walk to school had anyone who cared for them or their kittens. She felt as protective as a mother bird of the nest of baby robins in the Sharpe's backyard, something she would have scarcely even noticed days before. As abruptly as this consciousness appeared in her, it also entered completely and became second nature, penetrating all areas of her life as though it'd always been there.

On a Wednesday about a week and a half after Tolstoy's visit, Vivian was walking down the hall to her French class when she suddenly heard the tinkling of bells amid the slamming lockers and loud voices. She recognized the sound from somewhere – from inside the school – but she couldn't place where. The bells got more distinct and the other sounds receded into the background. She followed the sound down the steps to the first floor, to the Student Activities bulletin board, something she had never even paused at before. She stood in the busy hallway and the bells reached a crescendo, then stopped.

The Student Activities board was a messy, wide piece of cork, several layers deep with dozens of flyers, most outdated, ripped and weathered. Her eyes passed over the chess club tournament notices and the ancient school spirit days schedule until they revealed what she didn't know she was looking for: a simple, hand-drawn yellow flyer with a cartoonish sketch of a talking ear of corn that said in flowery purple letters:

"Hey, you! Did you ever wonder why true peace eludes you? Maybe it's because of what's on your plate. If you're interested in clean, healthy food and creating a compassionate lifestyle, check out the Center City High Vegetarian Club. Every Wednesday, 3:45, Room 202."

At the bottom of the page, someone had scrawled in red marker: *A.K.A., Freaky Tofu Eatin' Hippy Sprout Club!!!* Vivian smiled ruefully to herself, thinking that she'd never had tofu and she thought sprouts were disgusting. Maybe she wasn't a real vegetarian. She found herself scribbling down the room number on the back cover of her French notebook, determined to find out if that label applied to her. She made it through the rest of her classes with butterflies darting around in her stomach.

Finally, the last bell rang and Vivian sat in the student lounge, drinking a juice as she debated whether to actually go to room 202 or not. She was absent-mindedly doodling pictures of levitating pigs in her notebook, thoughts somersaulting around in her head, when a familiar voice startled her from behind, and a cool, dry hand suddenly covered her eyes.

"So now you're drawing pictures of floating pigs? You're a weirdo, Viv."

Vivian wheeled around, turning to face Kendra Brentwood, whom she'd known since they were in Brownies together in the second grade. In the years between, Kendra had evolved from a gangly, hair-sucking, freckled kid into a tall, athletic and popular girl with strawberry blonde hair. Despite their different placement in the social stratosphere of Center City High, they remained friendly, if not particularly involved in one another's lives. Kendra grabbed the chair next to Vivian and sat down.

"Oh, this. Yeah," Vivian said, covering the picture of Tolstoy with her hand as she flipped the cover over it, "I'm just trying to waste a little time. I've got somewhere to be at 3: 45."

"Where?" Kendra asked, her eyes widening. "Are you going to try out for the pom pom squad's open spot? You know I'm on that, right? That's the first step to being a full-fledged cheerleader. I could probably help you get in if you don't mess up bad or anything."

"No, I..."

"Oh, oh, I know." Kendra said, holding up her hand. "You're going to try out for next year's spirit squad. It's probably best to start out with that anyway. That's what I did. It's not too late for you. That way you can learn..."

"No, Kendra. I'm not trying out for either squad."

"Then, what?" she asked, then quickly gasped and clasped her hand around her mouth. "Oh my God, Viv, you're not going to an after-school club, like, the computer or math club or anything like that, are you? Geeky stuff? We're almost juniors. You've got to learn this, Viv or it will be too late."

"No, Kendra, it's not math or computer club," Vivian said, sighing, as she turned in her chair to look at the clock. "I'm, you know, going to go to another meeting."

"Which one?" Kendra asked, drumming her fingers on the table. "Tell me. There are only a few that are okay."

Vivian sighed. "Kendra, I'm not sure why you care."

"Why do *you* care if I care?"

"I don't; it's not a big deal." Vivian turned to look at the clock again.

"Then just tell me, already," Kendra said, swiveling Vivian's chair toward her. "Tell me."

"Fine," Vivian said, rolling her eyes with futility, mumbling. "It's just a vegetarian club meeting."

"What? Veterinarian...?"

"Vegetarian club."

"Vegetarian? Oh my god, no, you can't," she said, grabbing Vivian's arm emphatically, almost yanking her off her chair in the process. "That's way worse than chess. No, I know something about this. Listen to me. Do you know what they do to people there?"

"No. What?"

"Well, I don't know either," said Kendra, "but I think it's run by that weird girl, Wren Summer. The one who looks like she raided someone's closet from, like, 1968. I saw her putting up flyers for it once." She lowered her voice, eyes scanning the room. "I think she might be a witch or into voodoo or something. She creeps me out. In fact, she creeps everyone out."

Vivian shrugged, collecting her thoughts.

"Anyway, I don't think she has a single friend. Not even the dweebs or losers are that desperate. You don't want to be associated with that, do you?"

Vivian thought for a moment. Wren was a girl she passed in the hall, but she'd never had a conversation with her. Wren was a rare newcomer in the Center City school system. The gossip was that she had been taught at home until she was fifteen and had to be held back a year to catch up. No one seemed to know much about her, but whispers swirled around that her parents lived in the woods somewhere and that they were communists or hippies, living off the land. Or that her father was a famous artist, but that the whole family was crazy. Wren was in Vivian's freshman gym class one semester but managed to avoid the worst of it by arguing to Coach Shea that lacrosse and volleyball were competitive in nature, and she had an ethical and spiritual conflict with anything that pitted her against another being. The whole class all sat on the basketball court, exchanging looks and barely stifling giggles, while Coach Shea huffed and crossed her arms in front of her chest, asking Wren sarcastically what she wanted to do instead. Wren smiled serenely and said yoga with utter sincerity. Her bluff called, the gym coach couldn't do anything but oblige, though she made certain the rest of the class knew she thought Wren was a pain, rolling her eyes whenever she looked in her direction. Still, she got what she wanted. The other girls cursed her name every time they slumped pink and sweaty back into the locker room after class while Wren rolled up her yoga mat and got ready to go on with her day. Just to herself, though, Vivian had to admit that there was something about Wren – a natural grace, a luminosity, her obvious independent streak – that she couldn't help admiring in secrecy.

With her colorful, gauzy tops, long skirts, and dozens of rings, bracelets and anklets with bells dangling off them, Wren stood out in the monochromatic halls of Center City High. Whenever she was near, the delicate tinkling of bells and the scent of jasmine or lilac cut through the air. People inevitably snickered and stared as she passed, somehow never quite getting used to the novelty of the girl, but she always just walked by with a mysterious smile on her face, as if she was in on some private joke, gliding down the hall as though walking on a cloud, and her classmates parted like blades of grass as she passed. Another thing about Wren was that in a sea of faces that didn't vary much beyond ivory to light pink, her skin was decidedly caramel, and she had electric spirals of springy dark hair and almond-shaped eyes. Vivian thought that she was one of the most striking people she'd ever seen in person.

"It's no big deal, Kendra. I'm just going to check it out," she said, trying to look nonchalant as she glanced at the clock again. "I promise not to turn into a witch on you. I'm not making any promises about voodoo, though."

Kendra's eyes widened, gasping before she realized it was a joke. Then embarrassed, she said, "Very funny, Viv. You shouldn't even joke about that. It's one thing to *be* a vegetarian – it's another thing to, you know, hang out with them."

Vivian sighed.

Kendra pressed on, undeterred. "Really Viv, you'll thank me later. This school forgives no one, believe me." She lowered her voice. "Think about Sue Pentecost. She was so cool – best boyfriend, perfect hair, great clothes – and then she ate lunch with that dweeb who used to eat paste in grade school. Why on earth would she do that? One stupid lunch could have been forgiven, but then she went and did it again. That second lunch ruined her. Now she's not even cool enough to hang out with the paste-eater herself, not cool enough even for the Latin club."

She couldn't help but giggle at Kendra's earnestness. She covered her mouth.

Kendra put her hand on Vivian's shoulder. "Don't laugh. I'm looking out for your best interests, Viv, because you'll never have a chance to, you know, be popular if that Wren girl makes you a freak by association. You could certainly never be on the squad."

Vivian shrugged, rolling her eyes, finally courageous. "Maybe I don't want to be 'on the squad', Kendra."

"Don't be silly -- of course you do. Every girl does," she said, patting Vivian's arm. "You know I'm just saying this because I'm nice. Gotta go, though. We've got try-outs for the squad. Marci got kicked off because she couldn't get herself coordinated. We gave her a good chance, but it's still so, so sad. There are probably twenty girls trying out today. Meanwhile, Marci's calling me all the time because she's ready to slit her wrists. It's *exhausting*," she said as she dashed out of the room. "Don't forget what I said, Viv."

Vivian watched Kendra leave, feeling strangely indifferent to another person's opinion of her for perhaps the first time she could remember. For the first time in days, she felt unburdened and light. Instead of the gnawing uncertainty, a sense of clarity washed over her as she bounded up the stairs to room 202.

As she walked into the room, she thought at first that it was empty, and she was ready to turn and leave, but then Vivian saw Wren sitting by herself behind the teacher's desk, looking out the window as she snapped her fingers and hummed to herself. A silver anklet with bells jingled off her bare feet as she tapped them on the desk. Vivian blinked, standing there, as it sank in that this was the sound she had heard earlier, the one that led her to the bulletin board.

"Hey," Vivian said shyly, standing in the doorway, "is this the vegetarian club?"

Wren quickly turned toward her, her eyes bright and wide with surprise.

"Oh, my gosh, hi!" Wren said, jumping to her feet. "I didn't expect anyone, but, yes, this is the vegetarian club. Wow."

"Hi," Vivian said, looking around the room. "So, no one else is here yet?"

"Well, so far it's just the two of us, which is double what it's ever been. That's cool – in one day, the vegetarian club doubled attendance. Success! Come on in, Vivian."

"How did you know my name?" Vivian asked nervously, remembering Wren's reputation as the high priestess of Center City.

"It says so right there," Wren said, nodding toward the notebook Vivian clutched to her chest. "I've got good eyesight."

"Oh," she said, looking down and laughing with relief. "Yeah, that's me."

"So, come on in and let's hang out, Vivian," Wren said warmly.

"You can just call me Viv, by the way," she said, dropping her backpack on a desk and pulling a chair out. "Everyone does."

Wren perched on top of the desk across from Vivian, scrutinizing her in a friendly way.

"Your hair's so pretty." Wren finally said.

Vivian brushed a hand through it, embarrassed by Wren's directness. "Thanks."

"It looks like a sunset."

Vivian laughed a little in relief. "For a second I was afraid you were going to say that my hair looks like carrots. Carrot top. That's what everyone said when I was little."

"I like carrots too but what I immediately thought of was a sunset. Did you know that redheads need 20% more anesthesia to be knocked out? I read that somewhere or another. It's because you guys are more passionate. Oh, I can see I embarrassed you." After an awkward pause, Wren asked, "So, like, what do you want to talk about?"

"Umm, well, what do you usually do here?"

"Oh, usually I just sit at the desk and draw, but I left my sketch pad in my locker, and I can't remember the combination somehow today." Wren furrowed her eyebrows. "I guess I wasn't in the mood for drawing anyway. Astrologically I'm a bit messed up right now. Retrograde," she said, as though Vivian would certainly understand.

"Is that what you do here? Draw pictures?"

"Oh, no. Other times I write love letters."

"Really? Does he go to school here?"

"Who?"

"Your boyfriend?"

"No, I don't have a boyfriend. I write love letters to my husband," Wren said, nonchalantly.

"Wait," Vivian stammered, eyes widening. "You're *married?*"

"No, silly, not yet," Wren said, "but someday I might be. Or not. Anyway, I thought it'd be nice to write a bunch of love letters and give them to the person I might eventually marry, you know what I mean? Like completely romantic."

"So is that what you do here?" Vivian asked, confused.

"Oh, no," Wren said emphatically. "Sometimes I choreograph dances in my head, with music and everything. I just read a biography of Isadora Duncan so she's been on my mind lately. So I was choreographing when you walked in, but, anyway, who cares? It's so cool to meet another vegetarian. I thought that I was the only one."

"I don't get it," Vivian said, with some frustration she couldn't mask. "What is the point of the vegetarian club?"

"Well, I guess we get to decide that. There's never been more than just me, and I didn't want it to become a dictatorship. Anyway, I knew deep in my heart that some day another person would show up. This morning, actually, I was like not sure if I wanted to stay after school again just to sit here alone but then I reminded myself, 'Wren, today may be the day.' And look! Here you are, like magic," Wren said, snapping her fingers. "I've never met another vegetarian my age in town. So, when did you become one?"

"Um, about a week and a half ago, but I'm not sure that I am one officially."

"Oh, you didn't get an official registration packet in the mail yet?"

"No, I..." she stammered.

Just then, Wren started giggling.

"Oh," Vivian said, relieved and embarrassed. "You were joking about the packet, right?"

Wren nodded. "Anyway, you were saying about a week and a half ago..."

"Yeah, It just sort of happened one morning, and I didn't really have a lot to do with it. It's like I went to bed as a meat-eater and I woke up as a vegetarian," she said, feeling some comfort in describing things for the first time.

"Wow, with no warning?"

"Well, there was a little something that happened. It's complicated."

"That's so cool, though. You transformed overnight. Are your parents freaking out? I've heard that happens."

"A little. Not too bad, but they definitely know that something's up. They keep watching me, like I'm dangerous or something," Vivian said, with a nervous laugh. "Did your parents do that, too?"

"Oh, no, I was raised as a vegetarian. I've never had any of that dead stuff. My parents would love me no matter what I decided, of course, but they'd be disappointed if I ate meat, for sure."

"But aren't you curious about what meat tastes like?" Vivian asked, a little stunned to meet someone who'd never eaten meat.

"Oh, goddess, no. Ick! That's like asking someone who's never been exposed to radiation, 'Gee, aren't you curious about what a nuclear meltdown feels like?'" she said, laughing at her analogy. "Um, no."

"But your parents made you live as a vegetarian," Vivian said. "You didn't make that choice yourself."

Wren's eyes widened at this notion. "I did, Viv, and I make a choice every day as to whether I'm going to be a vegetarian. My parents can't control me. They know that I have my own mind. I'm very independent. Every meal of every day, I get to make a choice. Isn't that cool? This isn't some passive thing for me. So every day I get to say, 'Today I choose to be a vegetarian.' You know what I mean?"

"I guess I do," she said. This girl was making sense to her, Vivian realized with some nervousness.

"So…it's complicated?" Wren asked.

"What is?"

"Why you became vegetarian."

"Oh. Yeah," she said, hesitantly. "It's definitely weird. You'll probably freak out. Promise you won't."

Wren looked a little hurt at first, then solemn. "Of course I won't."

Vivian thought about it for a moment. Should she tell her about Tolstoy? Worried momentarily that Wren would think she was crazy, Vivian then realized this was a girl who wrote love letters to her imaginary future husband.

"Well, the thing is, I had a… visitor," Vivian said, looking down at her desk.

"A visitor," Wren repeated neutrally.

"Yes. A, um, pig came and talked to me one night," she said, trying to sound nonchalant.

"A pig," she repeated again. Vivian thought to herself that if Wren believed she was crazy, she'd just have to go into hiding or private school or something.

"Yes," Vivian said, avoiding Wren's unblinking gaze. "He was a floating pig spirit. Just appeared in my room and told me his story."

Wren smiled broadly in recognition. "Oh! You had an animal guide visit you. Gosh, you're so lucky. I've heard about that sort of thing. He traveled through realms of existence to meet you."

"Do you think?" Vivian asked, relieved.

"Of course," Wren said with absolute conviction. "Do you know how hard that must have been? So, like, what did your pig spirit say?"

"The spirit – his name's Tolstoy – he kind of talked to me but mostly I felt it."

"Felt what?" Wren asked, completely wide-eyed and captivated. "This is so cool."

"Well, I felt what he was talking about emotionally. I felt the pain and fear of him and these animals he lived with totally, like it was happening to me. I felt it in my body."

Wren leaned forward on the desk, speaking softly. "Whoa. You crossed the species border. True empathy. That's very cool."

"Do you think? I mean, I was starting to believe I was a freak," Vivian said, smiling for what felt like the first time in days.

"A freak?" Wren said, her expressive bright eyes flashing as she flung her arms up in exasperation. "That's what they called me when I wouldn't dissect a fetal pig in Mr. Roswell's biology class. I could hear the girls sitting behind me whispering, *Oh, the freak says she won't dissect.* Here they are, cutting apart a poor dead creature that they wrenched from its mother's womb, it's bobbing around in disgusting chemicals, and *I'm* the freak because I wouldn't participate. Man," she said, crossing her arms in front of her chest, "it shows you how screwed up our values are, you know?"

"Yeah, I think I know what you mean," Vivian said, slowly, recognition flickering inside. "But the thing is, I feel totally worried about every creature I see now. Every squirrel, every bird, every cat. I'd never really noticed them before, and now I can't stop thinking about them. Isn't that bizarre?"

"Well, I don't think so," Wren said, laughing, "but then again, I'm Center City's token weirdo, I guess. Of course I don't think caring about other beings is weird. In fact, I think the opposite is weird. Something opened up inside you. And you could just be making up for lost time."

"So," she asked, sighing, "am I always going to be like this then?"

Wren thought for a moment, hand cupping her chin. "I don't think so. I think what you need is an outlet for all your feelings."

"Such as?"

"Like when I get angry or sad or nervous about something, I draw, or dance, or write. Or whatever. Then I feel like I've released that feeling."

"I guess I don't know what my outlet is yet. Right now I'm just feeling kind of – um..."

"Blocked? Constipated?" Wren guessed.

Vivian nodded, a little embarrassed.

"No big deal. It'll flow out of you the way that it should soon."

Somehow, Vivian couldn't help being reassured by Wren and her total confidence. "I guess you're right. I need an outlet," Vivian agreed. "Oh, there was something else I was wondering about."

"Hmm."

"Milk and butter and cheese and eggs and all that stuff makes me sick now, too. Not just meat. I can't think about any of it without feeling like I want to throw up. Is that strange?"

Wren widened her eyes. "Are you kidding me?"

"No."

"That's awesome," Wren laughed. "It means that you're vegan, which is like a more productive vegetarian. I'm vegan too, but I usually just say vegetarian because people in Center City have a hard enough time wrapping their minds around that simple concept."

"So, I'm vegan. I never even heard that word before this conversation and now I *am* one. Is it safe?"

"Is what safe?"

"Being vegan."

Wren waved her hand in dismissal. "Oh, please. My mom has a ton of books we can give you to read on nutrition, but the short answer is yes, totally. Take a B12 tablet, eat a varied diet and you'll be great." Wren smiled gently at Vivian. "So, like, how do you like the vegetarian club so far?"

"It's pretty cool. It's been good for me to talk to you, actually. I feel like less of a weirdo, at least."

"You seem to worry about that sort of thing a lot," Wren said, smiling playfully. "Well, any time you want to feel like less of a weirdo, come talk to me. I'm sort of a benchmark for people for some reason. But who knows? One morning you might get out of bed and not even mind if people think you're weird," she said, her bracelets jangling as she pushed a springy spiral of hair away from her face. "You might even think it's a compliment, when you consider the source."

"So, not to be superficial or anything, but where do you get your jewelry? I never see that kind of stuff in town."

"Oh," Wren said, looking at her wrist as she twirled the bracelets around, "there's a great flea market twice a month in Prairieville that has all kinds of really cool cheap stuff, like twenty bracelets for two dollars. See this ring?" she said, holding up a finger. "It's antique, real lapis lazuli – also two dollars." Wren opened her eyes wide. "Hey, I just had a thought..."

"What?" Vivian asked, a little worried about what might follow.

"The next flea market is this Saturday. You should come with me."

Vivian got nervous. "I'm not sure if I can."

"Oh, come on," Wren said with a coaxing smile, "you'd have a good time."

Vivian thought about it. She was certain her mother wouldn't approve. Prairieville was only 20 minutes from Center City, but it was considered a pretty rough place. Lots of bikers lived there, and the *Center City Gazette's* police blotter would be pretty lacking if news from Prairieville weren't included.

"Come on. You know you want to go. If you ask really nice, I'll show you how to become exactly like me," she said, laughing as she twirled her bracelets teasingly.

"Um, I, uh, I don't know..."

"I can drive. I have a license. I can pick you up."

"You can drive already?"

"I am; I'm 17. I'm a year older than most sophomores. All those years of homeschooling and playing in the woods and making art were fun, but didn't amount to much as far as the school district here was concerned." She smiled, a little impishly. "So anyway, I may suck at math but I can drive. Take that, school board."

"I'm jealous."

"Don't be jealous. I'll show you what a stellar driver I am in person if you come with me to the flea market. Please? Come on. *Pretty please?*"

Vivian cracked a smile.

"All right," Wren said decisively as she clapped her hands together, "This is *so* it: you're coming with me. What time should I pick you up? It's usually best after 3:00 – that's when they start making the best deals. So I'll get you at around a quarter to three, okay? We're going to have a blast."

A FIRST GLIMPSE

Vivian managed to survive the rest of the week while brushing off her mother's attempts at grasping her daughter's new habits ("Another peanut butter and jelly sandwich?" she'd ask. "Haven't you gotten bored with those things?") with a patented blend of the teenaged vagueness and ennui Mrs. Sharpe had come to expect and at least reassured her that Vivian was still her daughter. Vivian also learned how to boil pasta that week, which was a great milestone, and she could always open a jar of marinara, and now that she mastered the can opener, beans were also available, improving her meal options greatly.

She did feel a lot better after meeting Wren, whose spirit seemed to give Vivian the lift she needed. Vivian was even inspired to buy a few sticks of coconut incense at Center City's lone hippie shop, Uncle Eddie's Emporium, the shop her father and most people in town referred to as "that place that sells those funny pipes," which also sold beaded curtains and the tie-dyed tapestries. Vivian didn't know why she felt compelled to go into Uncle Eddie's and buy the incense, and she didn't even know how to properly burn them, so they sat upon the desk in the pen holder Millie had made her for Valentine's Day.

When Saturday came, her mother was at the salon and Mr. Sharpe was with Millie at the library, looking up old county records for a new book he was researching on local fauna and flora. Vivian had just left a note about having gone shopping with a friend stuck to their refrigerator when she heard the car horn tapping outside her house. She sprang from the house and bounded into the little green hatchback covered with bumper stickers, anxious to fly under the radar of any nosy neighbors.

"Wow, Viv, you're in a hurry to get there, aren't you?" Wren said as she tossed a bunch of books and tapes off the passenger's seat onto the cluttered back seat. "I knew you would be."

"Yeah," Vivian said, looking over her shoulder as she buckled in, "this should be fun."

"This is so cool," Wren said, smiling. "I hope my favorite vendor – this lady who's got all these spooky old dolls – is there. I like to look at them and freak myself out, you know? I have to show them to you. There's one that I'm convinced is possessed – you need to see it. It looks like this mean girl in my history class: same eyes, same creepy expression. The actual real live girl is scarier, though, if you can believe that."

Vivian and Wren fell into a natural comfort in each other's company despite having just met, an ease in both conversation and silence. They spent the drive out to the flea market talking easily about their lives and families while Wren played strange music she said was *klezmer*, Jewish folk music. Wren was amazed that Vivian's mother owned *Looked Sharpe!*, though she'd never been there, and was equally intrigued by Mr. Sharpe's position with the historical society.

"My mom and I used to hang around there all the time when I was little. So your dad gets to be around all those amazing old clothes all day, the ones on the mannequins? How does he resist putting them on and playing dress-up?"

"Oh, my dad's not a 'dress-up' kind of guy," Vivian said, laughing at the image she'd conjured. "I'm pretty sure they smell like mothballs anyway. It's probably not so difficult for him to resist."

"Are you kidding? Between your mom's salon and your dad's job at the historical society, my parents would be playing in that stuff all day if they worked there," Wren said, laughing.

As they continued on their way to Prairieville, Vivian learned a few more details about Wren. Her mother was Jewish and African-American, and she ran an animal shelter and rehabilitation center in the countryside just outside of Center City, on their home property. She also was a musician in her spare time, and played violin in Green Earth County's only non-polka-playing ethnic band, the Prairie School Klezmer Ensemble, whose tape they were listening to in the car. Wren's father was a furniture maker and sculptor who used found objects, natural and recycled materials to build his designs. Wren had two older brothers, both of whom lived out of state. When she talked about her parents, she lit up with a natural radiance. Vivian imagined that Wren's family was full of the closeness, creativity and wonderful uniqueness that made her own seem as bland and boring as oatmeal in comparison.

As Wren and Vivian pulled up into the gravel parking lot of the market, following the directions of the bored-looking attendant with the orange flag, little pebbles scattered under their wheels and Vivian got a fluttery feeling in her chest, as though she were waiting for something to happen. Not necessarily a bad feeling, just one warning her to stay on guard, to be vigilant. She tried to dismiss it as they stepped out into the warm springtime air, breathing in the mix of car exhaust and popcorn, and for a moment or two she did. But then it returned, stronger than before.

Walking around the stalls, they squeezed between the rusted lamps, picture frames, and old dressers that jutted out all around them, careful not to knock anything over. Wren dug through drawers full of faded photographs of grim-faced Victorian-era men and women, postcards from around the world, tiny rusted buttons from long-ago political campaigns. Vivian took in all the strange little artifacts while Wren read to her from the back of a postcard from 1923, hoping aloud that Amelia made it back from her trip to Pennsylvania okay.

Vivian was distracted, though, trying to grasp her unsettling feeling of worry, which by then had morphed into a dull fear. While Wren was reading another postcard, Vivian found herself glancing back over toward the parking lot, where there were a couple of other vendors, and a man sitting on a folding chair and reading a newspaper next to a large, dented cardboard box. Something told her to go see what was in that box, and Vivian distractedly told Wren that she'd be back in a minute.

"No problem. I'll be around here somewhere. Oh, look – old Valentine's Day cards. Look at the two penguins. In love!" Wren said, holding up a card with cartoon penguins and puffy hearts surrounding them. "They're so cute. I love penguins." She clutched it to her chest.

As Vivian walked away from the building and toward the man, the feeling intensified, moving from her heart to her stomach. She knew that he, and whatever was in that box, was the source of her fear. She had to look inside.

As Vivian stopped in front of the box, the man didn't look up from his newspaper. He said, "You want a puppy?"

She looked down into the box, slowly. Inside were six black and brown puppies that almost looked small enough to fit in the palm of his hand together. Sleeping in the corner, they were huddled together with soiled, ripped up newspapers underneath them and crust caked around their eyes. One looked up and blinked at Vivian lethargically and glassy-eyed before going back to sleep.

"They don't really look well..." she said, haltingly.

The man looked up at Vivian, a bit taken aback, a small frown on his face. "They just need a bath. They're puppies, you know." He looked at his watch, then back to his paper. "They're fifty bucks each or two for ninety."

A voice emerged from inside her and rang clear as a bell, seemingly from nowhere, nearly startling her with its tone of confidence and authority. "Do you have a license to sell dogs?"

He looked up from his paper again, loudly snapping it shut, and looked at her with a full scowl on his face. "What are you talking about, license?"

That voice emerged again, this time even more confident than before. "I'm just asking if you are licensed to sell puppies. Are you?"

He looked her over for a moment or two, and Vivian met his eyes, unwaveringly. He picked up the newspaper again and said, "Look, either you want a dog or you don't, 'kay? Don't bother me again unless you're ready to buy one."

She paused a moment, squaring her shoulders. "Umm, really, that's not okay. I asked you a question because I'm worried about those puppies." After a minute of no response from him, she said, "I'm not leaving until you answer my question."

He turned a page of his newspaper sharply, muttering under his breath.

"Excuse me?" Vivian asked. "I didn't hear what you said."

"I said," his voice rising, newspaper clenched in red, tight hands, "that you don't know what you're talking about."

In a sense, he was right. Vivian didn't know *why* she knew what she was talking about, but somehow she did. In fact, she'd never felt a stronger conviction, pushing her forward.

"I do know what I'm talking about, sir. You're breaking the law, and those puppies are suffering."

A familiar voice spoke next to her.

"What's going on?" It was Wren, her forehead lined in confusion, looking in the box. "Oh..."

"He says that he doesn't need a license to sell dogs," Vivian told her, loud enough for the man to hear. "Look at them – they're too young to be away from their mother even if he did have a license."

"That's absolutely right," Wren said, nodding, still looking in the box. "They look about four weeks old, if that. Younger, I'd say. They're supposed to still be nursing." Looking up at the man, she added, "And you *do* need a license from the state to sell puppies."

By this point Vivian noticed that there was a small crowd gathered around them, maybe three or four people, just watching. The man continued to ignore them, snapping the pages of his newspaper over loudly.

"Listen," Wren continued, her voice rising with emotion. "My mom runs an animal shelter and she's a humane investigator. She's helped get people in trouble for this kind of thing. All I have to do is call her, and she'll be out here in a flash."

The man abruptly launched onto his feet, pushing his chair back, his eyes bulging and the veins in his forehead pronounced. Startled, Wren jumped back, grabbing Vivian's arm.

"Do you want trouble? Do you? Because I've asked your friend here to leave me alone and she keeps yapping at me. I couldn't care less about your mother. I don't need a license to sell dogs, and I don't care what your mom or the law says. Now, if you don't leave me alone, well, consider yourselves warned."

"Is that a threat?" Vivian asked, looking him straight in the eye.

"If you want to take it like that, " he said, sitting back down, "I suppose you can."

Wren turned toward Vivian and whispered, "All right, Viv, this guy's psycho. Let's go find the manager of this place."

"You go. I'll stay here," Vivian said, folding her arms in front of her chest.

Wren looked at her, surprised. "I'm going to go call my mother, too. Maybe you should come with me," she said quietly, looking sideways at the man.

"I'll be fine. Nothing's going to happen."

"Are you sure you don't want to come with me?" she asked, her eyes pleading. Vivian nodded.

"Viv…"

"I'm okay."

"I wish you would. He's like fifty times your size."

"I'm okay," Vivian said firmly. "Really."

"All right. I'll be nearby," Wren said, eyebrows knit. She started to walk toward the building, when she abruptly turned around and whispered, "Just walk away if he starts to get violent. Please." Then she hurried away.

The crowd, now about ten or so, stayed about eight feet behind Vivian in a silent arc, watching the little showdown, waiting for something to ignite.

"Listen," she said after a few moments, "I'm taking those puppies and I'm making sure they get the care they need."

He looked at her and laughed acidly. "Oh, really?" he said, smirking now.

"Yes. Really."

"How do you suppose you're going to do that?"

"Oh," Vivian said calmly, "I imagine it will be quite easy. Just like this." And she kneeled down by the box, grabbing it in her hands and cradling it in the crook of her arms. Vivian stood back up in the same spot, returning his stare.

He glared at Vivian, his burly body rigid and crimson with fury, his eyes like lasers. He stood up, towering over her, his chest puffed out. She looked back up at him, waves of peace running through her in a way she could have never have expected.

Without a word, he wrapped his thick fingers around the top of the box and pulled. Vivian didn't pull back, but just remained in the same posture, holding on. The man grabbed tighter and tried to jerk the box out of her arms, yanking to the side to knock Vivian off balance. Somehow she knew the worst thing to do was resist his pull, so she just moved with it, the box secure in her arms as he swung her to the side. He yanked again, even harder, with the same results. Frustrated, he pulled the box and Vivian up to him, and he bent down to stare her down, his eyes intense and bloodshot.

"You're going to let go of them," he growled slowly, inches away from Vivian's face, humid breath on her. She simply shook her head.

"No, I'm not."

The passing of time became impossible to gauge: they could have been standing there for ten seconds or ten minutes to Vivian. Abruptly, he stopped pulling, and pushed back against her and the box with the same brute force. Vivian staggered back toward the crowd surrounding them. She could hear some people gasp and someone nervously laugh as she reeled back, but instead of falling, her feet planted themselves onto the ground after a few steps back, and her arms, clutching the box of puppies tight to her, kept them jostled but safe. He stalked over to her, his hands clenched.

The two of them remained in that position, staring at each other. Vivian forgot about the flea market, the people whispering and gasping around her, everything: the whole world seemed to just contain her, this man and the box of puppies. Something shifted in his expression, just a little flash across his face and he looked away, spitting on the ground. He turned to walk back to his chair.

"Take 'em, then," he said, his voice gruff but quiet. "I don't got time for this nonsense. Those mutts aren't worth it. You're not worth it."

The crowd parted to let Vivian through, and she walked through the lot again, feeling their eyes watching her in disbelief, her body buzzing.

"Don't worry, babies," she said softly to the puppies, "I'll make sure you're all okay."

She was walking toward the car in a dazed calm when she heard Wren breathlessly call her name, rushing out of the flea market building toward Vivian, waving her arms, her eyes wide as she looked between her friend and the box. "What's going on? How did you get the puppies? I was worried about leaving you alone with that guy. Why didn't you come with me? Oh my God!" she gasped, breathlessly looking back into the box, "I can't believe you got the puppies." She seemed on the verge of hyperventilation.

"Yeah, well, I wasn't going to leave without them."

"I don't believe it..." she said again, shaking her head as she looked at Vivian incredulously. "Did he, like, threaten you or anything? I can't believe you wanted me to leave you alone with that guy. He was scary. Why did you do that? How did you get the puppies?"

Vivian smiled down at them. "Well, I just took them, I guess."

Wren broke out in a huge grin. "This is unbelievable." She stopped, looking over her shoulder to where the crowd was now dispersing, still watching them. "I'm glad everyone's all right," she said, looking in at the puppies, her hand on her chest. "I can't get my heart to stop racing."

"Just breathe," Vivian said, then erupted into laughter.

"What's so funny?"

"Just the idea of me telling you to 'just breathe'," Vivian said. "It's a little hilarious."

"You know that you kick butt, don't you?"

"I think that you're rubbing off on me," Vivian said, looking for Wren's car. "We should go now, though, okay?"

"Yes, yes, yes."

They walked to the car, and when Vivian sat with the box on her lap, a few of the puppies stirred and looked up at her, yawning. Wren made Vivian do a play-by-play of what happened with the man, so Vivian indulged her, but she was tired.

"So what went on inside?" Vivian asked.

"Oh, I knew my mom wasn't home this afternoon – she had a workshop she had to be at today, but I was waiting for him to call my bluff. So I found the flea market manager there instead and explained the situation, but she seemed kind of clueless. I got her card, though, and I'm going to have my mom call. She'll scare the pants off her. It'll be awesome," Wren said, admiringly.

"Good work," Vivian said, holding up her hand. "Look. I'm shaking."

Wren looked over at her, an unabashed look of wonder upon her face. "Well, you should be," she said, laughing. "I still can't believe what you did. I'm in shock."

"I can't really either," Vivian said, looking out the passenger window. "But you would do the same." Now her heart was racing.

She shook her head and said with disbelief, "I consider myself to be pretty brave, but I don't think so."

"You would, too."

After a few moments of them sitting silently, Wren finally said, "I'm so glad we met."

"Hmm?" Vivian closed her eyes with her hand to her fluttery chest, trying to will it to slow down.

"Never mind," Wren said, then squealed, her hands balled up. "You're like a superhero."

"Hands on the steering wheel, please."

ANOTHER VISIT

The puppies went home with Wren that afternoon, into her family's rambling house in the yet-undeveloped countryside near Center City. The property included a restored 19th century-era barn that had been converted into an animal shelter and rehabilitation center with everything they could want or need: heat, proper food, toys and warm blankets, as well as a small but dedicated core group of volunteers and a veterinarian who visited that very evening. The puppies had upper-respiratory infections and were indeed weaned at too young an age, but otherwise were fine.

Once Wren dropped her off back home after the market, Vivian just couldn't get back into the rhythm of the Sharpe household: everything seemed jarring and just a little too intense for her. Millie's TV show was too shrill; her father was flipping the pages of his book too loudly. Tucked away in her room, Vivian tried to read a book but couldn't get beyond skimming the same three sentences over and over before returning to her confrontation with the man at the market. She had just known that man with the puppies would back down. What if he hadn't? How was it that she knew exactly what she was talking about, with no experience to draw from? That sense of absolute calm in the face of an imminent threat – where did that come from? In the weeks since Tolstoy visited, Vivian had had all sorts of new perceptions, but her actions of that afternoon were the most unfamiliar to her. Where did she suddenly get the confidence she had, as though it were completely second nature?

After a couple hours of restlessness, Vivian did finally settle into sleep and, eventually, a deep dreaming state. In her dream, she was walking on the sidewalk outside her parents' house, going somewhere, though she wasn't sure where, and she started taking bigger steps, then skips, then small jumps. Gradually, her jumps became leaps up into the air and took on more of the quality of helium; she realized that without much effort, just a desire to do so, she could fly. Every time she'd gently flap her arms, she'd be soaring up through clouds that felt like soft, cool puffs of mist. Vivian could see the earth below her, becoming a pretty green and blue marble as she rose higher and higher, and she felt in her bones as if all she wanted to do was keep flying as high as she could.

She felt another's presence, and a bird appeared, a striking, serene-looking creature with iridescent, peacock-like feathers, nearly grazing her and then flying beyond her; she heard a *wssssh* as the bird flew past. Vivian started to follow the bird, and she called out to him, pleading for him to wait for her, her voice lost in the impossibly giant sky. Her arms flapping at the air couldn't keep up. She started crying as he shrunk into a little dot slowly swallowed by the vast powder blue sky, knowing he was going where she wanted to be. When the bird finally disappeared, Vivian suspended herself in the air, fluttering her hands to keep afloat, her heart sinking in disappointment.

A familiar voice spoke to her. "What troubles you?"

Vivian whirled around to see Tolstoy floating alongside her, a serene smile on his broad face. "Tolstoy," she shouted. "Did you see that beautiful bird?"

"Oh, yes," he said, his shiny eyes dancing. "Magnificent."

"Well, I just wanted to go where he was going. A creature like that has to come from a perfect place."

"I understand," he said, gently. "But it's not your time to go there."

Vivian became defensive. "What do you mean, it's not my time? You don't think I'm good enough to go where that bird is going?"

He smiled at Vivian softly. "Of course you are," he said. "But it's not time yet. There is much work to be done first."

"Where?" she asked.

"There," he said simply, looking down at the little speck of a sphere below them.

As Vivian looked at the blue speck below, she started gently floating down, through the clouds again – cool against her skin, soft between her fingers, the wind whistling in her ears – she passed the buildings and trees and houses until she was finally back where she started, standing on the ground, her feet adjusting to the earth again. As she landed, she realized the unexpected: it felt right to be there.

As Vivian stretched onto her side groggily, enjoying the first flying dream she'd ever had and feeling comforted to have seen

Tolstoy again, if only briefly in a dream, a strong sense made her open her eyes and adjust them to the darkness. There, once more, was the feather-light yet broad figure she'd hoped with all her might she would see again.

"Tolstoy," Vivian nearly shouted, bolting upright with eyes wide as she switched her lamp on. He held a hoof up to his mouth and she whispered, "You're here. I don't believe it. I just saw you in my dream again."

A rich laugh bubbled out of him. "It's funny how that happens, isn't it?" Then he lowered his voice, "Remember to keep your voice down or your mother will not be happy. I imagine that it takes some getting used to the notion that she can't hear me, but she can hear you. Just try this: think what you want to say instead of saying it aloud."

"But how will I know you heard me?"

"Give it a try," he smiled.

"Okay, do you hear me now?" She thought, feeling awkward, like she was speaking into a microphone.

"Um, yes."

She looked at Tolstoy and he grinned broadly back.

"Do you hear this?" she thought.

"As if it were in my own head," he responded.

"What is Millie doing right now?"

"Sleeping."

"What is my favorite color?"

He thought for a moment. "Green."

"What shade?"

"It is called emerald green. *Emerald*. What a pretty word."

They maintained eye contact throughout, Tolstoy looking peaceful but amused.

"Do you believe me now, Viv?"

"I do," Vivian accidentally spoke out loud, then thought, "I mean, I do. Actually, if it's okay with you, I'd rather speak. The other way is too creepy. I'll just keep my voice down, okay?"

"That's fine. I'll do the same. Not that anyone can hear me but you."

Vivian sat upright on the bed as Tolstoy moved to hover near the edge of her bed as he did the first time they met. She cleared her throat. "I've really missed you. There's a lot to talk about."

"Oh, yes," he said, his eyes sparkling. "There always is. I've missed you too, Viv, though I never was too far away."

44

"What do you mean? Like you've been following me around like a ghost?"

Tolstoy sighed, smiling wearily. "Are we back to this again? A discussion about ghosts?"

"No, I promise. It's just a little, you know, weird to realize someone is watching me. Is that what you're doing?"

"Well, it's not like I'm watching you exactly. Let's just say I keep informed."

"Like you get a report or something?"

"Oh, a bit like that, I suppose, but not really," he said, cryptically. "And how are you, my friend?"

Vivian said, "There's so much to talk about, but I'm really at a loss for words."

Tolstoy was silent for a moment, then said, "How have you been?"

"Well, you know, busy. Let's see...Where to start? I guess I could tell you about how weird I've felt, even though at the same time it seemed perfectly normal to feel that way, as bizarre as that sounds. Do you know what I mean?"

"I do," he said, nodding gently. "Very much so."

"Or I guess I could tell you about all these thoughts I've been having about the animals around me. It feels like I've just noticed them for the first time, you know? I mean, I knew they were there, but that was it. It's like a fog has been lifted."

"Delightful analogy."

"It's almost like developing a new sense. Now – ever since we met that night – it seems like I care as much about some little bird flying overhead as I do about myself. And it seems like I know what they're feeling."

"Fascinating."

"Yes," Vivian said a bit too emphatically, excited to have someone who seemed to understand. "Sorry, I'm still getting used to this. Anyway, it's like the squirrels who run by and just miss getting hit by a car, my heart is racing and all I feel is that I need to get on the other side of the street. Like I myself am in danger. The cats living outside are worried if they're going to have enough food for their kittens, and so am I. But it's not just like I think that's how they might be feeling – it's like I *know* that's how they are feeling, and I feel that way, too, inside my body."

"As though you two were one entity?" Tolstoy asked.

"Yeah. It's both: I can feel it inside my body but I am also aware of myself at the same time. It's not like I forget that I'm me and start thinking that I'm a cat or something. "

"That must be strange to adjust to, I imagine."

"Yeah, at first it was really overwhelming because it seemed to come out of the blue and I didn't know what to do with it, and I still don't, but I think I might have a hint."

"Oh?" he said, leaning in with interest.

"Well, today – you should know this because you've been watching from above or wherever you lurk, right?" Vivian asked.

Tolstoy laughed. "You're making me sound a little sinister, Viv. It's not quite like that, but, yes, I do know what happened today at the market."

"All I know is that when we were at the market, I felt in my bones that something was wrong. I mean, I've almost gotten used to feeling like that, these past couple of weeks. But this time the feeling became more urgent, different, like it was saying, *Prepare yourself.*"

Tolstoy nodded. "A crescendo."

"It was as if at first I could hear a train whistling in the background just faintly, and the longer I was there, the louder it got until I had to respond to it."

"Interesting. Why do you suppose that was?" he asked.

"I think because there was a crisis that needed to be addressed right then, and my gut understood it before my brain did. Like my senses were in a whirl and all I could focus on was finding the source of it. When I saw the man with the box, I just knew that was it."

Tolstoy leaned back, watching her. "Your sense of intuition is very keen, isn't it?"

"I don't think so."

"No?"

"Not really. Or at least, I never thought so. I mean, sometimes I'd feel like I didn't like a certain person, or I'd have a hunch about something or another, but it was never really strong. You know how some people say that they know that the phone is going to ring before it does? I was never one of those people. The thing about how this was different from anything I felt before is that it could not be ignored no matter what. It was like do or die."

"And you didn't find yourself doubting yourself?"

"That's another funny thing – no, not at all. In fact, I felt more confident than ever."

"Isn't that remarkable?" Tolstoy marveled, hooves on his legs.

"It was as though someone else was in my body for that time, but I was still me, somehow. Very strange. But even when that man started getting threatening, I wasn't afraid at all. Not even slightly. I'm not trying to sound all…"

"Like you're conceited?"

"Exactly, I just knew everything would be all right. That's not like me at all, Tolstoy. I mean, I don't go around starting trouble. I've never been in a fight in my life, barely even any arguments."

"Well, what do you suppose caused this sudden confidence?" he asked.

"I was hoping you could tell me," she said with a coy smile.

Tolstoy sat silently, conveying to her with his ever-patient demeanor that he would never do this.

Vivian thought for a moment, then spoke hesitantly. "The only thing I can guess is that it was meant to be. Like I was doing the right thing, you know? I don't think I would've been so calm if I were taking the wrong steps."

"A dance your body knew how to do but your mind had forgotten."

"Exactly," she said. "That's exactly it."

Tolstoy shook his head, smiling beatifically. "What a transformation you're going through, Viv."

"I know," Vivian said. "I guess I'm not as scared as I was in the beginning, but it's still pretty weird. It seems like it's natural for me to be living like this, though. And it's actually kind of, I don't know… fun."

"Fun being threatened by large strangers at the flea market?" he guffawed.

"Okay, well that would probably not go down on my list as one of the most fun activities of the last year, but the rest of it has been kind of neat. And, if it wasn't neat, it was kind of…"

"Interesting?" Tolstoy volunteered.

"Yes, interesting. It beats the pants off of boring and predictable, I'll say that."

"I should think so. And I noticed you made a new friend this week." Tolstoy said, expectantly.

"Oh, yes," she gushed, "how could I forget? Wren. She's just the coolest, totally unlike anyone I've ever met."

"She is quite a character. Wren seems like the kind of girl who makes you feel better just being around her."

"Exactly. Like how my mom says she needs that cup of coffee, you know, for pep? Wren's my cup of coffee. Isn't it weird that I was a little afraid of her at first? Now that feels like ages ago."

Tolstoy chuckled at the thought. "Why were you afraid of gentle little Wren?"

"Oh, I guess for superficial reasons," Vivian admitted, shaking her head.

"Like?"

"Everyone at school kind of thinks she's a weirdo, except for me now, of course, so they either laugh at her or they gossip about her. Or they pretend she doesn't exist. No one actually talks to her to her face."

Tolstoy shrugged. "Their loss."

"True, but I was afraid of the same happening to me because that sort of thing seems to be contagious, I suppose, but, you know, that matters to me less and less."

"She's quite a marvelous girl, isn't she? A great combination of strength and vulnerability."

"I hadn't really thought of her like that, but I think you're right, Tolstoy. Just to think, before last Wednesday, I was one of the many who thought she was a weirdo. I mean, I still do," she said, laughing, "but now that's not such a bad thing."

A peaceful smile slowly rippled across his face. "Another transformation. What a miracle it is," he said, almost to himself. "Once the perception can shift, anything's possible."

"I suppose it is."

"You and Wren could teach each other a lot, Viv," he said matter-of-factly.

She laughed. "I teach Wren? Like how to be boring and normal and ordinary? No, I don't think so. I'm afraid this learning thing is something of a one-way street."

"Oh, I don't think you're giving yourself enough credit, Viv."

Her eyes widened. "Tolstoy, really, I never thought I would say this, but she is so together. So confident. I mean, she's spent most of her life living the way she wants, so she's really secure in herself. Well, not tough, but strong. I feel like a baby bird still pecking her

48

way out of the egg next to her. Just barely pecking at that. Tiny little nibbles. I haven't even broken through yet."

"This isn't just false modesty, right? Because your qualities are so obvious to me."

"I don't think so. Perhaps you could enlighten me."

"Well," he said, thoughtfully resting his chin on his hoof, "for starters, you understand the world most people live in better than Wren does, given your upbringing. You understand what compels people to do the things they do better than Wren, because of your experiences. This is going to be of priceless value to you on doing the work ahead."

Vivian leaned forward. "And what 'work ahead' is this, Tolstoy? You mentioned that the first time you visited, too."

"Oh, we'll get to that in a moment," he said, smiling. "Another wonderful trait you have is just emerging: Your tenacity."

"What do you mean?"

"Well, today, for example, there was nothing that was going to turn you away from your mission. That sense of resolve and focus is also what you bring to your friendship with Wren, who can be a little..." he paused for the right word, "less committed."

"Are you done yet?" she asked, feeling slightly embarrassed with all the attention.

"Oh, heavens, no!" Tolstoy laughed. "But in the interest of brevity, I'll just leave it at saying that you are the ideal candidate for bringing about the change that needs to take place. This is why I'm here. This is why you're here with me. You need to be humble and confident at the same time, and today I saw ample proof that you could be both very nimbly. Not that I doubted you for a minute, I might add."

"So, okay, could you tell me what the heck you're talking about? I mean, this 'work' you keep mentioning. This 'change' I need to bring about. It's really driving me crazy."

He looked at her sympathetically. "You're right, Viv. It's time. I just didn't want to overwhelm you with too much too soon," he said.

Vivian laughed. "Tolstoy, if I weren't ready for what you are about to tell me after these past couple of weeks, I never would be."

"True enough."

She continued, not sure of where she was going. "You know, last week when I decided to meet with the vegetarian club, there was this kind of weird thing with this girl I know, Kendra. Anyway,

I told her what I was planning to do, meet with the club, you know, and she tried to talk me out of it."

Tolstoy nodded his head, chuckling in recollection, "Oh, yes. Funny girl."

She continued. "She was telling me how I'm going to be a geek, doomed to be a loser, blah blah blah. Well, you know. When she left, I knew in my heart that I had to go to the meeting. And I guess I would've been a lot more intimidated about it a few weeks ago. I probably wouldn't have gone. I would have jumped ship. On Wednesday, though, approval didn't seem to matter as much to me anymore."

"Just like that?"

"You could say so. I mean, being popular was never all that important to me, but it's a little scary to finally just reject all that in a really obvious way, you know? I felt like I was turning a corner by walking up those steps and going to the meeting. I mean, I know it sounds silly."

"No."

"Like it's not such a big deal, but it was to me. So, I guess that today wasn't the actual first time I felt like I was changing. I felt like that on Wednesday afternoon. I felt kind of grown-up in a way."

Tolstoy studied Vivian's face for a long moment. "So that's a good segue to talk about why I came to you."

"You mean other than the midnight meetings and deep conversations?" Vivian said playfully. "Yes, that'd be nice."

Tolstoy smiled at her. "Can you tell me why you think I'm here?"

Vivian rolled her eyes in exaggerated frustration. "Tolstoy, you come to me in the middle of the night and expect me to be insightful. You've got to cut me some slack. I mean, I'm not even a night person. Can I have the tiniest of a hint?"

Tolstoy laughed again. "Oh, Viv, I think you know why I'm here. Now use your recently discovered intuition and tell me what you think," he said, looking her straight in the eye. "Why am I here?"

She sighed. "Let's see...To make sure that I don't sleep too much?"

He shook his head.

"Okay, seriously, let's think here. Well, something to do with animals. I mean, after eating you for lunch that day – which I sincerely apologize for, by the way..."

"Apology accepted," Tolstoy said, tactfully.

"Well," Vivian continued, "ever since then, my, I don't know, my *awareness* has changed. I feel empathy for other beings in a much deeper way than before."

He nodded.

"And, well, I guess the reason you came to me has something to do with that."

He nodded again, encouraging her. "Dig a little deeper."

"It has something to do with animals and empathy, right?" she said, mulling it over. Suddenly, she had a flash. "Wait. Does it have to do with me protecting animals? Because that's all I ever think about these days."

"You're getting warm."

"Maybe helping others learn to have compassion?"

"Warmer still," he said, with an excited little wiggle, "so, so close."

"You can't just tell..."

He shook his head. "Try."

"I am trying."

"I know."

Slowly, Vivian said, "Through my example?"

He nodded.

"I can help others get in touch with their compassion?"

He nodded. "And together they would be?"

"So," she said, speaking quickly now, "through my example, I can teach others about compassion, help people move toward empathy."

"Does that feel right?"

Her arms felt tingly. "Yes."

"Then you're right on the nose," Tolstoy said, pointing to his snout. "Except that I would add toward their *natural* empathy."

"But – I don't understand – how am I supposed to do that?" Vivian asked. "I mean, how can you make someone else be compassionate?"

Tolstoy smiled patiently at her. "You can't. Isn't that marvelous? They have to do it for themselves."

"So my role is...?"

"I'm not sure exactly," he said serenely. "That will reveal itself when it's time."

"That's not helpful, Tolstoy," she said, unable to conceal the frustration in her voice.

"It may not be helpful," he said politely, "but it's true."

"In the meantime...?" she said with a small sigh.

"In the meantime you can use the skills you already have: Your humility, your commitment and compassion to help awaken it in others. You are able to communicate another's experience because you no longer have walls that separate you from understanding other beings. You no longer see yourself as separate."

"I still don't see how what I'm supposed to do is possible, Tolstoy. People are pretty prejudiced about how we treat animals. I mean, most people think it's natural to eat animals because they were raised to not think about them in any way other than as food," Vivian said.

Tolstoy considered this. "That is true, Viv. Remember, though, that evening we first met. When you went to bed that evening, you didn't know or feel any more than the average person about eating animals. You yourself said that up until that point, you really didn't care."

"So?"

"Well, clearly you made the leap."

"But I had you to help me, to guide me."

"I am not guiding, Viv. You are your own guide. All I did was support the natural compassion that was already there; you drew the conclusions yourself. It's not as though I cast a spell on you. You already had the tools. Everyone does except for a very, *very* small number. The awakening you had was entirely your own doing."

"Well, are you planning to do this for everyone in the world? Visit them while they're sleeping and help them understand?"

"Oh, no, Viv, that's not my work to do. The change has got to be carried out by the humans," Tolstoy said simply. "I first had to find a chief ally and ambassador, though."

Vivian pointed to herself, eyebrows raised. He simply nodded.

"So I'm supposed to change the world? Tolstoy," Vivian said, sighing, "I think you're underestimating what needs to be done."

"Oh, I'll have to respectfully disagree here: if you look throughout the arc of history, individuals have indeed prompted change that alters everything about a particular perception or presumption," he said emphatically. "What humans often fail to acknowledge, though, is that it is in the hands of the people, the mass of people, to want to change first, even if they're not consciously aware of it. Humans believe it happens from the outside in but it's really from the inside out. We can only influence and nudge and inform. That's it. But that is a lot."

He looked at Vivian's face, which was still skeptical, and redoubled his efforts.

"Vivian: I am essentially agreeing with you. The change has to be from within. What you *can* do is plant the seeds of compassion in the world around you, every opportunity you get. Awakenings will follow in your path, people will be so eager to be liberated from their inner prisons. The consciousness will grow like beautiful tulips," he said, spreading his arms overhead in an arc, hooves wriggling, "spreading over the globe."

She laughed with exasperation. "And I'm supposed to start spreading these tulips from Center City?"

Tolstoy shrugged and looked around the room, his face guileless. "Why not? This is as good a place as any."

Unsure of where he was headed, Vivian simply nodded.

"The thing is, Viv, you would be doing this whether I came to you or not. It's possible for you to achieve the extraordinary if you work from a place of pure love, pure intention. I think it would bring you comfort to study the humans who moved entire nations: look into Mahatma Gandhi. Look at Jesus Christ. It was possible for them to accomplish what others simply dreamed of because they remained anchored to their deepest convictions, and their convictions were rooted in a pure, loving place. Why couldn't you do the same? What's stopping you?"

She thought about this for a moment. "I'm afraid, I guess."

"That's natural, but do you think that these extraordinary humans didn't have moments or even days of doubt or fear? Of feeling overwhelmed by the responsibilities they took on?"

"I don't know."

"Of course they did," he continued. "We see the outside of the people, their accomplishments. It's easy to idealize them that way, to think that they were fearless, but they were just as vulnerable as anyone else is. The difference is they didn't let that stop them. The great ones decided that it would be far worse to maintain the status quo than to ignore what they knew was right. This helped them to stay anchored even through fear and doubt. You'll do the same. It would also be impossible for you to reverse course now. The momentum has already begun. "

She was silent for a few moments, thinking over what he said. "This is huge, Tolstoy."

He looked at Vivian with eyes full of compassion, as he softly spoke. "I know it is, Viv."

"But it needs to happen," she surprised herself by saying. "I know it does."

Tolstoy nodded solemnly. "We're on the precipice, Viv," he said with quiet conviction. "What the world needs is just a gentle tip, because it's really all right there, the tipping point, as they say. This will bring on a transformation of spirit the likes of which we've never seen."

"I've got chills."

"Strangely," he grinned, "I think I do, too."

A SQUIRREL NAMED BILLY
AND SOME DUCKS BY THE RIVER

School continued. Springtime started folding into summer, and the first warm days felt like an exotic gift from far away, like something discovered on a sandy beach when the tide rolled out. After enduring a typically long, cruel winter, Center City's young people were painfully distracted those last few weeks of school, and Vivian's classmates stared longingly out of any available window, in their minds already gone. School was not only almost over for the year, but spring was maddeningly there, ripening like a peach as the students slumped in uncomfortable chairs, breathing in the same entombed school smell they'd been inhaling all year, of gym shoes and French fries and deodorant. Usually Vivian had never felt as much of a surge as her friends when spring started easing into summer, more or less living every day as she had the previous one. This year, however, everything felt very different to her, almost as though the world around her had been just two dimensional to her before, it was all so suddenly vivid.

When she walked to school, Vivian felt that she had to take her shoes off and cross the lawn to Center City High rather than take the sidewalk; the grass felt so alive between her toes, it made her heart feel like it wanted to leap out of her chest from sheer giddiness. That spring, the songbirds seemed to be chattering to her directly; whereas once they were so drowned out by busy thoughts, traffic and other assorted distractions that she never noticed them, now they were distinct and rose to the forefront and everything else receded to the point of nearly disappearing. It wasn't as though Vivian had never felt distracted during school; she had, often. This year, though, her distraction had a different quality to it: she had a fierce sense of wanting to rush through school so she could get on with her life. Especially she wanted to go outside with the local bird identification book she found in her father's library and discover the differences between a male and a female red-bellied woodpecker. She eagerly soaked up the knowledge, excited to learn that males had longer tongues and bills.

Wren was always happy to join Vivian in her bird watching, and they started a new habit of walking partway together after school, splitting up when Vivian turned to her house. Wren usually went on to the Commie Café, the coffee shop that had opened in Center City thirty years before, where she worked behind the counter after school for a few hours a day during the week. On their walks together, Wren offered the kind of anecdotes a dry identification book couldn't provide, like: "Oh, look at that grackle up in the oak tree. Do you see him? Maybe he's a she. I don't know how to tell the difference. Anyway, once a grackle flew into our house and he wouldn't leave. He totally didn't want to go. My parents opened the doors and windows and turned on the fans to shoo him out but he really wanted to stay. My dad was like, 'Well, if he wants to live here, we can't force him to leave.' But my mom was all like, 'What are you talking about? The cats are going crazy and he's pooping on the floor.' Finally, he had been in our house for about a week, and I was going somewhere. I don't remember where. He flew onto my shoulder and as I opened the door, he took off. Whoosh. Finally. I don't know what that was all about. Just be careful if you ever see a grackle trying to get into your house."

There weren't any grackles trying to get into her home, but in her backyard, Vivian was excited to identify tree swallows, blue jays and eastern meadowlarks. It was almost as though this home she grew up in was entirely new to her, and the trees in her yard housed endlessly fascinating treasures waiting to be discovered. In this way, Vivian was like a child again. She took up an interest in her father's garden for the first time, helping him choose plants that attracted butterflies and dragonflies, and even though she knew it wasn't true, digging shallow holes for the seeds felt like it was the first time she had touched soil since she was a little girl. Rubbing the dirt between her fingers as her father happily prattled on about plants native to the region, Vivian stared at the rich soil, almost flustered by how alive it felt to her. It seemed as though it nearly pulsed with life.

She had once thought of all this around her as a flat background painted and repeated again and again, like in one of the cartoons she watched as a child. Now, ever since that day in

May with the ham sandwich, everything was different, shockingly vivid.

One day, not long after Vivian rediscovered her backyard, a squirrel started making overtures to her. Vivian sat on the lawn, and the squirrel, a bushy-tailed fox squirrel, circled her, making a slightly narrower circumference toward her as the minutes passed, until she could have reached out to touch him if she were so inclined. She didn't. Part of her wanted to, but she just couldn't get her hand to reach for the squirrel. Still, she found herself thinking about the squirrel for a couple of days after he first made himself known to her and that she thought looked like a Billy. One afternoon a couple of weeks after she first met Tolstoy, she suddenly felt so anxious to be in the yard with Billy and the birds that she walked through the front door, announced that she was home to Millie's babysitter of the day, kicked off her shoes, dropped off her backpack on the kitchen table, grabbed a bag of peanuts from the cupboard and walked out the back door. She sensed that he had something to communicate to her and she had a new idea about drawing him to her.

After she'd been quietly sitting on the lawn for about five minutes, Billy started running around Vivian, stopping occasionally to look at her, look away, and start circling again. Vivian had her bag of peanuts in her lap, and she started tossing them, shells and all, in front of her and to her side, in as casual a manner as she could muster. The squirrel stopped in his tracks. Vivian kept throwing the peanuts, whistling to herself the Nutcracker Suite's *March*. The squirrel stood perfectly still, seeming to weigh the advantages and disadvantages of going nearer to Vivian, who kept quietly whistling, a bunch of peanuts in her cupped hand. Billy edged closer, regarding the peanut nearest him and looking back at Vivian. He bent down toward it, seemed to sniff it, and looked at her again. This time, Vivian returned his gaze. She could see that it wasn't the peanuts that interested him after all. There was such an expression of solemn gravity on the squirrel, Vivian felt the smile drain off her face. He needed something, she was certain of that, feeling like she did at the flea market. The next moment, Vivian found herself upright, understanding that she needed to follow him.

The squirrel took off, pausing briefly to look at Vivian from under the willow tree in their back yard, then ran down the driveway to the Hanson's front yard and down the sidewalk of

Hickory Street with Vivian jogging behind him barefoot. He stopped every so often to look back, and, once satisfied that Vivian was behind him, resumed with a purposefulness she couldn't ignore. It was unlike anything she'd ever experienced; the closest analogy she could make was that it was as if she were being magnetically pulled.

They went down five blocks, and then crossed Lincoln Avenue – he waited for the light, bushy tail twitching, almost like any other conscientious pedestrian – to Capital Park, which was the main entry point in Center City for those coming to the Kickashaunee River, and one of the most striking areas of the town, with lots of old tall trees, some hills and meadows. Vivian kept following the squirrel, concerned now that she was amid the trees and other squirrels that she would lose sight of him. She increased her speed, trailing just a few feet behind Billy, but just as she did that, it became clear that she didn't need to worry about losing him. They passed a few other squirrels and Vivian noticed that Billy stood out as though he were illuminated somehow, like he had a spotlight inside him. At this realization, she relaxed enough to notice Kendra Brentwood sitting on a picnic table with a few of her friends across the field. Kendra had her hands cupped around her mouth and was shouting something to Vivian while her friends appeared to be laughing; Vivian waved distractedly and kept chasing Billy. She couldn't stop.

Vivian followed him through a grove of elm trees to a trail and crossed it, then went down to the more wild area of Capital Park, where the neat and managed area started to get thick with bushes and burly trees. Billy dashed between the shrubs and tangled roots as Vivian made her way behind him, and he still paused every so often to see if she could manage the increasingly demanding terrain; once he was satisfied she was up to the task, he continued on his way. Though she did get some scratches from branches, Vivian was sure-footed and agile in a way that surprised her; she found herself reminded momentarily of Nike, the goddess of Victory she'd studied last semester in the Greek mythology section of her World Culture class and she imagined wings flapping behind her. She didn't have long to indulge this particular fantasy of herself as a Titan-fighting goddess though, before she realized that Billy was most certainly heading toward the river. Vivian turned sideways, grabbing onto thick branches as she dug the sides of her feet into the ground, making her way down the steep slope of the riverbank, thick mud oozing between her toes. Once they got to the river, the water loud and speeding past them, Billy looked at her one last time and ran up a tree.

Vivian squinted up into the tree, shading her eyes with her hand as she tried to catch sight of that thick tail, curved like a question mark, or a flash of those determined eyes. She saw no sign of him, not even a branch moving, and she sat down on a log, her lungs still tingling, cheeks hot and flushed. Vivian considered the old tree, one that didn't have branches low enough for her to pull herself up onto, and rocked back and forth, her head, a little dizzy, cradled in her hands and her itchy eyes watering. The disappointment was crushing. Maybe she *was* crazy, believing that that squirrel was communicating with her. *He probably thinks I'm some lunatic*, she thought, *chasing him to the river like that*. As soon as she thought that, Vivian also realized that she had a strong compulsion to wash herself. She felt grimy and gross, like she had a sticky film on her body.

Then Vivian saw something move from the corner of her eye. It was a duck, a female mallard. She came waddling up to Vivian, and stopped just short of her. Vivian showed the duck her open palm. "I'm sorry, baby," she said, "I don't have any food."

The duck quacked at her with such an intensity, Vivian startled. "What is it?" The duck quacked once more, really more of a bark than anything, and one that sounded like the command, "Up!" As she issued the order, the duck ran behind her, pushing Vivian with her bill. She stood up, not sure what to do. The duck started excitedly quacking, and kept nudging Vivian along the river's edge. After a few feet, the duck ran ahead of her and hopped down the bank where a mass of tall prairie grasses, cattails and small sticks had been formed into a sort of cushion at the river's edge. On top were four ducklings, huddled together for warmth. Vivian blinked and squinted at them, finally rubbing her very itchy eyes.

There was something wrong. They were covered with what looked like black slime, their eyes barely perceptible behind the grease all over their bodies. As she looked at the ducklings, trying to figure out what to do, she was vaguely aware of a chemical smell that was making her eyes water. As soon as she noticed it, she became so queasy that she nearly fell over. She slumped onto a tree stump, steadying herself, her ears pulsing as she tried to breathe away the nausea. Each breath, though, made her feel sicker, pulling the chemical smell deeper into her. She looked at the ducklings and realized that she felt like them: overcome by chemicals, her senses reeling from it.

The mallard pulled her out of her stupor by quacking again, loud, right next to her ear. Just when Vivian was really starting to despair over what she should do, she saw Billy circling near her feet, and he ran, with Vivian trailing him, to a garbage can that was overflowing with trash. He stopped there, and Vivian stopped, too, just staring at the garbage can. He started running around it, chattering at her for the first time.

"What?" she said as though she expected a response. "What?"

Finally, the squirrel stood still at the base of the can, chattering loudly when she noticed a ripped open beer case that still had the bottom intact. In the next moment, she saw the ducks inside, and she had a mental image of herself running downtown. She saw this as clearly as if she were watching a film of herself. Satisfied, the squirrel ran off, Vivian scooped up the box, and she ran back to the riverbank where the ducklings were still on their bed of weeds, their mother watching for her next to them. Vivian bent down on her knees and started scooping up the ducklings, gently talking to them as she placed them in the box. Though they weighed almost nothing, she had to use both hands as she had a hard time loosening them from her palms.

"It's okay, babies. I'm here to help you," she murmured.

The ducklings didn't struggle, just flopped into one another in the corner of the box. Vivian could feel the heartbeat in one duckling, a tentative little pulse that felt like the smallest amount of pressure from her finger could have stopped it. The ducklings were together in a small mound, and, after wiping her hands on the grass, which did very little, Vivian stood up, cradling the box in her arms.

"Well, mama," she said to the mallard, "what should I do now?" The mother duck jumped and waddled up to the grass, puffed out her chest, quacked and spread her wings. In that instant, Vivian very clearly envisioned the mallard in the box with her babies, so she lowered the box to the ground and the duck hopped in. Vivian started running back to town, the box in her arms. She cut through the park and started jogging down the sidewalk with her arms in a circle, clutching the box into her. Occasionally a car would honk and the mother duck would quack back defiantly, and Vivian would imagine what she must have looked like, running down Center City's busiest street with a box with a mallard peering out of it in her arms. Running down the street in her hometown like this, her bare feet covered in mud, too, was embarrassing, she knew that, but that was all she could seem to do. She pushed ahead to a destination only her feet seemed to know.

She found herself downtown, and she stood at the corner of Main and Van Buren, her heart pounding, sweat beading on her forehead, her neck. She sat down on a bench, clutching the box into her, trying to get organized. As the world rolled by, somehow continuing as it always did, a city bus pulled up in front of her, brakes squeaking, and opened the door.

"Sorry, miss," the driver said, looking down at Vivian with a mixture of confusion and sympathy. "I can't let you on the bus with that duck. No animals on the bus but guide dogs."

Vivian stared at him blankly for a moment or two until she realized she was sitting at the bus stop. "Oh, no, I didn't want to get on the bus. I was just sitting here. Sorry." She stood up and with that, the bus continued on its way. As the bus pulled away, Vivian looked across the street and saw the familiar, grungy sight she had passed by on many occasions without ever stopping in: The Commie Café. She read the chipped, hand-painted wooden sign again and it remained the same: The Commie Café. Her heart leaped in her chest as she, barely aware of it, yelped out in glee. As she raced to the corner, she noticed Wren through the smudgy window right away, wiping down a table.

"There she is, mama," she said to the mallard, who then stretched her neck up from the box as if to look. "She's going to help us."

As she crossed the street, Vivian finally felt a heave of relief, like she'd found the answer she was racing for when she left the river. She knocked on the window with one arm, clutching the box into her with the other. Wren looked up and smiled in recognition. Her smile turned to open-mouthed confusion when she saw the box with the ducks in it. Still leaning over the table she was cleaning, Wren blinked at her friend a few times, not moving, until Vivian knocked on the window again and motioned with her hand impatiently for Wren to come outside. Wren left her cloth on the table and ran out.

"What is it with you and animals in boxes, Viv?" Wren said. "Hello, Miss Mallard."

Vivian was about to point out the ducklings, still huddled in the corner and mostly blocked from view by their mother, when Wren gasped.

"What? Oh …" Wren's voice trailed off as she put her hand to her mouth.

"I know. I found them at the river."

"What's that stuff on them?" She scrunched her nose. "God, they stink."

"I have no…" Vivian started to say.

"Here, let's wash them off in the kitchen. Eek. They look barely alive," Wren said, opening the door to the café, then looked at Vivian's feet. "No shoes today?"

"I guess not."

She held the door open for Vivian and walked quickly to the kitchen door. The café was empty except for a man with long silvery blond braids sitting behind the counter.

"What's up, Wren?" he asked, looking at Vivian and the ducks.

"I don't know. My friend found them," she said, opening the kitchen door, "and the babies have some kind of, I don't know, nuclear goop on them. Could you call my mom?"

"Call your mom?" the man with the braids repeated, now standing in the kitchen doorway. "And what should I tell her?"

Wren, looking exasperated, sighed and said, "She's an animal rehabilitator, Owl. Remember? Our home number's on the calendar," she said, pointing to a heavily marked-up, out-of-date calendar on the wall behind the counter.

"Oh. Right," he said, walking back to the wall with a phone in his hand.

Wren started filling the double sink with soapy water on one side and plain water on the other, and then she handed Vivian some tall rubber gloves, having already snapped hers on. As if this were something she did every day, Wren gently placed the mother duck in the plain water and picked up one of the ducklings, who immediately wilted into her cupped palm. The mother swam in nervous little circles.

"So," Vivian started, "I don't know what happened here, but I found them by the river. I think they were poisoned by something, don't you?"

"Yeah. But by what?" Wren asked. Still cupping the duckling, she started to carefully pour warm water over the bird with her other hand, reassuring him with a quiet, gentle voice. She frowned a little. "This stuff is hard to get off, whatever it is." She found some baking soda and made a paste of it in her palm. "This is helping a little." She rinsed that off and then used more of the dish soap until the water started to run clear. Vivian followed suit with another duckling, who felt as limp as a sock in her hand.

"You know," Vivian said, "we should probably keep some of this slime as a sample. We might need it. Don't you think?"

"Good idea," said Wren. "Let's get some from the last baby because we already started on these."

The water quickly turned into a noxious dark slime in the sink. Wren changed the water and they stood quietly side-by-side, gently lathering the ducklings with their fingertips and gagging at the smell. Vivian wiped her watering eyes on her forearms, and she sniffled as she worked. Not looking over at her, Wren asked, "Are you crying, Viv?"

"Crying? No. The slime is making me sick," she said, rinsing off the duckling with a plastic cup as Wren was, covering his eyes with a rag.

Owl poked his head back in the door. "Your mom's on her way, Wren."

"Cool. Thanks, Owl," she said, not looking up while she patted and wrapped the duckling in a dishtowel.

He came into the kitchen and bent down next to the mother mallard.

"Hello, ducky," he said, reaching in to pet her, "how are you this..."

The duck pushed up in the sink, making the water around her splash and chomped at Owl's hand, narrowly missing it.

"Whoa, princess," he said, jumping back. "I'll just leave you to your bath, I guess."

As he walked out of the kitchen, Wren wondered aloud how to save the slime on the remaining duckling.

"How about a spoon and aluminum foil to rub it on?" suggested Vivian.

"Perfect."

As Wren ran off from the kitchen to look for some foil, still holding the duckling she'd washed, Vivian felt like part of her ran down the drain with the slime they'd washed off. She couldn't shake the feeling of emptiness and loss even as she focused on drying off her duckling and finding some clean dishtowels for bedding in the box.

"Wren," she called out, looking around the kitchen, "do you have some more dish towels?"

Wren called back something she couldn't hear and just as she was about to go find her, Vivian was seized by an unavoidable instinct to look in the box, with nearly an equal measure of dread. Clutching the duckling she was drying into her, Vivian looked in the box and drew her breath in: the remaining duckling was slumped over on his side, his eyes half-closed and unblinking. As Vivian picked him up with her free hand, she realized that the duckling she had just cleaned, one she'd thought was very lethargic when she'd first picked him up, was actually brimming with vitality in comparison.

"He's dead..." she found herself crying, stinging tears streaming down her face, "Wren, he's dead."

The next few moments were a blur as Wren came running into the kitchen and the mother mallard started quacking manically. Wren took the freshly washed duckling from Vivian's hand, and Vivian collapsed into a chair, cupping the dead one to her chest as she sobbed into her arm.

"We should have helped this one first, Wren... He was the weakest...why didn't we wash him first?"

Wren bent down next to Vivian and hugged her silently as Vivian cried, heaving such big sobs her chest hurt. Then Owl's voice could be heard from the café, and a woman came hurrying into the kitchen with a small cage in her hand. Wren stood up and rushed over to her.

"Mom. One of the babies just died. We think they were poisoned."

Simone Summer, a tall, striking woman with hair like Wren's and darker skin, put her arm around her daughter and rushed over to Vivian. Vivian opened her hand for Mrs. Summer to see the duckling. She sighed to herself.

"Poor baby," Mrs. Summer said softly, shaking her head. She scrunched up her nose, looking like Wren did back she first saw the ducks. "What is that horrible stuff on him?"

Vivian didn't want to be holding the dead bird anymore. Wordlessly, she handed the duckling to Mrs. Summer and went to the bathroom to wash her hands and splash some water on her face, but she just sat in the dingy bathroom with the weathered, ancient anti-war posters, staring at her hands, stained green even though she'd had gloves on; she was no longer weeping but she had a pounding headache. After a few minutes, she heard a soft knock on the door.

"Viv?" said Wren gently. "Are you okay?"

Just the thought of having to have a conversation with Wren and Mrs. Summer made Vivian feel like she was ready to collapse. She had to leave the café at that moment. She had to go home.

As Vivian opened the door of the bathroom, Wren took her by the arm. "Viv, I'm so sorry about that duckling, but my mom says that she thinks the others are going to be fine. They're with their mom now. She's totally taking care of them."

Vivian pulled her arm away abruptly. "How can you not care about the one who died? Have you forgotten about him?"

Wren drew back like she'd been stung by a bee. "How can you say that, that I don't care? Of course I care."

Vivian shook her head, hating herself. "I'm sorry. I didn't mean that. I just can't take any more," she rasped.

Vivian could see Mrs. Summer standing by the sink, carefully lifting the mallard. "You don't even want to say goodbye to the ducks?" Wren asked.

"No," Vivian said, the lump in her throat almost painful at that point. "I wish I'd never found them. I just want to go home." She rushed out of the café with the screen door slamming behind her.

AT WREN'S AND MEETING WILL

At home that night, Vivian pushed her dinner around on her plate listlessly, dodged eye contact and conversation with her family and went to her room as soon as she could, shutting her door behind her.

"She's having one of those nights, dear," she could hear her father consoling Millie, who had had her heart set on playing tea party with her sister. "Would you share some Darjeeling with me?"

After lying for an hour in bed with the barest of feelings, as though she'd turned off a switch within herself that she didn't know she'd had until it stopped functioning, Vivian fell asleep early and slept hard. She dreamed for what felt like hours of being on a lifeboat with a basket of terrified kittens just beyond her reach in the ocean. The basket swirled in vortexes and Vivian watched in horror as kittens fell into the dark water and disappeared. She kept reaching for them, and the more she did, the more the water would churn and roil, pushing the basket and kittens farther away from her. She looked out in the water, and she saw more baskets and more pitifully crying animals whirling around like in the teacup ride at a carnival. The farther she looked out to the horizon, the more baskets she saw, bobbing and circling madly. She tried to paddle out to them with her arms in the murky water, but it just made everything worse. She woke early the next morning, already exhausted and with a whole day ahead of her.

Walking to school that morning, Vivian saw Kendra sitting on a bench outside the main entrance, talking to one of her friends, another popular girl named Vicki. In an instant of dread, she remembered seeing Kendra at the park the day before, and Vivian knew that Kendra would be unable to resist bringing it up. It was too late for her to turn around so she abruptly tried to turn her face away and become preoccupied with something in her backpack, but Kendra easily spotted her.

"Vivian!" Kendra shouted, jumping up and striding over to her. "Hey. Did I see you chasing barefoot after a squirrel yesterday at

Capital City Park? I was calling over to you, but you kept running. I know you saw me because you waved."

Vivian seriously considered denying it just to see how Kendra would react, but she didn't have the energy. Instead, she adopted an air of nonchalance, which was also certain to get under Kendra's skin.

"Yesterday, hmm?" Vivian said, looking thoughtful. "Yeah. That was probably me."

"What do you mean? Of course it was you, Viv," Kendra said grinning over at her friend Vicki, who was listening to them from the bench. "I saw you there. So why were you running after that squirrel?" Vivian had never noticed that Kendra could raise one eyebrow before.

Vivian considered her eyebrow for a moment and said, "I suppose because I felt like it."

Kendra clicked her tongue. "Don't be silly," she said, getting an impatient tone in her voice. "I'm just asking you a question."

"And I'm just answering it," Vivian said in more of a mocking tone than she intended, still annoyed from their conversation the other day. "Listen, I have to get to my locker." Vivian lifted her backpack off of her shoulders into her hand. "I've got stuff to do."

"Like chase squirrels barefoot?"

"We'll see what the day brings. Got to go, Kendra," she said, starting to walk past her.

Saying this, especially in such a manner, violated a subtle but important social rule at school: the popular kids were the ones who decided when to begin and end conversations. That fact wasn't lost on Kendra, who narrowed her eyes at Vivian like a queen with an impudent subject.

"What *is* your problem?" Kendra spat out, blocking her with her body. "What's going on with you?"

Vivian shrugged her shoulders and was ready to walk around Kendra and into the building when she heard the tinkling of little bells and saw a tanned hand with silver bracelets on her shoulder.

"Viv!" Wren enthused, eyes sparkling. "We need to talk. How are you feeling?" Wren looked over at Kendra, who had jumped back when she arrived. "Oh, I'm sorry to interrupt." Kendra suddenly looked terrified that Wren would start talking to her and ran back to the bench.

"Listen," Wren continued, unfazed, "we took the ducks home after you left and they are doing so well."

Vivian nodded foggily, looking at the sidewalk. Wren glanced at Kendra and Vicki, who were straining to hear their conversation, and she took Vivian's arm, walking with her into the school. They walked down the hall together silently and stopped at Vivian's locker.

"Listen. I'm sorry I yelled at you yesterday," Vivian said quietly.

"I'm sorry I wasn't more sensitive," Wren said. "For some reason, I didn't realize how upset you'd be about it."

"I couldn't help it," Vivian said.

"I know. My mom's worked with animals all my life, so I'm kind of used to the idea that not all of them make it. Part if me is, kind of desensitized, I think. She and I talked about that yesterday, and now I totally understand why you left the way you did."

"Why did I?" asked Vivian, a slight smile on her face.

"Because you were so sad, you know?" Vivian didn't say anything, so Wren continued. "Anyway, we took some pictures. We thought that would help. Do you want to see?" she asked, reaching for her bag. "They are already totally loving the pond in back. They took to it right away."

"The pond in back of what?"

"Our house, silly. Look at them. It's like they've always been there."

"You have a pond behind your house?"

Vivian flipped through the photos of the ducks in the twilight on the Summers' land. Seeing them walking through the tall, soft grass and the mother duck paddling with her babies in the pond, she felt as though she were looking at a greeting card. The land, of which she just saw a fragment in the photos, looked so different from anything Vivian had ever seen around Center City, with gentle hills and vivid purple, red and yellow wildflowers bursting from the earth. It looked like one of those Monet paintings she'd seen in her mother's coffee table book of Impressionist painters.

"It's so beautiful there, Wren," Vivian said, noticeably taken aback.

"Where we live? Thanks. My parents found the land years ago and decided that it was magical. It might be. It's why we're still in Center City. We call it Sevagram, after Gandhi's ashram. It means 'village of service.'"

"Tolstoy mentioned Gandhi before."

"Tol-?"

"The pig spirit," Vivian whispered. "He's mentioned Gandhi. I don't know much about him."

"Really? You should. He was monstrously cool."

"Well, I'm just still so amazed to know someone whose house has a name. We just have an address."

"We have an address, too. Addresses are fine."

A rare impulse bubbled up in Vivian and she found herself blurting out, "Can I go see it? Your home? I have to see it with my own eyes with the ducks there."

"Well, I'm not working after school today," Wren said, half-jokingly, as if she wouldn't expect Vivian to want to visit on such short notice.

"Today? Actually, today would be great. I don't have any tests coming up; I don't think that I'll have a lot of homework." Vivian said. "Do you mean it, Wren? I could see your place today?"

They agreed to meet at Wren's locker after school. Vivian kept thinking about the photos throughout the day. She couldn't help but feel that being on the land would ground her in way that her floating, distracted body instinctively craved. For the rest of the day, she felt peaceful.

In gym class that afternoon, while the class was getting ready to take a run, a girl named Kathy stooped next to Vivian as she was lacing up her shoes and said, in a straight-faced, cruel way, "Vivian, if you want to run really fast, just imagine that you're chasing a squirrel. I hear that's what you like to do these days." A couple of Kathy's friends turned their faces away as they giggled into their hands. Not too long ago, being laughed at would have devastated Vivian. This time, however, she simply smiled at Kathy and said cheerily, "You know, that's a really good idea. I think I will. Thanks for the advice." Kathy just stared at Vivian, with a look of confusion and defensiveness marking her face, as if she thought she was being mocked but wasn't certain. Vivian finished tying her shoes and started running, imagining Billy in front of her as Kathy had suggested, leaving her still stooped next to where Vivian had just sat. She made great time that day.

That afternoon, Vivian and Wren walked to the Summer's house together. It was a half-hour's distance from the school, down the streets with manicured lawns and houses side-by-side to an area where the land gradually became more unmanaged and the houses started spreading farther apart. Vivian marveled aloud at the fact that she'd grown up in Center City but had never known this part of it existed.

"Well, technically we're in unincorporated Center City, so it's understandable," Wren said, tactfully.

They turned down a dirt road and almost immediately Vivian noticed a giant structure in the middle of the meadow, with hubcaps, mirrors and bent metal pieces reflecting the sky and wildflowers and vividly painted pipes jutting all around like a crowded elevator full of sharp elbows. A little farther out, a graceful silver bird hung from a giant elm tree, his wings softly flapping in the breeze, shimmering in the sun. A beast of some sort – a dragon, perhaps – was lying in the sun, as if scratching his enormous back on the grass, his round chest constructed of thick and thin metal chains stretched towards the sky.

Noticing Vivian's reaction to the sculptures, Wren said, "I know. Aren't they cool?"

Vivian nodded. "Who made them?"

"My dad. He has a studio in the big barn – we have two – and he teaches there, too."

"Does anyone in town buy them? I mean, aren't they a little, I don't know, wild for most people in Center City?"

Wren smiled and nodded. "Yeah, most of his clients are in New Dublin or other cities, and most of his shows are there. But a lot of people from out of state come all the way out here just to meet my dad and buy his work. He's even in some art books."

Her house was a bright yellow A-frame with a wrap-around porch, striking against the blue sky. As they started walking down the road to her house, Wren grabbed the mail and whistled, then called out, "Hey, Bucky! I'm home." Within seconds, a scruffy, wheat-colored terrier pushed out of a dog door mounted into their front door and came bounding down the steps, panting happily.

"Hey, Buckaroo!" Wren said as he leapt up into her outstretched arms. He put his paws around her shoulders as if hugging her and leaned over to sniff Vivian. "This is Bucky, a.k.a. Buckers, Buckaroo, Buckmeister and Buckminster Fuller. Isn't he cute?"

"So cute."

"We found him when he was four or five weeks old, hiding under my dad's truck," Wren said, scratching his neck. "Luckily we heard this little bark so we didn't run him over or anything."

"How did he get here?"

"Who knows, really?" Wren said, shrugging. "He might have been the puppy of a farm dog and he got loose, or he might have been just dumped here."

"Dumped?"

"Yeah. When people find out you take care of animals, all of the sudden, you'll wake up in the morning to animals people don't want to care for, usually babies, sick or old ones," Wren said, matter-of-factly. "People just drop them off in the middle of the night. But can you imagine anyone dumping such a delight as Bucky?"

"I like his name." Vivian said, giggling as he leaned over to sniff her ear.

"Yeah, his original name was Lucky, but then we thought that was kind of, you know, rude, of us to name him that."

"To call him Lucky? Why?" Vivian asked.

"Oh, because we realized that we were calling him Lucky because he'd found us, which is presumptuous, you know? So we changed his name to Bucky, which fit, too, because he just sort of looked like one. Right, Buckers?" Wren asked him, kissing his fuzzy muzzle.

They walked up to the house and Wren put Bucky back down on the porch. They walked in and just as Wren was showing Vivian around, she heard her mom calling from outside.

"Wren?"

"Hi, Mom."

"Come out and see the ducks."

They walked through the long first floor of the house, through their kitchen with copper pots hanging from a rack on the ceiling and a huge painting of a rooster, and out the back door. Mrs. Summer was sitting on the grass by the pond behind their home, a notepad by her side.

"They're so sweet, I can't stop staring at them." Mrs. Summer turned to look over her shoulder as the door shut. "Oh, hello, Vivian. I didn't know you were coming over. What a nice surprise."

They walked over to the pond and Vivian, whose natural shyness was compounded by feeling a little embarrassed still for having run out of the café the previous afternoon, hung a little back.

"Do you see the way the mama is preening herself?" Mrs. Summer asked as the downy yellow and black ducklings watched the mallard. "She's been doing that all day. She's showing her babies how to waterproof themselves."

Wren sat down next to her mother and patted the ground next to her, motioning for Vivian to join them, which she did, relieved to not be standing awkwardly, not sure what to do with herself.

"She's such a natural mother," Wren said as the mallard settled into the grass with her ducklings. "I wonder if these are her first babies."

Mrs. Summer shook her head. "I have no idea. But most animals have an instinctive ability to care for their young, right? Unlike us."

"What do you mean?" Vivian asked.

Mrs. Summer looked surprised that Vivian spoke. Vivian was a little surprised herself. "Oh, I mean that human animals are the only mothers who think we need to read a thousand books and watch videotapes and buy expensive apparatus before we can adequately take care of our babies. Not that other animals have those things, but…"

"I know what you mean," Vivian said.

They sat quietly watching the ducks, enjoying the sun on their faces. Wren, who had taken off her shoes in the house, wriggled her toes in the grass and starting picking dandelions, absentmindedly tying the stems together as her mother breezily talked about the ducks she'd known. "They're curious but they don't really like to get too close to people. That's what's so remarkable about the mama coming to you for help."

"I think Vivian's discovered a new power," Wren said casually, tying another dandelion stem to complete a small loop. "Your majesty," she said, placing it upon Vivian's head. "The Dandelion Queen."

"My loyal subject," Vivian said in her best imperial accent.

"So," Wren said, brightly, "are you up for a walk? I could show you all around." She turned to her mother. "Viv thinks that we're cool, Mom."

"Really?" Mrs. Summer said, her eyes widening dramatically. "I've never been cool in my life."

"Me neither," Wren chimed in.

Vivian blushed.

"Look, I embarrassed her," Wren said. "Vivian's quite bashful. She's like one of the Seven Dwarves. Isn't that cute? I'm not used to someone this humble."

"I know. It's a rare quality, and a sweet one," said Mrs. Summer. She looked over at Vivian hiding her face in her hands. "Oh, boy, we've got a blusher on our hands. We've got to get you accustomed to a little attention, Viv. In the meantime, though, I think we can stop torturing you with our modest praise."

"I appreciate it," Vivian said, quietly, not quite sure if she appreciated their positive attention or if she appreciated that Mrs. Summer promised to stop giving it.

They walked to the garden first, what seemed to Vivian to be nothing short of a farm compared to her family's simple backyard garden. Flowers were already blooming, herbs and vegetables were in various stages of growth, neatly planted rows of green leaves had sprouted up from the ground.

"You should see this in July, August. It's really something then," Mrs. Summers paused, inhaling deeply, eyes closed; she looked just like Wren at that moment. "I can't wait."

"We eat off it all season," said Wren. "We can it and freeze it for the fall and winter. It's so much better than anything you taste anywhere else. Except the zucchini. You can keep zucchini for all I care."

"What is it with you and zucchini?" asked Mrs. Summer, fastening the gate with a rope as they left. "What did zucchini ever do to you? Attack you in your sleep?"

"I just don't like it. It's weird and squishy. And it has, like, no flavor."

"You could say the same thing about eggplant, but you love eggplant," said her mother.

"Eggplant tastes good, though. It's like tofu; it takes on the flavor of the dish. Do you like eggplant?" She looked at Vivian.

"Oh. I've never had it," she said casually.

Wren and Mrs. Summer both stopped in their tracks, looked at each other and said in unison, "You've never had eggplant?"

"Nope," said Vivian, feigning to stop to examine a flower. "I've never had zucchini either. I'm not even sure that I could point one out."

"What?" stammered Mrs. Summer. "I don't believe it."

"It's true," said Vivian, almost enjoying the attention despite herself.

"Well, what's your favorite vegetable?" asked Wren.

"Um, I don't know. Potatoes?"

"Oh, that practically doesn't count," said Wren. "What else?"

"Corn's okay," Vivian said indifferently.

"What about kale or collards?" asked Mrs. Summer.

"Never had 'em," said Vivian. "They're green, right?"

"Do you eat spinach?"

"Ugh, no. I don't know how anyone can stand that stuff. It's slimy."

"Spinach isn't slimy," said Wren, bewildered. "It's crisp and light like lettuce."

"The kind we get is slimy. It's in the blue and white can. I never eat it."

"Spinach in a can?" Mrs. Summer said, incredulously. "You eat spinach in a can? I didn't know they still made that."

"I didn't even know they *ever* made spinach in a can," Wren chimed in.

"Oh yes, it comes in cans and it's awful."

"Canned spinach should be illegal. It's a crime against humanity. A crime against nature," Mrs. Summer said, waving her fist to punctuate the point.

"Oh, great," Wren smirked. "Now we're going to have a new cause: fight canned spinach!"

"Free the spinach!" Her mom chimed in.

Wren giggled. "Okay, what about squash? Butternut, acorn, spaghetti..."

"I eat spaghetti," Vivian said proudly. "I like all kinds of noodles. I eat it practically every night. But noodles aren't made of squash, are they?"

"No, I mean spaghetti *squash.*" Wren said, laughing. Vivian looked at her blankly. "Oh my goddess, you've got to try spaghetti squash. It's so cool. You cut it in half and roast it – and then you can take out those seeds and roast them too – and then you scrape out these strands that are like skinny noodles with a fork. It looks just like angel hair pasta, my favorite. We mix it up with plum tomatoes, fresh basil, olive oil. It's my favorite thing about the fall, other than Halloween."

"So what do you eat, Viv?" asked Mrs. Summer.

"Well, I'm like you guys now. I don't eat animal foods."

"I know," Mrs. Summer smiled. "Wren told me. I was thinking that Wren might make it through her whole youth without meeting another vegetarian in Center City, let alone vegan. I mean, she meets other young people like her at conferences and that sort of thing, but never here."

"Well, I think a few people who go to the café are vegetarian. Owl's a vegetarian when he remembers that fish is meat," Wren said.

"No, but I mean peers like Vivian. Anyway, back to you, kiddo," Mrs. Summer said, looking at Vivian, "I know what you *don't* eat, but what *do* you eat?"

She shrugged. "I don't know. Pasta with tomato sauce. Peanut butter and jelly sandwiches."

"What else?"

"Um, that's about it," Vivian said. "Oh, and plain cereal."

"What do you mean 'plain cereal'?" Mrs. Summer asked.

"I don't drink milk anymore, so…"

"So just a spoon and a bowl of dry cereal?"

Vivian nodded.

"You don't know about soy milk? Or rice milk? Or almond milk? My goodness, child, we have got to *feed* you," said Mrs. Summer, exasperated.

"But I'm not hung- "

"I don't care if you're hungry or not," Mrs. Summer said firmly. "We have got to fill you up with vegetables and whole grains pronto. I can't stand it another second longer. You probably don't even know what you like to eat. Why do you think you were born with taste buds? You guys keep taking your walk and I'm going to the kitchen to make you something good to eat."

They walked a short, curvy path to Mr. Summer's studio, which was in an old barn that had been converted into a modern sculpture workspace, complete with various works in progress and all manner of torches and sharp instruments, all meticulously put away in several towering wooden cabinets stacked tall with cases and slim drawers. It was chaotic and organized at once. He was not in the studio at the moment – he was "scavenging" at an aluminum plant in Cooperstown, Wren told her – so Wren showed Vivian around his studio. They poked in drawers and looked at his charcoal sketches, which were taped to the walls. Vivian had never been in an artist's studio before, so it felt especially magical to her, like a wizard's workshop. The barn seemed to be buzzing with an electric alchemy, so much so that Vivian found herself lightheaded. She inhaled giant breaths as soon as they walked out of the studio, eager for the kind of oxygen she was accustomed to breathing. At that moment, the thought of eating something was very appealing.

"Maybe we should go back to the house and help your mom for a while."

"Oh, I think she's okay. If she wanted help, she would have said so."

"Yeah, but I'm feeling a little tired. I didn't sleep well last night. Maybe we could just hang out in the kitchen with her for a while," Vivian said. "Do you mind?"

Wren had a look of disappointment flash across her face momentarily, but then shrugged her shoulders and smiled.

"Nah. I'll show you the animal center some other time. No biggie."

"Thanks."

They walked back to the house as Wren chattered cheerily in her meandering way about the surroundings.

"See that elm tree over there? The tallest one? I fell off it when I was little, that big branch, and broke my arm. My dad came running out to help me and he stepped on a rake, which smacked into his head," she slapped her palm against her forehead, "and knocked him out. Can you imagine? It was like a cartoon. Then my mom hears all this commotion: me screaming under the tree with a broken arm and she came out running like this," Wren said, stopping in her tracks, eyes wide, mouth open in a look of shock, "and I remember thinking, 'Man, if I weren't in so much pain and my dad weren't hurt, this would be hysterically funny.'"

Vivian, doubled over and snorting with laughter, couldn't remember the last time she'd laughed so hard it hurt.

"You always have the best stories."

"You think? My life's pretty funny, I guess."

They walked up to the house where Bucky greeted them with a high-pitched bark, running in circles until he leapt up into Wren's arms. She wrapped one arm around him and held him at her side. In the kitchen, Mrs. Summer was standing over a cutting board on the counter, chopping broccoli, and a covered pot was simmering on the stovetop. A pan sizzled on the burner next to the pot, and it smelled a little like the Chinese restaurant on Van Buren near downtown. Vivian was a little nervous, both because of the expectation that she would be trying all this new food, prepared in a way she was not accustomed to, and also because she was uncomfortable with someone doting on her but she had to admit to herself that it she was intrigued.

"So what are you cooking?" Vivian asked.

"Well, I'm just working with what I have around, so we're going to have a simple stir-fry with, let's see, garlic, ginger, red bell peppers, broccoli and tofu over basmati rice."

"Ah, the mysterious tofu," Vivian said, feeling a little afraid.

"So you've heard of it before," said Mrs. Summer with a sly grin.

Vivian nodded grimly. "I've heard of it before but I've never had it. I was wondering if it would make an appearance today."

"Tofu is unfairly maligned, in my opinion. If you prepare it well, it will taste good, just like anything else," Mrs. Summer said, adding a few drops of sesame oil with a loud sizzle from the pan. "Here, sauté this for me, would you?" she said, handing Vivian a wooden spatula.

Vivian was tentative at first, unsure if she was moving things around right, but then fell into a comfortable place with herself, Mrs. Summer sprinkling tamari ("It's like soy sauce," Mrs. Summer said, "but better,") over the pan. They worked together in the kitchen with music chosen by Wren ("Etta James," she said, dreamily, "my favorite,"), Vivian happily stirring around the contents of the pan until the broccoli got to the bright green stage Mrs. Summer was seeking. They sat down around an oval, pale yellow table with red vinyl chairs with a starburst pattern on them. There were purple wildflowers in a glass vase. Vivian thought that it was the prettiest, most perfect table she'd ever seen.

"Well," said Mrs. Summer after Vivian's first bite, "what do you think?"

Feeling two sets of eyes on her, Vivian fought the urge to sink under the table. Instead, she chewed her food, bringing her napkin to her mouth. In her house, people didn't really talk about food. She took a sip of the iced tea Mrs. Summer had poured and said, "I'm not used to many vegetables to begin with, and I'm certainly not used to them being crunchy like this, so it's a whole new thing. But I like it. I could get used to it, I think."

"I'll take that as a compliment," said Mrs. Summer.

"Yeah. Viv thinks that she could get used to your cooking," Wren said, teasing.

Vivian turned pink, sputtering out that that was not what she meant.

Wren and Mrs. Summer laughed and they both assured Vivian that they understood. "It does take some getting used to when you change what you're familiar with, food especially for some reason. Of course it does," said Mrs. Summer.

The three sat and talked and Wren did an impression of her father in the morning (hair everywhere, eyes half-closed, taciturn: Vivian couldn't wait to meet him) and Mrs. Summer talked about Wren as a toddler, how she refused to wear anything but a pair of purple pajamas for a year. When they heard the doorbell ring, it was jarring, like a thunderclap out of nowhere. Bucky sprung off of Wren's lap with a peal of barks as Mrs. Summer left the room to get the door and a black and white cat who had just made a tentative appearance went darting off into the pantry.

"It's okay, Merlin," Wren said. "He's a bit of a scaredy cat."

Vivian could hear Mrs. Summer and a male's voice talking in the entryway. They talked for a few minutes before Vivian could hear them walking toward the kitchen.

"Oh, hi, Carson," Wren said warmly. "I was wondering who it was."

"Vivian," said Mrs. Summer, "this is my friend, Will Carson."

Will nodded in Vivian's direction. He was tall and angular with longish medium brown hair in a ponytail and oval glasses. He was wearing a t-shirt and ripped out jeans, and reminded Vivian of one of the Center City College students she might see idly strumming a guitar on Main Street downtown in the summer. His expression was unmistakably serious and focused, though, with no trace of the misty-eyed amiability of the downtown guitar strummers.

"Vivian was the one who found the ducks and took them to Wren," Mrs. Summer said, by way of explaining. Will nodded and grunted something, maybe some sort of acknowledgement, to Vivian.

"Carson, do you want something to eat?" Wren asked, standing up. "Drink?"

He shook his head, muttering something. The room became quiet, and after what felt like a few awkward moments, Vivian studied her stockinged feet (she'd left her muddy shoes on the doormat), hooked them together and rocked them back together until Mrs. Summer broke the silence. Everyone looked up a bit too eagerly.

"Will came over last night to take the sample you got off the ducklings. He works at the college and has a friend in the chemistry department. We wanted to get it analyzed just to figure out what we're dealing with." Mrs. Summer looked at Vivian. "Are you okay with hearing this?"

The ducks. Her chest sunk at hearing them mentioned but Vivian nodded, wordlessly, and looked back down.

Will took off his glasses and wiped the lenses on his shirt. "Of course the results are not back in yet as to what that substance was, but I have some suspicions. Did you say that you found the ducks on the river?"

She nodded.

"Where?"

"Not far from the entrance to Capital Park."

"See, the thing is, I think that sludge was a kind of chemical by-product run-off or dumping. Probably a dumping because this is very unfamiliar as run-off. I grew up in farm country. I know what it smells like. I know what it looks like."

Mrs. Summer frowned. "So what are you thinking? That someone poured it on them or something?"

Will shook his head impatiently. "No, no. I don't think it was intentional. We've been seeing other birds like this, fish covered in slime. I'm thinking it was a factory dump. Strongly."

"Do you mean Gordenner?"

Will took the band out of his hair and hastily looped it back around his hair, then started pacing through the kitchen. "Who else? Every time I think about this, I always come back to Gordenner. I can't imagine otherwise at this point."

Gordenner had been in Center City since the 1930s. It originally started as Universal Chemical Corporation by Jack Gorden and Harlan J. Jenner, and it was the town's largest employer, with more than 3,000 workers. Their name, slogan (*Helping America Grow*), and logo of a sheaf of wheat crossing an ear of corn, were seen throughout Center City, from the flags that billowed at their gleaming corporate offices downtown to the billboards that dotted the interstate to the Little League uniforms on the team they sponsored. Although Vivian had never given much thought to Gordenner – some of her friend's parents had worked there over the years but beyond that there was no personal connection – it was just taken for granted that Gordonner was completely entwined in Center City's history, as though the town never existed before the company was founded there.

"They have that plant out there on the river," Mrs. Summer said. "You think it could have come from there?"

Will inhaled, squinting. "Well, here's what I don't understand. I spent the day looking up EPA reports from the water samples they've taken around the plant, and it all came up clear. There was minimal pollution where the river meets the plant, no more than average. Downstream, that's where it starts showing up. Dramatically, I might add."

"But if it's not Gordenner, you don't want to keep focusing on them," Mrs. Summer pointed out.

"Oh, I'm sure it's them. Certain. All those dead fish washing up in the river. All those sick and dying birds. No one else is doing anything that dangerous. Remember eight years ago when they had to pay off that big settlement with the state?" Will looked at Vivian. "They got caught dumping chemicals into the river and got a huge fine."

"Not huge enough," said Mrs. Summer. "And they were dumping for years before that. But didn't they have to bring everything up to code as a result of the last suit?"

Will nodded. "They did, but I bet something happened. Like maybe one of their mechanisms is failing. Maybe they got lazy or more greedy. I don't know. I just know that when the water is tested right by the factory, it tests within an acceptable range, but, this is the thing, when it gets downstream a mile or so, it is totally polluted. Dead fish, slimy, noxious water. It's been like that for the past year."

"And there are no other factories or big farms in between?" Wren asked.

Will shook his head. "Nope. This is why I'm sure that it's Gordenner."

"Well, let's just say it is them. What do we do?" Mrs. Summer asked.

"First things first: we've got to prove it somehow. We've got to figure out how they're doing it."

"Then we've got to expose them to all the local media," Wren said.

Will snorted. "They own the local media. I think we've got to take it to something bigger. File a class action lawsuit or something."

"But that would take a lot of time," Wren interjected. "Maybe if we get the media and the *Patriot* involved right away, they'll get scared and clean up the problem."

"Won't happen," Will said, confidently. "It just won't. With a company like Gordenner, you've got to really hold their feet to the fire. They know that the local news is a joke. Even if we were to get any coverage, it'd be skewed in their favor."

"But how do you know that?" Wren asked.

"How do I know? I know because I wasn't born yesterday."

"Yes, but shouldn't we be considering every possibility?"

"Not if it means wasting time."

"I'm not interested in wasting time, Will. I'm trying to be effective," Wren snapped.

"Listen, we have to be strategic here. If we alert the media, they'll likely tip off Gordenner and there will be a cover-up before we could ever effectively expose them. They'll have beat us before we even started."

Vivian could see that Wren was getting upset and jumped in. "Okay, first we need to figure out what's really going on before we have a strategy. I think that we should go outside the plant tomorrow after school and just poked around. We could walk all around. I think it would give us a better sense of what we might be dealing with. Are you on?" she said, looking between Wren and Will.

Will frowned. "That works for me. After school, of course."

Vivian looked at Wren.

"Yeah, tomorrow should be fine. I'm off work"

Mrs. Summer frowned. "Guys, I am a little nervous. I have to say, this is trespassing. You could get in trouble."

"I promise we will be careful, Simone," Will said.

She looked at him a long time. "Promise?"

"Yes. Emphatically."

Mrs. Summer sighed. "Okay. Just, please, please be careful."

"We will, Mom." Wren reached over and squeezed her hand. "I promise."

Mrs. Summer smiled wearily, looking down at their hands, fingers now entwined. "I won't stop you."

Vivian looked at Will. "Should we say that we'll meet at the factory at 3:30? In front?"

"Works for me," he said.

"Me, too."

"Good, then tomorrow it is," Vivian said, surprised at the authoritative nature of her voice. It was the first time she'd heard it, other than the day with that man at the flea market. She excused herself to go to the bathroom and get ready to go home. She wondered again if Tolstoy was going to return. As she was walking out of the bathroom, something caught her eye in the mirror: she realized with a mixture of embarrassment and good humor that she was still wearing the dandelion crown Wren had made for her earlier.

"All hail the Dandelion Queen," she said to her reflection.

"Vivian," Wren called out from the kitchen. "Did you say something?"

"Oh, no," she said. "Just mumbling to myself."

TRESPASSING AND MEETING MS. COLLINS

Although Vivian had been withdrawing from her family for the previous month, she now found herself wanting to be closer to them. The things that irritated her about her mother – the way she forbade the family to use the guest towels, even though she was far too busy and particular about her home to even have company come over, the way she answered the phone ("Sally Sharpe here") – suddenly made her more endearing to Vivian. Vivian also felt the urge to play with her sister, even when she wasn't asked to, and found herself French braiding her hair with Millie's simple request that evening after she came home from Wren's house.

"Why are you suddenly so nice?" Millie demanded, smiling slyly.

"Oh, I don't know," Vivian said quietly, folding one soft section of her sister's hair over the next. "Something must have come over me."

She realized as she sat on the grass watching Millie play hopscotch, her braid bouncing, that she felt protective of her family, and that something in the past few days – finding the ducks, learning of the pollution in the Kickashaunee – spurred in her an instinct to draw her parents and sister close to her. It was enough of an abrupt behavioral shift that it became a topic of conversation at dinner the night before she was to visit Gordenner with Wren and Will.

"So," said Mrs. Sharpe after Vivian talked at length about Wren and her family, "is this the new you?"

"Does this mean you haven't succumbed entirely to teenaged angst?" asked her father.

Vivian felt her cheeks getting pink and hot. She was moments away from fleeing the room in tears when Millie chimed in, earnestly grabbing her sister's arm. "Don't pick on Vivian. It's not her fault if she's a teenager."

Vivian felt the hot embarrassment drain from her face, and had to smile at Millie's defense of her. Her parents looked at each other like they weren't sure if they should laugh or not, but then the whole table started laughing.

"She's right," Vivian said, looking at Millie, "I can't help it."

She had a stomachache the entire next day. She found herself wishing that she'd stayed home from school, annoyed that Tolstoy hadn't visited, nervous about that afternoon. In swim class she sat with her arms wrapped around her legs on the bench and stared at the water, imagining it filling with the noxious sludge she found on the ducks. Her throat clenched and her eyes watered at the thought, and soon, she was on the floor, kneeling. The next thing she knew, her swim coach, Ms. Hill, was crouched beside her, her hand on her shoulder.

"Are you okay, Vivian?"

Vivian sat upright on the cold tile, lowering her head to breathe, her fingers laced behind her head. After a few moments, she said, "I'm not feeling so well right now. I think that I should sit out…if that's okay."

Ms. Hill nodded distractedly and addressed the rest of her classmates, watching them from inside the pool. "Okay, girls, I want to see some elegant kicks now. No more sloppy legs. Slice through the water," she said, lifting and lowering her arms like a strangely robotic ballerina. She sent Vivian to lie down at the nurse's office.

After school, Vivian met Wren at her locker. For the previous hour, she had been distracted, trying to figure out a way to get out of going to the Gordenner factory that afternoon. She could legitimately say that she wasn't feeling well, but as soon as she started to feel some measure of relief imagining that she didn't have to go to the factory, her drive would kick back in and she'd remember the ducks on the side of the river, their quiet pulses. She could feel the pulse still in her fingertips. Her resolve came back, but it was fierce and unfriendly.

Wren was uncharacteristically subdued, too, which compounded Vivian's sense of doom. She had hoped that Wren would lift her spirits or at least distract her, but just looking at her friend slumping against her locker, it was all Vivian could do not to lie down in the middle of the hallway and take a nap. After a few minutes of walking silently – Wren's eyes downcast, Vivian distractedly kicking at a rock – they stopped at their bus stop and both drooped onto the bus stop bench. Wren could have driven, but Will was worried about their cars being discovered by security at Gordenner. And there likely *was* going to be security, she reminded Vivian solemnly. They sat in silence for a few minutes, then Vivian and Wren exchanged a glance and they both started laughing.

"We're a lively pair, aren't we?" said Wren.

"You're telling me. Are you nervous too? Is that why we're so quiet?"

Wren looked up at some geese flying overhead and sighed. "Yeah. I've never done anything like this. Just…yeah…nervous."

"Me, too."

"Well," Wren said, patting Vivian's knee reassuringly, "at least we're going into it together."

"Whatever 'it' is." Vivian said this grimly, not trying to be funny, but when Wren started giggling, she couldn't help but laugh, too. "What are we doing, anyway?"

"No idea. I was hoping you knew. Oh, we have bus, I see." Wren stood up, grabbing her bag. "Do you need any change?"

"Nope. I've got it," she said, already rubbing two quarters between her index finger and thumb. "Yippee."

They sat near the back of the bus and talked quietly about their plans, running over possible scenarios. If there was a security guard outside – Will had heard that there had been some vandalism recently at Gordenner, so there might be security – they would just keep walking. Otherwise, they would meet Will behind the factory, where pipes were pumping what Gordenner maintained was filtered water into the river. They were going to be stealthy and sly, they agreed. "Think like a cat," Wren said. "Well, not like one of my cats, 'cause ours are either lazy or feral. Think like a well-adjusted cat."

Wren pulled the cord near the last stop and walked to the rear door. "Have a blessed day," she called to the driver.

Startled, he turned around to face them. "What's that?"

"Have a blessed day."

He blinked at them, obviously not comprehending.

"Have a great day," Vivian intervened. "She was telling you to have a great day."

"Oh. Yes. You, too."

They pushed their way out of the door and started walking toward the factory, which Will had told Wren was west. He'd said that when they got off the bus, they'd walk until they came to a road on the right. Wren showed Vivian her compass, which was hanging from some pink yarn around her neck and had been under her shirt. "I don't really need it, but I thought it'd be fun to bring along."

"You're like Nancy Drew."

"Are your parents worried about you doing this?" Wren asked.

"What? Oh, gosh, I couldn't tell them. Do you think I could've told them? They probably think I'm off sulking somewhere by myself if they even notice I'm not home."

Wren nodded. "I sometimes think everyone's parents are like mine."

"So your parents aren't worried?"

"Nah," Wren said, kicking at some stones. "Maybe a little. But they trust me. Plus I've been taking self-defense workshops with my mom since I was eight. And aikido. There's part of me that's a little disappointed that I haven't been able to use it against anyone yet."

"Really?"

"Yeah, just a little. It'd be kind of fun to see if any of it really works outside of a classroom, you know? I don't want to learn today, though."

They walked along, making small talk and joking back and forth; they both were surprised with how quickly the road leading to the Gordenner building came up. It was a sprawling, grey structure with no sign in front or distinguishing characteristics. A locked gate enclosed the parking lot and factory, and it had a small sign attached to the fence stating that the lot was for Gordenner employees only and that trespassers would be arrested. There was a security booth in front of the lot, but it was empty.

They scanned the lot. Vivian took out a pair of her father's binoculars from her backpack.

"Now look who's Nancy Drew," Wren smiled. "All clear?" Vivian nodded.

"Will didn't mention this fence, but it's easy enough to climb over. It's like getting onto a horse," Wren said, putting one foot on the middle bar and swinging her other leg over. "Oh, you probably wouldn't know about that. Sorry."

Vivian followed, mimicking Wren's movements exactly, even the half-turn in her dismount. They crouched and darted between the cars in the parking lot until they reached the building, and kept going to the side.

At the back of the Gordenner corporate office building, they noticed that there was another building a bit behind and to the side of it, a much older and decrepit-looking structure but every bit as massive. "This must be the original building," Wren said. "Will said something about this. It's the factory." Vivian hadn't noticed until Wren had walked ahead to "scope out the back," as she said, that her eyes were itchy and tearing up again. She had assumed that her labored breathing – short, painful breaths – was from nerves, but when she noticed the tears she had been wiping away, she remembered that this was how she felt when she found the ducks on the river. She wiped at her eyes with the back of her hand as Wren motioned for her to come forward.

Behind the factory, they followed huge pipes that poured water out into the rushing river behind it. It was so loud, Wren winced and covered her ears as she walked near the pipes, and Vivian stayed back, noticing that she felt fine once again. As she was wondering why this might be, why the outflow of a factory that made her woozy wouldn't affect her in the same way, she heard something rustle behind her. Whirling around, she must have looked alarmed because Will quickly gestured for Vivian to be quiet despite the loud crash of river behind them. They walked to a patch of thick bushes and trees to the side of the factory and sat close together on the grass. He was carrying a small bucket.

"I thought you'd be a little while," Wren said.

"Yeah. I decided to ride my bike to get here quicker. So have you found anything?"

Wren shook her head. "No. I mean, I don't know what to look for exactly."

"Right. Well, it's not like a bunch of thugs in dark suits are going to make it easy for us like in the movies. We need to be on the lookout for chemicals being dumped. I don't know how it'll happen, but that's what we need to find. I brought a bucket and some containers for taking samples. Let's go back and wait for something to happen."

They started to stand when Vivian said, "Actually, I noticed something."

Wren and Will stopped to look at her.

"I noticed that when I was standing by the factory, my eyes got all watery and I was having a hard time breathing, but when we got out to the back, where the water is pouring out, I felt fine."

Will shrugged, wiping his glasses on his shirt. "So?"

"Vivian's an intuitive, Carson," Wren said, as though she were stating a plain fact, like the grass was green. She turned to Vivian, "So what do you think that means?"

Vivian looked back at the factory. "I think it means that Gordenner is creating something toxic inside, but that's not what's coming out."

"Well, we already know that they're creating toxins inside; they wouldn't deny that. It's probably legal for them to do, unfortunately," Will said.

"But somehow it's getting into the Kickashaunee. That's not legal."

"So how do you think it's happening?" Wren asked Vivian.

Will looked impatient. "This is entirely too speculative at this point. It's quite possible that Vivian's physical reactions were due to some plant she's allergic to that's near the front of the building and not in the back. Milkweed, pollen, whatever. We can't base our investigation on whether Vivian's eyes are watering. "

"But at this point we *should* be speculating," Wren argued. "We don't even know that Gordenner is the factory polluting the river."

"But they are," Will muttered.

"Who's speculating now? Prove it. Without a shadow of a doubt, prove it."

"Who else?"

Wren shrugged. "It could be accumulated run-off from big farms. It could be something else."

"It's not. We tested the residue from the ducks, remember? I got the results today: it's likely a chemical by-product, like an herbicide. I tested it against the others they sell and it wasn't one of them. It must be something new."

"Okay, Will, the point is at this point we should be open-minded. We have a thesis we're trying to prove – that the Gordenner plant is pumping poison into the water."

"A hypothesis," Will said

"What?"

"It's a hypothesis, not a thesis. A hypothetical argument constructed to test an assumed consequence."

"Right. Anyway, we should be following all leads right now, not discounting them out of hand."

Will shrugged again. Wren turned to Vivian. "So what do you think is happening, based on your intuition?" Vivian couldn't help notice Will rolling his eyes. She tried to think, but she was too self-conscious of Will's annoyance and Wren waiting for her, watching her as if she were an arcade fortuneteller, ready to spit out a prediction.

"I need a minute or two to think, okay?"

Will and Wren stood about ten feet away, looking at the pipes from behind the bushes, and Vivian sat in the grass. She tried sitting in the meditation pose like she'd seen Wren use in gym class but that felt awkward. After lying on her back and stomach, she finally settled with her arms wrapped around her shins, her head pressed against her knees, listening to the rushing water of the river.

In her mind, Vivian saw dirty water. Of course, there was water near her, so she shook away the image and tried to consciously conjure Tolstoy for the first time, hoping that he might offer some guidance. As soon as she could picture Tolstoy, though, the image of dirty water washed him away. She just couldn't hold on to Tolstoy and was about to give up when she noticed that the image of water that kept returning to her mind looked nothing like the Kickashaunee River. It was much more shallow, much less wide, slower moving. She tried to see past the mental image but all she could see was a thick woods surrounding the filthy water. As she examined the water, she noticed that it was not all dirty: it was clean up to a point, then it suddenly was filled with a sludgy liquid.

She joined Wren and Will, deep in conversation.

"Maybe they dump at night," Wren said.

"Possibly. That wouldn't explain why the river shows up as clean over here, though. See any 'visions'?" Will asked Vivian, squinting at the pipes.

"I saw water, dirty water, but it wasn't here at the river. Is there a creek nearby or something? In a wooded area?"

Will looked up, thinking for a moment. "Actually, yes. About two-thirds of a mile west. Colman's Creek. I saw it on a map when I was researching the area."

"Can we get there from here? Do you know the way?"

Will shook his head. "Just the general direction. I'm afraid that I would get us lost."

Wren said, "Viv, why don't you try to find it?"

"Me?"

"Yes, you," Wren said, like it was the most obvious thing in the world. "Use your intuition."

Vivian looked up and down the river and noticed that there was an old wooden bridge downstream. She started walking toward it. "Follow me."

Wren whooped and followed Vivian giddily. "This is like using one of those stick things to find water."

"A divining rod," Will muttered.

"Yes. One of those stick things."

"A divining rod."

"A divining rod," Wren repeated. "A stick thing. Whatever, word precision boy."

They crossed the bridge and followed a path between a row of trees that merged into a forest. Vivian tried to concentrate, acutely aware that there were two people following her, but she found that her feet just wanted to go a certain direction. When she let her mind take over and start trying to steer them in a different direction, veering away from the path her feet wanted to take, it reminded her of that childhood game, "Hot or cold." Not only did she stop feeling "right" – right in this case meaning her eyes were itchy and her throat and lungs hurt – but she literally got a cold feeling. So she found herself traveling over tree roots and through bushes in pursuit of that warm feeling with Wren and Will trailing close behind.

After they'd been walking for a while, Wren asked, "Are your eyes tearing up?"

"Yep. Also, what is it called? – my sinuses – my sinuses are throbbing."

"Good," Wren said.

"Thank you."

"Well, I just stepped in poison oak, I think," Will said, "and nobody seems too concerned about that."

Walking between trees and underbrush, Vivian started to get a sense of déjà vu, and she realized that this was giving way to the landscape she had imagined back at the Gordenner factory.

"This way. I'm sure of it," she said as they maneuvered through thick, tangled roots, thorns and bristly leaves. "Just follow me."

Finally, they heard it. Vivian pushed past bushes and down some flat rocks until she was at a creek, Wren and Will behind her. Before she even had a moment to marvel at her ability to find it, she was overcome with eyes and a throat that hurt so much they felt like bright orange hot coals. She didn't let the other two know how much it hurt, though. They had gotten this far.

Will sat down on a rock, taking off his socks and shoes, and rolling up his jeans. "This is nuts. If I didn't see it with my own eyes…" He balled up his socks and stuck them in a shoe. Wren kicked off her sandals, grabbed the bottom of her skirt and tied it in a knot on her hip. They both stepped in the water while Vivian sat on a rock and tried to calm her mind, which was racing with thoughts of trying to escape.

"Well, this is disgusting," she heard Will say. "Dead fish everywhere."

One of them retched. "It reeks," Wren said.

Vivian sat with her head cupped in her hands, elbows on her knees. She had never fainted before – couldn't even imagine what that was like – but it seemed to her that if she ever were to faint, now would be the appropriate time, and that losing consciousness would be the most merciful thing that could happen to her at that moment. She was also so tired and drugged feeling that she had to really focus to remember why exactly she was sitting by an odious creek in the middle of the woods.

"Viv? Are you okay?" Wren was kneeling by her side, her hand on Vivian's shoulder.

Vivian murmured weakly; nodding her head would take too much energy. "I'm just feeling so sick."

"I know. I know." She sat down next to Vivian, wiping her eyes with the bottom of her top. Will was scooping up dead fish into the bucket, making retching sounds. Vivian was vaguely worried that he was going to vomit because then it would be unavoidable for her to not follow in kind.

"Found a bird, too. It looks like a gosling but it's hard to tell with all the gunk on it. Looks like the same slime that was on those ducks, but even thicker."

Vivian could feel Wren shudder next to her.

"Well, I'm totally confused. This seems like spill from Gordenner, but how would it be getting here?" Will said, thinking out loud. He kept walking up the creek, naming the creatures he found matter-of-factly. "Fish. Fish. Frog. Fish. Bird. Something – a baby bird…I think. Sick. Frog…"

Vivian and Wren were leaned together, each holding up the other with their weight together, when something gurgled deep within Vivian's belly and she looked up at the creek. She stood up and pointed to a spot a few yards away from them.

"Look. What's that?"

91

Will loudly splashed out of the water and the three rushed over to that point at the creek, which had been murky but now was bubbling with a thick black slime in one area, as though an oil pipeline had accidentally been struck. It gurgled over the surface, spreading a viscous substance like squid ink in the creek for about a minute, and they stood together on the side of the creek, silent and staring. When it finally stopped, it took them a moment or two to shake out of their stupor.

"What just happened?" Wren repeated over and over. Will rushed around the creek, taking photos and samples of the still saturated water. "Eww. What is that?"

"I don't think you should go in there, Vivian," Will said. She didn't acknowledge that anything was said to her; she just walked right into the creek. It was like her sick, reeling self was still sitting back on the rock; the Vivian in the creek felt the kind of adrenaline that made her feel invincible as she walked to where the bubbling originated.

She bent down and felt around with her fingers, raking over pebbles, silt and rocks; she couldn't see anything through the filthy water. Then her fingers touched something different, a smooth metallic surface with some rough patches that didn't belong there. It was what she was seeking. Feeling around, it was a wide circle, maybe a little bigger than one of her mother's coffee cans. Reaching her arm deeper in, there was just water there, no rocks, no sand, deeper than where her feet were. She stretched her arm in up past her elbow.

"What is it?" Wren shouted.

"I'm not sure. Something round, like a hole. I think it's some sort of a pipe. Could it be a pipe?"

Will jumped back in the water and hurried over to where Vivian was standing, water splashing around him. He bent near her and put his arm in the water, frowning as he felt around. "Yep. That's a pipe all right."

"This is coming from the Gordenner plant," Vivian said. "It's practically a straight line from there. This is why the water coming out of the factory is clean. Because they pipe the toxins into this creek from underground."

Wren started jumping up and down, shouting. "That's it. That's it. This is what pollutes the Kickashaunee where the creek merges with it."

Will shook his head. "Just when you think that you couldn't get any more cynical…"

"But we've got them now," said Wren brightly, punching her fist triumphantly. "Vivian found the pipeline from the factory."

"So what do you propose we do?" Will said sharply, walking out of the creek. "Just start screaming at the top of our lungs? We need to have a plan here."

Vivian started walking out of the water, her arms and exposed legs covered with black slime. She was so nauseated now, her head swirling. "I think we should go now. I think we should go a little past the pipe and rinse off. We'd better get going," she said.

They walked some distance upstream of the pipe and rinsed off, needing to use their fingernails to scrape off some of the residue. It took about ten minutes to get reasonably clean. As they walked away from the creek, Vivian's head slowly began to clear up like silt settling, but she was still fatigued. Wren and Will, however, were completely energized from the experience. Vivian's ability to navigate their way back to the factory was much less pronounced than it had been finding the creek. She kept doubting her steps, sending them off into the wrong direction, walking them in circles until she said, "You know what? I can't do this right now. Can someone else figure out the way back?"

Will stepped to the front. "I think I can remember."

Wren walked with Vivian for a little while, gushing with excitement, but Vivian, still depleted, couldn't face her friend's energy. It just made her more tired.

"Do you just need to be quiet right now and collect your thoughts?" Wren asked.

Vivian nodded. "I'm just feeling overwhelmed. I'm sorry…"

Wren waved her hand like there was no need to explain. "I'm just going to go bug Carson for a while then," she said, rushing forward to catch up to him and his long strides. He actually seemed garrulous, far more animated than Vivian had seen him before, and he and Wren discussed the pipe back and forth as they made their way back toward Gordenner. Every once in a while, Wren would pause to make certain that Vivian was still behind them and wave to her. Vivian was grateful for a little respite, as she felt unable to even begin to formulate a thought. Like being distracted and reading the same line over and over in a book, in her mind, all Vivian could think was, "What do we do now?" again and again.

They found their way to the river and bridge without too much trouble with Will and Wren navigating together. Before they crossed the bridge, they waited for Vivian to catch up to them and Will said, "Okay. I'm going to have to hurry back because the lab at school closes at 6:00 and I want to get these samples in. What are your plans?"

Wren and Vivian looked at each other.

"I think we'll just take the bus home," Wren said.

"The last bus is at 5:03, right?" Vivian asked. "What time is it now?"

"It's 4:25," Will said, looking at his watch. "I've got to book."

"I think we're going to poke around here for a little bit," Vivian said, surprising herself.

Wren looked at her. "Are you sure?"

Vivian nodded. "I'm feeling better,"

Will became concerned. "Are you two going to be careful? I mean, we've gotten this far. Do you really want to push it?"

"We'll be careful. I just want to look at those pipes behind the building again."

"Why? We already know that they're pumping out a decoy," he said.

"There's something that is pulling me back. I can't explain it other than that."

"Just don't press your luck."

"Nah. In and out," Vivian said, trying to sound reassuringly relaxed.

"Well, okay," he nodded briskly. "Just be careful."

"We will."

They crossed the bridge and Will took off past the factory, running around the building until he disappeared from sight. They walked back to the factory.

"Are you sure we shouldn't just leave?" Wren asked. "I mean, we already found what we were looking for, right?"

"I think so. But I've got this feeling that there's something else to see or do here. If we leave, I'll be wondering about it all night."

"One of those 'you'll know it when you see it' things?"

"Exactly."

Vivian walked back toward the pipes, not sure what she was to be looking for as everything was the same as earlier. She scratched at her chin and squinted around the pipes, as though the appropriate quizzical expression might help to facilitate a breakthrough.

"So nothing's jumping out at you?" Wren shouted over the noise.

"Not yet. I just don't …"

At the same moment, Vivian and Wren looked over to see a man in a pale green uniform quickly approaching them, speaking into a walkie-talkie. The water was pouring deafeningly out of the pipes, so he signaled for them to stay where they were like a crossing guard with his palm out and fingers pointing up.

"You're trespassing. What's your business here?"

He was wearing mirrored sunglasses that reflected Wren and Vivian and the water gushing out of the pipes back to them. He had a badge on his shirt, SECURITY in large black type.

Wren started to say something but Vivian jumped in. "I came here to apply for a job but we couldn't get in through the front door. It was locked."

"A job? How old are you?" He motioned for them to follow him away from the pipes, close to the back of the Gordenner office building.

"Fifteen. I'll be sixteen in a month. I need a job for the summer."

"It's true," Wren chimed in. "Her parents run a tight ship."

"Did you come here 'looking for a job', too," he asked, his eyebrow cocked at Wren skeptically.

She looked at Vivian. "No. No, I just came along because I didn't want my friend to come out here alone."

"Do you girls have anything on you?"

"'On us'? Like what? We brought our book bags because we came from school," Vivian said.

"Open them, please. Empty your pockets, too."

Vivian unzipped her backpack and Wren opened the big drawstring bag she always had draped across her shoulders with a purple batik elephant on it. The security guard lifted their bags up one at a time and briefly thumbed through notebooks and textbooks, looking over lipstick and pens and, in Wren's bag, markers.

"What do you need these for?"

"Markers? I draw pictures with them sometimes. It helps me not get hung up on details. That's what's in the sketchbook in my bag if you want to see for yourself."

He looked at Vivian, holding up her binoculars. "What do you need these for?"

"We're birdwatchers," Vivian and Wren said in unison.

He handed them back their bags, then looked them up and down for a long moment. "You stay here." He walked about thirty feet away from them and called someone on his walkie-talkie. They talked back and forth for about a half-minute, incomprehensibly to Vivian and Wren, and he faced them the entire time, watching them.

Wren tried to look nonchalant as she smiled meekly at Vivian. "You really want a job here?"

Vivian pushed the hair off her face and nodded, "This was what I was looking for, it seems."

The guard walked back to them and put a hand on each one's shoulder, steering them back toward the building. "This way, please."

Wren looked at Vivian, her eyes wide in alarm, and Vivian gave just the smallest of nods back to her.

"We do have to catch a bus at 5:00, though," Wren said to the guard. He didn't respond. "It actually gets to this stop at 5:03, and it'll take a while to walk there. It's the last bus of the day."

He didn't say a word, just unhooked a set of keys hanging from his belt loop and unlocked three locks to open the back door of the building. Once inside, he gestured for them to stop and made a call on a phone that was mounted on a wall. This time his body was turned away from them. They could not hear what he was saying. When he hung up, the guard said gruffly, "Follow me."

They walked down a grimy gray concrete hallway and past a bunch of rooms with closed doors. It was loud inside, with motors whirring, hissing and spitting, and all sorts of loud noises Vivian couldn't identify. Her physical reactions were acute again, but she ignored them by imaging Tolstoy alongside her and concentrated on impressing him with her composure.

They stopped at an elevator and the security guard pressed the button.

The elevator, a cavernous, nearly room-size freight model, seemed to swallow the three up as they stepped inside, making Vivian feel both miniaturized and conspicuous. The security guard pressed the button for the second floor – they had been in the basement – and he stared straight ahead as the elevator slowly and loudly moved. When they reached the second floor, which felt like minutes later, he gestured to Wren and Vivian to walk out. "I'll be right behind you."

When they stepped out of the elevator, it was they were in an entirely different building. The walls were painted an eggshell blue, and the floor was covered with immaculate, wheat-colored carpeting. Here were people walking quickly in the hallway, engaged in conversation and discussing what seemed to be important matters, making it a sharp contrast from the machinery downstairs. Vivian's symptoms abated.

"This way."

They walked down one hall and turned down another, passing large offices with people on phone calls and drinking coffee, occasionally looking up to see them and, clearly too surprised by the sight of two teenaged girls followed by the security guard to avoid gawking a little.

They stopped in a lobby area at some couches set outside the largest office and they were brought to a receptionist, a handsome blonde man with periwinkle eyes in a linen suit Vivian's mother would probably admire, she thought to herself. He smiled at them in a convivial way, which Vivian was surprised by, and said, "It'll be a few minutes. They can have a seat." He looked at them. "You can take a seat."

The guard nodded at the man behind the desk and motioned for the two to sit on the couch. He remained standing, facing them, his face void of any discernable expression. He still had on his sunglasses. The receptionist spoke in a hushed tone over the phone, turning his body away from the window between them.

"Can you just tell us what's going to happen?" Wren asked, her voice surprisingly shaky.

For a few moments, the guard didn't say anything, looking as though he wasn't going to respond to her question, when he shifted his position and said, "I brought you here because you were trespassing. We're going to find out if your story checks out."

"What story? We don't have a story."

He ignored them and the two sat on the couch silently, Wren nervously crossing and uncrossing her legs, a soprano saxophone playing a grating version of "Over the Rainbow" on the stereo system. All Vivian could do was concentrate on remaining calm. She decided to imitate the Sphinx in the Egyptian section of her World History textbook, trying not to wonder what she could have led them into with this little excursion.

The receptionist spoke, startling everyone. "Larry, I just spoke with Robert," he said to the security guard. "He confirmed that it would be fine to bring Laura in on this. She's the one he requested."

"Mr. Fontaine doesn't want to talk to them himself?"

"He's not in town right now. He said Laura's fine to talk to on this."

The security guard nodded. They sat there for a few minutes more when a woman with short, spiky white blonde hair came around the corner wearing a skirt, jacket and shiny red heels. She glanced at Vivian and Wren, and walked straight to the security guard.

"So what do we know?" she asked, making no attempt to quiet her voice.

"Well, the one on the left, the redhead, she claims that she came here looking for a job. I found them back by the pipes."

The woman nodded impatiently, like she'd already heard this before. "How long ago?"

"About 15 minutes ago."

"And the other one," she said, nodding at Wren.

"She said she came because she didn't want her friend to come here alone."

"Names?"

"I didn't get the names. We came straight here."

"Did you find anything questionable on them?"

"No, ma'am. The one had markers, but she also had a sketchpad. The redhead had binoculars she said was for birdwatching."

The woman with the spiky hair turned to face them and walked a little closer. She was wearing deep red lipstick; she had high cheekbones and dark eyebrows with a strong arch, which made her look as if she were raising them in alarm even when the rest of her face was immobile. 'Chic but severe,' Vivian could almost hear her mother conclude.

"What are your names, girls?"

"I'm Vivian Sharpe; this is my friend, Wren Summer."

"And you expect me to believe that you were looking for a job when Larry found you out back by the pipes?"

"Really, ma'am..."

"You may call me Ms. Collins." She spoke sharply, crossing her arms across her chest.

"Ms. Collins," Vivian continued, "I'm so sorry for the misunderstanding and all the commotion. I came here looking for a job for summer and when we saw that the door was locked, we went around the side to the back. We were by the pipes when we stopped to figure out what to do, how to get someone's attention."

"It looks like you succeeded," she said, and Wren snorted, bursting out in laughter that was a little too vigorous. Ms. Collins looked at Wren, and she covered her face with her hands, quietly apologizing.

"And you want a job here?" she continued, eyes narrowed with skepticism. "Why? How old are you?"

"I'm 15..."

"You look younger."

"I know. Everyone says that, but I am fifteen. I'll be sixteen in July. I'm really interested in science and chemistry. I just thought this would be a great place to work."

Wren, recovered now from her outburst, said, "Vivian's a total science whiz. She's excellent at math too, a total brainiac."

Ms. Collins ignored her. "I still find it hard to believe that a fifteen-year-old girl would be looking for a job here. Why don't you work at the pool or something? Or as a camp counselor? Isn't that what girls your age do in the summer?"

"I can't swim very well and, as you can see, I'm a redhead. My skin can't tolerate too much exposure to the sun."

"Vivian gets red as a cherry tomato. She gets heatstroke like that," Wren said, snapping her fingers.

"Well, what would you do here? You're too young to work on the line."

"On the line?"

"Assembling, packaging, that sort of thing. You certainly couldn't work in any of the labs. What were you looking to do?"

"I'm very organized. I..."

"She's very organized. She organizes for fun..."

"I could help with paperwork, filing, you name it."

"But I thought you were interested in science," Ms. Collins said.

"Oh, I am. But I want to get my foot in the door. I just thought I'd work my way up from the bottom."

For the first time, though briefly, a smile flickered across Ms. Collins' face like a bolt of far-off lightning one sensed but could barely see. "Planning a long career at Gordenner, eh?"

"Oh, she is. That's all she talks about," Wren said.

"I can't say that I'd be here forever, but I'd like to get a chance."

Ms. Collins looked them up and down, and then, as though against her better judgment, smiled, shaking her head, and turned to the receptionist, who was listening to the whole exchange. "Kyle, could you give – what's your name again?"

"Vivian."

"Pretty name. Could you give Vivian an intern application?"

"Certainly."

Kyle stood to look through his file cabinets and Ms. Collins turned back to Wren and Vivian, sitting down on a chair facing them.

"Anything else you need, Ms. Collins? Run a background check?" asked the security guard.

Ms. Collins waved the notion away. "Not necessary, Larry."

"Then I'll get back to work if that's all right with you."

Ms. Collins nodded, and directed her eye contact to Vivian. "Let me tell you what I'm thinking, Vivian. This goes counter to everything I was expecting when I walked out here, but my gut is that you're being honest with me. That you really are sincere about wanting to work at Gordenner." She narrowed an eye at Vivian as though she were a fictional detective and then fixed it on her.

For her part, Vivian didn't flinch. "I am sincere."

Ms. Collins scrutinized her for a few more long moments, then she appeared to give in, relaxing her broad shoulders. "We had the budget approved last week to create a new position – a part-time assistant for me. Technically, the person would be an intern. Most of the work will be centered around a product that's going to be released soon.

"And what kind of work is it?"

"I'm director of marketing, so you'd be in the marketing department. Helping me schedule meetings, taking notes, taking messages, calling back clients. That sort of thing. How does that sound?"

"It sounds fantastic."

"We pay minimum wage; I can't say that you'd make much of a salary as an intern and at your age. And it's just part-time – thanks, Kyle – but I think it's a good place to start." She handed the application on a clipboard with a pen to Vivian, asking Kyle to make a copy for her.

"That sounds fine."

Vivian started filling out the application and Ms. Collins looked at the clock, saying that she needed to head back to her office and that she could just give her application to Kyle when she was done. She walked out of the room as she had walked in, at a fast, assertive clip that reminded Vivian of her mother.

Vivian handed her application to the receptionist and thanked him. Wren looked at the clock above his desk.

"Shoot. It's 5:13. I'm sure we missed that last bus. If there's one thing we can count on, people in this town are always on time."

"What should we do? It's too far to walk."

Wren turned to Kyle. "Do you think I could use your phone to call my parents and have them pick us up? We just missed the last bus.

He stood up and put Vivian's application on his desk. "I could give you two a ride. My day's over."

"Are you sure? We wouldn't be putting you out?" Vivian asked.

"Nah. Better than for your parents to come all the way out here."

Vivian and Wren looked at each other. "Sure. We really appreciate it," Wren said.

They went down the hallway to a different elevator, and walked out through the front entrance, impressive with its marble floors and tall potted trees, to the parking lot. There were a couple of men in the lot installing a video camera, the security guard standing next to them, talking.

"Ah. I wrote a memo about this last week. Looks like they're finally installing a video camera," Kyle said, unlocking the car doors. Wren volunteered to sit in back when they figured out that Vivian would be dropped off first. "We've been having some trouble lately."

"What sort of trouble?" Wren asked.

Kyle pulled up to the gate and started to get out of the car when the security guard waved him back.

"I've got it," he said, going into a station by the gate and pushing a button.

"Thanks, Larry. Have a good night."

Kyle turned out of the parking lot. "What sort of trouble? Vandalism. Paint splattered on the building – on the doors, actually – someone's been gluing the locks shut, pouring chemicals on the carpet…"

"Chemicals on the carpet?"

"Yep. Actually, the chemicals we produce."

"How do you know someone who works there didn't accidentally spill the chemicals?"

"Because it happens at night, up in the administration area, which is all locked up, of course, and not the same area where people work on chemicals. Also, whoever's doing it leaves behind a note."

"A note?"

"Explaining why they did it."

"Wow. And why do they do it?" Vivian asked.

"Because we're a big, evil corporation. Doesn't everyone go through this anti-authoritarian phase in high school or college?" Kyle said, laughing. "They're probably some bored anarchists from the college. I didn't think Center City had anything of the sort, but apparently it does. Makes things a little more interesting around here."

"How long has it been going on?" Vivian asked.

"Let's see...I started at Gordenner in November. I'd say it started in February. Two or three months now. That's why Larry got so bent out of shape when he saw you two at the pipes. Those are actually new pipes. Someone had bent the old pipes – don't ask me how – opened some first floor windows and turned the pipes back into the building. We had to shut down operations for a day because of the flooding, water damage. Now we have mold, I guess." Kyle said all this matter-of-factly, like what he was describing was a boring day at the office.

"So no one knows who is doing this?" Vivian asked.

Kyle shrugged. "Nobody knows. That's why we have a security guard now, but even he can't catch him. You can count on there being something vandalized at least once a week."

"Maybe it's someone who works at the factory," Vivian said.

"Or someone who was fired," Wren said.

"Maybe. No one's sure but everyone's a suspect, as they say in the movies. We've been advised to 'keep our eyes and ears open.' At least that was what I was told to type on our last security memo. You know, I'm not supposed to be talking about any of this. You'll keep it to yourselves, right?" They agreed.

Kyle turned to glance at Vivian. "Anyway, did you say that your last name was Sharpe?"

"Yes. Sharp like a pin with an 'e' on the end. Turn left at Elm, please, and then a right on Hickory. We're the colonial in the middle on the right."

He turned down Vivian's street. "You're not related to Sally Sharpe are you? *Look Sharpe?*"

"Yes, I am. She's my mom."

"Small world," he said, pulling over. "That's where I get my hair cut. Claudia's my stylist – sweet girl. It's the only salon in tow..."

"Worth considering," Vivian said, chuckling as she finished her mother's oft-repeated quote. It was a slogan referring to what Mrs. Sharpe called the "old lady" salons that used a heavy hand with the hairspray and did what she referred to mockingly as "hair-dos."

"Yep, they do pretty well." She opened the door. "It was very nice to meet you."

"Kyle Luddington. You can just call me Kyle."

"Thanks, Kyle."

"Oh, sure. Maybe I'll be seeing you soon."

"I hope so. See you," she said to Wren.

"See you," she said, scooting in front. "I'll call you later."

Kyle drove off just as Mr. Sharpe and Millie were riding up to the house on their bicycles.

"Was that Wren?" Millie asked.

"Yeah, it was Wren and this other person."

Millie took off racing on her bike after the car.

"Don't go past the block, Millie," Mr. Sharpe said. "Who was the other person?" He started walking his bike to the garage. Vivian walked with him.

"That was Kyle Lexington or something. He told me his last name but I don't remember it."

Vivian's father frowned a little. "How do you know him?"

"He works at Gordenner. I just applied for an internship there."

Mr. Sharpe stopped. "What?"

"I applied at Gordenner."

"You applied there? Why on earth would you do that?"

"It seemed like something to do."

"Something to do?"

Vivian shrugged.

"I don't understand."

"What's to understand?"

"Well, I never heard you mention Gordenner in your whole life, that's for starters."

"I don't have a job. I need something to do."

"So? Something to do? You could work at your mother's salon or even the museum with me. I didn't even know you were looking for a job. Why didn't you say anything?"

"I thought you would appreciate me being more independent. And it's just for the summer. It's certainly not something to make a big make a big deal out of."

"I'm just trying to understand, Vivian. It's way out there, almost out of town. How would you get there?"

"I'd take a bus like I did today," she said matter-of-factly. "The bus goes out there. Or ride my bike."

"What kind of job?"

"It would be assistant to the marketing director. I'd take messages, type up notes, that sort of thing. Just an internship."

"Why couldn't you be a receptionist at your mother's salon? It'd be the same sort of work and you could ride in and home with your mother."

"Because I don't want to, Dad. She already has receptionists and I want to do something different. I'd think that you would be happy I was doing this of my own initiative."

Mr. Sharpe squinted down the street at Millie, who was riding her bike back toward the house, standing up on the pedals.

"I am, honey, but this just seems to be coming from out of the blue. I'd never even heard one word from you about Gordenner before."

"I know. It's new to me, too. But it's going to be a good thing, Dad. Trust me."

Mr. Sharpe nodded, a skeptical look still on his face. Millie jumped off her bike and came running to her father and Vivian.

"Millie, don't just leave your bike in the yard. You know your mother doesn't like that. Bring it to the garage."

"I don't even have the internship there yet anyway," Vivian said.

"True," he said. "We are getting ahead of ourselves a bit."

Millie picked up her bike and ran back to them breathlessly. "I saw them. Well, I didn't really see Wren 'cause I was on the other side when they turned off the street, but I saw that man."

"Kyle."

"He's so handsome. I don't think I ever saw anyone so handsome with my own two eyes in person like that. Except you, Dad. He's not handsomer than you but he's pretty handsome."

"I should think not, but that's a relief. Thank you."

TROUBLE AT HOME

Mrs. Sharpe arrived home before too much longer and Mr. Sharpe, ever-wary of displeasing his wife, found himself occupied with refilling his drink when the subject of Vivian's day came up at the dinner table.

"Well, I think I may have found a job for the summer," Vivian said, trying to sound nonchalant as she ate the cheeseless pizza her father had made for her.

Mrs. Sharpe looked at her husband, who abruptly coughed and stood to get pepper from the kitchen, ignoring the shaker to his left on the table.

"Really?" Mrs. Sharpe said, one eyebrow raised at her daughter.

"Yes," Millie jumped in, rattling her table setting with her excitement, "with the second most handsomest man in the world."

Mrs. Sharpe looked between her daughters, uncomprehendingly. "What?"

"At Gordenner, Mom. I'd be an intern to the marketing director."

"An intern at Gordenner? Why? And who's this 'handsome man'?"

Vivian took a deep breath. "He's just a guy who works there, Mom. Kyle."

Mr. Sharpe walked back into the room.

"Why do you want to work there, Vivian? That just doesn't make sense."

Vivian traced the condensation on her water glass with her finger. "Because I just do."

"You'll need to do better than that, Vivian Sharpe." Mrs. Sharpe turned to her husband. "How much of this did you know?" At that precise moment, Mr. Sharpe was swallowing some food and had another coughing fit. Mrs. Sharpe glared at him before turning back to her daughter.

"So when did you develop an interest in Gordenner? This is the first I've heard of it."

"I just thought that it would be good to do something productive this summer. I can learn about marketing. I can learn how the business operates. I would have thought that you'd be into this, Mom."

Mrs. Sharpe sighed, shaking her head. "No, I'm not 'into' this, Vivian. This isn't sitting right with me. All of the sudden, you have some burning need to work at the Gordenner factory?"

"It's not the factory, Mom. It's the corporate building. I'm sorry that it's not sitting right with you, Mom," Vivian said, her voice cracking. "But I..."

"Listen, I didn't work so hard all my life so that my daughter would want to go work at a dirty factory, of all places," she said, looking at her husband briefly. "Your father and I have given you every opportunity and this is what you arrive at?"

"Honey," Mr. Sharpe said gently, speaking for the first time, "maybe you shouldn't take this so personally."

"How else am I supposed to take it," Mrs. Sharpe said, turning toward him with her eyes flashing. "It's a slap in the face. Do you know how many girls Vivian's age apply to work at *Look Sharpe*? Do you have any idea? Just to sweep up the hair, schedule appointments. Why would she want to work at a factory if it weren't meant to be a slap in the face? A filthy, old factory."

It was silent in the room, except for Mrs. Sharpe's rapid breathing and sighs. Vivian really thought that her mother would cry, and the thought filled her with a panic.

"You're not hearing me. I'd be working in the marketing department, Mom. And it's not like working in a factory. The factory is next door. It's a very nice, modern office building where I'd be. I was there earlier."

"That's true, honey. Remember all that they wrote all about the new building in the *Patriot*? It's supposed to be on the cutting-edge of technology."

"Wonderful," Mrs. Sharpe said, rolling her eyes. "Please pass the salad, Roosevelt. So you'd be helping to promote Gordenner and learn PR?"

Vivian nodded. "I think so. Mostly I'd be learning. It's a summer thing, just part-time anyway."

"May I be excused?" Millie asked, plate already in hands.

"Not yet. Who would you be working for? That man who drove you home? Which, by the way, I do not like and you are not allowed to do again."

"Kyle? No, he's a receptionist. I'd be working for Ms. Collins. She's really sophisticated and stylish. She reminds me of you in a way."

Mrs. Sharpe rolled her eyes at Vivian's obvious attempt at flattery. "And if you got offered this internship, I'll need to talk to this Ms. Collins before you accept."

"Yes, Mom. Of course. It's not that big a deal."

Vivian saw Mr. and Mrs. Sharpe glance at each other, her father shrugging his shoulders as Mrs. Sharpe squared hers.

"Well, I guess I can't stop you if you really want to do this, Vivian."

"I really want to do this, Mom," Vivian said, taking her mother's hand into hers.

Mrs. Sharpe smiled wanly. "And it's just for the summer?"

Vivian nodded.

"Because I wouldn't want it to affect your school work."

"It won't."

Mrs. Sharpe looked her in the eyes and squeezed her hand. Vivian, her body tight and tense, felt her muscles relax a little.

"It'll be great, Mom. You'll see."

Millie asked if she could be excused again, and, Mrs. Sharpe, as though forgetting her other daughter was in the room, startled a little and laughed at her reaction.

"Yes, Millie," Mrs. Sharpe said, patting her on the arm, "you could rinse your dishes and load them in the dishwasher." Millie hopped off her chair and dashed into the kitchen, as though she might get called back in if she didn't hurry.

"I just don't want to see this interfere too much with your summer, Viv. I'd like to see you go out with your friends more and have fun. There are only so many more free summers that you'll have."

Vivian nodded. "I know. I will."

"I mean, I think that it's lovely that you met this girl – Robin?"

"Wren."

"...Wren, but you should see your other friends as well."

"I know," Vivian leaned back, closing her eyes, rubbing her forehead.

"Tired?"

"Yeah. I'm going to finish up some homework if you don't mind. I'll probably go to bed early."

Mr. and Mrs. Sharpe nodded. They lingered in the dining room together speaking quietly while Millie played with her dolls in the basement. Vivian rinsed her dishes, then went up to her room and shut the door. Up in her room, Vivian felt for the first time that day that she could relax. Falling back on her bed, still full of the ruffles and the lacy pillows she had worn soft over her childhood, she felt like a boxer who has finally reached the end. The events of that day – the pipes leading to the stream, the dead animals, their discovery by the security guard, the offer of an internship – finally had the chance to settle within her so she could examine one after the other like strange shells she had found on a beach.

The telephone rang, jarring Vivian out of her luxurious solitude, and just as she was settling back in, her father knocked on the door telling her that Wren wanted to speak with her. She waited until she heard him walk down the stairs and the click of him hanging up the other phone before she said hello.

"Hey, Viv, can you talk for a minute?" Wren said, breathlessly.

"Sure."

"I just can't get over today. I can't stop thinking about it. Do you really think that you're going to try to get an internship at Gordenner? It's so weird."

"Yeah, I am. It seems like that's why we went back, you know?"

"Yeah, I know. But I just can't believe the way that I lied. I never lie. There I was, like, 'All Vivian talks about is wanting a job at Gordenner' and 'She's a total science and math wiz.' Blah blah blah. I mean you might be, but I don't know that."

"I'm totally not," Vivian laughed.

"I guess the point is that I never lie but I felt so comfortable doing it this afternoon. Should I be worried?"

"I don't think so. I don't know."

"Well, whatever, can we talk about Kyle for a minute? Is he totally gorgeous and charming or what? I think I have a crush on him. No, I definitely have a crush on him."

"He's way older, Wren. Like maybe even thirty."

"I know, I know. I'm not *interested*, interested, you know what I mean? I'm not going to pursue anything. I just think he's gorgeous, like an angel or a perfect sunset you only see once in a while. And he's so nice, too. It gives me hope for these next couple of years until I can get out of Dodge. It makes me wonder who else is hiding out here. I just can't believe that he lives in Center City."

"Or that he works for such an evil corporation."

"That's true."

"Do you think I did the right thing, Wren?"

"The right thing? About what?"

"Applying to be an intern there," Vivian sighed, slightly annoyed. "What am I doing?"

"Well, you must have realized on some level that getting an internship there would do something to help. I'm just not sure what it is, though."

"Neither am I. Maybe I just made a giant mistake. How am I going to know when I find it?"

"You'll know by your body, silly. When are you going to start trusting yourself? Every time you've made a discovery, your body led you to the answer and it's always been right on the money. This is a blessing, Viv."

"A blessing or a curse?"

"Maybe it's a blessing wrapped up in a curse, or it's a curse wrapped up in a blessing."

"What does that mean?"

"I have no idea," Wren said, laughing. "I'm tired. I guess that sometimes they're one and the same. What starts out as one can become the other."

"Great. So I'm cursed, too."

"I think you're only cursed if you don't do something with your blessing. Do you know what I mean?"

Vivian rubbed her face in her hands. "I don't know. You're starting to sound like Tolstoy."

The next day at school was a half-day; the next week, they would have just two more half-days of school and they would be out for the summer. That night, Vivian finished her homework, played "pretend school" with Millie, who loved any occasion to be the teacher. Vivian fell asleep early that night, just after nine o'clock.

Around midnight, she woke with a very dry, scratchy throat and got some water from the kitchen. Images from her dream, something about opening a desk drawer at Gordenner and finding it filled with dead fish, lingered in her mind. She fell back asleep without any trouble, though, and dreamed this time of birds, flying into a window somewhere – at Gordenner? at school? – leaving slimy brown splotches on the glass as they fell to the ground. On the ground, there were many others, a sea of dead and dying birds. Vivian tried frantically to open the window but found that it was stuck and rusted into place, as the while hearing the birds thump horribly against the glass, but all the windows were the same. Vivian turned and saw the security guard of that afternoon walking past her in the hallway, and she called out to him but he kept walking, seeming not to hear her. She turned back to the window, not wanting to look down but also not being able to stop herself, and she saw Tolstoy in the distance, standing back by the trees behind the factory. He was standing very still, looking at the birds on the ground, his head slightly bowed. Vivian knocked her hand against the window, crying out to Tolstoy, and he turned his head ever so slightly to look at her, his eyes making contact with hers. He nodded gently and sadly; then another bird smacked against the window and he watched the bird fall to the ground, soft feathers the color of charcoal smoke floating in the breeze. At last, Tolstoy looked up to a point in the sky and started disappearing, just as Vivian had seen him do before, in wavy lines. So did the birds piled up on the ground. When they were gone, all that remained was a slimy, unctuous landscape, one that looked like the aftermath or a toxic spill, and Vivian felt her heart heavy with grief, her hands and face pressed up against the cold glass of the window.

She woke to find her sheets gathered tight in her fists, woven between her legs. She loosened her grip and untangled herself, crying quietly. It was still dark out, not yet dawn. As she sat up to drink some water – her throat was scratchier than before – she heard a soft, polite cough in her room.

She whipped her head around, choking on and nearly spilling her water, when she saw Tolstoy sitting in her chair, facing her bed.

"Oh, jeez." she gasped, her hand on her chest. "You scared me, Tolstoy."

"I've got to figure out some way of materializing that is less abrupt, don't I?"

"I don't believe you're here. Where have you been?"

Tolstoy, his form somehow more incandescent than Vivian remembered, nodded serenely. "It has been a while, hasn't it?"

"Been a while?" Vivian sputtered, bolting upright. She set her cup down and lowered her voice to an angry whisper. "I'd say.

Tolstoy, I can't even begin to tell you what's been going on around here. I promise to keep my voice down."

"That's just fine."

"So where should I start? There's a lot to tell you..."

"You don't need to, Viv, because I already know. I knew it when it was happening. I'm not saying this to sound boastful," he said to her skeptical cluck, "but to let you know that you don't have to worry about updating me."

"Well, that's all fine and good, Tolstoy – could you move closer so we could talk easier?"

Tolstoy, as though waiting for the invitation, smiled and floated over to her bedside as he had done in the past. "That's better."

"It's all fine and good if you know what's happening, but that's not a lot of help to me at the time. Couldn't you just, like, show up?"

"I'm afraid not, Viv. It doesn't quite work that way. It can't work that way, at least not for the foreseeable future."

"But why not? Why can't you appear when I really need your help?"

"Hmm..."

"Like today. I was trying like mad to reach you, so hard I almost made my head explode, and you were nowhere to be found."

"Well..."

"Can you not see how that is frustrating? It would have really helped me out. And then you show up in the middle of the night, after everything's done. It's like we're out of synch."

Tolstoy shrugged. "You aren't going to like what I have to say, I'm afraid."

"Just tell me."

"It's not going to change anytime soon."

"Why not? I mean, if you can just materialize at will, why can't you..."

"Why can't I just do it when it might actually be of benefit to you?"

She nodded, and upon this, Tolstoy sat quietly, his eyes squinting as he thought.

"Well?" Vivian said after a minute or more of waiting for a response.

Tolstoy shifted ever so slightly and opened his eyes. "The truth of it is, Viv, that *you* have to do this work – the humans have to do this work for it to really happen. I can be an instrument of support insofar as I can help you think through your challenges and processes, but the truly significant work must be carried out by the humans."

Vivian let this sink in. "So, would you say that I'm wrong in feeling like this is a one way relationship? `Cause you show up occasionally and only when you want to?"

He smiled peacefully. "I wouldn't say that you were wrong; I'd say that there was a misunderstanding."

"Same thing to me."

"I hope you understand that you're not being persecuted. This is just the reality of the situation."

"Reality?" Vivian said, flustered, then lowered her voice again. "Tolstoy, you're a pig spirit who has come back to earth to personally guide me, a human being, in bringing an enormous change to the planet. You come to me – occasionally and never exactly when I could most benefit, I might add – and share your little bits of wisdom for me to interpret. The situation is already so unreal, and then you use a word like *reality*."

Tolstoy considered this for a few moments and then said, "It's unreal given the life you were accustomed to and your expectations that that life would continue more or less as it had, but it is the true reality once we disregard that."

"Disregard that I am talking right now to a pig spirit? That alone is cause for a thorough psychological exam. Disregard that I can feel what another being feels like to such a degree that it can cause me actual physical pain? Disregard that I just applied to intern at the Gordenner factory and that my mother seemed ready to pack up all my stuff and have me committed to a mental hospital when I told her? Disregard all that?"

"Hmm," he said, then paused briefly. "Yes."

Vivian threw back her head in frustration. "You see, Tolstoy? This is what I'm talking about. I feel like I'm being left high and dry."

Tolstoy nodded, a quizzical look upon his face. "High and dry. I'm not familiar with that phrase. It is an expression, right? Could you help me understand its etymology?"

"Oh, Tolstoy, it doesn't really matter," Vivian sighed, waving her hand. "That's not the point. The point is that I feel like I'm totally on my own, I guess. Like I got encouraged to stick my neck out, but then there's no one there when I really could use some help. Like I'm abandoned," she sighed.

"Abandoned? Meaning you have no one?"

Vivian nodded.

"Well, you know as well as I that that's not true. You have Wren to turn to, of course. Will, too, I would think. I am also always around, though I understand not as accessibly as you would like. And, of course, unfailingly, you always have yourself."

"Lucky me," Vivian said under her breath. "Well, seeing as I may have gotten myself into a little spot, I could really use some help plotting out what to do at Gordenner given that I might be interning there soon."

"Such an opportunity, Viv. How deftly you arrived at this result. Interning at the factory was just a brilliant turn of events."

"If brilliant means insane, then, yes. Anyway, it's not guaranteed, Tolstoy. I haven't gotten a phone call yet. I need to know what to do in case I get approved for the internship."

"Well, accept it, I say, by all means."

"I know, Tolstoy, but then what? Once I get my foot in the door, what then?"

Tolstoy sat pondering this, bouncing a leg as he thought. "Vivian, your intuition has taken you this far and you have not taken a wrong turn yet. Why are you doubting yourself now?"

"Because what if it goes away? I mean, this intuition appeared out of the blue – why not disappear? What if I take an internship there and I feel nothing? What then?"

"Do you think someone with a gift, say someone who is a remarkable artist, one day has that gift snatched away without warning? It just vanishes into thin air, as you humans say?"

"Why not?" Vivian said, shrugging. "I mean, you hear of people having a writer's block. Why couldn't I have an intuition block?"

"Oh, you could," Tolstoy said, a bit too cheerfully for Vivian's taste. "You could. It's just that having a block is not the same thing as having a gift disappear. It's not like you wouldn't have the gift anymore. It'd just be hidden, like the sun behind the clouds."

"Well, that's great news, Tolstoy." Vivian heard the sarcastic tone of her voice and immediately felt ashamed. "I'm sorry. I don't mean to be so rude." Tolstoy dismissed the notion with a quick shake of his head, then nodded at her to continue. "It's just, how do I find my 'gift' if it's hidden? Say, 'Come out, come out, wherever you are'?"

"That's a childhood game that you're referencing, right?"

Vivian nodded warily, not sure where this was going. "Hide and seek."

"I suppose it is a bit like a game of hide and seek, but more subtle. Gifts don't like to know that they're being searched for, so you've got to play a more nimble game, if you will."

At this, Vivian shook her hands up toward the ceiling, shaking her head. "Just give me answers, Tolstoy. I feel like I'm reading a fortune cookie and half the words are missing. Give me some direction."

"That's just it: there is no precise directive. It's not like I can say, 'Go straight. Turn here, go left,' and you'll arrive at a predetermined conclusion. If your gift is hiding, I would advise finding a back door to it. Dive into another area of your life wholeheartedly – your compassion, your empathy, your fears – and I believe that your gift will be rediscovered. It just became momentarily obscured by something else."

"But what if that doesn't work?"

"What if? You're trying to anticipate the future, Viv, and it's already having its effect on you," Tolstoy spoke quietly, as if he were speaking to himself. "Can you see that? You're becoming fearful. By all means, plan, strategize, be savvy, be careful, but don't doubt yourself. If everything else lines up – your intentions are pure, you are being mindful and compassionate – there is no reason for such self-doubt. Self-doubt will impede you at every step along the way if you let it, and you need to be working at full capacity."

Vivian absorbed this for a few moments, then said, "Okay, so let's say that I'm offered an internship at Gordenner and I take it. And let's say that I discover for certain that the underground pipe is theirs and that they know that they are polluting and that they are definitely covering it up. What do I do then?"

"Then," Tolstoy said looking at Vivian with a very serious expression that made the hairs on her arms stand up, "then it is time to strategize."

"With whom?" Before even waiting for an answer, she said, "I know, I know. Wren and Will. And you when you bother to show up."

Tolstoy seemed to not notice her barb, or at least he didn't mind it. "Exactly. You're not alone. This is terribly exciting, Viv," he said, eyes sparkling. "Think of what you can accomplish."

Vivian had to crack a smile. "I know. I think that it's exciting, too, actually," Vivian said, surprised even as the words were coming out of her mouth. "I've never done anything important before like this."

"Oh, I wouldn't say..."

"No, it's true. Nothing really, you know, meaningful. Nothing that mattered. This matters."

Tolstoy nodded.

"You know another thing, Tolstoy? As stressful and weird as things have been, as crazy and unexpected and sometimes scary, I've never felt more...bzzz!" She shook her hands. "...Alive. Like I have a purpose."

"Some search their whole lives for such an elusive thing," Tolstoy said. "For you to have found it at such a young age is a windfall beyond measure."

They smiled at each other shyly. Finally, Vivian sat up, entwining her fingers together and stretching overhead. "I hate to say this but I should be getting back to bed. I've got school tomorrow."

"Of course, of course," Tolstoy said, nodding politely. Then he changed tone and grinned impishly, "But before I leave, I have something for you."

Vivian sat up straight, eyes wide. "Oh, what? A trinket of some sort from the otherworld? A t-shirt?"

"You are funny," Tolstoy laughed, eyes sparkling. "No, nothing material. It's something I just thought of, a way to remind you that I'm always here, even if I'm not physically present."

"A picture?"

He shook his head. "Reach out and try to touch me right here," he said, indicating his chest.

Vivian paused for a moment, a confused look upon her face. "But I thought I couldn't feel you."

"You can't, I have no concrete form. But I do have a small sphere of warmth, right about where my heart would be. Try to feel it."

Vivian reached out and just felt her cool bedroom air, fingers running through Tolstoy's form. "I don't feel anything at all."

"Keep trying. Slow down. It's there. It's subtle but it's there."

"This is kind of weird, Tolstoy." Vivian kept reaching toward him, through his incandescent form until she suddenly stopped in mid-air. "Wait. Wait. Is that it?" She felt a little pocket of warmth right about at Tolstoy's chest level, surrounded by the regular temperature of the rest of her room. It felt comforting and pleasant, like a sock slightly warmed by a dryer.

"Yes, that's it," he nodded, smiling peacefully.

"Weird," Vivian said, keeping her hand on the sphere, molding her fingers around it like a doorknob.

Tolstoy spoke quietly, "Well, if you take that warmth and hold it to your heart, you'll be able to feel me with you when I'm not there, just as a cheerful reminder."

"Really?"

"Yes."

Vivian moved her hand back to her chest and held her palm against her heart, fingers spread wide. Her chest radiated with waves of gentle warmth, spreading from her fingers like rivers. "I feel it," she finally whispered, astonished. "You're right."

"So there I am," Tolstoy smiled. "I'll see you soon, Viv."

Vivian, her hand still on her heart, could scarcely speak. She nodded and whispered yes. Tolstoy held one hoof to his chest and began disappearing in wavy lines until all that remained were a few delicate sparkles, like embers after a fire. She moved her hand away after a minute or so, and the warmth was still there in her chest. Vivian realized that the last time she'd felt anything like that was when she first held Millie, her sleeping baby sister, to her chest soon after she was born, wrapped in her soft pink blanket. Vivian smiled to herself as she lay back down on her pillow, enjoying the warmth of that long-forgotten feeling.

AN INTERNSHIP

Vivian went through the next day in a glazed-over way, which was all that was expected of students these last few days of school. A few times, though, her history teacher, Miss Brown, a perpetually frowning woman who'd been teaching at Center City High School since before all their parents sat in her classroom, stopped abruptly mid-lecture in front of Vivian's desk and gave her a particularly bracing scowl, jolting Vivian into a straight posture and focused countenance. That lasted for a few minutes until she drifted off again to revisit her conversation with Tolstoy.

"Am I not entertaining enough for you, Miss Sharpe?" Miss Brown asked at one point. "Is Hiroshima not captivating enough for you? Shall I do a tap dance to better capture your attention?"

Vivian, mortified with so many eyes upon her, shook her head quickly and picked up her pen to scribble in her notebook. After short but effective silence, Miss Brown turned her attention back to atomic bombs and away from Vivian. Two hours left in the school day and it couldn't be over soon enough.

That afternoon when she returned from school, there was a note for her under a refrigerator magnet from her father. "Millie and I are at the library. Ms. Collins called from Gordenner and offered you an internship. Congratulations! Please call your mother at work and let her know. Dad." He'd written and circled Ms. Collins' number. Vivian started hooting and shaking at once, walking in circles around the kitchen, nearly hyperventilating, elated and terrified. She sat down to collect her thoughts and she noticed that her chest was radiating with waves of reassuring warmth, her parting gift from Tolstoy. The next thought she had was that she had to call Wren, who was working a shift at the Commie Café. Wren was characteristically ebullient.

"Viv, do you know what this means? You have their total blessing to snoop around and go into their files and stuff."

"Well, I don't know if I have their blessing to snoop, but I'm going to."

"Uh huh. That's what I meant."

"I have to be discreet, though. It's not like I can just gain access to all their information right away. I have to build up some trust first."

"Of course."

"So don't be disappointed if it takes a while before I start digging in."

"Don't feel pressured, Viv," Wren said with mock sincerity. "It's just that the future of our water supply depends on you."

"That's all."

"Oh, and the birds and fishes and frogs and turtles. We can't forget about them."

Vivian sighed.

"I'm teasing," Wren said, laughing. "Are you nervous?"

"Shouldn't I be?"

"A little," Wren said.

"Then I am," Vivian said, with a small laugh. "Am I allowed? I am a little nervous."

After hanging up with Wren, Vivian took a few deep breaths and called her mother at the salon. She waited for a few minutes on hold listening to four-and-a-half cycles of a recorded voice offering apologies for the wait, along with a listing of *Look Sharpe's* various goods and services, and then with a click, her mother came on the phone.

"Hi, honey. What's up?"

Vivian tried to sound casual. "Oh, not much. I just got home."

"Mmm. Hold on – Kathy, the man from the delivery service called – will you be able to let him in through the back with the new chairs in about fifteen minutes? Great," Ms. Sharpe took a distracted breath. "So what's up, honey?"

"I was just calling to say I was home."

"Oh. That's good." She waited a few moments for a response. "Is that all? I'm kind of busy at the moment."

"That's it. Oh. I almost forgot…"

"What?" Mrs. Sharpe said impatiently.

"I got offered the internship. Dad took the call. He left me a note."

There was silence on the other end.

"Mom?"

Mrs. Sharpe sighed. "I heard you."

Vivian silently waited for her mother to speak again, feeling shaky.

"I guess I can't stop you," she finally said, "but I'm going to need to call the woman there. What's her name? The one who you'd be interning for?"

"Ms. Collins."

"Ms. Collins. Let me get a pen…Nancy, I need a pen. Thanks. Paper? Thanks. Okay. I'm going to need to call Ms. Collins."

"That's fine. I…"

"You know, Vivian, it's not like I relish being your guard dog, but someone has to be looking out for you. If it were up to your father, you'd probably be running off to who knows where, no questions asked. But I want to find out Ms. Collins' expectations of you, what this internship is all about."

"I understand, Mom."

"If everything checks out, though, I've been thinking about it, and I don't think it's such an awful idea anymore. It'll give you some good experience," Mrs. Sharpe said. Vivian could hear her waking through the salon. "Hi, Donna. Oh, highlights today? Very flattering. Brings out the blue in your eyes. How's Dan? Getting the boat ready yet? Hold on, honey," she said to someone, perhaps Vivian, perhaps Donna. The whir of hairdryers in the background got louder as Vivian tried to picture where she was in the salon. Walking up steps – she was going to her office. Her feet on carpeting, no more heels clicking on the floor, with a whoosh it was quiet as the door shut behind her. "So, where was I?"

"You were saying that it will give me some good experience, that you're not so against the idea anymore."

"Oh, yes," she said. "That's right. It may be actually be a good opportunity. That being said, Vivian, don't take this the wrong way, but I don't think you should be talking about interning there too much to your friends."

Vivian was silent on her end, not sure where her mother was going with this.

"It's just that people think of Gordenner as an ugly old factory. Like how I reacted last night. You know, they make – what is it they make? – farm products and that sort of thing. Not exactly an interesting place to intern, I should think, especially not for a pretty young lady like you. I mean, I know that working there is important to you or you wouldn't pursue it, so I'm not going to stand in your way as long as everything checks out. But I'm just saying that you're kind of sweet and innocent, Viv, and you might be unpleasantly surprised if your friends react in a certain way when they hear that you're interning at Gordenner.

"Okay…"

"I'm just saying this for your benefit, Vivian. I don't want your feelings to get hurt. I know that you're excited to intern there, and, really, that is what's helped turn me around. It's great to see you have a passion for something, even if it's something I can't understand for the life of me. I'm just thinking that you may want to keep it under wraps that you're going to be interning there," she said quickly. "That's all I'm saying. Make your own decisions."

Vivian smiled, shaking her head. "I understand, Mom. I'll take that under consideration."

"I'm just looking out for you, Vivian."

"I know. For my best interest."

Vivian gave her mother Ms. Collins' phone number and hung up, slumping down into a kitchen chair in relief. She didn't sit there for more than a few seconds before she sprang up and called Wren again.

"Well, it looks like I'm practically in. My mom said that I can take the job."

"Woo! Viv, this is just fantastic. Oh, my goddess. You're totally Nancy Drew. You are. You're going to expose Gordenner…"

"Shhh. Wren, this has got to be a secret."

"Oh, nobody's here, not even Owl. He went to get some garlic, like thirty minutes ago and the grocery store is two blocks away, but he just called here to have me remind him what he was looking for. Oh well. Anyway, I understand. I will totally be quiet about it. I'm just so excited." She giggled. "Quietly excited."

When Vivian got off the phone with Wren, she went up to her room and grabbed a new spiral notebook – her mother always kept a supply on hand – and pen. She sat at her desk, and wrote Gordenner on the top of the page in capital letters and underlined it. She underlined it again, highlighted it, and started chewing on her pen cap, staring at the pale blue lines on the page in front of her, when the phone rang and made her jump. She knocked her notebook off the desk when she reached over for the phone.

"Vivian," said her mother. "I just spoke with Ms. Collins and she seems very professional. I think it will be okay for you there if that's what you want to do. You'll be mostly helping her in the marketing department, I guess, which will be good experience for you. It'll look good on college applications. So I'm all right with it. She seems like a very nice woman. She understands my concerns," she said briskly, pausing for a few moments. "Vivian? Are you there?"

She straightened her back, her mind racing. "Yes, Mom, I'm here. That's great."

"Okay, then. I'll see you tonight."

"See you later."

"So you'll call Ms. Collins and let her know you accept."

"Yeah, I will as soon as I get off the phone."

"Okay. I'll be home after six. We can talk then."

After they hung up, Vivian jumped on the bed and tried to call Ms. Collins several times, but her hand was shaking so much that she stopped. She breathed in deeply and tried to call again, but her hand was still shaking so badly that her fingers wouldn't push the right numbers. With her final attempt, she slowly pushed down the numbers, as if it were the first time she'd ever made a phone call. This time, she felt the warmth in her chest as she called, sending it in radiating waves through her body. As the phone rang, she wrapped her arms around her knees, trying to conserve the pleasant warmth.

"Ms. Collins here."

"Oh, hi, Ms. Collins," Vivian said breathlessly. "This is Vivian Sharpe. We met yesterday. I think you just spoke with my mom."

"Hello, Vivian," she said brightly. "How are you?"

"Great."

"I understand that you really want to intern at Gordenner. Your mother said that she'd never seen you excited like this about something."

"It's true. I'd really like to learn from you."

"So I think that it's safe to say that you will accept the internship?"

"Yes," Vivian said, lacing her fingers through the phone cord to try to keep them from shaking. "I accept."

"Okay, then," Ms. Collins said briskly with a squeak in the background, sounding like she was swiveling in a chair. "Let me find my notes. Here. It seems like your mother is concerned that this internship will absorb a lot of your time, and I assured her that it shouldn't. It would be three days a week, from 8:45 a.m. until 3:00. Monday, Wednesday, Friday. How does that sound?"

"It sounds good, Ms. Collins. I could do more, I think, though."

Ms. Collins laughed. "Now, Vivian, I don't want your mother to get upset. I think three days would be sufficient for getting your job done, really. Though I do appreciate your enthusiasm."

Vivian laughed airily. "Well, you know I am so looking forward to this."

"I can see that. So how does starting this Monday sound? Is that too soon?"

"No, no. That's fine. Oh, shoot. I have school. Wednesday's our last day."

"Why don't you start next Monday, then?"

"Or Friday. I could start Friday. I'd really like to start as soon as possible."

Ms. Collins sounded skeptical. "You don't even want to relax a little bit after finishing school for the year? Just hit the ground running?"

"Yep. I want to hit the ground running if that's okay with you."

"Who am I to say no?" Ms. Collins laughed. "You're a girl after my own heart. Okay, just come to the parking lot gate Friday morning and tell the security guard that you're here for an internship. Oh, you know what? I'll have Kyle send you a badge. I can also have him meet you downstairs Friday. You remember Kyle, right?..." her voice trailed off.

Vivian smiled. "Yes, I do."

"He'll meet you downstairs and bring you up to my office."

"Great, so I'll see you Friday morning."

"Yes, 8:45. See you then."

When Vivian reached over to hang up the receiver, she nearly dropped it, and that was the first time she noticed how sweaty her hands had become. Vivian heard Millie's muffled voice and her father's key in the back door; initially, part of her felt like crying because she just wanted some more time alone but as Millie's buoyant voice filled the house, she was mostly grateful for the distraction. She went downstairs, made herself a late lunch of a bagel with hummus – something her father had picked up at the grocery store ("I think you're going to like this, Viv," he said with a hopeful tone in his voice, eager to find something new for his daughter to eat) – and sat down with Millie at the kitchen table, making small talk about her morning at kindergarten.

"So, what was the funniest thing that happened at school today?" Vivian asked.

Immediately, a huge grin spread across Millie's face as she made a cracker sandwich with raspberry jam in the middle. "Robbie threw up, and that made Rachel throw up. Isn't that funny?"

"Hmm," Vivian was trying to choke down the bite of bagel that was already in her mouth. "Anything else funny happen at school today? Something not involving bodily fluids?"

"Bodily fluids?"

"You know, like vomit."

"Oh," Millie looked contemplative, then turned back to her cracker sandwich. "Not really. That was it."

They worked together for the rest of the afternoon playing with dolls and redecorating Millie's dollhouse, a family heirloom from their mother that still had a pretty pink comforter and oblong rugs, a little frayed at the edges, that Alma Wheeler had knitted for her daughter. Whenever Vivian played with the dollhouse – whether it was with Millie or years before when it was hers at Millie's age – she couldn't help imagining her mother playing with it as a little girl. Vivian imagined her mother as a little girl as having her mature mom's face and smooth, stylish hair on a child's body. It was a ridiculous image, Vivian knew: she'd seen photos of her mother as a serious-looking child in braids and plaid skirts, but it seemed to Vivian that she had always been an adult. Her mother had probably thought the same thing, she imagined.

That evening, they had a good-natured dinner together as a family, and Vivian's mother even flirted a little with her husband, calling him by her old pet name for him ("You look handsome tonight, Roosey Goosey," with a wink), which made Vivian blush and Millie burst out in a peal of laughter, repeating "Roosey Goosey" until she was told that that was enough. Mrs. Sharpe was particularly animated at dinner that night, giving impressions of all her least favorite clients, like Eleanor Beebe, who apparently had a squeaky, whiny voice, and was never happy with her hair but always came back; and Linda Crane, an affected middle-aged senator's wife, who came in every other month with pictures cut out from issues of *Vogue* and *Harper's Bazaar*, insisting that they cut her curly hair in whatever she considered au courant, no matter that it didn't suit her age or personal style or hair type. Vivian and Millie washed and dried dishes together that night, doing their favorite impressions of invented customers of *Look Sharpe*, like Big

Brassy Bertha Bonecrusher and Samantha with Sticky Salamander Skin.

The next morning, a bright Saturday, Vivian woke up energized. She was going to Wren's house to help plot strategies for her internship at Gordenner. After she showered, Vivian went down to have breakfast. Millie was already up, a half-eaten bowl of cereal in front of her. When she saw Vivian, she sprang up.

"You got something in the mail this morning."

Vivian blinked at her. "What do you mean?"

"Mail. You got something," Millie repeated, like it was the most obvious thing in the world. "A package."

"A package?"

Millie shrugged. "Yeah, Dad found it on our doorstep this morning," she said as she skipped over to the counter, picked up a small manila envelope and handed it to Vivian. Vivian turned it over in her hands. It had no postage, just her name typed on a sticker on the envelope, and the Gordenner stamp on the left-hand corner.

"What is it?" Millie asked.

"Hmm, I don't know. Ms. Collins said that she was mailing me a name badge, but this can't be it." There was something much larger than a name badge inside, something hard and rectangular-shaped. Vivian kept staring at the package, not sure what to do with it. She also wasn't sure why it made her stomach feel vaguely queasy and unsettled.

"Well, open it," Millie said with a squeal, like it was a birthday present, reaching out. "I'll help you."

"No." Vivian stepped away from Millie and started opening the envelope. She pulled out a black videotape with a note wrapped around it, secured with a rubberband.

"What's that?"

"Hold on," Vivian said, frowning. She pulled the note off the videotape, which didn't have a jacket on it. It was a typed note on Gordenner letterhead, dated two days ago. It simply said,

Attention: Vivian Sharp

Fully review tape before accepting internship.

There was no signature, simply those words and the Gordenner letterhead. Vivian read it over again to make sure she wasn't missing anything.

"What's that?" Millie repeated, reaching up to hold it.

"What?" Vivian, a little startled, had forgotten that Millie was in the room, and pulled back. "Oh, this must be a training video or something. Nothing exciting." She put it back in the envelope.

"Boring," Millie said in a sing-song voice, skipping back to her bowl of cereal.

Vivian put the package down on the counter near the refrigerator as she put some bread in the toaster. She picked it up again as the bread was toasting and examined it again as if it might reveal something new.

Mr. Sharpe walked in the kitchen, whistling and carrying a stack of books he was returning to the library.

"Oh, I see you got the package from Gordenner. Out of curiosity, what did they send you?"

Vivian looked down at the cassette in her hands. "This? Oh, I think it's just a training video."

"Too bad we haven't gotten around to fixing the VCR since Millie lodged her book in it," He glanced sideways at his younger daughter, who didn't seem to notice.

"It's okay. I'm going to Wren's house this morning and I'll see if they have one."

Mr. Sharpe mumbled something to himself as he walked to the refrigerator.

"What's that, Dad?"

"I was just saying that it was a strange thing," he said casually.

"What do you mean? What is?"

"The package. No postage; well, that's an easy explanation, I suppose. Someone must have dropped it by. But why the typing on the envelope?"

"Why is that weird?"

"Well, I would just think that a big, multi-million dollar company would have a more professional look. You know, a label that had your name printed on it from a computer. It's just a little strange, I think. They must have been in a hurry. But a typewriter would still take longer. I haven't seen typewritten words in ages."

Her father drove her to Wren's house after breakfast and for the whole ride, all Vivian could think about was the cassette. Several times Mr. Sharpe startled Vivian as she stared at the package in her hands, lost in thought.

"Vivian? Is something the matter?" he asked as he pulled onto the road toward the Summer's home. "You seem preoccupied."

"No. Nothing." Vivian tried to smile, look bright. "Thinking about the internship."

"Wow, this is really the country. Some of Center City's earliest settlers lived out this way. The Crenshaws, the Dubois. About a hundred years ago, there was an old mill not far from here. I think the road we're on is one of the originals. I'll have to check on the map back at the Society later."

"Really?" They pulled up to Wren's driveway. "I'll get out here." She got out of the car and, as was her custom when her sister was in the car, flattened her hand against the window to Millie in the back seat. Millie held her hand against Vivian's with the glass between them. "See you later, alligator."

"In a while, crocodile."

Wren and Bucky were sitting on the porch swing together, with the dog's legs draped elegantly across her lap as she combed her fingers through his fur. Bucky was whining quietly, like the sound of a far-off whistle, as Wren raked her fingers under his neck.

"Hi, Viv," Wren said. "I can't get up or Bucky will bolt. He got into some spurs last night and if I don't get these out, he'll get all matted." He whimpered again. "He's not liking me now, but he'll get over it. Much better than a date with the electric razor." She looked at the space next to Bucky on the porch swing. "Have a seat, girly."

Vivian sat down. Wren looked at the envelope in Vivian's hands, Bucky's fur between her fingers.

"What's that?"

Vivian took the videotape out, turning it around. "A video. Someone from Gordenner sent me a video."

Wren kept looking through Bucky's fur, her face scrunched up. "Really? Why?"

"See that's the thing. I don't know." Vivian took out the short note and read it to Wren. Wren looked it over.

"Wouldn't it be weird if they just sent you, like, an exercise video for no reason at all?" Vivian didn't say anything. "I'm joking, Viv. Look, they spelled your name wrong."

"I know. That's common. I told my dad I thought it was a training video, but I don't think it is."

127

"Why not?"

"Well, first of all, they just created this internship, so when would they have made the tape? Second, Ms. Collins never mentioned that she would be sending a tape or anything other than a badge to get in. It seems like she would have said something. Third, don't you think that the note is a little strange? Kind of, you know, abrupt?"

Wren nodded. "Yeah, but that doesn't mean anything. I take it that you haven't watched it yet."

"No. Our VCR's broken. I was hoping you would."

Wren opened her eyes up wide. "Are you kidding me? We don't even have a television. So where could we watch it?" She looked at Vivian with a sly smile. "I mean, I assume that I can watch it with you."

"Sure," Vivian said distractedly. "My dad mentioned the library, but something's telling me that we should watch it more privately. I don't want lots of people around. Also..." Her voice trailed off.

Wren looked at her. "What?"

"I just have a weird feeling again. Nervous, jittery, a little scared. Ever since I picked up this package I've been feeling this way, so that's part of why I don't think that it's just a simple little training video. It's almost like, you know those joy buzzer things, you know the thing that you hide in your hand –"

"And shock people with? One of my cousins had one of those."

"Yeah, exactly. Anyway, it's not like my hand is buzzing or anything but it just feels different when I touch the video. Like shaky and weird."

"Well, we should probably watch it."

"Right, but where?"

They sat thinking about it quietly for a minute or two.

"I know," Wren finally blurted out in a way that startled Bucky and gave him the chance to jump off the swing and run off the porch. Wren scarcely seemed to notice. "I know. They have a TV and VCR at the Commie Café. Sometimes Owl shows movies there and whatnot. It'd be the perfect place."

"But what about all the other people? I don't want other people to see this."

"The café opens at 11:30. Owl will get in at 11:00, start the coffee and stuff. We'll watch it in the kitchen anyway. It's – what time is it?"

Vivian looked at her watch. "Almost ten."

"Okay, so this is what we do," Wren said abruptly, standing up and shaking grey fur off her lap. "I have a bike. You can use mine and I'll use my mom's. We'll bike to the café: we'd be there in twenty minutes. I have keys to open up. Owl won't mind. If we leave now, we should have plenty of time. I'll just let my mom know that we're taking off, and we're gone."

THE VIDEO

Wren stood at locked door of the Commie Café, patting around her enormous purple batik purse, her hand beating around it like a small bird trapped inside, making them both nervous that she had forgotten her work keys at home.

"Man, I always have them in here. After this, I'm going to attach them to my house keys. Why didn't I do that before? Oh, he – no, those are the house ones again. Could you hold these, Viv? Darn it – oh, wait." Her face lit up with a big, relieved smile, keys in hand. "Yes. We've got keys. Phew," she said, pretending to wipe sweat off her forehead with the back of her hand.

Inside, the café looked much like it did when it was open during the day – quiet, comfortable and a little dusty, with sunlight streaming in the streaked windows. While Wren pulled the TV and VCR cart out of storage, for the first time, Vivian got a good look around the café, which was one large, brown room with a tin ceiling. Mismatched chairs with stuffing sticking out were pulled around small tables with glass tops and tattered, water-smudged paper menus underneath. There were framed posters throughout the room, of Janis Joplin smiling beatifically and Malcolm X looking intense in his horn-rimmed glasses. There were several low bookcases leaning against the walls that were stuffed full of books and disorderly with yellowed newspapers on top; it smelled like coffee grounds and cinnamon. Vivian was looking in the glass display case at the muffins and cookies when Wren stuck her head out of the kitchen door.

"All set up. Ready?"

She had two folding chairs set up in front of the TV back in the kitchen, and Vivian handed her the tape. Wren turned on the TV and a cartoon cat with a giant hammer chased a mouse.

"Here we go," she said as she pressed *Play*. It needed to be rewound, so they sat silently and waited as the wheels whirred in the VCR. The mouse hid on top of a Christmas tree and the cat tried to shimmy it, sending ornaments and pine needles tumbling to the ground.

"My cat did that once," Wren said, shaking her head. "But she wasn't chasing a mouse. Just for no reason."

Vivian could feel her heart beating in her chest, pounding against her skin, now clammy. She pressed a palm against her heart, trying to calm it down. She noticed that Wren was eating a bagel, sitting with one arm wrapped around a knee as if ready to watch a movie she'd rented from a video store. She saw Vivian looking at her and held out the bagel toward her, an offering.

"I'm sorry. I forgot to ask if you wanted one."

Vivian shook her head.

"It's vegan, of course. Sesame."

"No," Vivian said, shaking her head again. "Thanks. Not hungry."

The little wheels in the VCR clicked to a stop. With a jolt, Vivian leaned forward and hit *Play* again as Wren sat up, her bagel forgotten in her lap.

The first few moments of the video were of a grassy path and the occasional tips of muddy brown shoes, they looked like men's boots, appearing. After the initial disorientation this caused, Vivian realized that this was a camera pointed down at the feet of the cameraperson. The words *"JUNE 3"* appeared on the screen then faded away, and it was quiet but she could hear someone's labored breath in the background. The camera shakily came to a stop and then it lifted up to reveal a wall of green, which then came apart as the lens seemed to poke through it.

"What was that? A bush?" Wren asked.

"I think so. What is this?"

Leaves separated and they saw a large, grey out-of-focus building. The camera shot up and down and finally settled as if the cameraperson were kneeling or sitting down. Gradually the building came into focus and the camera panned down to three figures talking, one large figure and two smaller ones. The lens focused in on the three, a girl with bright red hair, another with brown spirals and a man in sunglasses.

"Oh, my God, Wren. That's us," Vivian whispered. She looked over at Wren quickly, and saw that her mouth was already open with her hand over it, eyes wide.

"What on earth?"

In the middle of the screen, the words, *"Gordenner Poison Plant"*, appeared for a few seconds and then faded as it had with the previous words. The camera pulled in tighter on Wren and Vivian, talking to the security guard as they had a couple of days prior, opening their bags for him. The security guard stepped away to make a phone call and the camera remained on the two as they tried to smile and look calm. The guard came back, put his hands on their shoulders, and they walked into the building together.

"What the...?"

Vivian, her face hot and heart pounding uncomfortably, couldn't look away. "I have no idea."

The camera remained trained on the building for another minute. "So they know, right?" Wren asked. "I mean, this is from them, right?"

"I have no idea," Vivian repeated.

The screen went abruptly blank and then opened again a few moments later on a creek, slowly filling with a slimy black sludge.

"That's it. That's where we were. That's where the pipe is," Wren said, staring at Vivian in shock. Vivian couldn't look away from the screen. Over the dirty pond, words appeared on the screen again. *"Gordenner claims to be taking every safety precaution with the disposal of Its toxic, genetically engineered poison, but It lies."*

The camera tightened in to a shot of a hand covered in green rubber gloves dipping a clear plastic cup into the creek and then holding up the cup, dark rivulets settling into it, until the water was tainted brown.

"In Reality, Its waste goes straight into an industrial pipe underground that leads into Colman's Creek, 2/3 mile west of the Factory".

The camera panned to two dead fish tangled in some reeds along the creek.

"The noxious, dangerous, poisonous, disgusting, despicable by-product of the bioengineered petroleum pesticide – not fit for consumption – is pumped into the creek, poisoning fish, waterfowl and other innocent beings and then joins the Kickashaunee River downstream, where it poisons the local water supply and unsuspecting citizens."

The camera panned to more dead fish and some sort of bird – possibly a gosling – covered in scum, lifeless on the grass nearby.

"You, Vivian Sharp, applied to intern at the wretched Factory and we feel it is in your best interest to know what the Factory is up to before agreeing to work at such an unfathomably foul place."

The image disappeared, and then it was inside somewhere dark with just a small concentrated circle of light, like a flashlight, pointing at a desk with some papers on it. A hand, still wearing the rubber gloves, picked up the paper and held it to the camera. The writing on it looked weirdly familiar to her, and it took a few moments to recognize the penmanship as her own: it was Vivian's internship application. She and Wren both gasped. Vivian felt her heart sink and she immediately imagined Millie, riding her bike up to a faceless stranger in a car who called for her. She shook her head as if to erase the mental image.

"If you care at all, you will withdraw your application. If you don't care, which is what we anticipate, expect repercussions worthy of such a vile place as Gordenner." The camera tightened in on Vivian's neatly handwritten name and address on the application.

After a few seconds, the screen went black and the words appeared in white, *"WE KNOW YOU."* Then the camera opened back on the desk, where the gloved hands picked up a bucket of dirty water – from the stream, presumably – and violently threw it all over a computer and keyboard, dead fish and dirty water splashing everywhere. The hands dropped the bucket on the floor, and pulled out a piece of paper with a little sketch on it in pen, almost a doodle, of a cat. The camera tightened in on the drawing, and then the hand slapped it on the waterlogged desk, the ink running into blurry, fat lines. In the last frame, the words *"The Lynx"* appeared and faded after a few seconds; then the screen went blank.

Vivian had chills like pinpricks on her arms and was turning to Wren when a male voice suddenly spoke: "What is this?" Wren dropped her bagel, letting out a gasp, as Vivian whirled around in her chair, nearly falling off. Owl was standing behind them, squinting at the television, bags of produce in his hands. "Do you know what that was?"

"How long have you been here?" Wren asked, jumping up out of her chair, her hand on her chest.

"A few minutes. Long enough."

Vivian, still unable to talk, wrapped her arms around herself.

"What do you mean, long enough?"

Owl put down his bags on the counter. "I mean long enough to know that you're in trouble. Or at least your friend here is in trouble."

Wren put her hand on Vivian's shoulder. "What sort of trouble? What do you mean?"

Owl sighed and didn't say a word. Vivian noticed for the first time he was drained of all color, that he looked so fragile, almost angelic. He smoothed his hair back into his ponytail and slowly shook his head, not saying anything.

"Owl? What? You've got to tell us."

He rubbed his hand roughly against his forehead and was quiet for long enough that it looked like he was going to remain silent, but then he spoke, almost as if to himself alone, so quietly they almost didn't hear him. "I can't believe that after all these years, he's back."

"Who's back?" Wren said. "You're scaring me, Owl."

"Well, you ought to be scared. Really scared." He looked around the room. "Look, I don't want to talk out here in the open like this. You've already exposed me to enough risk." He started walking to the pantry and then looked over his shoulder at Wren and Vivian, who didn't know he expected them to follow him. "Come on," he growled, impatiently.

They followed him into the pantry. His eyes were furious, bright. "Do you know what you've done? Do you have any idea how reckless you were to bring that video here?"

Wren and Vivian didn't say anything, just looked at him, incomprehendingly.

"I have worked years on the straight and narrow and you have no right jeopardizing me and my business the way that you have, bringing that thing in here. I thought I knew you better," he said, looking pointedly at Wren.

"Owl," she said, her voice cracking, "I have no idea what you're talking about. Vivian got this video from Gordenner and there was a note asking her to watch it. No one else had a VCR and we didn't think it would be such a big deal."

"Gordenner? Why would they send this videotape? That makes no sense."

Vivian finally spoke. "We know, Owl. But it was sent to me in a Gordenner envelope with Gordenner stationery. We were just trying to figure out what was going on."

"What's going on? What's going on?" Again Owl shook his head and smoothed his hair back again. "I'm not going to incriminate myself in any way. You need to get your mom here, Wren, and show her the tape."

"My mom? Why?"

"Because she knows."

"You can't tell us?"

Owl walked out of the pantry. "No way. I've already said too much."

Wren went up front to call her mother and Vivian sank back in the chair by the television. She sat bowed over, with her head in her hands, trying to concentrate, which was difficult with Owl muttering to himself as he angrily chopped celery and carrots in the kitchen, then she heard them sizzle in the soup pot. She absentmindedly picked up the letter from the Lynx and started reading it again. Before long, she felt like she was onto something – a fleeting feeling, but a deep one while it lasted – of profound anger, "righteous indignation" as her father would call it, mixed with rage, something she'd never felt before, the kind that could inspire someone to put a fist through a wall. Vivian realized before too long that the feeling had a distinct quality to it that made it different than anything that she was familiar with: it was a step away from her. She started to understand that the feeling came from the person who made the tape. Having this stranger's emotions inside her – someone who was totally foreign to her, who felt something she hadn't experienced before or ever wanted to again – almost sent her reeling. She steadied herself by concentrating on remaining in control when all she wanted to do was run from the Commie Café. Instead, she closed her eyes and counted backwards from one hundred, concentrating on the numbers, seeing them in her head, and the warmth in her chest reappeared.

When she was at number 21, Wren came in back and handed Vivian a cup of lavender tea. There was a knocking on the front door and Owl walked out of the kitchen.

"Calms the nerves," Wren said, nodding at the tea.

Vivian smiled weakly. "Thank you."

Wren put her hand on Vivian's arm. "I don't want you to worry. I can see that you're nervous. I think this person was just trying to scare you for some reason." She looked toward the door. "My mom will be here really soon. Hopefully that will clear everything up."

Vivian nodded.

"Do you want anything else? Some Moroccan lentil soup? It's *really* good. I can warm some bread..."

Before she knew it, Vivian was sobbing, hunched up on her chair. Wren took her teacup and put it on the floor; Wren stooped next to her, holding her close.

"I'm sorry," Vivian said. "I'm sorry."

Wren pulled away from her, "What are you sorry for? I don't blame you for being scared." She grabbed some napkins and handed them to Vivian. She stooped to hug her again. Vivian pulled away.

"It's just that I don't know what I've gotten into here. Why did someone send that horrible tape to me? I don't understand," she said, wiping her face. "I'm worried about my family, about Millie. She's not scared of anyone. He – whoever this is – knows my address now. I can just see her talking to some stranger who shows up..." She started shaking, her breathing too rapid.

"Take a breath."

"I can't."

Wren shook her head. "You can."

Vivian closed her eyes, took a breath.

"Viv, don't torture yourself. My mom will clear everything up, I promise you. It's probably not that bad."

Vivian breathed deeply and sighed. "I feel like such an awful person. Owl hates me; I got him all mad at you, too." They could hear Owl talking in the front of the restaurant, presumably with Mrs. Summer.

Wren dismissed the thought with a wave of her hand. "Oh, please. Don't even worry about him. That's just his way sometimes. He overreacted and he'll apologize in, oh, about seven minutes," Wren said, looking at the clock on the wall. "He always does. You have no idea how many times he's blown up at me."

Vivian sniffled, smiling a little. "Really?"

Wren's eyes widened. "Yes, totally. He gets a little paranoid sometimes and freaks out. I used to take it seriously but it never lasts long and now I just let it slide. You should, too."

Now they could hear three voices in the restaurant – another male voice, as well as Owl's and Mrs. Summer. Wren cocked an eyebrow and gently pushed open the swinging kitchen door.

"Oh, hey, Carson. I didn't know you were here. What are you guys doing out here? You should come into the kitchen."

Owl, Mrs. Summer and Will walked back to the kitchen. Owl and Mrs. Summer were looking grim-faced and serious, while

Carson was bright-eyed and energetic, just as he was when they returned from Colman's Creek.

"So the tape's rewound. Do you want to see it?" Wren asked.

"Listen, I'm supposed to open in about ten minutes," Owl said. "How should we handle this? I don't want anyone to know anything about this."

"Well, first of all, the movie's only a couple of minutes long," Wren said. "Second, even if it went longer, there's no talking. No one would hear it."

Everyone looked at Owl, who slouched against the counter, shaking his head slowly. "Well, it goes against my better judgment..."

"We can go somewhere else if you don't feel comfortable, Owl," Mrs. Summer said.

"I have a VCR," Will offered cheerily. "I'm not far..."

Owl shrugged. "No use wasting your time. Let's get it over with. I'm not watching it, though."

"You don't have to," Mrs. Summer said.

"I don't want to bury myself deeper into this."

"We understand."

"I just don't need any trouble, especially not from him after everything."

"Owl," Mrs. Summer said, in a way that made it sound like she was near the end of her patience. "We understand. Now can we watch this and get it done with before you open?"

Owl nodded but made no attempt to leave. Wren pressed *Play*, and her mother and Will moved in closer to watch.

They watched the video again; Vivian was too afraid to see Mrs. Summer's reaction to look at her. She stood up and walked away to the sink when the camera opened on the desk and her application. Owl was still standing where he had been when they started the videotape.

For a few moments, no one said anything. Vivian looked over at them, and she could see that while Mrs. Summer looked even more grim than before, Will had a wide smile stretched across his face. He was the first to speak.

"I don't believe it," he said, a smile slowly spreading across his face. Vivian hadn't noticed before that he had a dimple, but then again, she'd also never seen him smile before. "I can't believe it, I never thought I'd see it, but he's back."

"Who's back?" Vivian asked. "Who is this?"

"The Lynx. Didn't you see that drawing? His trademark? The Lynx is back."

Vivian saw Owl and Mrs. Summer exchange glances. "But who's the Lynx?" she asked.

Mrs. Summer straightened her back and took a deep breath. Owl and Will were both looking for her to answer Vivian's question. "Who is the Lynx?" she said finally, a tired, grave smile on her face. "Oh, that's a long story. Are you ready for a long story?"

Vivian rejoined the group and turned a chair around to face the others, as did Wren. Will grabbed a couple of folding chairs that were leaning against the wall and carried them over, setting them to face Wren and Vivian. "You want a chair, Owl?" he asked.

Owl shook his head, irritated. "I've got work to do. I've got to open." He carefully closed the swinging door behind him as he walked into the restaurant. They could hear him walking toward the door and then they heard footsteps coming back. He opened the door to the kitchen and poked his head in. "Just keep it down, okay?" he said.

Mrs. Summer started talking a couple of times, only to lose her train of thought and become silent. Vivian glanced at Wren, who had a concerned look on her face. Clearly, she was not accustomed to seeing her mother flustered like this. Mrs. Summer bent forward and pressed her fingers onto her chin. At last, she took a breath again, this time ready to speak.

"Girls, the Lynx lived here a long time ago, like twenty years ago, and he was a saboteur."

Will jumped in, presuming correctly that Wren and Vivian would be confused. "A saboteur is someone who sabotages. Specifically, the Lynx would sabotage agribusiness, polluters, animal abusers."

Mrs. Summer nodded. "He was based in the Center City area..."

"Center City?" Wren asked, her jaw dropped, looking between them both. "Nothing ever happens here."

"Yep, Center City, but he would travel the county, sometimes the whole state, finding various places to sabotage. And he'd always leave behind his little calling card, the drawing of a lynx, like the one you saw, but no one knew who he was. No one ever found out either."

"That's so cool," Wren murmured.

"Yes, that's what we thought at first, too. He was like Robin Hood to us in those days. I mean, it's hard to imagine this now, but back then, we had a pretty vibrant community of activists, partially because of him. You know all those protest signs and the flyers I have boxed up in the attic, Wren? That was from back then, and the Lynx really helped give us the courage to push our issues front and center. Animal rights folks, environmentalists, we were all working together harmoniously, mostly because of the Lynx, though we never met him. It's so hard to imagine that today."

"But what did he do to help make it happen?" Vivian asked.

"Well, we saw what he was doing – it was in newspapers and on the news everywhere, not just around here. It was big news that this rogue character, the Lynx, managed time and again to outfox the best, most complex security systems just as simply as a child would knock over some wooden blocks."

"Not only that," Will interrupted, excited as a little boy, unable to contain himself, "but he would totally stick it to them. If they were polluting, he would make sure that the executives had sewage backing up into their sinks at their homes, their bathtubs. Not only the executives, but he also went after investors. He would get his hands on the list of investors for whatever company and target them, too. It was a brilliant strategy, making these CEOs and boards of directors completely terrified. If someone was cruel to animals – that was really where his heart was – he would, like, there used to be this horrible old horseracing track here…"

"Heartland Park," Mrs. Summer said.

"That's it. 'Heartless Park' was what the Lynx called it in his letter to the press. He sabotaged it so that none of the gates would work, so they couldn't race the horses. They fixed the gates – at great expense, from what I understand, and they never figured out what he did to disable them – and then he did it again, immediately, the same thing with new, expensive gates. They never recovered from that and they closed down that spring."

"Will, how do you know about all this? Were you even born yet?" Wren asked.

"Yes, but I was only a toddler when all this was going on. I studied him later, when I first became an activist in high school. The Lynx is such an almost mythic figure it was hard to separate fact from fiction, but the libraries always have the old articles on him if you knew how to look for it. You should dig around for some of what was written about him twenty years ago. We're really not doing him justice here. He was into everything. Really had the local profiteers in a bind."

"Yeah, in about a year's span, he probably infiltrated and sabotaged, I don't know, dozens of companies."

"Thirty-seven," Will said. "There might have been more, but some at the end were likely copycats. There were 37 that were consistent of the Lynx's work."

Mrs. Summer shrugged. "That could be right. I know there were a lot of businesses he targeted, and it's not like he only sabotaged them once and then was done with them. He'd return sometimes a dozen times to one location. He'd have several going at once. And apparently he did it all single-handedly, too. If anyone was an accomplice, no one was talking, then or now. It was weird at the time – we were all wondering if the Lynx was someone we knew or knew someone we knew."

"So what happened?" Vivian asked. "I mean, where did he go?"

Mrs. Summer shrugged. "He disappeared as suddenly as he arrived. And not a moment too soon."

"Hmm," Will said.

Mrs. Summer looked at him. "Hmm, what?"

Will hesitated for a moment, then said with a small laugh, "I was just thinking that he left too soon."

"Really? You weren't here, Will."

"I understand that, but why were you glad that he stopped?"

"Because he destabilized and then destroyed all that he and we had created. I mean, what's going on now in terms of activism? Even at the college, Will, there's nothing going on."

"And you blame that solely on the Lynx?"

She dismissed the thought impatiently. "No, not at all. I do think, though, that we were nearly at a point in which we were a viable, productive force to be reckoned with and then he went over the edge, pulling us along with him by association."

Will cocked his head. "What did he do that was so over the edge, I mean, considering everything? Considering who he took on, those industry apologists and criminals?"

"Oh, Will. I'm surprised that you can even ask that, knowing as much as you do about the Lynx. He clearly had no regard for human life."

"Are you talking about the pipe bomb?"

"Pipe bomb?" Vivian and Wren repeated, looking at each other.

"Well, yes, that, but he was violent before that, too." Mrs. Summer turned to Vivian and Wren and said, "He sent a pipe bomb to a laboratory on campus that was vivisecting animals and a janitor had the misfortune of having it explode on him. Blew off one of his arms from the elbow down."

"He got sloppy," Will said, almost defensively.

Mrs. Summer shook her head in disbelief. "You don't get sloppy with such violent means, Will, not when it involves lives. You just don't, end of story. That man could have easily been killed; as it is, he was maimed."

Will didn't say anything.

Mrs. Summer's eyes flashed with anger. "How could you be so callous? It was totally inexcusable and that poor man's life was ruined. I can't believe that I even have to explain why that was wrong. Before that, Lynx had become almost as dangerous but thankfully nothing worse had come of it, other than destroying property."

"Destroying property is not violence, Simone. We're going to disagree on this. These are inanimate objects we're talking about, but objects that also have the potential to harm the planet. It sends a powerful symbolic message."

"Yes, blowing off that janitor's arm certainly sent a message," Mrs. Summer said, her voice getting very deliberate. "People who care about animals despise humanity. What a lovely legacy that's been left for us, for those of us who have to still work with the public to improve animals' lives."

Will became angry, too, but, unlike Mrs. Summer, his voice rose with it. "It isn't his fault that people are so stupid and unsophisticated that they believe that if you protect animals, you naturally hate people. How is that his problem? That's faulty reasoning and no matter what the Lynx did, people would use their own mental shortcomings to understand his actions."

"So you think it'd be an 'unsophisticated' conclusion to come to that blowing off someone's arm to make a point shows disregard for humanity?"

Will sat upright, his hands gripped tight across the seat of his chair. "You're twisting my words, Simone. That package was not meant to be intercepted by that janitor. That was a fluke thing – frankly, I don't think that the Lynx should have taken that risk, either, but that janitor wasn't the target. The target was the guy running the vivisection lab. That's whose name was on the package. If it had gone the way he had planned – and imagine that one horrible bastard did indeed get his hand blown off or worse and so the school decided it was too dangerous to keep the lab going – all those beagles, all those rabbits and mice would not have been tortured and killed. If it had gone the way it was supposed to, everyone would have thought that it was totally justified."

Mrs. Summers set her jaw, her eyes blazing, and she spoke very slowly, enunciating every word. "Will, I have cared for those animals from that laboratory at my sanctuary. I have nursed them back to health and changed their bedding and socialized them and spent money out of pocket for their medications and surgery bills. I have held some as they were euthanized because there was no hope for some of ever having their suffering relieved. Please do not pull this holier-than-thou attitude on me because I'm not having it."

"Mom, it's okay…"

Will exhaled. "I apologize."

She took a few moments to calm down, then sighed. "Look, I'm not arguing with you as to whether something is justifiable, Will. I'm saying that the Lynx went this particular route, and look at where we are now. Objectively, look at it. Are the animals better off now than they were when we were active? Are we able to educate people, or is the door slammed in our face before the conversation starts because we're still associated with someone considered to be a terrorist? I'm just pointing out the reality of our community today as opposed to twenty years ago, when we were on the cusp of creating something significant. I mean, activists in San Francisco, New York – everywhere – looked to this little town, Center City. People moved from there to here – to Center City, to this boring little nothing town – to be a part of a movement that was happening. Can you even imagine that? People don't move *to* here, not if they can help it. They move *from* here."

Will looked frustrated, deflated. "Look, Simone, the industries, the executives, the investors: they deserved to be harassed. Do we disagree? Look at who he targeted – not an innocent one in the bunch. Debold Chemicals. Fisher Laboratories. The Coopertown Hatchery. The Dixmoor Power Plant. They *deserved* it. And much worse. Corporations are just constructs, but as long as they have the power to destroy, they're fair game."

"But, Will, strategically, does this make the most sense? When we have to win over hearts and minds? I mean, I agree that some of that at first was good and it was effective. His acts of sabotage, when he started, got people to notice the things that went on behind closed doors and it helped to generate enough interest that concerned people came out of the woodwork. Then the activists could jump in after he got everyone's attention and educate and make our voices be heard. We could piggyback on him in a way that was synchronized and smart. I agree that it was an impressive beginning."

"So when, in your opinion, did that change?" he asked.

Mrs. Summer was silent, thinking. "I'm not sure if I can pinpoint it, but probably when he became threatening. When children were afraid to go to sleep at night because of what their daddy or mommy did for a living. Afraid that they might not even wake up in the morning."

Will threw up his hands, unable to contain his irritation. "But those parents did not deserve to have their crimes against the others concealed from their children. Why should they get to go home and have little Bobby or Susie look up to them as heroes? I think that it was masterful to rip away the curtains and expose them as what they were: Animal torturers. Polluters. The worst of humanity. Why shouldn't they have had to face their children as what they truly were?"

Mrs. Summer blinked a few times, looking more tired than before, and spoke slowly. "Because, Will, then the children have become innocent victims. Can you not see that? The very thing that we condemn in their parents – that they would perpetrate violence against the innocent – is what we are re-creating. Is that fair? Did the child commit the crime?"

"No," Will said, "but what is the greater crime, Simone? That some scumbag is exposed for being exactly what he is, or that animals get tortured behind closed doors, that Center City becomes more polluted?"

Mrs. Summer didn't say anything. Will was on a roll now, and he leaned forward for emphasis. It became clear to Vivian that they didn't even need to be there, that he would have been happy to rage to an empty room.

"When someone decides to benefit financially by hurting animals and the earth, it's a choice they made. Come on..."

"Don't talk to me like I don't..."

"It's a conscious choice. To me, to respond swiftly and decisively, and, yes, harshly, perhaps, is justifiable. This is an example of 'by any means necessary': if the kids are sad when daddy or mommy is exposed as an animal torturer or the one who poisoned the town's water, so be it. Is that the end of the world? The greater good is that their parents are shamed out of their line of work. If shame isn't enough of a motivator, then they are intimidated. By no means is that the equivalent of the violence or damage that they cause."

"Do you see what Will is trying to do here, girls?" Mrs. Summer asked at last, looking at the silent Wren and Vivian. "He's trying to frame an argument in such a way that I have to become an apologist for the very people I work day in and day out against, since before he was born. Isn't that interesting?"

He shook his head vigorously. "No, Simone, I'm not. I'm just disagreeing with you."

By now, Owl was back in the kitchen, leaning against the wall by the door. No one knew how long he'd been there as he had a way of slipping in and out of rooms, undetected for the most part.

"Well, could you at least dial it down a bit, Will?" Mrs. Summer said, rubbing the skin on her hand. "I'm just having a hard time with the proselytizing. Do you need to be standing on a soapbox every time we discuss this? My grandfather was a preacher; I've had enough preaching for a lifetime."

Will looked genuinely taken aback. "I'm sorry, I didn't realize I was doing that. I'm just really excited, I guess. It seems like I've been waiting for this my whole life and I'm overzealous, perhaps."

Mrs. Summer was about to say something when Owl coughed, clearing his throat. "Well, I don't know about anyone else, but I'm wondering what we should do now. For all we know, the café is bugged and he's listening to every little word. Or the FBI has bugged us and is doing the same. I can't afford this."

"Afford what?" Will asked.

"Losing the café," Owl said impatiently, like this was obvious.

"Owl, I sincerely doubt the café is bugged or you'd end up losing your café over this video. I mean, no one knew that we'd end up here of all places to watch this, right?" Will said.

"How do we know that? I just feel like we're all marked right now."

"What is this, some kind of thriller?" Will snorted with a mocking little laugh. "Espionage? Extortion? Like the Lynx is some
144

sort of boogeyman lying in wait?" He rubbed his hands together in an impression of a sinister cartoon character. "Bwa ha ha!"

Owl moved in toward Will, clenching and opening his fists, veins in his forearms pushed out like ropes. "Listen, dude, you don't insult me. Don't come into my place and insult me. I don't even know you – you're just a kid and you somehow consider yourself some sort of 'expert' on the Lynx and activism. Don't forget that I lived right here while this was going on in the first place. Have you ever had the FBI show up at your doorstep? Look through your files and mail? Nothing that you've read about radical activist theory in one of your classes is going to trump my experience."

Will started to respond, a grin still on his face, but Mrs. Summer jumped up and stood in between them. "Owl, I think that we're all a little tense and on edge right now. Let's calm down."

Owl walked back to where he'd been standing before, muttering to himself, and slammed his back against the doorframe making the pots hanging above the stove rattle a little, his arms folded across his chest.

Mrs. Summer broke the silence with a quiet voice, spoken like she was just thinking out loud. "It's amazing to me that after all these years, he still has the power to divide like this." She looked at the girls, and almost seemed surprised to see them there. She clucked her tongue, sat down again and looked at Vivian. "I'm sorry, honey. I think that we all got caught up in the drama of the morning and we neglected you, how this has to be affecting you. I'm sorry."

Vivian was still so stunned by the video and the tension in the room, all the new information, she had a hard time speaking. She tried to a few times, but no words came to her. Mrs. Summer looked at her sympathetically and patted her knee. "I understand, Vivian. Take your time."

Growing self-conscious about everyone looking at her, waiting for her to speak, Vivian, her throat dry, finally rasped out a few words, the inadequacy of them making her instantly ashamed. "What should I do?"

"I guess I don't understand why you received this videotape in the first place," Mrs. Summer said. "What do you have to do with the pollution at Gordenner? I mean, what do you have to do with Gordenner at all?"

Wren looked expectantly at Vivian and she nodded, looking down. Wren explained to them that Vivian had been offered and accepted an internship at Gordenner, and told them about the pipe they'd discovered when they were at the factory earlier in the week. Owl occasionally glanced out the window of the swinging door, a nervous look on his face, and Will, who had taken a spiral notebook out of his backpack, was scribbling down notes.

Mrs. Summer listened to the story, folding and unfolding the pretty tasseled scarf she'd been wearing around her shoulders on her lap. She was silent after Wren finished telling her story, and Owl was silent as well, still leaning against the doorframe. The only sound came from Will, furiously writing in his notebook with a ballpoint pen.

"Vivian, is this something that you're sure you want to do?" Mrs. Summer asked. "I don't think that it's too late to back out of this internship and this video will probably be the last time you'll hear from the Lynx, if that's what you want."

At once, Will stopped scribbling and looked up, watching Vivian. She briefly imagined calling Ms. Collins to turn down the offer and she shook her head. "No. That's not what I want. I don't want to endanger my family, but this really feels like what I'm supposed to be doing. Interning there, I mean."

Will nodded. Owl walked back into the restaurant and Mrs. Summer watched him, interlacing her fingers. "I'm not sure what to tell you, Vivian. If the Lynx is indeed back on the scene, he's unpredictable and who knows the repercussions? He could have even grown more violent over the years away. I guess my question is, what is your goal at Gordenner? Is there really something you could accomplish working there?"

"Well, I haven't given it much thought beyond the fact that they are polluting the water and killing animals. I need to stop that somehow."

"Of course. I understand. I appreciate that. But is interning there the most effective route?"

Will jumped in. "It is, Simone. That way Vivian would have access to information without having to sneak around. It's nearly as good as having their consent."

Wren, who had been uncharacteristically quiet, nodded her head and chimed in. "I agree, Mom. How else would Vivian have the freedom of movement she needs to get to the bottom of what's going on there?"

Mrs. Summer smiled politely. "Well, we know what Will and Wren think. You'd be the one sticking your neck out, though. What do *you* think?" she said, pointedly looking directly at Vivian. They all turned in their seats to face her. Owl came back into the room and stood against the doorframe again.

"I think," she started saying, then her thoughts went blank, like water swirling down a drain. She sat quietly thinking, and started again. "I think... What was the question?"

"Do you need to be interning at Gordenner to do this work?"

"Sorry. Thank you. Yes, I think that I have to be there, for the reasons Will and Wren gave and also just because that's just what my heart is telling me, even after this videotape."

Will nodded and impatiently tapped his notebook with his pen. "Look, Vivian, I started working on a plan of attack. I don't want you just to go there with no back up. Now that we know that the Lynx is following this, we've got to figure out a way to get him on board, to understand that you're on his side."

Vivian felt her body tense. "I don't know if I want to work with him, Will."

"Why not?" He sounded personally insulted.

"Well..."

"Yes? What's the worst that could happen?"

At this, Mrs. Summer let out a guffaw and soon everyone in the room was laughing, with the exception of Will, who looked genuinely confused by such a reaction. As the realization washed over his face – he turned from looking confused to being irritated – he crossed his arms in front of his chest and sulked.

"Oh, Will. Come on. You have to have a sense of humor about this," Mrs. Summer said, still laughing. "How are you going to be in this for the long haul if you can't laugh once in a while?"

Wren put her hand on his shoulder and said with her eyes opened wide in faux-sincerity, "Will, maybe the Lynx will find you through Viv and he will totally adopt you as his son. You guys could wear matching sweaters and get family portraits taken together. Wouldn't that be cool?"

Grudgingly, he had to smile a little, even as he shook off Wren's hand. Owl walked back to the cooler and quietly added, "Except it would be just Will in his sweater and this other sweater beside him with no one in it because the Lynx could not be photographed. He'd be like the Invisible Man standing next to Will."

"Okay, I get it," Will said. "Har dee har har. What's the worst that could happen – um, grave bodily injury. Can we move on?"

The bells hanging from the front door of the café started jingling and the air whooshed as it closed. They stopped talking, listening to bodies shuffling in and pulling out chairs, voices chattering. Owl looked stricken again, as though customers stopping in was highly suspicious. Vivian picked up the cup of now-lukewarm tea that Wren had given her right after they'd seen the video, and she stood up.

"You know what? I'm going to be okay. I think we should just let Owl have his café back and go on with the day."

"We could meet somewhere else to strategize, Vivian," Will offered. "There's a lot of work ahead. There are all sorts of rooms at the college library that are never checked out. Should we go there? To the library on campus?"

Vivian shook her head. "I think I need a little time to just think about this by myself. I'm going to go ahead with beginning the internship Friday like I never saw this video. I think that that's the best thing that I can do right now."

She felt them all looking at her, unblinking.

Mrs. Summer spoke first. "Are you sure, Vivian? I mean, going up against Gordenner and possibly the Lynx: those are formidable adversaries. More preparation might make you feel more confident going in."

Vivian thought about this for a moment. "No, I'm all right. I promise that I will keep all of you in the loop..."

Owl coughed, almost choking.

"Except you, Owl. But I think I just want to get started on this. Something is making me feel like that's the right approach right now. I mean, this whole thing is weird and all, but, I don't know, I just want to get moving now and prepare for Friday by making sure I'm rested. Does that make sense?"

Mrs. Summer looked at Will and Wren, studied Vivian's face. She smiled very subtly, her face brightening briefly. "It's your call, Viv. I don't there's any harm in what you propose: taking time by yourself is a very mature decision. I just want you to know that you can call any of us..."

Owl coughed again, louder this time.

"Especially Owl," she laughed, "any time. He wants you to call him from public phones in the loudest voice you can manage. I'm kidding, Owl. Relax. Jeez. All joking aside, Vivian, I just want you to remember that we're here for you."

With that, Owl started back out into the restaurant, but he stopped right before walking out. "Um," he started, looking at Vivian and then down at the floor, his voice quiet. "I'm sorry if I yelled at you before. It's just…"

"I understand, Owl."

He nodded his head, still looking at the floor. "I got spooked. I still am, to tell you the truth."

"I understand. I'm sorry."

"It's just that he turned everything upside-down. You have no idea how bad it was." His voice trailed off. He looked at Vivian until she nodded.

He mumbled something else, something not intended to be heard it seemed, and walked into the restaurant. The door had barely shut when Wren jumped up in excitement. "See? I told you that he'd apologize. It took a little longer than usual, but he did do it. Everything's all right in the world again."

"Because Owl apologized?" Will asked.

"Yep, because he apologized. Otherwise then it would be certain that the planets were totally out of alignment and meteors might start crashing around us at any moment. Forget Gordenner: we're talking tsunamis. Earthquakes! The fact that Owl apologized makes everything all right again. We're back in balance." As she was wont to do, Wren said this in such a straight-faced way that it was impossible to know if she was joking or serious. "I can relax again."

"*Oookay,*" Will said. He reached into his backpack and pulled out a bunch of brochures, handing them to Vivian. "Here, I think you should see these."

She turned them around in her hands. She had three different brochures from him, glossy and bright, each with scenes of bucolic farmland, tractors and outstretched hands carrying fat tomatoes, knobby carrots.

"What are these?"

"Greenwashing pabulum from Gordenner. They all basically say the same thing: that they exist to feed the world, to help the noble farmer, that they are an essential part of the fabric that connects us with our agrarian roots, blah blah blah. All nonsense, of course, greenwashing nonsense. Anyway, they have these all over campus, like in the student commons building and the science building, which they basically own at this point through their donations and various grants. I'm almost certain that they're going forward with Miracle Wheat again. They've been working the 'feed the world' angle like gangbusters lately, which makes me suspect that they're up to something major."

"You said greenwash. Is greenwash a product of theirs or something? What is it?"

"Oh, sorry. I assumed you were familiar with the term. Basically, it's when a corporation gives itself an environmentally conscious image makeover that is all about appearances, nothing of any real substance. Gordenner never paid much attention to their corporate image before and now all of the sudden they don't want to be perceived as the boogeyman. So that makes me wonder what they have up their sleeves. You're going to be neck-deep in greenwash with their marketing department. What a stroke of luck," he marveled with a low whistle.

Vivian thanked him and put the brochures into her purse; she turned to hug Wren and Mrs. Summer goodbye.

"I think I'll walk home. I've got some errands."

She didn't really have any errands, but she felt bad about lying so she stopped at the drugstore on the way home to buy something, which turned out to be cotton balls. She just needed to walk by herself.

SCHOOL'S OUT

For the rest of the weekend, Vivian spent most of her time in her bedroom, trying to think. The videotape sat on her desk in its envelope, which she'd wrapped in masking tape, as though that were going to give her some level of protection. She found herself often staring out her bedroom window, which faced the street, and didn't notice anything out of the ordinary. No strange cars, no one hiding in the bushes. She didn't sleep much at night, though, and even went downstairs and quickly poked her head outside shortly after midnight with her heart pounding wildly to convince herself that there was no one lurking behind their door. Vivian was relieved to wake up Sunday to heavy, dark clouds and sheets of rain, which kept Millie indoors and off her bike. Vivian picked up her spiral notebook and opened it to the page she'd started when she first accepted the internship, still blank except for the heading 'Gordenner' underlined twice. She was starting her apprenticeship in less than a week. She stared at the blank page several times before she noticed her sophomore English textbook on her desk and decided to write a haiku.

Gordenner poisons.
What am I supposed to do?
Wait and see, I guess.

Vivian scratched it out angrily, then ripped the page out, balled it up and tossed in her wastebasket. On second thought, she reached back in, opened it up and ripped it into tiny pieces.

The rest of the week went by quickly for Vivian; the last day of school was Wednesday and the students were raucous and reckless, setting off the fire alarm twice in one day, the boys shoving each other into lockers. Vivian didn't mind as it brought her out of her nervous mind briefly, and it also gave her and Wren something to roll their eyes about in the cafeteria.

Wednesday morning the students cleared out the last remnants of the year from their lockers and were issued their yearbooks in homeroom. The rest of the day, more or less, was devoted to getting yearbooks signed in the gymnasium, which had been set up with streamers, balloons and popcorn and cotton candy machines; Center City High's most popular band, Photosynthesis (they met during biology class), laughed uproariously at the feedback they created on the stage. Wren and Vivian sat near the top of the bleachers, their feet crossed on the row below and thumbing through their yearbooks as the student body buzzed and circulated below them.

"What do you think of the band?" Vivian asked.

"Oh," Wren looked over at them as if she hadn't even noticed that they'd been playing. "Not really my thing. They're fine, though, I guess. And you?"

Same."

"This girl – the one with the short bangs – Cindy McDougall. Do you know her? She's super mean," Wren said, pointing at a picture. "Page 82. She tripped me on my first day here – just stuck her foot out plain as day and tripped me as I was walking down the hall. Can you imagine that? I spilled my books everywhere."

"Oh, yeah. She's always been mean," Vivian said, glancing over with a grimace. "She rubbed paste in my hair in kindergarten. On purpose, of course. May I?" She drew a little moustache on Cindy McDougall. Wren scribbled in a triangular beard and devil horns and they erupted in laughter, then quickly turned the page.

From their perch in the bleachers, they looked down at the crowd, moving around one another like ants, yearbooks outstretched or clutched to the chest, looking around for the next person to sign it.

"This whole concept of getting your yearbook signed, it's like a popularity contest, isn't it? I'm still new to this high school culture thing."

Vivian nodded. "Yep. You get the right people to sign it and it's like your existence is justified."

Wren laughed. "Well, we should still sign one another's yearbooks, shouldn't we? I don't care about anyone else signing mine."

"I reserved the whole thing for you," she smiled.

"Don't you want to save some room for your other friends?" Wren asked.

"I seem to have neglected the 'other friends' aspect of my life."

"I feel bad."

"Why?"

Wren turned serious. "Well, I hope that I haven't been keeping you away from your other friends."

"Nah. It's my own choice. Quality over quantity, right? We're taught our whole lives that we're supposed to have tons of friends and I think that's silly. Now fork over that yearbook, girl."

"Having no forks, I'll just hand it to you," Wren said, holding it out to Vivian.

"That'll do just fine." She handed Wren her yearbook. "I think a fork would be an awkward tool for passing it anyway."

Wren nodded. "A spatula or two would be a better choice. A set of sturdy tongs, even better."

They sat side-by-side, scribbling in one another's yearbooks and trying to sneak glances. Wren finally turned her body away from Vivian and propped the book up on the bleacher row behind them, still using her arm to further prevent any stray glances ("No sneaks," she admonished).

Vivian felt inarticulate suddenly so she stumbled around in a scrawling, rambling paragraph. She finished long before Wren, who had Vivian's yearbook for more than a half hour, occasionally giggling to herself before she'd write more, so she spent the rest of the time leafing through the pages. Until a few months ago, Vivian had considered the social world of this little universe with frustration and envy, like it was a secret society with its own language and secret codes that she couldn't hope to ever crack, but now she couldn't be less interested. Flipping through the yearbook, Vivian turned to the photo of Wren, with her calm smile in her class photo and her unself-conscious, unabashed grin as the sole member of the Center City Vegetarian Club – the shot was taken before Vivian met her – and Vivian smiled back. She couldn't help feeling like she'd found her perfect match in a friend.

By the time Wren finished Vivian's yearbook, the last bell of the school year rang. Students whooped and hollered, slammed shut lockers in the hallways, sent their backpacks skittering across the floor like bowling balls. Wren looked up and started handing Vivian her yearbook, then reconsidered.

"One last thing," she said, barely opening the book as she quickly scribbled. "I forgot to sign it. Okay, it's ready now."

Vivian started to open her yearbook, but Wren pushed it shut. "Read it later," Wren said. "Could you?" She looked around the gym nervously. "We've got to get going or we might get locked in here all summer. Can you imagine? Heaven forbid."

They walked out of school together, carrying the last remains from their lockers and laughing about their early impressions of one another of just a few weeks ago.

"When you first walked in the room," Wren said, as they both stopped abruptly to avoid a passing football, "I thought at first that you'd come to the wrong room by accident."

"What do you mean?"

"When you first came to the Vegetarian Club meeting. But that I was determined to persuade you to hang out even if you were at the wrong room."

"Why?"

"'Cause you looked different."

"Different?"

"In a good way, yes, different. Anything different here is a compliment, silly. Then I was totally flustered when you said that you were actually looking for the Vegetarian Club, but I tried to be low-key about it because I didn't want to scare you away."

Vivian giggled. "Really?"

"I can be overly enthusiastic sometimes I guess."

"No, well, I just felt like such a moron and, well, you've always seemed so poised. I guess it's good to know that I'm not the only one who felt idiotic. You made me feel comfortable right away, though."

Wren brushed her hair out of her eyes. "So what do you think brought us together? Like, do you think it was fated to happen, or just one of those happy accidents? We could have gone through all of our school years without really knowing one another."

"I don't know. What if..."

A sharp voice was calling to Vivian and as she turned around, she saw Kendra Brentwood running across the lawn toward her, waving one arm, the other wrapped around her yearbook.

"Oh, great," Vivian muttered under her breath. "Kendra." She and Wren stopped.

Kendra ran up to them, gasping for air. Vivian looked back to where she had run from, and she saw a group of three of Kendra's crowd standing close together, watching them.

"What's up?" Vivian asked.

154

Kendra smiled in such a way that made Vivian instantly guarded. "Well, Viv, I was wondering about your summer plans. We don't talk much these days and I was just wondering."

Vivian looked at Wren and didn't say anything at first. She shook her head. "Why?"

"See, I have a cousin who's going to be visiting for a few weeks starting in July and maybe I can set you two up. He's totally cute, seventeen, tall. What do you think? Should I introduce you? I heard that redheads are his type..."

Vivian shrugged, genuinely baffled. "Umm..."

"I mean," Kendra said, opening her eyes wide, "I assume you still date boys, right? Or, come to think of it, I don't remember you ever having a boyfriend."

Vivian didn't say anything, just stood silently trying to figure out what Kendra was getting at. Kendra smirked a little before adjusting her face to look more serious. She asked Vivian in a conspiratorial tone, "So, just out of curiosity, do you even like boys?"

"What are you even talking about, Kendra?" Vivian bristled. She couldn't help noticing that Kendra steadfastly refused to meet Wren's gaze.

Kendra ran her hand through her hair. "It's not big deal these days if you don't like boys, Viv. I was just wondering. You can tell me."

Vivian could feel her face get red and hot. She glanced back at the group, still watching them. "Listen, I know what you're trying to get at. At least give me the credit to know when I'm being made fun of, Kendra."

Kendra protested. "I was just wondering..."

Vivian felt the anger boiling up. "Oh, don't give me that innocent act. You couldn't care less about what's going on in my life. You're just entertaining your little followers over there. I'd think that you'd have better things to do." It was like slow motion to Vivian, telling Kendra off like this, and she didn't know if she was more terrified or thrilled. She started to storm off and Wren hurried up to join her.

"Vivian," Kendra called out, "why are you being so defensive? Are you hiding something?"

"Excuse me," Wren said, whirling around to face Kendra, curls springing like coils. "Vivian has nothing to hide. You just need to pay attention to your own life."

Kendra, momentarily stunned, blinked a few times. "Um, I wasn't talking to you."

"Um," Wren said, matching Kendra's imperious tone perfectly, "if you're talking to my friend that way, then you *are* talking to me." She put her hands on her hips.

"Whatever, witch," Kendra said, turning to walk away.

Without skipping a beat, Wren said, "Whatever, word that rhymes with witch." She started walking away, then turned and shouted, hands cupped around her mouth for amplification, "In case you were wondering, the word starts with a 'b'."

Vivian felt her face turn hot, both laughter and tears just below the surface. They walked together to downtown Center City, where Wren was about to start her shift at the café. They walked slowly, letting it sink in, and then sat together on the bench across the street from the café for a few minutes.

"So, I feel weird asking this and all," Wren said quietly, "but it's on my mind and you know how that is."

"What?"

"Do you think you might be better off staying away from me? I don't want that pack of mean kids to make your life miserable because of me, you know."

"No way. That would be awful. I never fit in with them anyway so I may as well go for broke. Sometimes it just takes a while to adjust to something new."

"I can't imagine that anyone as awesome as you was ever even slightly, *slightly* friends with that idiotic Kendra girl. I mean, who am I to judge, but she's pretty evil, am I right?"

"That would be a 'yes'. She's gotten more like that, apparently."

"So do you want to change the subject?"

Vivian nodded eagerly.

"Suits me. So are you ready for interning Friday? You haven't said much about it."

"I think so," Vivian said, frowning a little. "The Lynx has definitely added to my..." she fluttered her hand over her heart.

"Understandably."

"...but it feels like the right thing to do. Ask me again when he tries to bomb my house."

Wren winced. "Shhh. Don't even joke about that. Everything's going to be fine."

"I know, I know. It will. I'll be fine. I'm sorry."

Wren sighed and started gathering her bags. "All right, girl. Bagels don't toast themselves, as I have learned, though that would be a neat innovation. Will you call me after work on Friday? I'm going to be dying to hear about it."

"Sure will."

"Where are you headed? Home?"

"No, to the library. I've got to do some research before Friday. See you soon."

Wren stood there expectantly. "No hug?"

Vivian looked around. "Are you sure?"

Wren laughed and nearly tackled her in a bear hug. "This is proof that you don't like boys anymore, Vivian. Take that, Kendra," she shouted, "We're loud and proud."

Vivian pulled away from Wren, laughing. "Well, goody gumdrops. I needed a little more drama in my life. I need it from every possible direction. Thank you."

She walked on to the Center City Public Library, because her mind kept wandering back there. She went up to the second floor to her favorite section, a little room off of the periodicals section, with big comfortable chairs and lots of sunlight. She sat in the otherwise empty room for a few minutes when she remembered the brochures that Will had given her, still in her purse. Glancing through them, they didn't look very controversial and certainly not like something from an agricultural chemical company. They looked more like some of the vacation destination glossies her mother got in the mail for traveling to Mexico or New England. There were lots of photos of cows standing in gently rolling pastures, and robust looking farmers driving their tractors and spreading seeds by hand. The scant text the brochure had focused on the reputation Gordenner had built up for the past 60 years, one of giving farmers the means to feed a hungry world.

As Vivian was glancing through the last brochure, a passing librarian, pushing a wobbly cart of books, stopped in her tracks.

"Isn't today the last day of school?" she asked Vivian.

Vivian, a little startled, nodded her head. "Yes, it was."

The librarian opened her eyes wide. "And you decided to come to the library to celebrate?" She shook her head, and prepared to push her cart again. "Kids today."

Vivian, feeling very conspicuous now, put her brochures away, walked down to the first floor and she found herself looking up old articles about the Lynx on microfiche. Dozens of articles popped up, most occurring within a yearlong period almost twenty years before. She skimmed through all the articles, reading about the explosion that nearly gutted a local car dealership attributed to the Lynx and offices being ransacked at the agricultural department of Center City College, also attributed to him. All the articles referencing the Lynx followed more or less the same formula: the police were called in when workers discovered the damage in the morning. The pattern was one of escalation, starting with broken windows and locks when a place was first targeted, building to explosions on repeat visits.

Vivian sat in front of the microfiche for hours, her shoulders growing very sore, her eyes dry and tired. She couldn't turn away, though, and by the time she'd finally read every article, more than two hours had elapsed. She rubbed her eyes and went to sit outside the library on a stone bench, trying to clear her head. All she could think about was the Lynx, and an image she had conjured in her head of an obscured, furtive figure lurking in the shadows, one that she couldn't see. She saw the rubble of an exploded building, laboratory equipment strewn everywhere, from the photos she saw. Vivian was ready to go back inside when she heard a familiar voice calling her name. She whipped around and there was Millie running across the expansive lawn toward her, and her father not far behind with a surprised look on his face.

Millie ran to Vivian, her arms outstretched, and leaped at Vivian in a flying embrace. "We were waiting for you at home and after a while I got bored and Dad said that we could check out a video at the library for tonight. Do you want to see a movie? I want to see if there's one with pirates. Billy Cole is having a pirate birthday party next week so I need to learn about them."

Vivian was still adjusting to the abrupt change in mood when Mr. Sharpe caught up to them. "Well, isn't this a surprise. I wouldn't expect to find you at the library on the last day of school, Viv. Millie and I were set to take you out to lunch to celebrate."

Vivian just realized that she'd forgotten about lunch. "Oh, I must have forgotten to mention that I had some things to check out."

"That took you all afternoon? What did you get?"

Vivian looked at him, not understanding.

"What books did you check out?"

"They didn't have what I was looking for so I just sat around reading."

"No harm in that," Mr. Sharpe said. He studied her face, something he'd started to do more often, looking for something unspoken, as if there were a clue hidden there.

She shrugged. "What?"

"Nothing."

Millie jumped off her lap and ran toward the entrance. "Come on."

Vivian went upstairs and collected her bags, then met Millie and her father in the lobby, a movie already in her sister's hand. Millie skipped down the sidewalk to the car talking about her last day of kindergarten, the cake with yellow frosting and strawberry ice cream that Miss Walsh handed out to Millie and her classmates. Next year, Millie breathlessly gushed, she would be a big kid and would need all sorts of new things: a backpack, new notebooks, a pencil box. Vivian listened to Millie prattle on, still dazed a bit from spending the afternoon in front of the microfiche, and unable to get the Lynx out of her mind. Pulling up to the house at last, Vivian was relieved to find it as it was when she left that morning, not reduced to a smoldering pile of ashes.

That night after dinner, Vivian was sitting in her room in front of her blank notebook again when she realized that she hadn't read Wren's yearbook inscription yet. Lying on her belly on her bed, she reached over and grabbed her yearbook, staring at the page as though it were in Sanskrit. Once her eyes adjusted, though, she saw that Wren had in fact drawn her a pictogram of their friendship: when they first met at school, going to the flea market, washing off the ducks in the sinks at the Commie Café, all drawn with in ballpoint pen in Wren's loopy, loose style. At the bottom of the page, she signed it and included a quote from Carl Jung: "The meeting of two personalities is like the contact of two chemical substances; if there is any reaction, both are transformed."

THE FIRST DAY

Vivian spent the weekend getting ready for Gordenner. She picked out her outfit early in the morning – brown knee-length skirt, a white blouse and a pair of shiny black shoes with a short heel – folded the clothes neatly, and had them ready on her chair with her Gordenner badge, which had arrived in the mail earlier in the week, on top. She experimented with jewelry and hairstyles, deciding on a simple silver chain and hoop earrings for the former, a cute headband for the latter. By the time she had planned all that out, it was not even ten in the morning. She had nearly a full day before she would begin her first day at Gordenner. She stared at her neatly folded pile of clothes and felt her heart start to race until she looked away.

Vivian managed to distract herself most of Sunday, getting the bus schedule so she'd know when to leave home in the morning, going to the bookstore to skim through magazines, and finally deciding to walk around Capital Park, the place where she'd followed Billy. It was a warm, sunny day, and she sat on a small hill overlooking the river for quite a while, raking her fingers through the grass. She relaxed for the most part but became concerned whenever she'd notice a squirrel nearby. Thankfully, the squirrels seemed to be content to just stick to their own business that day, so Vivian spent her time watching the birds, filling her spirit with what felt like their essence: freedom, soaring lightness, confidence. She realized that she'd been so busy the last few weeks, she had neglected the source of her inspiration – the animals – and she basked in them, like someone needing the sun after too many cloudy days.

She went to bed early that night and woke up far too early, before sunrise. She'd been hoping for a visit from Tolstoy but it never materialized. Her mother, always an early riser, was startled to see Vivian leave the bathroom in her robe at six in the morning, already showered and her hair blown dry.

"I knew I'd heard something," she said, a confused look on her face. "I thought that you didn't start until 8:45."

"I do. Just wanted to get an early start," Vivian said brightly. Mrs. Sharpe was still watching her as she hurried down the hall to get dressed. For the finishing touch, she lifted her hair up and put the elastic cord of the Gordenner badge around her neck. Something made her look in one of her vanity drawers, and she found some mascara and tinted lip balm her mother had given her from her salon, neither of which Vivian had ever opened. Opening her mouth into a small O as she had seen her mother do when applying cosmetics, Vivian brushed on her mascara, slightly worried that she might inadvertently blind herself by poking herself in the eye. Looking at herself in her oval dresser mirror, the same mirror she'd used when she was a small child playing dress-up with her mother's makeup and jewelry, Vivian realized that here she was, ten years later, playing dress-up once again.

She ate her toast with peanut butter and jam quickly, then went back to her room, eager to avoid any conversations. She brushed her hair a few times, packed and re-packed her purse, practiced smiling in front of the mirror and then, finally, sat on her bed, careful not to crease her skirt, thinking about beginning her first day at Gordenner until she couldn't take it any more. She put her lip balm in her purse, thought again, and removed it.

She sat at her desk and took a deep breath. No matter how nervous she might be, she decided that she would make an extra effort to be friendly to Kyle: he was a likely ally. She would not talk a lot, just listen and observe. Wasn't that what Tolstoy advised her to do? She wondered how she would begin the process of whatever it was that compelled her to take an internship at Gordenner. Suddenly, Vivian felt very alone and regretted not taking Will up on his offer of a strategy session. She picked up the phone and called Wren's house. Mrs. Summer answered the phone at the first ring.

"She's still asleep, sweetheart. It's not even 7:00."

Vivian glanced over at the clock. "Oh, I'm so sorry. I woke up so early today, I thought it was later. I hope I didn't wake you."

"Me? Oh, no. The animals wake me up at sunrise. Is there a message or something you want me to tell Wren when she wakes?"

"No, nothing really. I was just nervous because I'm starting at Gordenner today. Butterflies in my stomach, you know. Plus," she laughed at the absurdity as the words tumbled out, "I don't really know what I'm doing."

"You'll do just fine, Vivian. Trust your intuition but be careful," Mrs. Summer said with characteristic solemnity. "You'll know what to do."

After hanging up with Mrs. Summer, Vivian felt ready to go downstairs and face her parents. She could hear that they were both in the kitchen. They were standing together near the counter, talking quietly about something, and she could hear coffee gurgling in the coffeemaker.

"Well, look at you," Mr. Sharpe said, too bright for Vivian. "Wait a minute," he said looking closer. "Are you wearing make up?"

She blushed and immediately turned away. "Just a little, Dad. Whatever."

Mrs. Sharpe elbowed her husband in the ribs, somehow not disturbing her cup of coffee. "I told you not to embarrass her."

"I'm sorry. I just reacted. It's just that she looks so grown up all of the sudden."

"I *am* grown up."

"I didn't mean that you're not a grown up, Vivian. I just mean, I don't know," Mr. Sharpe looked at Mrs. Sharpe with desperation in his eyes, "I just meant..."

"You meant that you saw your daughter in a new light," Mrs. Sharpe said. "You're not used to seeing her dressed up like this." She took a sip from her cup and she looked her daughter up and down, an appraisal. "I think you look lovely. I like your hair off your face. You've got such lovely cheekbones and little mascara just makes your eyes pop. It's understated but pretty." She tilted her head, still staring. "Maybe it's time to start getting your eyebrows shaped, though..."

"Mom!"

"What's wrong with her eyebrows?" Her father squinted at her like an archeologist with a new discovery.

"They're a little...unkempt. Most are. Listen, Elizabeth Taylor's eyebrows didn't just happen: they needed to be coaxed into the right shape. 'Eyes are the windows to the soul and eyebrows are the window treatments.' I was taught that in cosmetology school years ago. A little wax, some cloth, one-two-three, *zzzt*." she said, ripping off imaginary brow hairs. "It's over."

"Could you two stop it?" Vivian said, covering the now-conspicuous eyebrows she'd never really noticed before with two hands. "You're both creeping me out."

"Wouldn't want to be creepy, dear," said her father said drolly. "Keep in mind that I think your eyebrows are perfect as is."

"I'll fit you in for a brow shaping next week," her mother said.

They made small talk and her mother gave her some pointers ("Stand up straight – slouching doesn't make a good impression," and "Be sure to repeat peoples' names back to them after you are introduced; it helps you remember and it shows an interest in the person.") A few minutes later, Mrs. Sharpe offered to cut "some cute wispy bangs" for her daughter. Vivian decided that though she would be early, she was ready to go wait for the bus. She kissed her parents and promised to call if there were any problems. Just before she left the room, her mother jumped up.

"Vivian, I almost forgot," she said as she ran to the living room, "I have something for you." She came back to Vivian, holding out an 8 X 10 family portrait they'd shot last Christmas in a pretty silver frame. "I got this frame for you. I thought you could keep it on your desk."

"Oh. Thanks, Mom." Vivian said, genuinely touched.

"I just thought it would look nice on your desk. I want people to know that you come from a good family."

Vivian sat at the bus stop for twenty minutes, until she could finally see it turn down Lincoln Avenue. As the bus got closer, she could see that the driver who had taken her and Wren to Gordenner the previous week was driving. He pulled up and nodded his head in recognition as Vivian put her two quarters in the fare box. There were a few other people on the bus, but all had gotten off by the time it reached the Gordenner stop on Plank Road. Vivian pulled the cord and the bus driver looked up at her in the mirror.

"You going to Gordenner?" he asked, surprised.

Vivian stammered for a moment. "I – yes, I'm going to be interning there for the summer."

"Ah," he stopped the bus and Vivian walked to the front to go out the door. "My grandpa was a farmer. Got all his fertilizers and herbicides from Gordenner."

Vivian nodded. "Yep. They've been around for a long time."

The bus driver scratched his chin and said, "I still remember their old jingles on the radio. They used to play them during the

Corinthian Eggs Playhouse Hour. 'Keeping America strong and able, Gordenner helps bring food to the table.'"

"I never heard that."

"You wouldn't have," the bus driver smiled. He looked to be a little older than her parents. "You're too young. Well, have a good day, young lady. Help them to keep bringing food to the table."

Vivian thanked him and crossed the street, walking toward the gated parking lot of Gordenner, his voice singing the jingle still in her ears. Near the parking lot, the security guard from last week was sitting in the security booth. Noticing Vivian, he walked out the door. He was wearing the same mirrored sunglasses as he had when they first met. Vivian pulled out her badge so he could see it. Her heart was fluttering.

"I'm supposed to start here today with Ms. Collins."

"I heard," he said, scarcely glancing at her, and he pressed a door opener he carried in his pocket; the gate slowly swung open. Without another word, he walked back to his booth. Vivian hurried inside the lot and the gate shut behind her with a clang.

The door to the building was locked, but she could see Kyle sitting near the entrance, reading a book and waiting for her. There was also an older woman at the front desk, drinking coffee. Vivian pressed the bell and the woman looked up, buzzing her in.

"Hello, sunshine," Kyle smiled, snapping the book shut. "Ready for your first day?"

Vivian nodded. "Yeah, I hope I'm not late."

Kyle shook his head. "No, no. You're right on time. A little early in fact," he said, glancing at a clock and standing up. "Ms. Collins asked me to meet you here and bring you upstairs. Got a chance to bother my friend. Vivian, this is Betty Clark," he said, extending his arm to the grey-haired woman behind the desk.

"Nice to meet you, Ms. Clark," Vivian said, remembering her mother's advice about repeating names.

"Oh, you can call me Betty," she said, smiling. "Nice to meet you, too."

"Vivian's going to be a new intern here, working with Ms. Collins."

"Well, very nice to meet you, Vivian. I'm sure she'll keep you very busy upstairs."

"Don't let her innocent looks deceive you, Vivian," Kyle said with exaggerated gravity. "Betty is the eyes and ears of this organization. Nothing happens without Betty knowing it first."

Betty waved off Kyle, laughing. "Oh, please. I wish I were that alert."

"She may charm you with photographs of her grandchildren, but she's really secretly taking your fingerprints."

Betty laughed some more.

"See you later, Betty," he said.

"Don't get into any trouble now, Kyle," she called off after them. They walked down the gleaming marble floor to the elevator.

Kyle said, "If you need anything today and you can't find Ms. Collins, feel free to come to me. Ms. Collins is running around, so she's not always so easy to find."

As they waited for the elevator, a voice shouted for them to please wait. A deliveryman with a few big boxes on a dolly caught up with them.

"I've got a new computer and printer here," he said to Kyle, looking at his order. "These go to your office, right?"

"Oh, good. Finally. Yup, follow us, Pete. They go to my office." Kyle turned to Vivian and pointed his thumb at the deliveryman. "Pete clocks in about as many hours here as I do. He's the delivery guy."

He leaned against the back of the elevator, careful to keep the boxes balanced and nodded at Vivian.

"You've got some new equipment?" Vivian said. Butterflies swirled in her stomach.

"Yep," Kyle said, pushing the button. "I'd wanted an upgrade, but I didn't think it would happen this way."

Vivian must have looked at him curiously, because he gave a subtle little shake of his head.

"Here we are," he said, pressing the button to hold the door open. "Do you know Ms. Collins' office? It's just down the hall and on the right. Third door in. You can't miss it. Her name's on the door."

Vivian nodded and reminded herself to smile.

"So, why don't you go ahead because I've got to get this stuff set up?" He put his hand on her shoulder. "See you later. Follow me, sir."

Walking down the hall, Vivian became aware of a slight throbbing behind her temples, but it was nowhere approaching how uncomfortable she'd felt during her previous visit. She convinced herself that the headache was of the variety that could easily be shaken if she became occupied enough. She was determined to become occupied.

Ms. Collins was sitting at a desk in a simple-looking office, where Kyle said she'd be, engrossed in a phone call. Noticing Vivian, she waved her in and held up one finger, indicating that she'd be a minute. She didn't stop talking the whole time.

"No, Martin, we'd need the comps in sooner than that. I'd say by next Thursday, latest. If we don't have them by Thursday," she said flipping through an appointment book, "we'll have to wait another week after that for all of us who need to sign off on them to be here. That would be cutting it too close. Is that possible?" She smiled a little at Vivian and pointed at a chair across from her desk for her to sit at. "Good, thank you. I appreciate it. Try your best. Also, these printer costs are exorbitant. Can't it be done for less?" She took a sip of coffee and looked at a sheet on the desk, going over items with a highlighter. "Could you look into that, then? I need to know if we get a price break if we order more, because we'll need more posters down the road. I don't need Accounting breathing down my neck about this. Thanks. Look into that. Okay, my 8:45 is here. Got to run."

She swiveled in her chair. "Welcome, Vivian," she said, changing her tone only slightly from harried to friendly. "How are you?"

Before she had a chance to answer, Ms. Collins stood up and sat on the desk, facing Vivian. "It's a busy day, so let's hit the ground running, shall we? That's your preferred mode of operation, right? Redheads," she smiled, shaking her head. "Just follow me and I'll be getting you oriented. Did you get here okay?" she asked, as she picked her jacket up off the desk and put it onto a coat hook. "I forgot to ask how you'd be getting here every day."

"Oh, I took the bus. It gets here right on time."

"The bus, hmm?" she repeated back, distractedly, running a hand through her spiky hair. "I didn't even realize Center City has buses. Kyle found you okay?"

Vivian was mesmerized by her silver eye shadow. She tried not to stare. "Yes. He had to go back to his office with some computer equipment."

Ms. Collins nodded quickly and said, "Okay, well, the space here used to be one big office, but we divided it up like this when I got the budget for an assistant. This," she thumped on the desk, "is yours. This phone here – when it rings in here, answer it. You can see in that little window on the top if it's an outside call or an in-house call. Answer it either way. You could answer it, 'Ms. Collins' office.' To dial out, press nine first and wait for the dial tone."

"What do I do if someone's on the line for you?"

"Ask the person's name and then say you have to check to see if I'm in my office. Put him on hold. You can either call me – my extension is five – or walk over and ask me. Don't call out to me from your desk, okay, because I hate that. I had an assistant at my old job who did that and it really drove me crazy. Very unprofessional. If I'm not in my office, to page me, hold down on the blue button right over here and talk. All this stuff is on a laminated sheet in your top drawer. There's a protocol. Don't be afraid to refer to the sheet a lot at first. Everyone's extension is in there and there's also an owner's manual for your phone if you need it. Occasionally you'll need to write down a message – I prefer that to messages on my phone because I can get overloaded with those – so let me show you to the supply room so we can get some pens and message sheets and that sort of thing."

"Okay."

"You don't mind if we start out like this, do you? Or do I need to be more slow and methodical?"

"No, this is fine."

"Good. I like fast learners. No coddling. That's my way, too. Follow me." With that, Ms. Collins turned abruptly down the hall and Vivian followed closely behind her. "I generally take lunch at noon, usually for about an hour, so I'd like you to take your break a little earlier or later, if that's okay, so there's always someone in the office. You're entitled to an hour."

"Oops..."

"What?" Ms. Collins looked irritated.

"I just realized that I forgot my lunch," Vivian said. "Oh, well."

"Well, you shouldn't go without lunch. There's a cafeteria on the first floor. There are also vending machines and break rooms on each floor with refrigerators and microwaves and that sort of thing. Personally," she lowered her voice, "I don't like the cafeteria food. Today a bunch of us are ordering in together from Rizzo's downtown. They have a passable antipasto salad. Also, subs – turkey, tuna. What do you think?"

Vivian's stomach lurched a little, but she tried to seem unaffected. "Oh, um, you know, I only have a couple of dollars on me."

"Oh, I can spot you for the day, Vivian," Ms. Collins said, laughing, dismissing her with a wave of her hand. She stopped at a door and pulled out her keys. "It's really not a big deal."

"You know, I had a really big breakfast so I think I'll just get a granola bar or something if that's okay with you."

"It's your choice," she said, opening the door. "But good luck trying to find a granola bar here."

She pointed around the narrow supply room. "Okay, here you'll find pens, highlighters, white-out, notebooks, message sheets, staplers. Paper clips. Office supplies. Let's get you a good variety here so you don't have to keep coming back. Oh, I should mention that we'll give you some keys once you've been here for three weeks. Until then, you'll have to borrow mine or someone else's – don't be afraid to ask."

Ms. Collins walked around the supply room, collecting items and handing them to Vivian.

Okay, I've got two notebooks, a package of pens – do you prefer ballpoint or felt tip? Blue or black ink?"

"Oh, anything would be fine."

Ms. Collins gave Vivian a look like that was an idiotic thing to say.

"Black felt tip, please."

"Certainly." Ms. Collins continued collecting. "It's important for us to have opinions, don't you agree? Okay," she thought out loud, "I've got a pen cup, a highlighter in pink and one in yellow, a book of message sheets – do you want one of those erasable calendars? – yeah, I'd better get you one."

Vivian's arms quickly became overloaded so Ms. Collins started nestling stuff in the crook of her own arm. "I've got a stapler, staples, tape dispenser and tape. What else?" She looked around the room before noticing a clipboard hanging from the wall near the door. "Oh, shoot. I've got to sign everything out." She sighed and put everything down onto a box and grabbed the clipboard, scribbling as she continued talking. "We've got to account for all this stuff – every last eraser. They're maniacs about keeping the inventory straight."

She looked around the room one last time and clapped her hands before picking up the items she's put down. "Okay. We've got a good start," she smiled at Vivian. "Let's drop this off and work from there."

They started down the hallway again and Vivian started getting accustomed to Ms. Collins' fast pace. She walked about twice as quickly as Vivian's natural speed, making her feel like she was about to lose control on a treadmill.

"Let's take a little detour first," she said, turning abruptly into an office. Vivian had to brace herself so as to not crash into Ms. Collins. It was a large room filled with copiers, printers and scanners. There was a woman with brown hair back in a tight ponytail and glasses on the edge of her nose waiting for copies as the bright light flashed underneath. "Oh, hi, Nadine. This is Vivian. She's my new intern."

"Nice to meet you," Nadine said, pushing up her glasses before she held out her hand, then she noticed that she had some paperclips in it, so she dropped them into her other hand.

"Nice to meet you, too."

"Nadine is our tech lady. If your computer malfunctions, Nadine is the one to call. Extension 17. She also runs the copier room. If you need copies of anything, just bring it over to Nadine and she'll take care of everything. Nadine, could you let Vivian know the copy room rules?"

"Of course," she said, in a harried way. "To maintain the integrity of our equipment, I am the only one authorized to make copies and prints. If you need something, even just one page, fill out this green request form and put it in the wire basket," she said, showing her a large desk piled with forms. "I do things on a first-come, first-serve basis, so if you need something right away, get it to me right away. Um, what else?" she looked around the room. "If I'm not busy with something else, I'll get to it right away. If not, it'll be in your mail slot as soon as I'm finished."

"Thanks, Nadine. We'll see you later," Ms. Collins said as she left the room. Vivian hustled to catch up.

"I'll let you in on a little secret," Ms. Collins said as soon as they were a good distance away; Vivian nearly had to jog to keep up with her. "If you just want a copy or two of something and you don't want to wait, go to Kyle's office. He's just on the other side of the floor from us. He has a good copier in there and you don't have to go through all the rigmarole. Everyone does it and Kyle doesn't mind. Just be discreet about it. Act like you were stopping by his office to talk to him for a minute. Anyway," Ms. Collins grinned, winking, "you didn't hear it from me. Nadine has control issues."

They walked back to the office and splayed everything out on Vivian's desk. "Okay, what time is it?" Ms. Collins said, frowning up to the clock. "9:13 already. I've got to get ready for another meeting, so why don't you get yourself set up in here for a little bit. Familiarize yourself with the phone," she said, pulling out the manual from the drawer and tossing it on Vivian's desk. "If you need anything, just page me because I won't be in my office."

"The blue button, right?"

"That's right. Hold it down and talk. Remember that as long as you're pressing the button, people can hear you throughout the building so please sound professional. If you get confused, just let go of the button and start over. Oh, and you should leave a little message for yourself on your phone. Like, 'This is Vivian Sharpe, assistant to Ms. Collins. Please leave a message and I'll get back to you as soon as possible.' Something like that, okay? Oh – be sure not to mumble. I hate when I can't tell whose extension I'm leaving a message on."

"I will speak clearly."

"Good," Ms. Collins said. "So I'll be back in about 45 minutes." She hurried out the door, grabbing a large black folder and glancing at the clock as she left. "Don't be scared." She started to leave then rushed back in for her cup of coffee before running out again.

Vivian started to unpack her pens, arranging them in the penholder like flower stems as she glanced out the window into the hall that faced her desk. She hung the calendar up on a nail and set up the photo her mother had given her that morning. She fiddled around with her desk and put the notebooks away neatly. She had her message pad in the top drawer and she put her stapler and little plastic box of paperclips on her desk, lining them up several times until she was satisfied with how the top of her desk looked. She noticed a water cooler in the corner of the room, next to the door leading to Ms. Collins' office, and, as she poured a cup of water into her new Gordenner mug, the big bubble rose to the top and burbled, almost embarrassing her even though no one else was near. Vivian noticed that her headache had receded until it was almost not noticeable. She peeked into Ms. Collins' office and saw a sparely decorated room – minimalist, her mother would say – with a large desk neatly stacked with papers and a couple of chairs. On the walls, she had several framed posters of Gordenner products from many years ago. In the back, there was a large window facing out to the woods and the pipes leading to the river where she, Will and Wren had wandered earlier.

"Hello?" A male voice spoke.

Vivian spilled her water a little as she whipped around. "Oh, hi," Vivian said to the man in the grey suit standing in the doorway. He had short, light-brown hair and a very pale, almost grey face. He looked to be around Kyle's age, in his thirties, carrying a stack of papers.

"I didn't mean to startle you. I'll grab some paper towels." He walked out of the room and was back moments later. He handed them to Vivian; his hand was so cold Vivian almost flinched.

"You must be Victoria, is that right? Veronica?"

"Vivian," she said as she stooped to wipe up the water.

"Vivian, yes. Ms. Collins told me you'd be starting today. I'm Kevin Newell. I'm the director of New Product Development."

"Nice to meet you."

"Is Ms. Collins around?" he asked, craning his neck to see into her office.

Vivian shook her head. "Not right now. She had a meeting she started about five minutes ago. She should be back around 10:00. Should I have her call you?" She rubbed her arms, suddenly cold.

"Oh, that's all right," he said. "I'll just pop in later. Thanks," he started to walk away when he turned back. "On second thought, yes, could you give her a message to call Kevin Newell?"

Vivian grabbed a pen and wrote what he'd said. "That's it? Just call Kevin Newell?"

"That's it." For the second time, he started to walk away again when he stopped again. "Vivian, just out of curiosity, how old are you? You're in high school, right?"

"I'm 15. I'll be 16 in a month."

"That's what I thought. You don't know any college-aged kids, do you?"

Vivian shook her head, then remembered Will. "Oh, yes. I know one. I'm sure he knows others."

Mr. Newell nodded distractedly. "Mm. We're trying to put together a focus group of young people for a new product, but you're a little too young and most of the students at the college are gone for the summer now. Maybe we can still give it a try, though."

After he left, Vivian found herself wishing she'd brought a sweater along. Even though she had on long sleeves, her arms were so cold she could barely loosen them enough to record the greeting on her phone. She waved her hands under the vents in her office, and there was no cold air coming out of them. She couldn't keep from shivering.

After about fifteen minutes, Vivian had finally warmed back up. Ms. Collins came back to the office, her heels clicking on the floor, sipping iced coffee, this time from a to-go cup.

"So how did everything go? Did you record your greeting? Your desk looks nice."

"Yes," Vivian said, handing Ms. Collins the message she had taken. "Mr. Newell came by. He wants you to call him."

Ms. Collins nodded absentmindedly and tucked the message behind her fingers, which were holding her folder. "Is that your family?" she asked, nodding at the picture on her desk.

"Yep."

"Kyle told me that your mother owns *Look Sharpe!* Is that right?"

"Yes, that's her."

"Interesting. I do my hair in New Dublin because I go there most weekends. I kept my condo there. It's good to know there's a decent place in town, though. Does your dad also work there?"

Vivian almost laughed at loud at the idea of her father wielding a scissors and hair dryer. "No, he's a historian."

"A historian. How interesting. What is his area of expertise?"

"Center City. He is president of the Historical Society, lectures, and writes books and that sort of thing."

"He writes books? About Center City?"

"Yes."

She squinted at Vivian as if this were the most bizarre thing she'd heard for a while. "I can't imagine a more boring place to write about. Well," she smiled, shrugging, "good for him. He must not get easily bored. Me, on the other hand, I'd be clawing out my own eyes if I had to find something interesting enough to write about Center City, let alone whole books on it."

"It's not so bad," Vivian said, a bit more defensively than she'd intended.

"Oh, I'm sorry," Ms. Collins said. "I can see I insulted you. No, I'm sure it's a great place to grow up. Safe streets and picket fences and clean sidewalks. I get that. I don't have children, though, so I've never had to think about that sort of thing. Don't feel bad. I grew up in a small town, too. A town of 575 people, way smaller than here. I've been a city dweller as soon as I was old enough to move out and go to college 20 years ago and it really is where I'm

172

happiest. Center City is fine for what it is, though. Have you been to New Dublin much?"

"Oh," Vivian shrugged, "yeah, a few times. I haven't been for a couple of years. The drive is a little far."

"But it's worth it. The restaurants in my neighborhood stay open until three in the morning. There's always something going on, an art fair or big museum exhibit opening. You'd love it. There's so much to do. I think I'd go crazy if I didn't have my weekends there, and the drive's not so awful. I get a book on tape or two and it goes by in a snap. I guess after all these years away, it's been hard for me to readjust to a smaller town."

"How long have you been in Center City?"

"Good question, Vivian, because it gets into our work together," Ms. Collins pulled a chair up to Vivian's desk and sat down. Vivian was discombobulated for a moment, seeing this kinetic creature stop moving. "I was hired just over six months ago to develop and direct the Gordenner marketing department. Can you believe that – after being in business for 60 years – Gordenner did not have a marketing department? I mean, they had people do what could be called marketing, in its own way, but there was no actual department, no one knew what they were doing. There was no plan. Isn't that insane? This multi-million dollar company and they, well, they just made stuff and sold it. The incentive of coming out here to develop a marketing strategy for this company was too tempting. They had just developed a line of products that are poised to help hungry third world nations and needed a whole new, revamped image. We're not talking about boring old sprays and seeds anymore: this is something that can save the world. Gordenner is on the precipice of something huge."

"Wow." Vivian got the shivers again, and was not sure if the hair on her arms was standing up because she'd gotten the chills again or because Ms. Collins spoke with such conviction.

"Wow is right," Ms. Collins laughed. "Now, without going too much into the details yet, this is going to be rolled out early next spring, but before it comes out, we've got to make quite a splash. We've got to get the newspapers writing about it, we've got to get celebrities and world hunger activists supporting it, we've got to get important people buzzing about it, we've got to make the product – which you'll learn more about soon – not only seen as this great humanitarian effort, but also something *sexy*. Something international, sophisticated. Yes, it's a farming product, but this farming product helps raise healthy, beautiful children who then love our country because Gordenner is from the U.S.. So it's a peacemaking product, too, at its heart. That's our story."

"But it's something that grows food better?"

"Yes, of course," Ms. Collins shrugged dismissively, "but that does not make a sexy news story. A globetrotting celebrity helping to distribute bags and bottles of this product, though, *that* is a sexy news story and that's the angle that we're pursuing. Sure, people have warm feelings about the old farmer planting seeds and the farmer's wife collecting eggs in her apron, but market research has let us know that people pretty much know that imagery is a fallacy now. It's a story we like to tell, like Washington chopping down the cherry tree, but it no longer reflects reality, and people know that. Furthermore, it's irrelevant. What matters now is two things: that people feel good about the company and that we're doing something interesting, something compelling."

"Hmm."

Ms. Collins' eyes shone. Vivian wondered why she hadn't noticed this before. "Well, Gordenner had it down as far as people liking the company – I mean, they've been around for sixty years, Gordenner was an important piece of the link to our agrarian roots, blah blah blah. You know, try not to fall asleep. I mean, people didn't have extreme warmth for Gordenner because it is perceived as sort of boring, but at least the feelings are more warm than negative. More neutral than anything, really. Think mashed potatoes: fine, you know, in a pinch but no one really gets excited about them. Gordenner was mashed potatoes. As far as doing anything interesting, though, this company was a complete disaster. They would have ugly little boring ads in farmer catalogues and magazines, but that was about it. And until a couple of years ago, administration here was fine with the status quo. Then, Robert Fontaine was hired as president of Gordenner U.S.A."

Vivian remembered the name from the day the security guard brought her and Wren in. Kyle had mentioned him.

"Mr. Fontaine was the one who hired me away to Gordenner. Anyway, he is the one who helped turn Gordenner around into this company that's going to be on the leading edge of farming technology. Actually, I hate that word – farming. I'm going to have to come up with another word. I don't like 'producers' or 'growers,' either. Anyway, Gordenner is now poised to become a truly modern business. It's part of the ten-year plan to phase out of

Gordenner U.S.A. into Gordenner International. And, as my intern, you would be part of that team, of that growth."

"I don't know what to say," Vivian said, rendered a little breathless by the intensity of Ms. Collins.

Ms. Collins slapped her hand on Vivian's desk, making her flinch a little in her chair. "Say that you're excited. Say that you're thrilled. This is an incredible opportunity, Vivian, especially if you want to go into marketing down the road. Mark my words: our campaign is going to change the world. When you're in college, you can tell your friends that you worked on this campaign and they'll revere you."

"Wow."

"You're going to have to come up with something better than that if you want to generate excitement, Vivian," Ms. Collins smiled, "but I'm feeling forgiving because it's your first day. Actually now that I think of it, a thesaurus would be a good addition to your office." She grabbed a pen from Vivian's desk and scribbled a note for her on a sticky note and stuck it on Vivian's desk. "The thesaurus is essential to a marketer. We have some extras in the supply room, I think."

Vivian spent an hour learning the phone system and getting familiar with the floor plan, which was laid out on a few laminated sheets ringed together that Ms. Collins handed her before she took her lunch break. She also gave Vivian an employee manual, which included a couple of pages on Gordenner's history, dress code for employees, procedure for sick days: anything she needed to know as an intern. Vivian skimmed over the manual, catching little details as she read.

There were nearly 3,000 people who worked at the Gordenner facility in Center City. Almost 1,500 were in Vivian's building, known as the "new building": people answering phone calls, taking orders, selling products, producing advertisements and in promotions; scientists creating and studying new products were in the state-of-the-art laboratory on the bottom floor. The rest were assembly line workers and forklift drivers who worked in the factory, the original Gordenner building, now referred to as "the old building," which was the one behind the new facility.

Gordenner had factories in two other states, Idaho and Mississippi, as well as several enormous packing and fulfillment facilities, and employed almost 12,000 people altogether, but the facility downstairs was their crown jewel. Under the leadership of

Mr. Fontaine, a cutting-edge laboratory was built when the new Gordenner building was completed the previous year, six floors tall and massively wide. According to Vivian's employee manual, no outsiders were permitted into the laboratory, even other Gordenner employees, without an interview, a new background check, and express written consent, and they had to sign a legally binding non-disclosure form. Glancing back over the floor plan of the laboratories, Vivian noticed that unlike the other floors, there were scant few details of the layout provided of the laboratory, only the words New Product Laboratories and Development, and grey lines delineating rooms.

After Ms. Collins came back from her lunch, she put a pile of papers on the corner of Vivian's desk for her to file, but when she reached for them, Ms. Collins gently chided her, "Vivian, it's time for your lunch break now. We can go over filing when you get back. See you in an hour, okay? The cafeteria's on the sixth floor, down by the big sculpture."

Vivian nodded her head as though she knew what sculpture Ms. Collins was referring to and started down the hall. Ms. Collins called after her, standing in the hallway with her purse, grasping the strap as she would the leash of an unwanted dog.

"Honey, don't ever leave your purse at your desk," she said, handing it to her. "It's just not safe like that. Remind me that we need to talk about safety procedures after lunch, okay?"

The letter from the Lynx flashed through her mind; Vivian flushed and thanked Ms. Collins before she continued down the hallway. Several people sped past her, men and women with the gait of Ms. Collins, all dressed in business attire, polite but fast-paced as they hurried down the hall. This pace was something Vivian was not accustomed to seeing in Center City. She glanced into the offices as she passed, and they were all done in a contemporary design, clean and subdued: rooms with muted oatmeal-colored walls, full of people, most on the phone or typing, some chatting around desks in groups of two or three. A few looked up as Vivian as she passed and looked at her quizzically, a couple smiled and nodded politely, but almost everyone continued working without taking notice. One room was larger than the other offices, easily the size of her school cafeteria, full of cubicles with people talking with headphones on, typing into laptops; the noise was almost deafening. "Good afternoon, Gordenner, U.S.A.," one person said after the next. "Twelve digit customer ID number, please." In another room, the lights were turned off and door was shut. Vivian was able to make out figures watching images on a screen, a shot of a crop of wheat and workers harvesting it. It crossed Vivian's mind as she walked to the elevator that whatever it was that people were talking, meeting and typing about was what she needed to learn.

"That's all," she smiled to herself ruefully, and at that moment her headache reappeared.

On the sixth floor, she wasn't sure where the sculpture was that Ms. Collins had mentioned, so she asked two women walking down the hall, engrossed in a deep conversation. One, a brunette, looked momentarily annoyed at having her conversation interrupted before seeming to think better of it and she smiled archly at Vivian. "We're headed that way."

They turned down a series of halls to a large room, like an atrium, with a sprawling bay window and a view over the trees framing the Kickashaunee River. Tall potted plants added to the dramatic effect of the room, but the centerpiece was the soaring bronze sculpture that nearly reached the vaulted ceiling. It was the figure of a farmer hoisting a bundle of wheat over one shoulder, his biceps bulging and the veins in his neck swelling under the strain. The women continued on their way, and Vivian followed the sound of trays being collected and water spraying until she found the cafeteria.

Far bigger than her high school cafeteria, Gordenner's was immense to Vivian's eyes; she'd only seen a cafeteria this big at the history museum she'd gone to when she was in New Dublin as a child. About a third of the tables were full, but Vivian could see that she'd missed the rush; cafeteria workers were picking up abandoned trays and dishes at the empty tables. She walked through the food line – as Ms. Collins had warned, the food did not look appetizing to her in the least. There was fried chicken under a warmer, pink roast sandwiches wrapped in plastic and tucked together in a bin. Vivian started to feel her stomach lurch so she quickly moved down the line to get a drink and a bag of pretzels with the change she scraped together.

She'd just sat down at a table when she heard someone call her name.

"Vivian." Kyle waved his arm from a few tables away. She hadn't noticed him. "Want to be my lunch buddy?"

Vivian blushed and felt relieved to see a face she knew. "Hi, Kyle."

"Well, come on," he said, gesturing broadly at his table. "It looks like I have an open seat. Or two. Or three."

Vivian moved over to his table.

Kyle shook his head. "Don't tell me that's all you're eating. A bag of pretzels and a soda."

"Oh, you call it soda," Vivian said. "I remember hearing that people from the East Coast call it that. Soda rather than pop."

He smiled. "That's right. I'm from the South originally – we say pop like you guys do – like *y'all*, rather," he grinned, "but my family moved to the Boston area when I was in sixth grade. The word soda just stuck somehow. So anyway, missy," he said, taking a mockingly stern tone, "that's all you're eating for lunch?"

"Well, I'm not really hungry."

"Please don't tell me you're on a diet. My niece, she's a little younger than you, thirteen, but she's always on a diet."

"Nope. No diet here, just not hungry."

"Nerves?"

"A little," Vivian admitted, "but I'm not on a diet."

"Good, 'cause you're skinny enough. I don't want to have to worry about you. Too many girls on diets." The natural light in the cafeteria made Kyle's blue eyes illuminate even more. Kyle seemed to notice her staring, which she tried not to do but couldn't resist, and he looked down at his tray. "So how's your first day?" he asked, taking a bite of his sandwich.

"Okay," she said. "There's a lot to learn, a lot to remember."

Kyle nodded. "I started here in November and I'm still learning all the intricacies. Don't stress about it, though. If you make mistakes, they just make you take a weekend intensive on Gordenner protocol."

Vivian's eyes widened. "What?"

"Oh, it's no big deal," Kyle said nonchalantly. "That and an essay you have to write and read in front of this tribunal. That's pretty easy to connive your way through, though: just hit the right points and you're golden."

"I have to read an essay to whom?" Vivian could feel her pulse racing. "How many times do I have to screw up to do this?"

Kyle started to answer her, then broke into a huge grin. "I'm sorry, Vivian. I was just funning with you. You're easy to tease, you know that?"

She took a deep breath, pretending to fan herself in relief.

"So, Vivian, how is your day going? Are you able to keep up with Laura? She's a dynamo."

"Laura? Oh, you mean Ms. Collins? Fine. Yes, she's got a lot of energy, but I think that I'm keeping up. Or I'm faking it okay for the moment."

"You've got the right idea: fake it 'til you make it," he smiled, winking, then turned serious. "It's a steep learning curve. Just when I got used to my other computer and programs, I got a new one, so I'm having to learn all that now. I hope I get the hang of it quick, because Bob – Mr. Fontaine – is coming back Monday. He was in southeast Asia for three weeks."

"Well, you must be doing well if you already got a big upgrade, right?"

Kyle paled for a moment, then pulled his chair in, lowering his voice. "It was not exactly planned, Vivian."

Vivian didn't know what to say. She wasn't sure if Kyle wanted to keep talking about it or not. She decided to stay quiet as she got the sense that this was something she wanted to hear.

Kyle kept scanning the rest of the cafeteria as he leaned in a little to talk quieter. Vivian turned toward him discreetly, too.

"We had another break-in last week. Thursday night. This was the first time anyone got into the offices. Anyway, whoever this was destroyed my computer and printer, threw some nasty sewage all over it. He, she, they, whoever, grabbed all of this paperwork out of my files and off my desk and shredded them and threw the pieces all over the place." He winced at the recollection. "It was a disgusting mess."

Vivian got goosebumps and could barely speak. Kyle's office had been the one that the Lynx had targeted, the day Wren and Vivian had been apprehended by the security guard and brought to his office. That was what she had seen in the video.

"All the color's drained out of your face, Vivian. I didn't mean to scare you. Are you okay?"

Vivian tried to collect herself, coiling her hair around a finger in a look of nonchalance. "Why do you think someone did that?"

Kyle shrugged. "I don't know. Maybe someone got passed over for a job. Maybe someone doesn't like our logo. It could be anything. I didn't mean to worry you, though. Maybe we shouldn't talk about this."

"I just don't understand what Gordenner could be doing to inspire such anger," Vivian continued quietly. "I mean, it's a farm supply company."

"I don't know either. You know, they do a lot of important work here. They've got a lot of projects going on that their competitors would love to get a preview of, I'm sure," Kyle looked around the room. "Anyway, I shouldn't even be talking about any of this."

"Don't people already know about it?"

Kyle nodded and took a sip of his drink. "Some do, but no one will really talk out loud about it. It's weird, like a dysfunctional family. People whisper about the break-ins and the vandalism, but other than that, kind of ignore it. There are no memos. There aren't even any police reports. It's just like, 'Tell Karen in HR that you need a new computer and printer. Get the latest model while you're at it.' Then they get new locks. Always with the new locks. Must cost them a mint."

"Wow."

Kyle started to straighten his posture when he thought twice of it and slouched back down. "Please don't mention this to anyone, though. For some reason we're supposed to pretend that it's not happening, and I'm fine with playing along for a paycheck. Okay?"

Vivian nodded earnestly. "No problem."

Kyle smiled and looked over at the clock on the wall. "Well, all good things must come to a screeching halt," he said, standing up and gathering his lunch tray together. "My lunch hour is over. See you later, kiddo."

Watching Kyle walk off, Vivian tried to steady herself but it felt like her head was spinning. She looked around the room and saw a bunch of strangers eating lunch, talking, taking sips from cups. Maybe one of them was the Lynx, she thought, concealing his true motives, just like her, punching in and out every weekday at Gordenner. Maybe it was the man in the grey jacket, the one who caught her looking at him and then quickly looked away. Maybe the Lynx was the man sitting in the corner, the one who steadfastly avoided her glance. Vivian mashed up the pretzel bag, popping it, and tossed it in the garbage can as she left the cafeteria. She still had a lot of time left in her lunch hour. She decided to do a little wandering.

Outside the cafeteria, the main room split off into two hallways. Vivian walked down one; a brass plaque next to the door called it the *Community Research and Outreach Wing*. She noticed that, though the rest of the Gordenner was sleek and contemporary, this wing had a markedly different look. There were oak-framed black-and-white photos on the walls of the hallway, and gold identification tags, labeling them as events and individuals throughout Gordenner's history. It looked more old-fashioned and comfortable in this wing, and there was soft music playing out of speakers, Queen Anne chairs placed at regular intervals along the hallway. The effect almost made Vivian imagine that she was at a hotel.

The first photo Vivian saw was of two men standing side by side in white laboratory jackets. One was short and stocky, with dark hair and thick eyebrows; the man standing next to him was tall and thin with light colored hair, rather elegant looking. They both held test tubes. The engraving read *"Louis Gordon, left, and Coleman Jenner, right, founders of Gordenner Seed Science, which became the Gordenner Chemical Company in November 1948 and Gordenner U.S.A on June 14, 1960."* Vivian walked up and down the long hall, looking at each photograph and identification tag. On the first wall, most were pictures of original Gordenner building, the factory. There were photos of the staff day at the Heartland Park racetrack in 1950 and photos of women with stiff-looking hair sitting at desks with phones, dated 1954: the inscription noted that Gordenner was the first major business in Center City to employ women. On the other side of the hall, the photographs were more contemporary and in color. There was a picture of the 1968 Miss Center City posing with the workers in the laboratory; men with bushy sideburns in the 1970s and oversized shirt collars leaning against the doorframe with their coffee mugs. The last photo in the hall was of Robert Fontaine, Gordenner CEO, smiling as Center City's Mayor Fred Doogan cut the ribbon with an oversized pair of scissors when the new building was completed last year.

Vivian was so absorbed in the photographs that at first she didn't notice the rooms that opened up into the hallway, ten in all. Vivian looked into one and it was quite a bit larger than the space she shared with Ms. Collins, with an oak floor, an area rug and comfortable looking chairs around a big oval table, more like a dining room than something in a work place. The back of the room was covered in dark glass, and next to the wall, there was a small table with two empty pitchers and a tray of white mugs with the Gordenner logo facing the front. A microphone hung from the ceiling over the center of the oval table.

The next room was identical, but the door was shut and there were people – about fifteen, maybe more – sitting around the table, listening to a woman in a light green suit talk in front of the glass window. She was holding up large cards with pictures of hungry-looking African children and another woman was sitting next to her, scribbling down notes. Everyone seated around the table was listening to the woman and some were nodding. All had a drink in front of them and a paper plate with a doughnut; Vivian noticed a donut box, mostly empty, on the table that was up against the wall. The woman who was talking suddenly looked up and had eye contact with Vivian, peering through the window in the door, so she hurried back to the atrium. As she was leaving, a woman carrying a clipboard and a pen behind her ear briskly brought another group of people down the hall, leading them into another one of the rooms with the oval tables.

Vivian returned to her office a little early but she didn't think that Ms. Collins would mind. Other than briefly turning down a wrong hallway and nearly colliding with another office worker (she apologized and mentally reminded herself to pay better attention to her surroundings), Vivian did not have any trouble getting to her office. She could hear Ms. Collins in her office talking to someone, a man, about something that seemed important: Vivian could make out words like 'focus group' and 'promotion'. Vivian was studying the floor plan, all the dizzying layouts with room after room, when Ms. Collins came out of her office carrying her schedule book. Kevin Newell, the man who was looking for Ms. Collins earlier, followed her.

"You're back early," Ms. Collins said, glancing at a clock.

Vivian stood up. She couldn't tell if that was a criticism or a simple observation. "Um, yeah. I got anxious to do some work, so I came back. I hope you don't mind."

Ms. Collins snorted. "Mind? Not at all." She turned to Mr. Newell. "Vivian's a go-getter."

Vivian blushed, feeling a wave of guilt. She then noticed that she had gotten cold again, and she shivered, unable to avoid it.

"Is something wrong, Vivian?" Ms. Collins asked. "You're probably hungry…"

"I'm fine. I found something to eat."

Ms. Collins looked at her skeptically. "Usually wrapping one's arms around oneself and shivering is a universal sign of being cold."

Vivian looked down. She loosened her grip but she couldn't let her arms completely go. "Yes, I guess I am a little cold."

"Hmm. Well, it feels pretty comfortable to me and I know that they don't turn on the central air until later in the month, so I don't know. Are you feeling like you're coming down with something?" She scrunched her nose sympathetically.

Vivian shook her head. "I'm sure that I'll be fine. I'm warming up already," she lied, mentally begging her teeth not to chatter.

"So you met Mr. Newell already, right?"

Vivian nodded. He seemed to be scrutinizing Vivian in a way that unnerved her, giving her a strong feeling that she had been discussed in Ms. Collins' office.

"Mr. Newell had an idea for something to do with you, Vivian, something that will help Gordenner launch that new product I was telling you about. Would you be interested in a doing little market research?"

"Sure. I'm not really sure what that is, but I'll do anything to learn more about what's happening at Gordenner." Vivian had to use all her willpower to resist shivering again.

Mr. Newell cleared his throat like he was about to make a speech. "Market research is the way that a corporation like ours can find out consumers' responses to new products. Now it may be something material, like a new cracker or a new diaper, or it may be a concept. We're trying to assess the marketing of a new product line. That's what we're doing with this research: testing our marketing direction."

"I saw that area after lunch, I think. Those rooms with the big tables. So they were conducting..."

Mr. Newell nodded impatiently. "Yes, they were conducting market research in there. Now, what I was wondering with you, since it's a lot of work to get a focus group of young people together, I was wondering if we can run some preliminary concepts past you before it's even taken to the market research stage. This would help us craft our approach before we take it to a larger group."

Vivian nodded, wishing again that she'd brought a sweater. She made a mental note to bring one along Monday. "Sure."

"We are interested in your opinions because you're almost within the demographic we're trying to reach. A little young, but close enough. This will help us figure out what works before we see the larger group."

Vivian grabbed her purse. "So should we do this now?"

Ms. Collins beamed with something like pride. "What did I tell you about her being eager, Kevin? No, we were thinking Monday," she said, looking over her planner. "Is that okay?"

"I don't have anything else scheduled," Vivian said, looking at her blank calendar. "Do I?"

Ms. Collins shook her head. "Nope. Kevin, we'll talk Monday morning and schedule something. Maybe early afternoon?"

"Sounds good."

Mr. Newell started to walk away and Vivian almost had to brace herself against her desk: it was as if a cold, winter wind blasted by her. She'd never felt anything like it before, and she had to do her best to not visibly react. She intuitively reached for the papers Ms. Collins had given her for filing earlier, thinking that they were going to flutter into the air with the cold blast, but they remained entirely undisturbed on the corner of her desk. She was the only one in the office who seemed to be experiencing this miniature weather system. When the phone on her desk started beeping, she jumped a little.

"Well, don't be scared, darlin'," Ms. Collins said. "That just means you got a message or two. Nothing to be afraid of: just look in your phone manual and you should be fine," she said, returning to her office.

Vivian read the manual and entered her new code for message retrieval. There were two messages, and Vivian grabbed her message pad and a pen. The first message was from someone named Emily, who worked at a news station. She left her number for Ms. Collins to call her back. The second message, it took a moment to realize, was from a typically breathless Wren.

"Hey, girl. I can't believe you already got an extension and all that. I didn't expect that you would so soon but I called anyway and this nice lady figured out who you were and sent me through. It was so weird hearing your voice on the answering machine thingy," she giggled. "Anyway, I'm sure that you can't talk now but I wanted to check in with you and – oh, my gosh – you *have* to call me tonight. I'm dying of curiosity here." She started to hang up the phone when she gasped and said, "Oh! Did I say that this was Wren? I mean, you probably figured, but just in case. Okay. Call me. Maybe we can get together tomorrow."

When Vivian hung up the phone, Ms. Collins was standing behind her. "Any messages?"

"Yep," Vivian handed her the one she had jotted down.

"Great," she said, reading the message and not looking up. "That's all?"

Vivian almost lied but changed her mind. "Oh. A friend of mine left a message here. She was wondering how my first day was going and all. I'll call her back when I get home."

She thought for a moment that she noticed a flash of disapproval on Ms. Collins face, so she kept talking. "I don't know why she called me here. I didn't ask her to do that. I think I'll tell her not to call me at work any more."

Ms. Collins picked up the papers she had left on Vivian's desk, nodding distractedly. "That's fine, Vivian. Should we file?"

Ms. Collins took Vivian through the filing process; she explained that the papers were several months of reports from testing the new product line. The papers, stapled together in bunches of three or four pages, were stamped 'confidential' in red, but Ms. Collins didn't seem to mind Vivian filing them. They were to be sorted chronologically and then put in the folder marked *BW: Market Research*. Vivian sat at her desk to arrange them in order, glancing at the pages surreptitiously as Ms. Collins quickly typed and talked on the phone in her office. There were a bunch of percentages within paragraphs Vivian felt too nervous to linger over, so, while pretending to drop one report on the floor, Vivian slipped it into her purse, looking over her shoulder towards Ms. Collins' office. She wasn't sure why, but she wanted to read one of the reports that night in the safety of her home. Ms. Collins wouldn't notice that one was missing overnight. She'd slip it back in Monday when Ms. Collins was on break. Vivian felt an odd pang of guilt bothering her until she stopped to think about it: she reminded herself that she was there to accomplish a job. With conflicted feelings nagging at her, Vivian buried herself back into organizing the reports, and she soon found distraction in it. She also realized that she was no longer cold.

Once the reports were properly filed, she was sitting back at her desk, ready to study the manual again, when Ms. Collins came out of her office – like every movement she made, she made her way from her office to Vivian's in one seemingly enormous but graceful stride, almost like she was ice skating – and pulled up a chair next to Vivian's desk. She had another cup of coffee with her.

"Great. You filed that whole stack?"

Vivian nodded.

"Excellent," she took a long sip from her coffee cup. "Now, Vivian, it's almost time for you to go, but I wanted to talk to you a little bit about some safety precautions here at work before you leave."

"Sure." Vivian felt her throat tighten.

Ms. Collins looked momentarily pained, clearly dreading this conversation. She reminded Vivian of her mother's expression when she first nervously initiated the "birds and bees" discussion with Vivian a few years back.

"Remember before you took your lunch break when I told you to always take your purse with you? Well, any time you leave the office, even to make copies or go to the restroom, you're going to have to remember to take your purse along at least until the three weeks are up and you can get a key to lock the door. The top drawer of your desk locks – here's a key..." she said, handing her a tiny key, "- but it's too narrow for a purse."

Vivian put the key in her purse, zipping it in a little pocket.

"I know that Center City is a safe place so you probably don't think this way," Ms. Collins continued. "There are thousands of people who work here, and, yes, we try our best to only hire trustworthy people, but, well, things happen. You don't want to find out the hard way that you should have watched your purse better."

"I understand."

"There's more," Ms. Collins said, lowering her voice. "We've had some vandalism lately. It usually happens at night and that's why we have a security guard service now. There are security cameras that are going to be installed inside the facility soon. I'm just saying this to let you know that it's nothing to be worried about, but you should be cautious. When you leave here after work, if you see anything or anyone strange, let the security guard know. We tell all employees this."

"Like what should I be looking for?"

Ms. Collins raked her hand through her hair. "Oh, say, a car driving slowly around the outside of the plant. I assume that you're taking the bus back?"

Vivian nodded.

"Okay, if someone you don't know comes up to you and starts asking about Gordenner. Anything out of the usual. Specifically, this would be a man, probably in his sixties. I can't say that much more than that. Just be on the alert. And, I feel weird saying this, but, as mother always said, don't talk to strangers. If you have any questions about anything, talk to me or a supervisor or the security guard in front, okay?"

"I got it," Vivian said. She decided to push further. "So you think it's just one man who's doing this vandalism?"

Ms. Collins looked circumspect for a moment. "I wouldn't want to speculate. We just don't know enough yet, but it seems to point to one man from what I understand. One thing that I would ask is that you don't talk to anyone outside of Gordenner about this. In fact, talking about it *inside* Gordenner is discouraged too because it hurts morale, builds a culture of paranoia and gossip. Really, if you have any questions, you can just come to me, okay?"

Vivian nodded.

"Also, Vivian, I'm going to ask that you keep all Gordenner materials, your manual, any in-house memo or that sort of thing, to yourself. We've got some very ambitious projects that we're working on and confidentiality is a must."

"I understand."

"Which leads me to this," Ms. Collins walked back to her office and Vivian could hear her opening a desk drawer. She returned with a form and pen for Vivian. "This is your standard non-disclosure agreement. It essentially means that you agree to keep any and all information you have been privy to while interning at Gordenner to yourself. It is not to be shared with others, especially non-employees. This is just a formality everyone working at Gordenner has to agree to in order to protect our interests. It's nothing to be scared of, though. If you want to read it through before signing it, feel free."

All the words seemed to run together into unintelligible legalese; it may as well have been written in Sanskrit. Vivian skimmed it because she felt she should and signed it, crossing her fingers reflexively under the table as she did. She smiled at Ms. Collins, handing it to her, and waited for her to say something. Ms. Collins glanced at it then up at the clock. She took a deep breath and smiled with obvious relief.

"Well, Vivian, I think you've had a great first day. Do you agree?"

"Yes. It's gone well." Vivian was feeling fatigued but she tried to channel Wren and sound upbeat. "I've loved it, Ms. Collins." She almost winced at how perky she sounded.

Ms. Collins didn't seem to notice. She glanced at the clock again, then said, "Well, you'd better hit it if you want to catch the bus back home. It should be here in about ten minutes, right?"

Vivian grabbed her purse. "You're right. How did you know that?"

"I called the bus company, silly. I didn't want you to be standing out there with no bus in sight. So I'll see you Monday at 8:45?"

"See you then. Oh, I was wondering if I could take the manual and floor plan home with me to study over the weekend."

Ms. Collins' eyebrows knit together a little as she thought. "I don't see any harm in that, but, remember the agreement about keeping our materials private, okay? It's for security purposes."

"Got it," Vivian said, grabbing her purse maybe a little too nervously, knowing that the papers stamped confidential were inside. "Are you going to New Dublin this weekend?" *Stay calm*, she told herself. *Smile.*

"Of course," she said. "There's a gallery opening tomorrow night I was invited to and a good friend of mine is going to be having a brunch Sunday morning. Her husband's a former chef – he's just amazing – so I'm looking forward to that. He's got a frittata with my name on it. I go hungry all week and then devour everything in sight when I get back home." She started walking back to her office. "I'll see you Monday."

Vivian said goodbye to Betty at the front desk and stepped out into the sunshine as she left the building, a little stunned by the brightness of the day and the chirping robins after being boxed in all day. The transition from indoors to outdoors was so abrupt it almost knocked her over. The birds seemed more vocal than ever, their voices rising in an almost impossibly loud crescendo. Vivian rubbed her ears, walking through the parking lot, when she noticed the security guard watching her from his booth. Once again, Vivian told herself, this man has to see me doing something weird. She gave him a little friendly wave as she walked closer, letting him know that she noticed him watching her rubbing her ears and was unbothered by it. The expression behind his sunglasses remained frozen in stony-faced gravity.

"The birds are really loud today," Vivian said.

He looked at the sky and frowned almost imperceptibly, saying nothing.

"I guess that's their prerogative," Vivian said in a cheerful voice. "Have a nice weekend."

He gave the smallest of nods and pressed the button for the gate to swing open. Walking to the bus stop, she thought that the best she could hope for at this point with the security guard was that she was just perceived as a hopeless ditz and not much of a threat to Gordenner security. She realized that this would not be too much of a charade for her to pull off.

Vivian was grateful to see that a different bus driver was picking her up because she was hoping just to stare out the window and not have to make any small talk with the jingle-singing driver of that morning. She leaned against the window and watched the town pass by, changing from trees and wide expanses of public parks to construction crews and office buildings as they moved toward downtown Center City and, finally, Vivian's stop.

Back at home, she could hear Millie and another child playing in the den, and she could hear another voice – a young woman's, presumably a babysitter – with her, talking on the phone. She walked up to her room and quietly closed the door behind her, hoping to be undetected. Remembering the report she had put in her purse earlier from Gordenner, Vivian climbed on her bed and read it while lying on her stomach, ankles crossed in the air.

April 14

Eighteen people (six men, twelve women, 34 – 45 years old) were part of the Gordenner Bountiful Wheat Market Research #7 of April 12. The purpose of this Market Research was to assess consumer response to the genetically enhanced component of Bountiful Wheat and Bountiful Spray.

We began with the short (eight minute) film presentation of The Promise of Bountiful, showing participants the regions of Africa and India that would most benefit from the nutritional and financial support a Bountiful Wheat crop could yield. After viewing the film, three participants stated that they were "moved" by what they saw in the film and everyone expressed an interest in learning more about the Bountiful Wheat innovation. During the screening, participants displayed body language associated with a positive reception of the information (nodding heads, leaning towards the screen, etc.) and two women were observed dabbing their eyes as they watched the film.

Recommencing after a short coffee and bathroom break, facilitator Lauren K. asked the participants what they thought of the possibility of feeding the world's poor. One man expressed that he thought it was a good idea, but not at the expense of feeding "our own" [this country's] poor. A woman spoke up and said that she has traveled to Central America through her church to help build schools and wells and did not see what helping people in one nation would take away from our own nation. The man argued that this meant that funds that could be applied here would be applied elsewhere. Lauren then asked if this was a product that would have no negative affect on U.S. citizens, if this would be a product they could feel good supporting. All participants agreed that they could.

By a show of hands, thirteen people responded in the affirmative when asked if they felt it was every citizen's responsibility to end worldwide starvation. Of these, eleven responded in the affirmative that access to a single plentiful and nutritious crop is more important for impoverished people than any other concern. Those who disagreed with this statement said that concerns such as access to clean water, vaccines, and a variety of crops would be as or more important.

Lauren then asked the participants if they would approve of a seed that had been enhanced to contain a day's recommended daily allowance of B-vitamins and folic acid. One woman, a former nurse, remarked that a deficiency of folic acid in one's diet can lead to birth defects such as spina bifida. Lauren responded that one of the reasons why Gordenner was so excited about the promise of Bountiful Wheat was the effect it could have on reducing birth defect rates worldwide, especially in impoverished nations.

Lauren then asked the participants if they would have any reservations about supporting a crop that could feed the world's poor and help individual farmers and villages find self-sufficiency if that crop had been nutritionally enhanced using new, cutting-edge technologies created in the Gordenner laboratory. The sample was evenly divided: nine people stated that they had no concerns about any such enhancement, and nine responded that they would need to have access to more information. They were asked if the technology had been granted generally regarded as safe (GRAS) status by the USDA and FDA but was considered a new technology with some potential and minimal risk factors, would the benefits (feeding the hungry; self-sufficiency) outweigh the potential drawbacks. Of the eight, three agreed that the benefits would outweigh the risks and five stated that they would need additional information.

Vivian read this page over twice, rubbed her eyes, then read it again. Will had mentioned a wheat from Gordenner when they met to watch the video from the Lynx. The second page of the report was a series of percentages: how people responded to questions the facilitator asked and how it broke down into age brackets, males and females. No matter how many times Vivian read this page, how much she concentrated, the numbers all collided into each other and she couldn't make sense of it. She was going to try again when she collapsed in a heap. After a few minutes, she was going to read over this second sheet again when she remembered that she'd promised to call Wren.

"Oh my goddess," Wren nearly shouted into the phone. "I'm so glad you called. I've been thinking about you all day. How did it go?"

"Okay."

"Like what do you mean 'okay'?"

"You know. *Okay.*"

"Listen here, missy. You don't infiltrate a giant corporation and tell me that your first day was 'okay'. I mean, what happened? Did you make any discoveries? Did the creature from the black lagoon jump out at you? Details, Viv, I need details."

She giggled. "Okay, first of all, it's like, as you said, a giant corporation. It's not like there are undercover agents and characters out of James Bond lurking behind every corner. It's like a big building filled with, you know, professionals and whatever."

"I guess you'd fit into that 'whatever' category."

"Of course. Me in my trench coat."

"You wore a trench coat?"

"I was kidding," Vivian said. "Isn't that what spies and undercover agents wear?"

"Oh, yeah. I guess. Anyway."

"Anyway, it's mostly sort of a big, boring office building. You know."

Wren sighed, sounding exasperated. "How am I supposed to know what a big, boring office is like? I mean, honestly. My mom runs an animal shelter and my dad is a sculptor. Haven't you heard? We're hippies. I work at a coffeehouse from the Paleozoic era. A corporate office setting as unfamiliar to me as, like, the Serengeti or the Great Pyramids. So, like, what are we talking about?"

"We're talking about cubicles and a giant cafeteria and Muzak and everyone racing around with cups of coffee..."

"Ick. I hate coffee..."

"We're talking about filing papers. We're talking about making copies and filling out the right form in the office supply room so the inventory doesn't get screwed up. That's what I'm talking about when I say 'boring office'."

"Ah," Wren murmured. Vivian could almost see her nodding her head with an eyebrow raised, impersonating a detective. "So did anything interesting happen at all, or do we have to wait for this whole thing to reach some sort of crisis before you can uncover what's going on?"

"Okay, Wren, I've been there for one day, okay? It's not like, you know, this is going on six months or something. But I will say that something is definitely up."

"Finally you toss me a bone. Oh, yuck. Bad expression. I don't want a bone. You toss me a celery stalk. Okay, so what is making you say that something is definitely up?"

Vivian thought for a moment. What evidence did she have that not everything was as it seemed at Gordenner? "Well, for one, the people there are paranoid." Vivian found herself lowering her voice. "Like, you remember Kyle, the guy who drove us home?"

Wren sighed melodramatically. "Swoon."

"Yep. The swoon-y man. Well, Kyle was telling me that no one is allowed to talk about what the Lynx is doing to them. It's all hush-hush… like that will make it go away."

"Wow. Did he say 'the Lynx'?"

"No, but that was who he was talking about. He just couldn't say it."

"Sounds like a dysfunctional family."

"That's just what Kyle said."

"See? We were meant to be together."

"Anyway," Vivian said impatiently, "remember in the video, that bucket of sewage he threw on the computer and keyboard? That was Kyle's desk."

"No," Wren gasped. "My Kyle? I guess that makes sense, though, because that was where he found your application, right?"

"Right. So, it's kind of paranoid there. Ms. Collins was also really stressing to me that I was not to talk about anything that happens at the facility with anyone else, unless it's with her or the security guard or a supervisor. And she hinted at the Lynx, too."

"How was Ms. Collins?"

"She's nice, actually. Hyper and demanding and kind of intimidating, I think, but I like her for some reason. She kind of reminds me of my Mom."

"Oh, and that security guard. Did you see him again? He's scary."

"Yes, actually. I think I'm throwing him off my trail by just being kind of a dweeb, though."

"Good strategy."

"Thanks. It comes naturally to me, which is nice."

"No charade necessary."

"He does seems to be seconds away from frisking and cuffing me at any moment though."

Wren laughed. "Anything else?"

"Oh, plus I had to sign this form – what did Ms. Collins call it? – a something-something agreement. Uh: non-disclosure agreement. Basically saying that I wouldn't do what I'm doing right this moment."

"Excellent. Continue."

"Also, there's this guy there, his name is Mr. Newell, and the weirdest thing happened with him twice. Maybe you'd know what it was about."

"What?"

"Well, both times it was in my office, when he came in to talk with Ms. Collins – you go past my desk to get to her office, you know? Anyway, both times I talked to him, out of nowhere, I started just freezing when he was nearby. Like there was an air-conditioner going on at full blast, but no air blowing, just ice cold. Like my blood just froze. And I'm pretty sure that I was the only one who felt it, too. The second time, it nearly knocked me over."

Wren was quiet, absorbing this until she said, "Weird. Why do you think that was?"

"I have no idea. I was hoping that this would be more in your area of expertise and you might know."

"I've never heard of anything like that. Are you sure there wasn't a vent blowing on you or something?"

"Yes. I checked that first. There was no air blowing around. It was weirder than anything. The second time, Ms. Collins was in the room with us too and she didn't notice a thing."

"Hmm. I'll do some research into that. Anyway, can you meet tomorrow? We should talk in person," Wren said.

"Sure. You don't work?"

"Nope. Day off. Where should we meet?"

"Well, Millie has camp in the morning and my parents will both be at work, so maybe you could come here. You haven't been here yet."

"Sounds good. What time?"

"Should we say ten?"

"Works for me"

Vivian managed to spend the rest of the day holed up in her room for the most part, trying to skim through the employee manual. She kept finding herself conjuring an image of herself, radiant with courage, confronting the CEO, Robert Fontaine, whom she imagined as a tall, imposing figure, with her knowledge of Gordenner's secret pipeline of poison. Her skin and eyes glowed with her passion, but her voice was eerily calm, and all Mr. Fontaine could do when faced with her righteousness was promise to cease all polluting operations. When Mr. Sharpe came home, though, and then her mother, it was expected that Vivian tell them about her day at Gordenner, so she joined them in the kitchen as her father put a roast chicken in the oven and she heated up some water for pasta for herself.

She had a hard time at dinner that night watching her parents and sister slowly strip the flesh away from a bird's skeleton, so she answered their questions quickly and efficiently, eager to jump out of her seat, rinse her plate and get back to her room. Vivian hadn't realized how tired she was until she found herself putting on pajamas and washing up at 8:00.

She was asleep almost instantly. She had so many dreams – scattershot, fragmented and insensible – that the process of dreaming so hungrily almost wore her out by itself. In the morning, Vivian recalled images of Ms. Collins and Kyle, piles of forms scattered across her desk, a folder stuffed with important papers she tried to hide and take home with her, but all the papers kept slipping out and falling out of her reach, almost getting her caught.

ANOTHER LETTER

That morning, her parents left for work early, leaving her with Millie until the camp bus would arrive just after 9:00. Vivian sat in the backyard with a glass of orange juice and watched the birds fly from tree to yard to bush to tree. This was always her favorite time of the day, when everything was quiet and sometimes foggy and dreamy. She closed her eyes and listened to the birds chirp until Millie sneaked around the side of the house and turned on the sprinkler. Vivian, her hair wet and plastered to her face with water up her nose, couldn't get mad as she saw her sister run giggling into the front yard. Vivian chased her and, rounding the corner, she saw Millie standing still by the front door, turning an envelope over in her hands. Vivian froze where she stood, wet hair dripping on her shoulders and immobilized with a chill running down her spine, when Millie's voice brought her back to the present.

"Vivi, I think you got a letter from work again."

"Where did you find that?" Vivian said finally, willing herself to move as she rushed over to her sister.

"On top of the steps," Millie said, gesturing to the front door. "It wasn't in the mail box or anything."

Vivian grabbed the envelope from her sister. Her name was typed across, misspelled as it had been on the videotape package she got in the mail. Her hand was shaking as she reached for Millie's arm.

"Let's go inside. Now."

"I don't want to," Millie said, pulling back. "What's the matter?"

"Nothing, Millie: just listen to me and come inside now."

Millie pulled her arm away but could tell from Vivian's tone that she was not open to negotiation. She stomped into the house, Vivian close behind her, and ran to her bedroom. Millie slammed her bedroom door just as Vivian shut the front door to their house and locked it. She could hear Millie taking out her toys in her bedroom so she went in the bathroom upstairs, shut the door behind her and opened the envelope. Feeling woozy and with her heart racing, she sat on the floor, her back braced against the wall. She unfolded the piece of paper inside, which had been folded into thirds. At the bottom on the typed page was a sketch like the one she saw with the videotape of a lynx. Her hands shook as she read the note, and it was as if she were tunneling into her own body, hearing herself breathing from the inside.

That vile corporation you now work for poisons your town, your sister, your mind, yourself. How despicable one must be to decide to help It poison more easily. You are helping It sicken, pollute and kill: can you sleep with this knowledge?

We were hoping that a young person like you would take a stand against those criminals at Gordenner once you were exposed to the truth of Its evil deeds, but apparently you are already so corrupted you don't care. That's all that we can conclude, in fact. In that case, prepare yourself for the consequences of the choices you have made. Every choice and action we make have consequences, Miss Sharp, and we believe we must restore the natural order. As is the natural order, Choice + Action = Consequence.

The Lynx

Still clutching the letter, Vivian bolted from the bathroom and ran down the steps, nearly slipping down two. She checked the lock on the front door, shut the shades in the living room and the blinds in the kitchen, while Millie stood holding her doll by one limp arm at the top of the stairs.

"What's going on, Vivi?"

Vivian ignored her.

"Why did you shut the shades?"

"I can't talk now. Go back to your room."

"Vivi?" Millie started crying. "What's wrong? Are we in trouble?"

Vivian checked the back door and the side door; they were all locked. Millie was still wailing at the top of the stairs, her doll slumped on the floor. Vivian ran up the steps and sat on her knees a couple stairs of below, hugging Millie around the waist and looking up at her.

"I'm sorry, Millie. I can't explain right now. Everything's okay, though. It's all okay."

"Are we in trouble?"

"No," she said harshly, causing Millie to sob. Vivian kissed her wet cheek. "I'm sorry. I got worried. I was being silly for no reason. Let's play upstairs until your bus comes. Let's play in my room. We never play in my room." Vivian's bedroom faced the street and she needed to look out; Millie's room was across the hall.

Millie considered this, wiping her eyes. "Is everything okay?"

"Everything's okay."

"You promise?"

"I promise."

She sniffled, wiped her face with the back of her hand, and sighed with relief. "What should we play?"

"I don't know. Whatever you want. How about school? You can be the teacher. How's that?"

Vivian put the letter in her desk drawer underneath a bunch of other papers and stood in the corner, looking out her bedroom window. There was nothing unusual. Three little neighborhood girls were outside playing jump rope. Somehow that peaceful scene made Vivian even more nervous. She closed the shades and pulled out the desk chair for Millie to sit in.

"Okay. Should we do some homework, students?" Millie said.

"Yes, Miss Sharpe. Can we work on the alphabet today?"

"Certainly." Millie handed Vivian a pencil and a notebook. "I'd like to see capital and lower-case letters of the whole alphabet, please."

Vivian sat on her bed and wrote the letters out. When she got to G, she peeked out the behind the shades.

"Young lady, I did not say that you could get out of your chair yet," Millie reprimanded.

Vivian took a quick glance – nothing had changed, the girls outside were still jumping – and she scampered back to her bed. She wrote out all the letters and Millie was correcting them as she saw fit with a red pen when Vivian heard a car honking nearby. Her heart in her throat, she ran to the window and saw the camp bus parked in front of their house. She had completely forgotten about it.

"Oh, Millie, hurry. The bus is here."

They ran down the steps and were almost to the door when Millie stopped abruptly, shouted "My bag!" and ran back upstairs, grabbing her backpack with her bathing suit and towel. Vivian took a deep breath and opened the front door. Nothing was unusual, the girls were still jumping rope and there was only the bus on the street. Vivian could see the bus driver craning his neck in his seat, looking impatiently at them. No one appeared to be behind the bushes.

"Come on, Millie." Vivian awkwardly half-shielded Millie with her body as they hurried down the front walk to the bus. If Millie noticed anything weird, after the past half-hour of strange behavior from her normally placid older sister, she didn't say anything. Vivian bent down and hugged her close before Millie got on the bus.

"I'm sorry I was so weird," she whispered. "Have a great time at camp."

"I will." Millie bounced up the steps onto the bus. "Weirdo."

Vivian watched the bus take off and the girl jumping rope while her two friends twirled waved at Vivian. They were jumping to the Cinderella Dressed in Yellow rhyme, seeing how many kisses Cinderella would receive before the jumper would get tangled in the rope: one, two, three, four, faster, faster... Vivian waved back and ran inside, locking the door behind her. She rushed upstairs to read the letter again, sufficiently giving herself goosebumps. It would be an hour before Wren would be there. She checked each door again, locked all the windows and closed all the shades upstairs, which took less than ten minutes. She didn't see how she could make it for nearly an hour by herself so she called Wren to soothe her nerves. Speaking cryptically, she told Wren that she got another letter that morning and she was very nervous. Wren said that she'd be over right away.

While waiting in the kitchen, which seemed like the safest room with its proximity to two doors in case she needed to flee, Vivian glanced out the window that faced the backyard as she held on to the phone. Less than an hour before, she was enjoying the beautiful, sunny day, sitting on the grass and easing into the day. Now she imagined a stranger's dirty brown boots on the grass of their yard, crouching behind the cover of the raspberry bushes. She ate some crackers, not tasting a thing, then organized the family spice rack alphabetically to try to take her mind off things and was halfway through organizing her father's considerable tea collection when the doorbell rang. Vivian peered out the peephole of her front door and felt a tremendous wave of relief when she saw Wren's jumble of corkscrew curls.

Vivian let Wren in and quickly shut the door behind her.

"Before we do anything, I've got some stuff for you." Wren started pulling dropper bottles, tea bags and vitamins out of her enormous purse and lining them up on the dining room table. "I've got valerian root capsules, a vervain blend and chamomile tea. I've also got this calming blend in glycerin that my mom puts together for the animals, but it's totally safe for human use as well." She handed Vivian the dropper bottle. "Twenty drops under the tongue." When Vivian made no move to do as Wren directed, she said, "Come on. It tastes sweet. Bottom's up."

Vivian did as she was told.

"This way to your kitchen? I'm going to start some tea."

She nodded and trailed behind Wren.

"So, the thing about the cold, you know?"

"The cold?"

"You know how you said that guy at work made you feel cold? Tea kettle is…?"

Vivian reached in the cupboard and pulled it out. Wren filled it up at the sink.

"I think it's because of your intuition or empathy. This is just a hunch, but I'm thinking he's someone to avoid. He makes your blood run cold. That can't be a good thing."

"You're probably right."

"So that's it." Wren looked around. "Nice kitchen. Lots of light. Well, there would be if the window shades were open." Wren turned to Vivian, nodding at her hand. "Is that the letter?"

Vivian looked down; she hadn't realized that she was still holding the letter and the phone. She handed the letter to Wren and set the phone on the counter. Wren sat at the kitchen table and read it.

"Hmm. Well, he sounds pretty angry."

"Yeah, I got that, too. Angry like blow-up-your-house-angry? Or angry like fire-off-an-outraged-letter-angry?"

"I'm not sure," Wren said, shaking her head slowly. "It could go either way, I suppose."

"Oh, great."

"No, I mean, I can't read his mind. I can see why you're so upset, though."

The kettle started whistling, making Vivian gasp and clutch her chest. Wren raced to the stove, switched off the burner, then took down two teacups, and poured some tea for them.

"So what am I supposed to do, Wren? I mean this guy knows where I live and everything."

Wren handed Vivian her teacup. She leaned against the kitchen counter, thinking to herself. All Vivian could think was that she really didn't like tea all that much.

"I wish that we had some way of communicating to him that you're infiltrating Gordenner, you know? Like send out a smoke signal that you're not just an intern. Or – how about you leave him a letter at your house?"

"Do I want to get involved with this guy, though? I don't think so. Also, I can't leave a letter here that my parents could find."

"You're right." Wren nodded, her hand around her teacup. "Listen, Viv, I have a question. Do you think it would be okay to invite Will over? He's dying to talk to you about your first day at Gordenner, and he might have some thoughts about the Lynx and this letter. What do you think?"

"I don't know. I'm already feeling pretty exposed and nervous as it is."

"I understand. I just think that Will would be able to help."

Vivian thought about it. "I guess I don't see any harm in it."

"Great. I told him that unless I called, to come over by 11:00. I hope that's okay."

"Yes. Fine."

The two sat at the kitchen table. Wren went into the other room and brought back her boxes of tea and bottles of herbs.

"I'm going to leave these for you. They'll help with your nerves. If you parents ask, just tell them that you've been having trouble sleeping. Do you have a pen and paper?" Wren jotted down instructions for Vivian on how to take the herbs. "If you don't feel nervous, you'll be able to think more clearly about what's going on, you know?"

It was clear that Vivian didn't want to talk about the Lynx anymore, so Wren cheerfully suggested that she take a tour of her house, starting with the kitchen pantry.

"I love looking in someone's pantry. I feel like I get to know the people through seeing their cupboards. See? Like this?" She pulled out a box of cocoa packets. "We don't have things like this at my house: cocoa mix." She turned the box around and looked at the ingredients.

You mean you've never had cocoa?"

"No, I've had cocoa, of course I've had cocoa. What I mean is that in our kitchen, we have the cocoa powder. This is already mixed together, right? Cocoa powder and sugar together. At my house, we combine them on our own."

"So then what's the big difference? Two packages instead of one?"

"Well, I hadn't thought of it like that. I guess my mother would say that she just likes to make her own mix rather than buy some corporate cocoa. You know?"

Vivian nodded. She didn't know.

"Somebody here is a tea lover," Wren commented, looking at all the boxes that Vivian had recently organized.

"Yeah, my dad mostly."

"This summer I'll give you lemon verbena and lavender and peppermint that we grow in our garden. You can dry it yourself: just tie a bunch together and hang it upside down. Easy as pie. If your dad is a tisane guy, this makes much better blends. Trust me. He'll never go back to this boxed kind. It has no flavor, comparatively."

Wren looked at Vivian a little guiltily.

"Do I sound judgmental? I'm sorry. I can come on kind of strong sometimes and you're like my one link to the way the rest of the world lives. I have a lot of catching up to do with how the rest of the world functions sometimes. I guess I don't always know the right thing to say."

"You're fine. I'll just accept that our kitchen is full of corporate cocoa and bad tea. It's not personal. You didn't even say anything about the disposable plastic cups in the pantry..."

"Well, I had to show a little restraint."

"...which, for the record, I've stopped using."

"Good for you," Wren laughed. "Okay. Can I judge, I mean, see, the rest of your house now?"

"Certainly."

Walking through the house with Wren, as she looked at the family photographs on the walls (Millie was "cute as a bug, but one of the nonviolent, beneficial bugs that don't sting," Wren declared) and admired the porcelain figurines in her living room, Vivian was able to forget about the Lynx for a few minutes and enjoy her company. Every once in a while, Vivian would forget why the window shades were drawn, and the harsh, visceral memory of the letter would flood her senses again until Wren, who asked a lot of questions, could distract her again. Most of her questions were about Vivian's family, and most she didn't know the answer to, like what were their astrological signs and their favorite colors.

"I think that my father's must be tweed, but I never really asked him. He just wears brown tweed all the time. I don't think he probably has one, though."

"Really?" Wren asked, studying his face in a picture with Mrs. Sharp at his high school reunion. "I would have guessed him to be a steel grey or a cobalt blue. You should buy him something in one of those colors and see how it changes his personality. Or buy him something really bright and cheerful, like orange. I'd bet you'd see a whole different side of your father. Like my mom was wearing this yellow top one day last week and she was in a really bad mood, snipping at everyone. Not being herself. Finally, I told her, 'Mom, put on some purple already,' and she did and she was back to her normal self, much more centered."

"Hmm."

"Your mom probably wears a lot of primary colors, I would guess, especially reds. It's because her personality's so strong. What's her sign again? Oh, you don't know. When's her birthday? Wait..." she threw up her hand like she was stopping a car in traffic... "don't tell me. I love guessing signs. She's a Leo or Scorpio."

"I don't know. It's August 12."

"Ha, she's a Leo," Wren clapped, jumping a little. "I knew it. That makes sense from what I see and you've described. She's dominant, proud, strong-willed. Your birthday's in July, right?"

Vivian nodded.

"See, that's what makes you perfect for infiltrating Gordenner. You're a Gemini – the twins. Your sign represents duality – do you know what that means? Duality?"

"Dual? Meaning two?"

Wren nodded vigorously, "Yes, which means that you'll be able to present a public face when you go in to work and conceal the part of you that is working undercover. No other sign would be as good a fit as a Gemini. Lots of actors are Geminis."

"That's good to know."

"Wait: you're not a Gemini. You're a Cancer," she said frowning.

"And?"

"It's still good. Cancers operate from their emotions, from protecting their homes and families. It all really depends on your moon and ascendant and all that other stuff anyway. What time were you born?"

"In the morning. Like eight, I think."

Wren frowned a little. "Your chart changes minute by minute so you have to be precise. Next time you get your birth certificate, look up your time of birth, okay? I could do your whole chart. You'll love it."

"Sure thing."

Vivian was showing her around the upstairs when Wren suddenly stopped and shook her head. "Oh my goodness, do you guys have three bathrooms?"

Vivian thought for a moment. "No, four. There's another in the den downstairs."

Wren chuckled to herself. "One bathroom per person. I've never seen such a thing."

Vivian was about to show Wren the balcony off her parent's bedroom when they heard the doorbell ring. They both jumped a little and then raced downstairs, giggling and frightened.

"Who is it? Who is it?" Wren whispered loudly as Vivian looked through the peephole.

"It's Will."

Vivian opened the door and was about to say something when Wren grabbed his arm, pulling him inside the house. Vivian quickly shut and locked the door.

Will looked back and forth between them. "What's up? Why are all the shades shut? I thought that no one was home for a minute there. It's so dark in here."

"So much to tell you, Mister Will," Wren said, taking his arm. "Here, let's sit in the kitchen."

Will seemed apprehensive but followed Wren's lead to the kitchen. Vivian turned on the light and grabbed the letter from the kitchen table where Wren had left it with the teacups.

"I got another letter from your friend the Lynx."

Will took it and sat down in the chair. "When did you get it?"

"My sister found it this morning. It was on our front steps."

He read it silently a few times over. He looked up at Vivian. "Hmm."

"Yes. Hmm, indeed."

"Well, what do you suggest?" Wren said, with more than a hint of impatience in her voice.

"I'm still absorbing it. I don't know. Clearly the Lynx thinks that you are working for Gordenner now, though, I have to say, I don't know why he'd want to bother some nobody there."

"Thank you very much."

"No offense."

"Being called a peon is not meant to be offensive?" Vivian laughed.

"No, what I meant is that there are thousands of people who work there, all with much more powerful titles than yours as a marketing intern. You're pretty much the bottom of the totem pole. He usually goes after the guys in charge: the CEOs, CFOs, the high-up executives. What does he have to gain by going after you? You don't have the authority to really influence anything."

"She may not have the authority," Wren said, defending her friend, "but she's going to influence plenty at Gordenner."

"But the Lynx doesn't know that. If he did, he would know that she's working against the corporate goals and he'd leave you alone. Anyway, this note... I think that the best thing to do would be to try to reach him somehow and let him know that you're on his side."

"That's what I said to do," Wren said, jumping in her seat with excitement.

Will ignored her, turning to Vivian. "What do *you* want to do?"

"I think," she paused. "I think it's dangerous." Will started to disagree, but Vivian cut him off. "I don't think that I want to begin communications with a known terrorist. Is that so hard to believe?"

"Oh, please. He's not a terrorist," Will said, waving his arm in dismissal. "I love how that word just has lost all meaning. He wouldn't bother you once he knew where you were coming from. And we could get the Lynx on board with us. We totally could. He could guide us." Will started to get that feverish look he'd had the other day at the Commie Café. "He could mentor us."

"Oh, I don't think that's wise," Wren said.

"Why not?" he said, his chair squeaking as he turned to face her. "Do you know how many activists around the country – the world, even – would die to be in Vivian's shoes?"

"Is that really the best expression? 'Cause right now, her shoes aren't looking like the safest pair in the world."

Will continued, ignoring her, "To be this close to the Lynx, this legendary figure? It's all I can do not to stand outside with a megaphone to let everyone know that the Lynx is on the move again. We can't let this opportunity pass us by."

Vivian almost choked hearing this. "Opportunity?" she coughed. "The opportunity to be threatened by a stranger who's known for using violence to get his message across? I would prefer other opportunities, like straight 'A's or a cute boy asking me out, or something like that."

Wren laughed out loud. Will shot a sharp look over at her, causing her to cover her mouth, but she still continued laughing.

"I'm trying to be serious here," he scowled.

"I mean, really, Will, I *am* serious," Vivian said. "I just fail to see how this is just such a wonderful opportunity for me."

Will took a deep breath, as though it required all his patience to explain his point of view to Vivian and Wren. "Listen, Vivian, I would be happy to leave you some articles about the Lynx."

"I read them at the library. Somehow they didn't make me feel more comfortable with his presence in my life."

"Hear me out, please. Articles in respected, balanced publications. Books that reference the Lynx. I would be happy to provide you with ample proof that the Lynx is a highly regarded figure, a seminal, deeply important..."

"He's Seminole? I didn't know that. My mom's one-quarter Seminole..."

Vivian and Will both looked with confusion at Wren.

"Seminole Indian. Isn't that what you said? That he's Seminole?"

Will looked so exhausted suddenly, like he was ready to curl up and fall asleep. Instead, he spoke very deliberately. "No: *seminal*, like one of the original guys who created the monkeywrenching movement."

They were quiet for a few moments.

"Okay, I'll ask," Vivian said finally, looking at Wren. "What's monkeywrenching? I'm going to assume that it does not actually involve monkeys running around with wrenches, right? 'Cause if so..."

Will almost started laughing, then regained his composure. "No monkeys are involved, but there may be wrenches. Basically, monkeywrenching is using whatever tools we have to stop industries and the government from poisoning our communities.

Usually, it's a form of sabotage, creating financial hardship or destruction against corporations."

"So…" Vivian said.

"It's using a factory's wastewater to flood itself, for example, something that the Lynx has done. It's disabling the means of destruction or exploitation, whether that means pouring sugar in the gas tanks of logging trucks or liberating animals in a fur ranch."

"Cool," Wren said admiringly.

"In any case, the Lynx is considered, if not *the*, than *a* major progenitor of this style of activism. Anti-whaling ships sinking whaling ships, spiking a road so logging trucks cannot access the forest: a lot of it can all be traced back to the Lynx in one way or another. He did much less high-profile, high-visibility assignments, though. He was all about working undercover locally."

"Think globally, act locally," Wren chimed in cheerfully.

"What a community guy," Vivian said.

"Listen, I know that you're being sarcastic, but he was. Is. The fact that the Lynx has you on his radar after so many years completely underground, well, you should be flattered. The activist community across the country – across the globe, really – is going to be so energized when word gets out that the Lynx is on the move again. It's going to have an amazing ripple effect. His reputation and mystique has only increased during his years underground. To think that this all just landed on your lap…"

"Like a hand grenade," Vivian muttered.

"– it's miraculous in a way. Anyway, I absolutely encourage you to strike up a correspondence with the Lynx so we all can work together to topple Gordenner."

"What would I say? Like, 'Hi. Please don't bomb my house. Let's be best friends forever!'"

"Vivian, if you can't be serious…"

"I *am* serious, Will. I am taking this very seriously. I am the one being threatened. I'm truly at a loss."

"Do you want me to write something for you?"

"For the Lynx?" she asked.

"Yes. A letter to him," Will said.

"How would I get it to him?"

He shrugged as though this were simple. "We'd do it."

"I'll write it." Vivian tore a sheet from the grocery list pad and took the pen that was on the table in front of Will. "Do you mind? How do I start? 'Dear Lynx'?"

"I wouldn't say 'dear'," Wren said. "Too...I don't know...."

"Me, neither. Too goody-goody."

"Then what should I put here to begin my note? 'To The Most Noble and Venerable Lynx'?"

They all silently pondered this for a minute.

"How about just 'Lynx' then start your letter?" Will offered.

"Is that too abrupt? Rude?" Vivian asked.

Wren wrinkled her nose. "I think it is."

Will frowned, thinking. "I don't think that such pleasantries matter much to the Lynx. I'd cut to the chase. I think he'd respect that."

"Okay," Vivian said. "'Lynx, comma. I'm not who you think I am.' How's that for an opener?"

"It sounds a little melodramatic to my ears, but under the circumstances, I think it's fine." Will said.

Vivian wrote that line out and stared at it for a few minutes, occasionally writing and crossing out words, without speaking. Wren rummaged around in her purse for something or another, and Will drummed his fingers on the table.

"You know, I think that I'll do better at this when I can just have some time alone to concentrate."

"But you will write a letter to the Lynx?" Will asked.

Vivian nodded.

"Soon?"

"Yes. Tonight."

"Promise?"

"Will, if I said I was going to do something, I'm going to do it."

Will looked at her for a moment or two, as though to gauge her sincerity, then he nodded. "Okay. So could we talk about Gordenner? You're up in the administrative offices, right?"

"Yep. I'm Ms. Collins' intern. She's the head of marketing."

"Whoa. Laura Collins? I guess I knew that, but I hadn't put two and two together."

"Why? What do you know about her?" Vivian asked.

"Just that Gordenner hired her a while back from some big marketing firm in New Dublin. There was something about it in the paper and her name stuck with me."

"Not that he's obsessed or anything," Wren said.

"Okay," Will said, ignoring her, "so you work with Laura Collins in marketing. Anything interesting happen yesterday?"

"Not really. It was my first day..."

"Wait," Wren shouted in mock-seriousness. "Vivian signed a legally binding non...what was it called?"

"Non-disclosure agreement."

"You did? They had an intern sign one? They must be pretty paranoid."

"Yeah, I signed it, but I crossed my fingers, which legally blocked my signature, I think."

"It would totally stand up in court," Wren said, crossing her fingers and feigning wide-eyed innocence. "But your honor, I did crossies."

Vivian laughed. "So anyway, they do seem pretty paranoid. You're right, especially about anything that has to do with the Lynx. Apparently people cannot even mention his name out loud without getting in trouble. Kyle was telling me all about it."

"Kyle," Wren sighed.

"Now who's Kyle?" Will asked, shaking his head and frowning a little.

"Kyle is the assistant -"

"The gorgeously handsome, perfect assistant, created by God's personal paintbrush..." Wren said under her breath.

" - to the big guy there..."

"Robert Fontaine."

"That's right. But he's really nice and pretty open about things. I think he's a good ally. He seems to like me." She shot a look at Wren, feeling herself blush. "Not in that way."

Will rubbed his jaw, looking concerned. "That's all fine and good, Vivian, but you can't let your guard down, not even for a second. I wouldn't tell this guy anything about why you're really there. Not a thing. His loyalties are with Gordenner and Fontaine. Don't ever forget that."

"You don't know that, Will," Wren said. "He may not be all that loyal to Gordenner."

"Wren, this is really serious," Will said, slapping his hand on his leg. "The only person Vivian can really trust at Gordenner is herself. Period. I cannot stress that vigorously enough. Not only could Vivian fail to accomplish her goals if she is exposed at Gordenner as an infiltrator, she could get in deep trouble personally. She signed a non-disclosure agreement, for crying out loud." Will looked at Vivian. "Do you agree?"

Vivian nodded. "The thing is that I like Kyle and −" Will looked like he was going to interrupt, so she kept talking louder, "-

actually, I kind of trust him, but no way am I going to reveal to anyone there that I am anything but a dependable little intern who minds my own business."

She must have said this with conviction, because Will looked noticeably relieved. "Okay. So what else?"

"We need to figure out how to get a letter to the Lynx."

He shrugged. "Right now I have no idea. I'll think about it, though. Short of leaving it on your front step in the off chance that he'll come back and find it, I don't have any thoughts at the moment."

"Okay. What else? Um, I got an employee manual..."

"Do you have it here?"

"Yep. I knew that you'd ask. I had to get permission to bring it home." She went up to her room and brought it down. Wren was refilling the tea kettle when she returned to the kitchen. She placed the manual on the table in front of Will.

"Okay," Will mumbled, leafing through it. "Good."

"Oh, also I have this report. I actually took it from work without anyone knowing and I have to return it Monday. It's some sort of market research report."

It was stuffed inside the manual binder, so Vivian flipped through the pages and pulled it out, handing it to Will. He wiped off his glasses on his shirt and frowned at the report in front of him.

"I knew it," he said coldly, still looking at the report.

"What?" Vivian and Wren both asked.

"I knew it," he repeated, his voice rising. "They're bringing back Miracle Wheat and Miracle Spray. Those scumbags are really doing it." He shook his head in disbelief, but Vivian thought that she saw excitement in his eyes, too. "They are set to destroy any ecosystem this poison touches. Even given their appalling history, it's still a shock."

"What is Miracle Wheat?" Wren asked, looking at Vivian.

Vivian shook her head. "I don't know much about it."

Will slammed the report on the table. "Miracle? What is Miracle?" He started riffling through his bag while talking. "Miracle Wheat and Miracle Spray are now being called Bountiful Wheat and Bountiful Spray. It's the latest configuration with the bio-X microorganism." Vivian and Wren stared at him blankly. "The microorganism is a natural by-product of creating this seed, which they do in giant vats. At least, that's how they did it with Miracle; that's the most efficient way for them. The waste product of these seeds in inevitable: you cannot produce the seeds without it, and that has been a huge marketing problem for them. This waste product is thought to be carcinogenic, a dioxin."

He pulled out a blurrily photocopied magazine article and handed it to Vivian. "Years ago when these products were called Miracle Wheat and Spray, they couldn't sell them domestically, not even with our lax standards and regulations. The stuff's too toxic for us, so the foreign market is where they're going to push it, specifically developing nations. This here," he said, tapping a finger on the report, "this is trying to gauge public opinion so they can preemptively dismiss any criticism. I'd heard rumors that this was what they were going to do, but this is the first real evidence I've seen."

"What's so bad about it, though? I'm not being argumentative. I just don't know." Vivian said.

"Well, for one, it's a patented seed, and that has all sorts of ethical implications. Like, how can we patent life? Beyond that, it's simply horrendous. The seed itself – it's genetically engineered; it's not sufficiently tested and has the potential to spoil crops and indigenous food systems through genetic drift. They police themselves instead of there being third party oversight. They have been given pretty much of a free ride from the governmental agencies to conduct their own tests. Anyone can see that the integrity of a test is going to be compromised when it's being 'tested' by those with a vested interest in a product going to market."

"But how can that be allowed?"

"Welcome to the real world, Vivian. I'll tell you based on Gordenner's past what they're going to tell the public. They are going to say that this wheat can feed impoverished communities, but it's all hype as far as I can see. In order to consume enough of this wheat to get the nutritional boost they claim, you'd have to eat boatloads every day. I remember with Miracle, it was thirteen loaves of bread a day to get the RDA of folic acid that it's enriched with. *Thirteen.* A villager could get her RDA of folic acid just from eating a variety of plant foods."

"Thirteen loaves a day? That's per person? Impossible."

Will nodded. "Yep, except they're not going to admit that aspect of things. Instead of giving poor people the means to grow the native plants that have sustained them for thousands of years, they're deceiving them into becoming sharecroppers for their fiefdom and encouraging monocropping." He paused. "I suppose probably you don't know what monocropping is, right?"

Vivian shook her head.

"It's growing one crop, one kind of plant, over and over. What happens if that crop fails? What if it doesn't take to that particular climate? There are so many variables that could occur, and one is all that it would take to totally torpedo a local economy. And the thing is, the thing that makes it so evil and sadistic, is that the people Gordenner is going to prey upon are the poorest of the poor. Their message to the public is, 'Oh, those poor little native people. Through our generosity, we'll get them started on these seeds for free.' What they're not saying is that then they'll be dependent on – what was it?..." he looked down at the report "...Bountiful, because virtually nothing else will be able to grow. They'll be beholden to Gordenner's fiefdom."

"What about the spray?"

"The spray," Will leaned back in his chair, head resting in his hands as he savored the moment. "The spray will make all other chemicals look like nectar from the gods. A liquid ambrosia. You ever hear of Agent Orange?"

Vivian and Wren shook their heads. "Was he like a spy or something?" ventured Wren.

"No. It was an herbicide – a defoliant – developed back in the 1940s by the chemical companies Dow and Monsanto. It was used by the U.S. military in Vietnam as part of its program of chemical warfare. Agent Orange destroyed almost every plant in its path. It was also a carcinogen."

"What does that have to do with Bountiful Spray?'

"Vivian, how much have you read about the history of Gordenner? How much do you know?"

Vivian shrugged. "A bit."

"If you researched Gordenner, you would find that they started as a chemical company. The sprays can be made of chemicals that have been banned here but we're still exposed to them because the crops they're sprayed on get imported here. Look at the stickers you see on the produce. 'Grown in Chile,' 'Grown in China.' We may ban certain chemicals here, but other countries may not and they can get sent back here."

"I never thought about that."

Will nodded. "Few do. Gordenner shifted their focus from chemicals to farm chemicals to nutraceuticals about ten years ago.

They've been a secretive company historically, so it's hard to find much on them, but there have been a couple of quality pieces, mostly chapters in books. I could get you some information to read." He made a note to himself. "Your dad's an historian, right?"

Vivian didn't remember sharing this. Maybe Wren did.

"Well, maybe he has access to stuff of value about Gordenner."

Vivian shrugged. "You said a word before – nutra-something."

"Nutraceuticals?"

"Yes. What is that?"

"Seeds supposedly enhanced – that's a key word they use, *enhanced* rather than genetically engineered, because that turns people off – with nutritive components: vitamins, minerals. It's incredibly profitable. The problem is that this particular product – Bountiful, just like Miracle ten years ago – is that it's potentially a health risk and ecological disaster. They're going to try to spin it into them helping the world's poor, though, and that's why this is so patently evil."

"Why are they doing it? If it's so evil and everything?" Wren asked.

Will looked at her incredulously. "Because they're a *corporation*, Wren. Because they stand to make a veritable goldmine. It's not that hard to understand. They make a troublesome product, but if it's shipped overseas to people who don't have access to decent sanitation let alone a good lawyer, they have a *great* deal. They wheel and deal and get lucrative, binding contracts. Gordenner gets all the positive P.R.; meanwhile, back in some village in the Philippines, a terminator seed and spray are killing every other plant, the entire ecosystem, and they're fully dependent on it. And that's not even taking into account the potential health risks."

Wren started to say something, but Will interrupted.

"And it's not just that village in the Philippines. No, we're talking about villages in Africa, all over Asia, South America, Central America. The global repercussions of this one product are mind-boggling."

"So now what?" Vivian asked, throwing up her hands in frustration after a few moments of awkward silence. "What on earth am I supposed to do with this information? A fifteen-year-old in Center City."

Will leaned forward. "This is why we have to strategize. Do we go to the media right away, leak it to the biggest, loudest environmental group we can find, or keep it under our hats until we know a little bit more?"

"Well, okay," Vivian said, biting her lip until it hurt. "This all leads me to another question. Apparently I'm supposed to be a part of a market research session about Bountiful Wheat on Monday. Should I be honest with them about what I think – given what I know now – or give them the answers I think they want so they don't suspect anything? The thing is, I could have the opportunity to speak out against it, but I don't know if that's the best idea or not."

"I don't know either," Wren said. "It's about whether you want to live a total lie or not."

"I disagree," Will said, frowning. "It's about whether Vivian wants to approach this as a strategist or not. If you alert them to the issues that you and others might have about Bountiful, it could tip them off that they need to devise a plan to deflect criticism. If they're not tipped off about this, we have more of a chance to upset their apple cart. You know what I mean?"

They all sat with their heads in their hands, mirroring one another silently, as they contemplated this. Finally, Vivian broke the silence. "I'm just going to wing it. We're all going to have to trust that I'll do the right thing. I'm not going to know the right approach until I'm sitting there in the room with them. But you're going to have to trust me."

Wren nodded. "I think that's the best solution for now. Vivian always does the right thing, but it's not like she can plot this out. She functions on an intuitive, gut level in these situations."

Will didn't respond for a few moments then agreed almost grudgingly. "Okay. This is your call, Vivian. I'm going to trust that you'll do whatever's best."

Wren started to talk when Will interrupted her.

"The only thing is that I would urge you to use a lot of caution. You know, think of this in a long-term win sort of way. Yeah, you could tell off those Gordenner executives, but is that the best for the long-term goal of keeping this toxic waste out of the third world?"

"I plan to be cautious, Will."

"Vivian's very cautious," Wren agreed.

"But don't be *too* cautious," he said emphatically. "You've got to do something."

Vivian agreed.

Will seemed suitably reassured because he nodded and turned back to studying Vivian's employee manual, occasionally muttering to himself and shaking his head when he came across something disagreeable. Not long after, it became clear that Will was only interested in concentrating on reading the manual, so Wren turned to Vivian and said brightly, "I think we should open the shades. It's like a cave in here."

"I don't know. Do you think it's safe?"

Will didn't look up from his reading, but responded nonetheless. "Yes."

"It's just that if you think of yourself as a prisoner, that's what you will become," Wren said. "If you think of yourself as free and safe, you'll put out a vibe that's much less vulnerable."

With a look of annoyance on his face, Will finally looked up. "That, or you could just realize that there's no real threat against you and move on." He returned to the manual once again.

"You guys are right," Vivian said as she stood. She was starting to open the kitchen shades when the doorbell rang, and she froze in shock. Wren jumped up and looked at Will, his face suddenly pale. Vivian realized that they were both looking to her to do something, and she was just standing still, her hand on her heart, immobilized with fear.

"No one dangerous would just ring the doorbell, right?" She tried to sound calm and she motioned to Wren to sit back down, but she was a little short of breath to be convincing. Wren looked at her uncertainly; Will wordlessly nodded. She walked to the front door.

Looking in the peephole, she could first see a woman with her hair in a headband. At first Vivian didn't recognize her but then it dawned on her that she was a neighbor from across the street, Mrs. Hannigan, a preoccupied-seeming, pursed-lipped woman with ash blonde hair who always had a look like she'd just taken a bite out of a lemon. Mrs. Sharpe was not friendly with her – the Hannigans moved in two years ago and Vivian's mother knew only a few of the neighbors because she was usually busy with work, but they were politely pleasant to one another at their annual block party.

"Hello, Mrs. Hannigan."

She squinted at Vivian. "I just came by to see if everything was okay. I was working in the yard this morning when I noticed all the shades were drawn, then my Megan told me that she saw a young man come in."

Vivian was at a loss for what to say. "Oh," she managed.

"Is everything okay?"

Vivian smiled as calmly as she could at her neighbor while her brain raced for a suitable answer. "Everything's fine, Mrs. Hannigan. We just..."

"And I noticed that your parents weren't home so I became concerned."

"Oh, no. We're fine." Vivian remembered with an almost too-enthusiastic sense of relief reading somewhere that people with migraines are sensitive to light. "Yeah, my friend Wren came over, but she has a bad headache so we shut the shades because the sun was bothering her."

Mrs. Hannigan raised an eyebrow. "All the shades? I noticed that the shades upstairs were drawn too."

"Well, Wren was helping me rearrange my bedroom. Really, everything's okay."

Mrs. Hannigan stood there, showing no sign of moving.

Finally, Vivian awkwardly said, "Would you like to come in?" She could see Wren race back to the kitchen table from the doorway. "There's really not much to see."

Mrs. Hannigan seemed to consider this for a moment, but Vivian could see that her mind was already set. "Well, you know, it's not like I want to be a snoop or anything..."

"I understand."

"But I'd feel terrible if, well, if there was, you know, something going on and I didn't do anything."

"So you'd like to come in?" Vivian opened the door a little wider.

"Thank you."

Mrs. Hannigan, her eyes adjusting to the darkness, just stood in the entryway until Vivian led her to the kitchen.

"My friends are in here."

Will and Wren sat at the kitchen table, Will with a book in front of him and Wren with sunglasses on. They both looked up when Vivian walked in with Mrs. Hannigan as though they were surprised.

Wren stood up. "Oh, hi. I'm Wren. Nice to meet you, Mrs. Sharpe."

Mrs. Hannigan looked momentarily confused, then understood. "Oh. I'm not Vivian's mother. I'm her neighbor from across the street."

"Well, that explains why you and Vivian look nothing alike," Wren said very quickly. "And why you rang the doorbell. Nice to meet you anyway," She extended her hand to shake, which Mrs. Hannigan did reluctantly. Wren touched her sunglasses offhandedly. "I'm sorry about my sunglasses. I don't mean to be rude. It's just..."

"Vivian told me. You have a migraine."

"That's right. Headaches run in my family. Vivian was so thoughtful to shut the shades for me, too."

"And we haven't met yet," Mrs. Hannigan said to Will, who was skimming a textbook. He extended his hand awkwardly, almost as an afterthought.

"I'm Will. I'm a friend of Wren's mother."

"You look quite a bit older than Vivian and Wren," Mrs. Hannigan observed, squinting at Will.

He looked at the two. "Yes. I'm in college in Center City."

"Do you mind if I ask why you're here?"

Will pointed to his textbook. "I'm tutoring Vivian and Wren in chemistry."

Mrs. Hannigan blanched at this. "Over the summer? Wasn't school just let out? Surely summer school hasn't started yet."

"It hasn't," Vivian said. "It's to be ready for chemistry in the fall."

Mrs. Hannigan pursed her mouth even more than usual and seemed to turn this over in her mind. "Hmm. Seems strange to be spending your summer indoors being tutored in a class that you're not even taking."

"I guess it might seem strange," Vivian concurred.

Mrs. Hannigan took one last, long look around the kitchen then stared at Vivian, as though she was going to wait until she heard a more honest answer. Vivian stood firm and offered some lemonade.

"No. Thank you. I should be going. Nice to meet you...?"

"Wren."

"Have you taken any aspirin, Wren?"

"Aspirin? For what?"

"For your headache, dear."

Wren flushed for a moment, then giggled nervously. "Oh, sorry. No. I don't believe in them. I do acupressure. Except at the moment, I'm not."

Mrs. Hannigan nodded slowly like she had the answer she'd been expecting. "Well, have a good time studying. Nice to meet you, Will."

She started to walk out of the room when Wren stood up and said, "Thank you. I'm starting to feel a little better. We could probably open these shades any time," she said to no one in particular.

"Have a nice day," Mrs. Hannigan said as Vivian walked her to the door. Her mouth was set in a grim little line Vivian couldn't interpret.

"See you later, Mrs. Hannigan."

As soon as she left, Vivian shut the door and watched through the peephole until she crossed the street. Once Mrs. Hannigan was in front of her own house, Vivian slid against the door with her back, legs like rubber. She knew that she was drained of all color.

After a minute or so, Wren called from the kitchen. "You okay, Viv? I'm sorry about that aspirin thing. My mind just went blank."

Vivian took a deep breath; all she wanted to do was go upstairs and hide under her blankets. "Yeah. It's okay. I'm okay," she said, struggling to stand. She walked to the kitchen and leaned on the doorframe. Wren's sunglasses were already folded on the kitchen table.

"Sorry," Wren repeated. "I'm not used to this whole spinning webs of deceit thing."

"Do you think that I am?"

"No," Wren looked taken aback. "That's not what I meant."

"I know," Vivian mumbled. "I'm sorry."

"Are all your neighbors such busybodies?" Will asked, sounding annoyed with Vivian.

"Not all. Just three out of four or so." Vivian looked around the room. "I'm going to open the shades because that scared me worse than the guy hiding in our bushes."

"The imaginary guy hiding in your bushes," Will called out.

Vivian and Wren silently walked through the house, opening the shades with a *fffft*, while Will remained in the kitchen, reading. As Vivian was opening the last shade in Millie's room, finally filling the last room with light, she said very matter-of-factly. "I don't know if I can pull this off, Wren."

"What off?"

"This whole thing. I've got threatening messages from the Lynx, suspicious neighbors, deception. I just don't know."

Wren absorbed this in a very calm manner as she turned off the light, then quietly spoke as she followed Vivian out of the room. "Of course you can pull this off. You're the only one who can."

MARKET RESEARCH

The next day, Vivian slept in, went for a bike ride through town and then stopped in front of the movie theater downtown. She looked at the posters for a few minutes and noticed that one was about to start. She'd never gone to see a film by herself and made a point to enter the theater during the previews so it was dark and she could just sneak in. As much as she was embarrassed about seeing a movie by herself and potentially committing social suicide once again, it was something she really wanted to do. The movie itself – something about three teenaged girls who assume false identities and take a whirlwind trip to Europe where one falls in love with a prince – didn't matter. It was stupid and predictable and she enjoyed it thoroughly. Just to sit still for a couple of hours and stop thinking was a huge relief. Walking out into the late afternoon sun – thankfully it was a film popular with twelve-year-old girls and she was not recognized by anyone – she felt lighter. Riding her bike home, Vivian felt better than she had in months, but as she got closer to home, a bad feeling began to gnaw at her. She hurried home, legs churning, her mind racing with worries.

As soon as she walked into her home, she saw her mother sitting on the couch, looking as though she'd been crying, with balled up tissues on her lap and her father sitting next to her, looking very tired. Standing frozen in the doorway with her parents staring at her like she was a stranger, Vivian's heart pounded. Had the Lynx done something? Where was Millie?

"What, Mom? What's going on?" she said, looking back and forth between her parents, panic in her voice, and her hand still on the doorknob.

"Vivian, we need to talk," her father said gravely. "Come inside and shut the door."

Vivian stood still, immobilized with her anxiety. "What? What? Tell me what's going on."

Mr. and Mrs. Sharpe looked at each other. Mrs. Sharpe coughed a little, then sniffed. "Vivian, you have some explaining to do about yesterday. Mrs. Hannigan told us what she saw and we need to know your explanation."

Vivian never thought she would feel such a deep sense of relief under the circumstances. "You mean that my friends were over? That? Mrs. Hannigan blew that all out of proportion."

Mrs. Sharpe bolted upright, her eyes shiny and furious, pointing at her. "Shut that door right now. I'll be damned if the whole world is going to be exposed to this."

Vivian did as she was told, but remained frozen where she stood, her back pushed up against the door.

"We need to know what happened here. You had a young man over, from what I understand. A college student. I also understand from Millie that you were acting strange, running from room to room and shutting all the curtains. And that's how Mrs. Hannigan found you, in the house with the window shades drawn and a young man, a stranger to us, in our kitchen. With that Wren girl," she sighed then sniffed, "another friend we have never met."

Mr. Sharpe looked at his wife and she nodded. "You know fully well we would have never allowed this to happen – a young man in our home – unless there were an adult present. I'm surprised at you," her father said, and he looked at her in such a way, with such naked vulnerability, that she saw him in that instant as a child, the way he looked in the black-and-white photo of that skinny, serious-looking little boy sitting with his grandfather on a porch swing that sat on her parent's dresser. Her chest filled with the warmth she received from Tolstoy the last time she saw him and all she wanted to do was hug her father. She walked away from the door and sat in the chair facing her parents, her fingers interlaced.

"Can you explain yourself? Vivian, we're so very disappointed," Mrs. Sharpe said.

"I'm sorry," Vivian nearly whispered. "I tried to explain to Mrs. Hannigan that there was nothing to worry about, but I could see that she didn't believe me."

"Why should she have believed you?" Mrs. Sharpe almost shouted. She caught herself and lowered her voice again. "And what was this about that young man tutoring you in chemistry? Who is that boy?"

Vivian took a deep breath. The warmth in her chest was still there, helping her stay calm. "His name is Will. He's a friend of Wren and her family."

"Is he her boyfriend?"

"No."

"Is he your boyfriend?"

"No. No. He's just a friend."

"Why was he here without our permission, without us meeting him?" Mr. Sharpe asked. "I didn't realize that you needed a tutor."

"She doesn't, Roosevelt. That was a lie," Mrs. Sharpe said, rolling her eyes at his naïveté.

"It was a lie," Vivian calmly admitted. "He was here and Wren was here just to talk and visit. He's very interested in Gordenner."

Mrs. Sharpe laughed shrilly. "Interested in Gordenner? Another one? Nonsense. Who do you take us for? *Nobody's* interested in Gordenner. I have lived in this town my whole life and this is the most I've ever heard anyone talk of that place."

Vivian shrugged. She had nothing to say.

"Why were the shades drawn? And why did you run through the house doing that in a panic? Millie was scared out of her mind."

Vivian was silent for a moment. "I can't explain that, but I did have a reason."

"Are you in some sort of trouble?" her mother asked, very gravely.

"No. Mom, everything's fine. I just had to for a reason I can't explain right now."

"That's another lie. You told Mrs. Hannigan that Wren had a migraine, that's why the shades were drawn. I have never known you to lie, Vivian, not once." She stared at her daughter. "What are you hiding from us?"

Vivian rubbed her face, then realized that anything she did, any small gesture, would just make her look more guilty in her mother's eyes. "I can't talk about it but you're going to have to trust me."

"Trust you? Trust *you?*" Her mother sputtered. Mr. Sharpe put his hand on her wrist but she shook it away like a housefly. "First you have two young people come over to our house without our permission. I haven't even met either of them. Then you're running around shutting all the shades..."

"I actually did that first."

"– then you lie to our neighbor *twice*, who is genuinely concerned about what's going on. Why on earth should I trust you?"

Vivian felt her face get hot and her eyes sting. "Haven't I given you fifteen years of evidence that I could be trusted?" She rasped.

Mrs. Sharpe seemed to be anticipating this and pointed at Vivian furiously. "Do not pull that manipulative garbage on me, Vivian Sharpe. Oh, no. We are talking about the *here* and *now*," she punctuated the words by slapping her hand in the other open palm. "If you cannot give me a reasonable explanation of what happened yesterday, I am just going to have to go by the assumption that you can no longer be trusted."

Vivian looked at her father and he quickly looked away. She tried to maintain her composure, but tears were already blurring her vision. Her mother was crying now, too, something Vivian had only seen once or twice, and that made her cry more. She couldn't speak: her throat had clamped up. The three sat like that, Vivian and her mother crying and sniffling, Mr. Sharpe looking off into space, until he spoke after a painfully long silence. His voice was quiet and gravelly and strangely uncertain sounding.

"Vivian, I feel that you deserve the benefit of the doubt. You've always been a nice girl."

Vivian crossed her arms in front of her chest, insulted and embarrassed. She looked down, everything blurry, and tore at her tissue rather than respond. Mrs. Sharpe shot him a look, and he straightened his posture.

"We have to take a stand against this recent behavior, though, Vivian, especially as you've given us no reasonable explanation, as your mother said."

"Except that you could trust me," she croaked between sniffles.

"I'm sorry, Vivian, but that's just not sufficient given everything. We're your parents and you've never before really given us cause for alarm, but you are now. Unless we can understand and accept the reasons behind your behavior yesterday, we'll have no choice but to take some actions that we feel are necessary."

"Such as?"

Mr. Sharpe looked at his wife. She blew her nose and looked out the window.

"Vivian, we have given you a lot of latitude, but we're going to end that for now until we can see that we can trust you again."

Mrs. Sharpe joined in. "We don't like all this time you've been spending with that Wren girl."

Vivian felt her chest snap back like a rubber band. "That Wren girl," Vivian repeated, incredulous that someone could be so dismissive of her, "she's only my closest friend."

Mrs. Sharpe squared her shoulders. "Well, we're going to insist that you spend time apart, at least until the end of the month. We'll take it from there with consideration of your behavior for the next few weeks."

"Can I talk to her on the phone at least?"

"No. That is part of the deal. You two need a clean break for a couple of weeks. I need to see improvement first."

Vivian could feel her voice catch as she said, "Could I at least call her to tell her that I *won't* be calling her?"

Mrs. Sharpe looked at her husband; he shrugged. "I guess so. A quick call."

Vivian stared at the tissue she was compulsively pulling at in her hands. "And?"

"When you finish work at Gordenner, you come straight home or you tell us where you would like to be for our authorization," her mother said.

"I have to be *authorized* to go anywhere but here?"

"You did this to yourself by lying, Vivian. You did it to yourself. Believe me, we don't relish policing you any more than you want to be policed. We're your parents, though. If we find you in violation of any of these rules – contacting Wren, going someplace without our consent – we will revoke your internship at Gordenner, which was what I wanted to do in the first place but your father talked me out of it. But we are dead serious about all of this."

"I got that impression."

"Do *not* be sarcastic to us, not now," her mother warned, folding her arms across her chest. "You're in no position for that."

Her fathered quickly interjected, "We know that you're a good kid, Vivian..."

"Oh, dad. Please don't..." she hiccupped, red-faced.

"Don't coddle her, Roosevelt. And don't make me into the bad guy again, either."

"No, really, hear me out. We know that you're a good person." Mrs. Sharpe shot him a look that said she didn't know where he was going with this, so he straightened his posture and cleared his throat. "It's just that we're seeing things that alarm us and we have to nip this behavior in the bud for everyone's best interest."

Mrs. Sharpe nodded, temporarily mollified by her husband's choice of words. "This is not just for me and your father, Vivian. This is for you, too."

Vivian didn't say anything. Her temples throbbed and she felt like throwing up. They could hear the squeak of the screen door on the side of their house opening and Millie's fast little steps on the kitchen floor with another pair of feet. She was squealing with laughter with a friend. Mr. Sharpe looked grateful for the diversion. "Well, I should start dinner."

Mrs. Sharpe looked like she was going to say something to Vivian, then thought better of it. She stood silently and grabbed her discarded tissues with one hand.

"I guess that's it." She walked without another word into the kitchen.

Vivian went upstairs to her bedroom, shut the door and sat at her desk. She sat looking at the yellow telephone that just an hour ago would have been a direct line to Wren and for the first time in her life, she understood that it would feel supremely gratifying to throw her phone against the nearest wall with a loud, violent clank. She resisted that urge, knowing that that was all that stood between her and being forced to withdraw as an intern at Gordenner, and, instead, she took out her pen and stationery from her desk.

Lynx,

I realize that you think that I am just another loyal Gordenner employee, but I am not. It's too complicated to explain in this letter, but I know of their horrible activities. I also know about their plans for the future and they are indeed evil. I am working there to "infiltrate." You're going to have to believe me on this as I have no proof.

In the meantime, please stop sending threatening letters to me. This has been distracting me from my goals of exposing Gordenner. I have a little sister and parents and if I have to worry about their safety, my work will be much more complicated. I understand why you wouldn't have a reason to trust me on this, but you're going to have to so I can get my work done.

If you need to contact me again, please do not send letters to my home, where they can be easily found by someone else. My parents are very much on edge lately, and if I had to quit at Gordenner because they were worried for my safety, I could not be able to complete what I am there to do.

Thank you.

Sincerely,

Vivian Sharpe

She read the letter several times, mildly embarrassed by the pastel purple stationery with her monogram adorned with pink and yellow roses around the edges, but it would have to do. She sealed it in an envelope and hid it between some folders in her desk drawers, then she imagined Millie going through her desk, as she often did, so she took her letter, the two letters from the Lynx and the video and she put them in an old shoebox of hers that was stuffed with old mementos in the corner of her closet. Vivian remembered the locking drawer at her desk at work, and made a mental note to bring these with her the next day to Gordenner. She pulled her phone over to her bed and tried to call Wren, but no one answered the phone, and she was relieved for the most part. She was too enervated to face an endless stream of questions. She also realized that her parents' mandate wouldn't actually be that harsh: she could still talk to Wren from Gordenner. Vivian spent the evening moping and avoiding all contact with her parents. Wren left messages on the home line for Vivian that she had to ignore.

The next morning, Vivian woke up with a slight headache and vague sense of dread when her alarm rang at 6:30. She lay in bed, trying to figure out what was bothering her as the sunlight streamed in her bedroom and she heard a kitchen chair scrape against the floor, someone pushing away from the table. She came up empty. She just felt terribly alone. She remembered with some consolation that her mother would be at her early morning racquetball class at the health club that morning. At least she wouldn't have to face her.

After showering and getting dressed – she decided on a light grey dress her mother had bought her during a trip to New Dublin last year – Vivian went back to her room and transferred everything from her small purse to the larger shoulder bag. She shut the door and she moved the letters and videotape into her new bag. She zipped it shut and hung it from her chair as she started to go downstairs to the kitchen. Thinking better of it, she grabbed her bag and took it down with her. Millie sometimes liked to play dress-up with her bags, and though she most likely was still asleep, Vivian couldn't take that risk.

Vivian wordlessly joined her father in the kitchen. When she put her bagel in the toaster oven, Mr. Sharpe looked like he wanted to say something, but Vivian looked away. Once she realized that she was not angry with him, really, just embarrassed, it dawned on her that he was as well.

"Orange juice?" she asked as she poured some into her glass. He had an empty juice glass in front of him. He looked surprised, then grateful. He nodded.

"Thank you."

With the initial awkwardness vanquished for the most part, Mr. Sharpe pulled out the *Patriot*, Center City's daily newspaper, already folded open to the front page with a photo and caption. He handed it to Vivian.

"It looks like Robert Fontaine of Gordenner is back from his tour of Southeast Asia," he said. "Maybe you'll meet him today."

"I doubt it, but maybe," she mumbled. In the photograph, Mr. Fontaine was being greeted by someone – perhaps an employee, maybe a friend – at the Midland Airport in Center City, his suitcase in hand and a broad smile on his tanned face. The caption read:

Robert Fontaine, President of Gordenner, U.S.A., returns to Center City after a three-week business tour of Southeast Asia. (See story, page 9).

Vivian turned to the story. "Could I read this?"

"Of course." He rinsed his dishes and then walked out to the back yard to water the garden.

Yesterday marked the return of Robert Fontaine, president of Gordenner, U.S.A., to native soil and Center City. Mr. Fontaine, 42, spent three weeks touring Southeast Asia, spending time in Thailand, Laos, Myanmar (formerly known as Burma), Indonesia and Malaysia. The purpose of his travels? Being a beach bum? Enjoying the local cuisine?

"I toured Southeast Asia purely for business," Mr. Fontaine told The Patriot. "I fell in love with it once I was there – it's very beautiful, of course – but my purpose was to build a relationship between Gordenner and Southeast Asia."

Although Mr. Fontaine declined to elaborate, he did say that big news would be shared with the public in the coming weeks.

"It's a little early to get into now," he said, "but let me assure you that the news is pretty exciting and something I'm sure that all of Center City is going to be interested in learning about it. Gordenner is poised to become globally recognized as a leader in the fight against world hunger, and I'm very excited about our future."

Mr. Fontaine, the big-city boy is now dedicated to building Gordenner into a state-of-the-art facility and business, is certain not to disappoint.

Vivian had no appetite but forced down the rest of her bagel. She went back to her room and then remembered to bring a sweater along, as she would was expected to meet with Mr. Newell, and she made herself a hummus sandwich to bring to work for lunch.

As she waited at the bus stop that morning, the headache began to press into her temples. She took out the last letter from the Lynx, still in its opened envelope, and her letter to him. She had no idea how she was going to get this letter to the Lynx; it wasn't as if she could look him up in the phone book. Thinking about it, she turned the envelope from him over in her hands, studying the way it was folded, and took the letter out, the squarish black letters slightly smudged on the oatmeal-colored Gordenner letterhead. With the letter in her hands, she closed her eyes for a moment and rubbed her temples, trying to ease the headache, when she saw a flash of something in her mind: something green and pointy like a plant, a fern. Seeing that, just for a millisecond, filled her body with a flash of anger, like a thunderbolt. She opened her eyes, baffled, wondering if she had fallen asleep for a moment. Vivian closed her eyes again, and the plant came back, this time with a slightly wider scene around it, of a few more plants and water. Vivian felt very much like she could be losing her mind. She opened her eyes to check for the bus, and, it being nowhere in sight, closed her eyes again; what she had seen in her mind's eye looked familiar to her, and, without realizing it at first, made her hands clench in rage and her pulse quicken.

It went back-and-forth like this, and Vivian became frustrated with the headache and the picture that would emerge every time she closed her eyes, because all she wanted to do was concentrate on how she was going to reach the Lynx. As soon as she'd try to concentrate, the same sequence would repeat, like there was a hidden magnet pulling her mind a certain way without her control. In a flash, she got an idea: She put the letter from the Lynx down on the bench and she closed her eyes, concentrating on the question of how to contact the Lynx. This time no picture emerged and her emotions remained unchanged. She just heard the sounds of the street traffic passing her. Vivian picked up the letter again, held it in her hands, and closed her eyes, again asking herself how to reach the Lynx: this time, a clearer picture came to her, of plants and dirty water and dead fish in a stream. This time, the anger made her shake. Her eyes popped open as she heard the loud rumble of the bus pulling up and the door opening; she realized that she had seen the stream with the pipe in it behind the Gordenner plant, and she had experienced it through the eyes of the Lynx. It also was clear to her that this stream was where she needed to leave her letter for him to find.

As she put her change in the bus meter, the friendly driver from Friday smiled at her, "Daydreaming, were you?"

Vivian was still a little stunned and slow in returning to her body. She didn't know what to say, so she didn't say anything.

"I saw you a block away sitting at the bus stop with your eyes closed," he said, pulling back into traffic, his eyes in the mirror. "I could have sworn you were either daydreaming or asleep."

"Oh. Yeah," she yawned. "I'm still adjusting to my new schedule."

She sat near the back of the bus and practiced holding onto the letter while keeping her eyes open to see if she could still get the same sort of response as she did when her eyes were closed. She thought about the Lynx, what she imagined of him, a big, enraged figure with wild eyes and unruly hair. She cobbled together this form, and it felt false: nothing resonated. She had no emotions, no images jumped to her mind. When she held the envelope and just let it unfold by itself, feeling the grainy paper between her fingers, she was able to reach that state she was in when the bus arrived. Even with her eyes open, she could faintly see the plants and water, as though through a veil, and, the next time, with her eyes closed, she saw very clearly a big boot splash through the water, and she thought she heard it as well; it was so vivid she almost jumped. It was the same muddy brown boot she saw on the video he sent her. Vivian opened her eyes to see the bus driver looking at her through his mirror. They both looked away immediately.

She spent the rest of the bus ride in a daze – a little frightened, a little excited – and barely remembered getting off the bus or being buzzed into the parking lot by the security guard. She must have, though, because she found herself being greeted by Betty, the woman behind the front desk, dressed in a bright red dress, after she was buzzed in.

"Good morning, hon. Vivian, right?"

"That's right. And you're Betty?"

Betty smiled. "That's right." Then she stood up and lowered her voice. "Hold out your hand. I have a surprise for you."

Vivian obliged and Betty placed a small chocolate cookie in her palm. "Just made them this morning," she said. "It's my Monday morning tradition. Makes getting through the week..."

The instant that the cookie was placed in her palm, all Vivian could feel was misery: chickens driven crazy in their cages, a cow screaming for her calf. The images flashed through her mind at lightning speed, nearly knocking her over; she was also acutely aware of Betty standing in front of her, still talking, but Vivian couldn't hear her. It was as if there were a Vivian doll standing there in her place and she was outside it all, watching. Vivian held it together the best she could, attempting to approximate a smile, trying to not look horrified. Her heart raced; she felt like a captive animal. In her mind, she saw a chicken, her skin rubbed raw against metal bars, blink from behind a cage, and Vivian's skin burned at the bottom of her feet. Betty stopped talking and looked at her quizzically, her head cocked to the side.

"I'm going to have this at lunch. Oh, I'm late," she looked up at the clock. "Thank you, Betty." Vivian hurried to the elevator and dropped the cookie in her purse until she could safely throw it away. Shaking as she opened her purse, she realized that her other hand still was holding the letter from the Lynx, so she put that away first. As soon as she did, the images, the terrible sounds, disappeared, as though running down a drain, even though she was still holding the cookie. She touched the envelope again to see what would happen, and it all flooded back into her again. Vivian wasn't aware that another woman was waiting at the elevator with her. When she got inside, all she wanted to do was take a deep breath and lean against the wall for a few moments, but she couldn't. She had to smile politely. As soon as she got off, though, she rushed to the women's restroom and threw the cookie away. Then Vivian washed her hands and sank into a chair against the wall. She didn't want to cry – she felt really nervous about being discovered crying in the bathroom – but she couldn't avoid it. She went into a stall and cried, hoping that no one else would walk in but not able to stop herself either.

She splashed some water on a paper towel, dabbed her face with it, took a few more deep breaths, and walked back out onto the main floor. It felt like being awakened from a bad dream. Walking down the hall, which was starting to become familiar to her, she realized with a little relief that her headache was gone.

Vivian walked into her office, and it felt so strange to identify the space as hers, though it was. She walked over to Ms. Collins' office and saw her on the phone; Ms. Collins waved to her, rolled her eyes melodramatically and made a mouth-moving motion with her hand. Vivian smiled and slid the market research report quickly into its folder, locked up the materials the Lynx sent her and then checked her messages. There were twelve messages, all for Ms. Collins, and Vivian diligently followed the format as outlined in her phone manual and message pad. She found comfort in doing rote work. There was nothing particularly noteworthy in any of the messages; they were mostly from various printers, a few newspaper reporters wanting more information for stories, and a couple of people returning her calls without much of a message. By the time Vivian had finished jotting down the messages, Ms. Collins – with her short hair spiky and magenta lipstick and shiny lime green pantsuit, she seemed electric – was standing by her desk, tapping her foot in her high heels a little impatiently.

"Hi, Ms. Collins. I've got your messages here." Ms. Collins very briefly skimmed the messages, occasionally mumbling to herself.

"Why is she calling me again? Oh, okay. Mmm," she looked up. "Good morning, Vivian," Ms. Collins said, folding the paper in quarters and then absent-mindedly tucking it between her middle and index finders. "So, let's talk about today, shall we?"

Vivian nodded.

"All right, Kevin – remember, Mr. Newell? Well, we've got you scheduled to meet with the two of us at 1:30 for that market research we talked about. So, why don't you leave for lunch a little earlier than usual, like 12:30, so afterwards, just go down that hallway past the sculpture to where the market research rooms are, and we'll meet you in room 604 at 1:30. Is that okay?"

"Sounds good. Anything I should bring with me?"

"Nothing. Just an open mind," she said, running a hand through her hair. "So this morning, I'd like you to concentrate on getting some copies made for me up in the copier room, and then, could you drop this off with Kyle?" She handed Vivian a yellow envelope. It had Mr. Fontaine's name written across the front. "Oh, this reminds me. Mr. Fontaine is back today. I'm sure that you won't meet him, but in case you notice people being a little more busy than usual, that's why. I'm supposed to be meeting with him this morning, probably for an hour or so. If you need me, well, don't page me unless it's absolutely necessary. But you remember how to page, right?"

Vivian nodded and pointed to her phone. "The blue button."

"That's right." She pulled out some papers. "I'll need 12 copies of this, front and back, and another 12 copies of this one." Ms. Collins grabbed a package of sticky notes, writing down the number and sticking them to the papers. She looked up and took a deep breath, then wrote *Room 604, 1:30* on another. Almost as an afterthought, she said, looking up, "And how was your weekend, Vivian?"

"Oh, fine. Kind of boring. And yours? How was New Dublin?"

"Lovely, lovely." She handed the papers back to Vivian. "Now you remember how to get to the copier room, right? Good. When you get back from the copier room, I've got some more for you to file, just like you did last time. Chronological. I'll just leave it on your desk. Okay?"

"Got it."

"Okay, Vivian, I'll see you when you get back unless I'm with Mr. Fontaine, in which case I'll see you after that."

"Sounds good."

"Thanks," Ms. Collins said before heading back to her office.

Vivian took a detour into the women's restroom with the papers in tow. She sat in a stall reading them; one was labeled "Strategic Plan: Phase One of Bountiful Wheat" and the other sheet was labeled "Media Plan: Phase One of Bountiful Wheat." She could hear someone in the stall next to her and the water running at the sink, so she was unable to concentrate. She would have to find a way to smuggle one of each home, too.

In the copier room, Vivian found Nadine standing with stooped shoulders amid the dozens of machines, many of which were spitting out paper in a staccato order or flashing bright lights as they worked on their assignments, all whirring fans and beeping. Nadine, her glasses edging down her nose, squinted at Vivian like she couldn't quite place her.

"I met you Friday..." Vivian said helpfully.

Nadine moved closer, not able to hear Vivian, looking vaguely annoyed.

"I was just saying that I met you Friday. I'm Ms. Collins' intern, Vivian."

Nadine nodded in such a way that it seemed like she still didn't remember meeting Vivian but that was neither here nor there.

"Are you here to make some copies?" she asked, looking down at Vivian's papers.

"Yes..."

"And did I teach you the system?"

"Yes, you did. I was just coming in to fill out the forms now." Vivian started writing, filling out the form, when Nadine sighed. It was the sort of sigh that made Vivian look up, thinking that she meant for it to be noticed. Nadine ran a palm across the stray hairs that had come loose from her ponytail.

"Now that Mr. Fontaine's back in town, suddenly everyone has to make a million copies of their various projects. I sent out a memo last week asking people not to overwhelm the system today, but I guess it went unnoticed." She had little black specks of mascara already dusting her cheekbones, and looked genuinely fatigued at just after 9:00 a.m.

"Oh, I'm sorry. I'm just..."

"I know," she cut Vivian off. "You're just doing what you're told, as you should. It's not your fault. I'm just a little aggravated. I'll get over it." She started to say something else but a machine started making a disquieting *thwap-thwap-thwap* sound, adding to the polyrhythm of the room. Nadine whipped around on her heels, like a teacher ruffled by a disobedient student, craning her neck and scanning the room to locate the errant copier. "Jammed again," she sighed. "*Again.* Just leave that in the basket. It probably won't get back to Ms. Collins before this afternoon at the earliest the way things stand."

"Okay," Vivian said. Then she felt that she should say she was sorry, so she did, but Nadine was kneeling by a copier and pulling out jammed sheets of paper with a grimace, so she couldn't hear her. Vivian hurried out of the room to Kyle's office.

"Hello, young miss," Kyle smiled from behind his enormous desk. "And to what do I owe the pleasure of your visit on this lovely morn?"

Vivian nearly blushed. Instead, she fumbled around for the envelope Ms. Collins directed her to give him. "This is for you, from Ms. Collins. Actually, it's for Mr. Fontaine. For you to give him."

He scanned the envelope quickly and set it on his desk. He glanced back at Mr. Fontaine's office with the door shut. "Still in a meeting. I will get it to him ASAP, though. How was your weekend?"

"Uneventful. And yours?"

"Oh, I did a lot of yard work, which was fine but not very exciting."

"Do you live here in town?"

He nodded. "Yeah, we've got an old Victorian we're restoring not far from where you live, actually. Bought it for a song two years ago. It's on Lincoln, near the old Lutheran church there."

"Oh. I know where you mean."

"The yellow one with the wraparound porch. A big magnolia in front."

Vivian thought for a moment. "I'm pretty sure I know the one. It's really pretty. Do you live there with your wife?" She immediately was embarrassed for asking such a personal question, but Kyle seemed unfazed.

"Nope. I'm not married. Just a roommate and two little yappy dogs, one elderly dog and one grouchy cat."

"That's cool. Thanks for getting the letter to Mr. Fontaine for me."

"Oh, you're welcome, Vivian. See you later."

Just seeing Kyle, with his smile that always seemed to convey that they were in on a secret joke together, made Vivian feel better, a little lighter. Walking back to her office, she was thinking about him, how he was the sort of person who put everyone at ease, the sort of person who always seemed unbothered by the world – perfect for Wren, really, except too old – when she remembered the letter in her purse that she would have to try to get to the stream behind Gordenner for the Lynx to find. Fear and dread settled into her stomach like a hot stone.

She organized the reports, which went back in time to when Ms. Collins started at Gordenner, and they seemed to average three or four market research reports each week. Some were about how the public perceived Gordenner (*"Seven of the ten surveyed agreed with the statement, 'Gordenner is a company that cares about feeding the world', while three stated that they had no proof of that assertion,"*) and others were about specific products (*"Ten of twelve in the survey agreed that a warning on a bottle of herbicide that one's yard would not be safe for use for four hours after spraying would make them apprehensive about purchasing the product."*). Vivian took her time filing them in the cabinet and checked her messages. There were two for Ms. Collins and one for Vivian, from Wren. Her heart sunk a little hearing her upbeat voice, not knowing that Vivian had been barred from communicating with her, not knowing any of it. Vivian returned her call when everything was filed, her heart feeling like it was anchored low in her chest.

"Hey, Vivian. How's it going?" Vivian could hear a dog barking in the background. "Shhh, Buck. I've been calling you at home but no one answers. So are you at work? What's going on?"

"Yep, I'm here. I can't talk long, though."

"I understand. So what's new?"

"Nothing much." She didn't know what to say.

"So how's everything? How are you?"

"Okay…"

"You sound weird. Is someone in the room?"

"No."

"Well, something's the matter. You don't sound like yourself."

Vivian looked out into the hallway from her office. No one was nearby. She swerved in her chair sideways from the window. "Oh, yeah, I guess I got grounded. Can you even believe that?"

"Grounded? Why?"

Vivian lowered her voice. "Because – well, it's a long story – but my parents found out that you guys were over Saturday…"

"So?"

"Well, I guess that Mrs. Hannigan – remember that neighbor of mine?"

"Yes?"

"Well, she made a big production out of coming to the house and finding you guys there with the shades drawn. Like I was doing something wrong, sneaking behind their backs or something."

"So she didn't buy that I had a headache?"

"I guess not. And she got my parents all upset, so I'm grounded. I've almost never even been grounded before. I have to come home after work every day or get permission for anything else…"

"No," Wren sounded aghast.

"Yes. And," she added quietly, as if her parents might overhear, "I'm actually not allowed to talk to you, either."

"Why not?"

"I don't know," Vivian sighed. "Like I think that they think that you were secretly responsible in some way. I have no idea. Like I was such a good kid until I met you."

"What did I do?"

"Nothing. Nothing. They're just trying to understand what's going on, I guess, and I can't tell them anything to explain things, you know?"

"Huh..."

"So I can't talk to you for the month."

Wren was silent, stung. "Well, it doesn't sound fair at all. You're trying to do the right thing and you're getting punished."

"I know but I can't explain anything to them."

"You don't think that my talking to them would help at all?"

Vivian got a mental image of Wren in her tie-dyed dress trying to talk to her mother and chuckled a little. "No. I don't think that would help the cause."

"So what then? This is awful."

"Well, I know. It is. But I'm trying to stay positive. I think that it'll give me a chance to really concentrate on what I need to do here, you know? Like, I figured out that I'm going to leave my note for the Lynx at the creek out in back..."

"No! The one with the pipe?"

"Yep. I'm going to leave it there for the Lynx, and I think that I really need to be able to focus to get this done. It works out for the best, I think, just being on my own for a little while."

"A: that totally hurts my feelings," Wren said, her voice choking, like she was going to cry.

"No, Wren..."

"It's not you, it's me, right? Anyway, a: that totally hurts my feelings and b: do you think that is safe? Going out to the creek by yourself? What if he's there?"

Vivian hadn't considered that. "I guess I'll have to just deal with him if he is. He's fine. It's fine. And I don't want you to worry or have your feelings hurt."

Wren was quiet for a few moments, until she sniffed. "How can I not? And that dude is *not* fine."

"You're just going to have to trust me," Vivian said, shaking her head at how often she'd had to say those words recently. "I will take care of myself and I will be careful. You know that I'll be careful."

"Uh, Vivian, I don't know that. Like with that guy at the flea market? That wasn't careful."

Vivian was surprised: she hadn't thought of him for weeks. "I am not going to fight with the Lynx, okay. I'll do what needs to be done. I will take care of myself. You have to trust me."

"Couldn't we at least do something like if I don't hear from you by a certain time, I'll call the police or something? What time do you think you'd be back?"

"I'm not sure. Maybe 2:45? I have a market research thing straight afterwards and I have to leave by 3:00." Vivian didn't like the thought of Wren calling the police, but she felt that she had to compromise a little. "Let's say I'll call you by 2:45, okay?"

"That sounds okay," Wren said grudgingly.

Vivian lowered her voice again. "You know, also, Wren, you're my best friend and I don't want you to ever think that I'm trying to shut you out. This is just a temporary setback. You're my best friend and I totally think the world of you." Vivian realized that she hadn't told anyone she was her best friend since she was in fourth grade. She felt a little embarrassed, but she was glad she said it.

Wren sniffed and the phone sounded muffled, like she was wiping her nose. "And you're mine. I don't know what I'd do without you. That's why this has been so sad to hear. I thought that I was finally going to have a friend my age to hang out with this summer."

"Come on. Don't be sad. Don't be sad. This is all going to go away soon and we're going to still have a terrific summer."

"Do you promise? After your whistle-blowing exposé on the evening news, right?"

"Well, yeah, but still. I promise. We'll have a great summer after everything."

Neither said anything until Vivian said, "Well, I'd better get going."

"Okay. Call me later."

"I will."

"Be safe."

"I will."

"Promise?"

"I promise."

Just as Vivian was ready to hang up the phone, Wren called out to her.

"Yes?"

"Just don't... don't..."

"I won't do anything stupid."

Vivian took a few minutes fighting back tears, reassuring herself that this was only temporary, and then she answered the phone for a bit, taking messages from busy people, until it was time for her lunch break. She unlocked the drawer and took out the last letter from the Lynx and the one she wrote him, writing his name across the envelope. Almost as an afterthought, she took a roll of tape from her desk and put it in her purse. She grabbed her sweater for later and took the elevator down to the first floor, passing dozens of offices full of talking voices, ringing phones, the harsh beeps of numbers on speakerphone being dialed. Opening a back door, she heard the gush of water pouring out of pipes into the river, and she saw the place where she had stood with Will and Wren a couple of weeks before. She quickly walked down to the bridge over the river, crossing it, and resisted the urge to look over her shoulder. Her headache was back but she had to keep walking; each time her foot stepped down, her head throbbed a little more. She decided that if she were discovered, most likely by the security guard, she would tell him that she was just taking a lunch-hour walk. She didn't think that there were any rules against taking a walk in the woods. At least she hoped there weren't. Vivian distracted herself from the headache and the gnawing fear by making mental lists: of her favorite ten movies, of her favorite ten songs, of her least favorite to her most favorite holidays (her least enjoyed was Thanksgiving now that she was a vegan; her favorite was still Halloween), the five reasons she'd give the Lynx to trust her. This last one was hardest.

It seemed to be a quicker trip to the creek this time. She started to know it was nearby when she noticed the change in the environment around her and could faintly hear water trickling. She felt like she might actually enjoy this walk if it didn't make her feel like vomiting. Before walking through the bushes, Vivian reached in her purse to get the letter from the Lynx out to see if she could pick up anything, but she couldn't find it anywhere. She had her letter back to him, but his to her was nowhere to be found. She must have left it back in her office, she realized with no small amount of anxiety, but she had come this far: she would have to leave the letter behind anyway. She found a stick with a pointed end and held it close by her side, her hand tight around it. She walked between the bushes out to the creek.

"Hello?" she said, tentatively at first, then growing louder. "Are you there? Actually, I don't care whether you are or not. I'm leaving you a letter, okay?" Nothing noticeable changed, and the sickening, putrid stench of the creek made her almost reel. Her heart racing, she breathed out of her mouth as she found another stick to tape the letter on to, her eyes tearing. "Sir, I don't know if you're here or not, but this is for you. I'm here to try to stop this, too." She jammed the stick in the dirt and taped the envelope onto the end of it. She thought she saw something move, and she inhaled as she gasped, making her cough, but it was just a little flash in the water, probably a fish floating past. She was determined not to look into the water as she was sure that would sap whatever strength it would take to get back to Gordenner. "Okay, this is for you. I'm going now." She took one last little breath. "Please read it, okay?"

With that, Vivian hurried back between the bushes, heading back to the building. Her headache diminished as she walked, and, just as last time, her stomach hurt. Once she had walked for a few minutes and there was a reasonable distance between her and the creek, she sat on a log with her head hanging down between her knees. Finally standing with wobbly legs, Vivian almost found herself wishing that she would throw up so she could at least get some relief. The farther she walked from the creek, though, the more she noticed the feeling recede. By the time she was back to the building, she was almost fully recovered. She checked the time – she had twenty minutes left before she'd have to leave for the market research meeting – so she want to the restroom and washed her hands, wanting to wash off the smell of the creek in case it was on her somehow. She had no way to know if the awful smell clung to her clothes or not, but, going into the cafeteria and sitting in the corner, no one seemed to pay any special attention to her. As usual, she was barely noticed at all and had to hurry out of the way a few times to avoid being walked into by people walking and talking with their trays in front of them. Vivian sat at a corner table, ate the sandwich she had stashed in her purse, and watched the clock. A few minutes before she was due in room 604, she wrapped up the other half of her sandwich. She wasn't hungry but her stomach felt more settled after she had eaten so she was grateful for that as she walked to the room.

Mr. Newell, wearing a dark grey suit that made his bluish complexion look quite stark against it, was already in the room, reading some notes when Vivian walked in. Ms. Collins was not in the room yet, and, as Vivian walked in, she was instantly reminded of the strange phenomenon of Mr. Newell: the blast of arctic cold she felt in his presence. He looked up, a faint frown on his face at being distracted, muttered a quick hello, then turned back to his papers. Vivian, unsure of what to do, stood there for a few moments until he looked up distractedly and said, "I still have some more reading to do if you don't mind. Have a seat and when Ms. Collins gets here, we'll get started."

Vivian sat down and quickly threw on her sweater. Every time Mr. Newell turned a page, the cold air intensified. She tried to distract herself but all she could think of was the prickly sensation in her arms where her goosebumps pushed into her sweater like pinpricks, and she vowed to bring a thicker sweater next time to keep at work. Vivian wished that she had something to read, just something to occupy herself with, when she glanced around the room and saw that there was a coffee and hot water station set up with tea. She was not particularly fond of tea – and the few sips of coffee she'd ever had made her gag – but she wanted something to do and something to warm her up.

As Vivian was throwing out the tea wrapper, Ms. Collins rushed into the room and closed the door behind her, glancing up hurriedly at the clock. "Sorry I'm a few minutes late, Kevin. There was a misunderstanding I had to clear up with the printer. Idiot. Hi, Vivian." Ms. Collins threw her bag, papers and folders onto the table loudly. "You guys almost ready? Oh, that looks good. Vivian, could I get a cup of coffee? Black's fine."

"Give me a minute, Laura. Just getting up to speed. Thirty seconds," Mr. Newell said, tracing the lines he was reading with a finger. Something crossed Vivian's mind with the tone of his voice and the little pushing away from the table he did as Ms. Collins walked in: *he doesn't like her.*

She carried back the two drinks and sat next to Ms. Collins, who looked up from her appointment book and thanked Vivian, then turned back to it for a second before she noticed her intern again in her sweater. "Cold again? You look healthy otherwise. You must be thin-skinned. I used to think I was, but maybe I'm not anymore."

"Maybe that's it."

"Drink up." She clinked her coffee cup against Vivian's cup playfully.

Mr. Newell tapped his papers together against the table, organizing them. "Okay, I'm ready." He looked over at Vivian. "Thank you for being here. Now, you understand what we're doing, right?"

"Market research. Is that what you mean?" Vivian tried not to shiver.

"Yes, that's right. Our purpose today is to try to gauge a young person's point of view about a new product we're releasing. Market research is particularly crucial at this stage of the game, before we finalize our PR plan." Mr. Newell stood and walked toward the corner of the room where a tripod stood with a large black portfolio balanced on it. Mr. Newell's effect on her was not so severe when he crossed the room, Vivian realized with some relief. She sipped her tea and concentrated on staying calm – she felt as if there were a hummingbird darting against her ribcage – while Mr. Newell opened the portfolio, took out a large spiral-bound book and leaned it on the stand, opening it to a graphic of the earth.

"Now, before we start, I would like to ask that you speak honestly, Vivian," Mr. Newell said. "Remember that we are simply trying to get your natural responses to what we show you. It's very important for our data that you do not try to tell us what you think we may want to hear. There are no right or wrong answers."

"Just be honest," Ms. Collins added, taking a pair of red-framed glasses out of a case in her purse and putting them on. Vivian nodded; she had never seen her wear glasses before.

"Okay," Mr. Newell said, pointing to the picture, "this is Planet Earth. On this earth, there are oceans and mountains and tundras. Those of us in the room live in what many call the 'breadbasket of the world'. The soil is rich and crop growth is abundant. Not everyone is so fortunate, though. Many people, either due to poverty or drought or crop failure, cannot feed themselves or their families. They become malnourished and die prematurely, maybe even starve to death," he said very woodenly as he glanced back at his notes before continuing. "In the past, people would have thrown fundraisers or given loans to these countries, and that might help them for the short term, but not for the long term. Gordenner is committed to feeding the world, though, and we think that we could eradicate world hunger with..."

"And starvation, Kevin. Don't forget to hammer that home. Not just hunger: *starvation*." Ms. Collins smiled a little apologetically to Vivian. "Sorry."

He lost his place and looked stricken for a moment. Then he glanced back at his notes, wrote in a word and continued. "We could eradicate starvation and world hunger - "

"Thank you."

"- with just two products. Two products that the best and the brightest scientists have labored over for years to bring to market." He turned the page to another sheet, one with a drawing of a bag and a spray bottle on it, both with colorful packaging. "Bountiful Wheat and Bountiful Spray." He paused to look at the image on the paper as though that was stage direction he had rehearsed. "Vivian, I'd like to pause for a moment to ask, what does the word 'bountiful' mean to you?"

Vivian was taken by surprise. She wasn't expecting to speak so soon. "Bountiful? Um. Plenty. Abundant."

"Very good," Mr. Newell said, like a high school teacher. "The name of our new product line was very consciously chosen because our research shows us that our products will help to create an abundant yield for the farming communities using them. People who even a year ago would have been in serious jeopardy with a bad crop season will now be able to not only sustain their families, but keep them in good health and relative prosperity. All thanks to some seeds and a simple spray application."

He paused as though to wait for Vivian's response. She nodded. "Mmm…"

"So, Vivian," Ms. Collins said energetically, turning to face her, "what we want to know is what are your feelings at hearing this? Hearing that Gordenner has developed a breakthrough technology that can feed the world in virtually any climate. I remember in the 1980s seeing images of starving Ethiopians with their bloated bellies, and it was the saddest thing ever. I felt so helpless. With Bountiful, there would be no Ethiopia. I mean, there would be an Ethiopia, of course," she laughed a little, "but there would be no starvation in Ethiopia."

"Well, I'd think that that was a good thing."

"A good thing indeed. And it's not only creating a reliable food supply, but as Mr. Newell hinted at, this product, these seeds, are enhanced with folic acid, to ensure healthy babies, and various other vitamins that might be scarce in more impoverished nations. So they'd not only be fed, but be fed well. How does that make you feel? What do you think about that?"

Vivian was quiet, thinking for a few moments.

"Tell us quickly. We need your gut reaction," Ms. Collins prompted.

Vivian paused, then said, "I think that's incredible."

"You're right. Anything else?"

"Not right at the moment."

Vivian thought that Mr. Newell might have rolled his eyes at her. "Okay, Vivian, now I want to go into greater depth about this. When partnered with the spray, our Bountiful seeds grow wheat crops that are resistant to both drought and flooding: that means they can be grown in very dry or very wet conditions. And the seeds are enriched with crucial B vitamins – without which you'd have chronic fatigue and heart palpitations – as well as the RDA of folic acid, which prevents birth defects. Spina bifida. The spray will knock out any kind of threat: it's a very potent insecticide, plus an herbicide. It kills any weed that might threaten it for miles around and..."

"Hmm," Vivian said.

"Yes?" He looked irritated and a little surprised at being interrupted by her.

She was determined to ignore the sharp line between his eyebrows. "If it kills any weed, isn't that a threat to other crops?" Vivian remembered what Will had said about monocropping and making the other nations dependent on this one food source.

"Umm..." Mr. Newell looked down at his notes. Ms. Collins crossed her legs impatiently.

"I mean, these other countries, they're going to grow crops other than this wheat, right?"

Mr. Newell looked perplexed, then smiled unexpectedly, an expression that looked like he could have pulled it out of his shirt pocket, it seemed so unnatural on his face. "See, Vivian, that's the beauty of this seed and spray. Working together, it's incredibly efficient. The spray will knock out any threat, and the seed – this single seed – will produce all the RDA of folic acid and other B vitamins. They won't need other grains because they can get all they need from one source."

"Oh, I understand," Vivian nodded.

"Okay, so what I was..."

"But, it's just...hmm."

"What, Vivian?" Ms. Collins asked. "What is it?"

"I don't quite get it," Vivian said, and as she spoke, she became less and less concerned about Mr. Newell's furrowed forehead and Ms. Collins' impatient legs shifting. It was like Vivian's mouth was moving and the words were coming out, and it felt like she knew what she was saying, but she had no idea *how* she knew what she was saying. "What about those who are wheat intolerant? What if this Bountiful Wheat becomes the main crop of a country and because all these other grains have been neglected for Bountiful to thrive, what will those people eat for their B vitamins?"

"We're working with a pharmaceutical company to develop a new product for that very concern, Vivian," Ms. Collins said, tilting her head quizzically and staring at Vivian for a moment. It was clear that she was caught off guard. "It will help those with gluten intolerance to better digest the wheat and absorb the nutrients. That should be out at the same time the Bountiful products are released."

"Won't that cost something? I mean, if you're talking about impoverished people…"

"Yes, it'll cost something," Ms. Collins said, squinting at Vivian with some irritation, "but those details don't matter right now. We need to focus on Bountiful." She nodded at Mr. Newell, who started talking again when Vivian interrupted and said,

"I'm sorry. I don't mean to interrupt, but I have more questions."

Mr. Newell pantomimed a little wheel with his hand, indicating that she should continue.

"Okay, so my next question is what if there is a crop failure? What if some unforeseeable thing happens…"

"Nothing unforeseeable will happen, Vivian," Ms. Collins said emphatically, shaking her head in disbelief. "Gordenner has been studying this and all possible variables and scenarios for years now. This is not some junior high science project or something."

"So I'll just assume that you're right. But what about other factors? Like what if there's one sort of bug that pollinates the citrus plants, for example, and the Bountiful Spray kills all them? Then they've lost their vitamin C source. Or what if the spray attacks the, I don't know, carrot crop as a weed. What about their vitamin A and their eyesight?" Vivian just had to assume that carrots supplied vitamin A and that that was responsible for vision because that was what she was saying so assuredly.

Ms. Collins smacked her hand down on the table, and Vivian wasn't sure whether it was in anger or to emphasize her next point, but it was startling enough to give her a jolt. She spoke calmly but with obvious annoyance. "Vivian, dear, I assure you, these details will have been addressed by our science department. That is not why we're here. We're representing marketing and product development here. I appreciate your concerns, but our main point today was to get your initial reactions to our product."

"I understand but I can't tell you that unless I ask these other questions."

Ms. Collins looked at Mr. Newell and he, very consciously to Vivian, scratched his chin and adopted a more thoughtful mien, like a hammy actor in a play. "This has been very helpful for us to understand what issues people might have, Vivian. Thank you."

Vivian shrugged. "You're welcome."

"Before we get into all the nitty-gritty of the questions you're asking, though, I just want to know if we're on the same page about something: That starvation is an atrocity. Do you agree?"

"I do."

"I mean, it must be difficult for you to imagine what it's like, a comfortable high school student in the United States, never having gone hungry, what starvation might feel like, and I think that this is why you're having these doubts and problems grasping the seriousness of the issue."

Vivian didn't say anything.

"I am interested to know, though, if you can imagine what it would be like to starve to death. To watch your family starve to death, your future children."

Vivian shook her head.

"Well, I hope that you will never have to face that particular challenge, Vivian. Robert Fontaine, our CEO, just returned from Southeast Asia, where he saw starvation up close and saw how these new products would have an immediate and positive effect on the communities there. You can't imagine the poverty there; it would be beyond your comprehension. The reason why we are so eager to release these products is so that we can do our part to put an end to starvation. Pure and simple. We are giving people not only an immediate way out of the cycle of poverty and hunger, but also a tool for the future for their self-sufficiency."

"See, it's not just a concept to us, Vivian," Ms. Collins said, nodding enthusiastically. "We're trying to stamp out starvation with these Bountiful products and encourage self-sustaining communities. Can you imagine if your generation didn't have to worry about feeding the world because that problem was solved? That would be one less thing to worry about, a quality of life improvement that would be so invaluable, so unimaginable up until now, it cannot be fully grasped at this point. It'll be huge. Enormous."

Vivian wasn't sure what to say: in her mind, she saw an image of the ducks she found in the river and the sewage pumping into the creek. She nodded.

Mr. Newell turned to another page, one of a red dirt road with a brown-skinned woman and her baby sitting on her lap. The baby was crying, wet streaks running down his dusty cheeks, and the mother had her hands stretched out, seemingly pleading to the photographer, asking for something.

"So, Vivian, have we established that you believe it's unacceptable that people are starving to death in this day and age?"

"Yes."

"I'm going to break from script a little more, if you don't mind," he said to Ms. Collins. She frowned a little but nodded. "We're figuring out the other research group based partially on this one and I want to see what works best."

He fiddled with his notes for about a minute. Vivian and Ms. Collins smiled awkwardly at one another, then Vivian occupied herself with her cup of tea and Ms. Collins got more coffee. Finally looking up, Mr. Newell said, "Do you agree that feeding hungry people is worth anything, Vivian?"

Vivian knew that she was being led somewhere. She remained silent, looking at him like she was unsure of his question. She had to just accept that she might look stupid in their eyes.

"In other words," Ms. Collins jumped in, understanding where he was going, "that above everything, that hunger and starvation must be eradicated."

Vivian nodded.

Ms. Collins said, "Regardless of extenuating circumstances, the main drive is to keep people alive and healthy. Right?"

Vivian took a sip of her tea to try to calm her heart, which started thumping madly. "Do you mean that there are circumstances related to Bountiful?" she asked as calmly as she could.

Mr. Newell looked at Ms. Collins, but she seemed very intent on avoiding his eye contact, and she kept hers locked on Vivian. "What I mean is that the benefits of Bountiful Wheat and Spray would override any potential…"

"Criticisms," Mr. Newell said.

After a few moments, Vivian said, "I guess I would have to know what those criticisms are before answering."

Ms. Collins pressed on. "Vivian, if you came across someone today, say, on your walk home from the bus, and that person said to you, 'Young lady, I am hungry, I have two children and I have no food,' would you play twenty questions with the person? Would you ask this and that?"

"Probably not."

"Right. You wouldn't," Ms. Collins said gently. "You've got a big heart; I do too. The reason I came to Gordenner in the first place, quit the job I loved in New Dublin to come here is because I wanted to use my skills to get this product, which is really going to change the world, out to the public. I want to get it out there and in communities so that we can change the world."

Vivian got goosebumps again, and she wasn't sure if they were from Ms. Collins' emphatic way of talking, or Mr. Newell, who was tapping his foot a little in the corner of the room. "I think that's really exciting, Ms. Collins. I just would think that I'd have to know a little more about Bountiful."

"Vivian," Mr. Newell said, "out of curiosity, what is it that is making you reluctant? We've described what we think is a win-win product to you, and yet you seem to be apprehensive."

"I'm sorry…"

He held up a hand. "Wait. I'm not angry with you. I just need to know this for our future research studies. What is keeping you from being excited about what we're telling you?"

Vivian thought for a few moments.

"Answer quickly," he said, a shade more sharply than he may have intended.

"It's that if there are 'extenuating circumstances' and that sort of thing, I would need to know. As a potential supporter, that's important."

"Did Ms. Collins using those words 'extenuating circumstances' make you suspicious?"

"Not suspicious exactly. I would say 'concerned'."

Ms. Collins shot a look at the blacked-in window at the back the room, something so inconspicuous Vivian almost hadn't noticed it, and said, "Please note that."

"No, it's not that," she hurriedly said. "I just think, that if this is such a wonderful product, why do you need to convince me of it?"

Ms. Collins tapped her pen on the table. "We're very thorough, Vivian. Our scientists have put years into the research and development of Bountiful, and we need to make sure that every angle is covered before the product is released. We're not selling a new flavor of bubble gum. We cannot afford any missteps. Frankly, your reception is confusing to us. Unexpected, too."

"I understand that. I just am wondering, you know, based on what you said, if there are drawbacks to Bountiful. What should those of us whose thoughts are being researched know about? That's going to affect our opinions and you won't know the honest answer until we get all the information."

Neither of the other two said anything so Vivian continued. "I just thought that you wanted my truthful response to something so you could release Bountiful without any concerns about unpredictable reactions. I thought this was what you wanted."

If this were a movie, Vivian thought to herself, Ms. Collins and Mr. Newell would exchange furtive and squeamish glances. As it was not, Ms. Collins looked like she was at a loss for words – something it was clear she was unaccustomed to – and Mr. Newell gave a strange choking sort of cough, then walked over to pour some water for himself; the cold air as he passed made Vivian shiver a little. No one spoke and Vivian wondered if she might have pushed it too far.

Mr. Newell finally took a long sip from his cup and said, "I've had lawyers in here doing market research, Vivian. You're a tougher crowd than any of them." He said it in such a way, she couldn't tell if he was impressed or angered. She assumed that it was both. He stared at her, his expression unreadable.

"I'm just thinking that if you want the support of people in the research, you should be able to answer all their questions. I think a lot of young people might have similar concerns."

"I don't..."

Vivian was unsure what he was going to say, if Mr. Newell was going to be hostile or contrite, because his voice rarely changed and because Ms. Collins cut him off.

"You know what, Kevin? I think what she's said is legitimate." She pointed her pen at Vivian like she was an exhibition at a museum. "I think that what she's saying has some merit. A lot of merit, actually. It's just that we are not prepared – we don't have the framework down yet – to address the issues you are raising. We didn't factor all this in. No one's at fault," she pulled out an enormous date book from her purse. "We're going to have to reschedule for Wednesday. What do you think, Kevin?"

He sighed, his shoulders collapsing a little. "Was this just a big waste of our time?"

"No, no," she waved away the notion like an annoying mosquito. "To the contrary. This is a gift. I think that Vivian's just brought our attention to a line of questioning that we were naïve to try to ignore. We need to do this right. We need to face it straight on. I feel it right in the center of my being that this is the right thing to do," Ms. Collins thumped a hand on her chest. "We need to be thorough with this." Mr. Newell shook his head in frustration and she said, "Listen, it's a pain far better to be doing this now. Vivian was good enough to alert us to some holes in our marketing strategy and we need to follow through with that. How's Wednesday, same time, same place?"

Mr. Newell looked through his book as well. "Well, I have a meeting with Janice from R and D scheduled for then..."

Ms. Collins scribbled in her date book, not looking up. "It's important? Can't be rescheduled?"

He looked up from his date book at Ms. Collins, visibly offended. "Of course it's important. All my meetings are important."

Ms. Collins met his eyes. "That's not what I meant. You know that. I meant that this needs to take priority. The press conference is Thursday. Can you reschedule?" When he didn't say anything, she said, "Listen. I have to reschedule a meeting, too."

He shook his head and sighed again. "I'll look into it." He scribbled loudly in his date book.

Ms. Collins snapped hers shut and tossed it back in her purse. "Do. Let me know ASAP because we've got to get moving on this." She changed to a gentler tone and smiled at Vivian. "So, we'll meet again Wednesday, same time, same place, okay?"

"Sounds good."

Mr. Newell cleared his throat. "We'll need to make sure that the room is open and book it."

Ms. Collins stood and shrugged. "Have your secretary do it then. If it's not, just get another. The room isn't important. Thanks, Kevin. You ready, Vivian? We'll walk back together."

Mr. Newell loudly snapped the spiral book on the tripod shut and Ms. Collins walked out of the room, leaving her used coffee mug on the table. Vivian was unsure what to do with her mug – it was all so abrupt to her – so she hurried out the door behind Ms. Collins and left it behind. She picked up her pace to catch up to Ms. Collins, which she was able to do, but it really took all of her concentration. She made a note to herself that she should start exercising on the treadmill her mother bought a few Christmases ago. Rounding a corner at a breakneck speed and hoping she wouldn't collide with anyone, she said to Ms. Collins, "I'm sorry if it didn't go the way you were hoping."

Ms. Collins looked like she was going to say something then thought better of it. "Everything's all right, Vivian. You didn't do anything wrong. You did what you were supposed to do."

"Mr. Newell seems pretty annoyed."

"Mr. Newell," she said, a cryptic smile on her face, "Mr. Newell has to be more prepared for everything not going his way in life." Ms. Collins, perhaps aware of Vivian's labored breathing, slowed her pace a bit and talked quietly, almost conspiratorially, to Vivian. "When you graduate magna cum laude from an Ivy League school and your parents have money, little disappointments can really rock your world, I guess." She giggled a little. "If you ask me, I'd say that people who face disappointment early in life have it better in the long run. I'll take a scrappy person over a spoiled one any day."

She rounded another corner, said a brisk hello to a passing woman with a handful of folders pressed into her chest, and pushed the elevator call button. People clearly reacted to her, Vivian observed; they smiled and stared at Ms. Collins as she made her way down the hall. Vivian leaned against the side of the elevator when they walked in, exhausted from the day, which Ms. Collins mistook as apprehension. Walking off at their floor she said, "He's a big boy, Vivian. He'll get over it. It's okay to speak your mind. It's always okay. "

Back in their office, Ms. Collins quickly walked back to her desk, shut the door and started dialing numbers on speakerphone. Vivian looked for the letter from the Lynx and found it on the seat of her chair. Relieved but angry with herself for being so careless – she could only imagine what Will would say – she put it in her bag and called Wren. She answered the phone breathlessly on its first ring. "You alive?"

"I am," Vivian said, trying to sound cheerful. She turned from the window and spoke quietly. "No boogeyman seen."

"*Phew.* That's good to know."

"I just dropped off the letter and left."

"You must have been scared out of your mind."

"I was," Vivian almost whispered. "I wish the two of us could talk. I feel so exposed here." She could hear Ms. Collins talking in the next room, laughing loudly, so she felt relatively safe as long as no one came into the office. She watched the door and the office workers passing by in the hall as she cradled the phone on her shoulder.

Wren didn't say anything for a few moments. "So how long is this embargo supposed to happen between us?"

"Just until the end of the month. I'm going to keep calling you from work, though."

"I guess your parents never said specifically that calling from work was off-limits."

"Well, they did say that we could not speak for a month. I'd have to assume that talking from work fell under that umbrella. But still..."

"Still."

"If they didn't want me to call from work, they could have said that directly. 'And no calling from work, either, young lady!' It's understandable that I'd be confused."

"Completely. I would be in a similar circumstance," Wren said.

"And neither of us is exactly stupid."

"Nope. Not stupid."

"It's not my fault if their rules were vague."

"That's *one* thing that can't be blamed on either of us."

"One thing for which we shall remain blameless."

"Blaming stinks. You know what, though? I blame that neighbor of yours. I feel justified in blaming her for ruining my summer," Wren said, a tinge of bitterness in her voice.

"It's only a month."

"That's forever."

Vivian started to laugh.

"No, really, Viv, butterflies are lucky if they live a month. They're positively ancient if they make it that far. They're like, 'Listen, you little whippersnapper, when I was a caterpillar, these lavender flowers weren't even blossoming yet...' So a month is a long time."

"But we aren't butterflies. Well, I'm not. As for you..."

"I am a monarch," she said emphatically. "That's one of my totem animals, at least my mother's sister, my Aunt Phonecia, said so and she's as psychic as they come."

"Then it must be a fact. Anyway, we have July and August..."

"And then back to school," Wren sighed melodramatically. "I hate that place. Why did I decide to stop homeschooling and insist on Center City High? To do math I'll never need in my lifetime – shoot me, please, if I have the sort of career that requires it, okay? – and read one-sided history books? To have strangers hate me at first sight just because? Gah."

"To meet me. That's why you stopped homeschooling. And we're going to kick butt next year at school. We might even get a new member at the Vegetarian Club."

"Are you actively recruiting? My little club: how it's blossomed."

"Not yet. But we'll have that. And we can also laugh at the boring, shallow people. We can do that. We'll have an endless supply of that, for sure. And hatch plans. We can hatch plans. We'll have a lot to do."

"You know what would be cool?" Wren said with a playful tone.

"Hmm?"

"To have boyfriends next year. Or at least a date. One measly date. Or maybe two guys will move here next year, like foreign exchange students – does Center City get them? – from, like, Portugal and Spain. Or Zimbabwe. Or Norway. Or Trinidad. Or even New Dublin..."

"That's practically a foreign land."

"Anyplace but here. And they will totally fall in love with us and take us cool places – okay, pretend that we don't live in Center City and there are actual cool places – and cook us awesome vegan food. Wouldn't that be cool?"

"Yeah. My guy can have a pierced ear and maybe, maybe he's into skateboards. He's an artist, too." Vivian said, wistfully, gazing out the window, "and his hair's a little on the long side. Or it's short and spiky. Oh – and he has a cute accent, too. We can all go..." Ms. Collins' office was suddenly quiet, so Vivian hushed her voice. "I should go. I'll call you Wednesday, okay?"

"Sounds good."

"Talk to you then."

"Be safe."

"I will. Bye."

"Bye."

Vivian finished writing down Ms. Collins' messages for her. She was going through her last details of the day when she remembered the reports she'd had copied earlier in the day and thought it was wise to check her mail slot. She needed to get copies of each of those papers to bring home with her. Ms. Collins was sitting at her desk, looking through a folder, so Vivian quietly knocked on her door. She looked up and nodded.

"I've got some messages for you." She put them on Ms. Collins' desk.

She mumbled something and frowned a little as she glanced at the messages then she turned back to the folder, flipping through the pages as she looked for something.

"And, um…"

Ms. Collins didn't look up from the folder. "Yes?"

"I was going to check my mail thingy before I leave..."

"Your slot?"

"That's the word," Vivian said. "Would you like me to check yours, too?"

Ms. Collins looked uncomprehending for a moment. "Oh. Uh. Sure," she shrugged, looking back down to her folder. "That would be fine, Vivian."

Vivian went to her mail slot, which, aside from a memo about a company softball game and another one admonishing employees for dirty dishes in the kitchen break rooms, was empty. Ms. Collins' bin, however, had dozens of items, including the two reports she'd had copied in the morning, which were on the top; Vivian found them easily and with relief. They were clipped together neatly with a print of the copy order Vivian had filled out. She went to the bathroom with all the paperwork and unclipped the two master copies, then she walked to Kyle's office. He was sitting at his desk, frowning at his computer and tapping repeatedly at something on his keyboard when he noticed her waiting for his attention.

"Oh, hi, Vivian. This new computer is a pain if you ask me." he grumbled, then looked away from the screen. "Got to love technology. It simplifies our lives so much. Anything I can help you with, darlin'?"

Vivian fumbled through all of the papers she was holding for Ms. Collins and pulled out the two reports. "I guess we'll need one more copy of each of these. I'm sorry; I must have written down the wrong number for Nadine and she seemed really stressed today so I was wondering..."

"Wondering if you could make a couple copies here? Sure." He took them from her. "Just one each, right?"

"That's right."

"Laura must've told you about my copy machine."

Vivian grinned. "She did."

"It's just an open secret at this point," he grinned, putting the first sheet under the top. "So, do anything exciting today?"

"Not really. I was in some kind of market research earlier, but not much more than that."

"Market research for Bountiful?"

She nodded.

"You watched the market research or participated?"

"Participated. I guess they wanted to talk to someone around my age."

"That must have been exciting in its own way. It's pretty big-time stuff. We're pushing into high gear soon on promotion," He lowered his voice. "You know not to talk to anyone outside of Gordenner about it, right? About Bountiful?" He took the second sheet out of the copier. "Top secret stuff."

"Oh, yeah. I know."

He handed the reports back to Vivian. "Well, here you go, missy. Will I be seeing you Wednesday?"

"Yep. Thanks, Kyle."

Walking back to her office, Vivian stopped in a different restroom – she was starting to know where all of them were – folded and stuffed the copies from Kyle into her purse and clipped the original reports back with the copies.

Back at the office, Ms. Collins was on the phone again. It was time for Vivian to leave to catch the bus, so she stood in the doorway of Ms. Collins' office, pointed at the wall clock and, pointed to herself and made a motion of walking legs with her fingers. Ms. Collins nodded, covered the mouthpiece and whispered, "See you Wednesday." Vivian carefully placed the stack from Ms. Collins' mail slot onto her desk and waved goodbye.

Out in the parking lot, the security guard let her through to the street, and, with a minute to spare, she caught the bus. She was tempted to read the reports on the ride home but decided that it was too risky; she was already taking too many chances in bringing them home in the first place. Once again, she found herself looking forward to calling Wren when she got home, only to remember the disappointing reality. She immediately thought of her mother, talking on the phone all day at work, able to call a friend without a second thought, and felt resentment churning in her chest. She'd never been restricted like this by her parents before, and she realized there was also a part of her that also found the whole thing kind of thrilling.

As she walked off the bus and down her block, she saw Millie, one of her friends, Cassie, and her babysitter, a friendly, freckly college student in her twenties named Abby, running through the sprinkler in the front yard. At first Vivian was annoyed by what felt like an intrusion – she just wanted to be at home by herself – but then she remembered the Lynx and she was immensely relieved that she got the letter to a place she was sure he would find it. That alone eased her mind so much that after a brief stop indoors, she came outside in her bathing suit and joined in. After chasing Millie and Cassie through and over and under the sprinkler for ten minutes, Vivian lay in a straight line on the cool grass and the two girls took turns shrieking madly and jumping over her. Staring at the clouds as their little legs ran in circles around and over her, tanned ankles and pink-bottomed feet leaping up and down, she felt so peaceful at first she was sure that she could fall asleep right on the spot, the grass soft beneath her. She reminded herself of the reports, though, folded, hidden and smuggled from work less than an hour ago, sitting in her unassuming brown bag on the living room couch, the couch where she used to build forts, and the lightness faded. When she saw a cloud formation roll past that looked unquestionably like a duck and ducklings to her, she went inside and holed herself up in her bedroom with her reports.

Media Plan: Phase one of Bountiful Wheat
- *Write letters to key magazines for publication in April editions. If monthly, send by* **February 15***; if weekly, send by* **March 15***. Have drafts completed by beginning of the year, and finals approved a week before sending.*
- *Write press release for local newspapers. (To be released by* **April 1***).*
- *Write separate press release for national newspapers* **(also April 1)***.*
- *Write op-eds for all major national newspapers (NY Times, Washington Post, LA Times, New Dublin Chronicle, etc.) starting in January. Have*

drafts ready by **November 15** and finals approved/market researched by **January 3**. Start rolling out after **January 15**.

- Spots on public and commercial radio, starting in April, filming **March 8** and editing week of **March 21**. (See script drafts filed under Radio Drafts in Progress. Finals by no later than **February 15**.)
- 30-second commercials for public and commercial television and cable, starting in May. Have lists of media outlets by end of March. Have storyboards and final drafts completed by **April 1**. (See script drafts filed under Short Television Commercial Drafts in Progress.)
- 60-second commercials starting in June. Have lists of media outlets by end of March. Have storyboards and final drafts completed by **May 1**. (See script drafts filed under Long Television Commercial Drafts in Progress.)
- Blitz all local, regional and national radio and television programs with appearances and call-ins starting in **January**. Janine will have updated producer contact list by end of year.
- Find local and national celebrities to align with ASAP. Contact agencies/Patty
- T-shirts sent to all relevant celebrities. Design complete by beginning of the year.
- Launch date: **May 15**

The list went on in this fashion with each asterisked point followed by several action items and more deadlines. Vivian, sleepy again, rested her head on her desk for a few minutes and then picked up another report, this one a year before.

Strategic Plan for PR Framing of Bountiful Wheat
Cc: Marketing, Sales and Promotion staff; Robert Fontaine
According to the preliminary market research thus far, feedback has pointed overwhelmingly to people responding positively to framing BW as a global humanitarian effort. (See summary: May 23.) **Support has been overwhelmingly positive in our 20-plus market research sessions so far.** *We conclude that emphasizing the promise of BW in terms of world hunger, malnutrition and poverty is the best, and only, approach. In a recent survey by R.R. Donleavy and Associates (released in April of this year), 43% of respondents said that they do not trust corporations. In light of this, focusing our PR unwaveringly on the humanitarian effort aspect of BW is the best way to earn public trust and foster good will.*
All members of Gordenner staff in Marketing, Sales and Promotion will be given Key Strategy Talking Points in the coming weeks, and these should be

used when discussing BW with all relevant clients. **ALL media requests must be directed to Laura Collins for her discretion: only Ms. Collins and Mr. Fontaine have clearance to speak with members of the media.** *If there is any uncertainty, contact Ms. Collins at ext. 5. Unauthorized individuals speaking to members of the media is grounds for immediate termination.*

Reminder: the strategy and marketing cohesion retreat is scheduled for the weekend of August 19 (see memos of 4/11, 5/15 and 5/23). Please put this in your date books now if it's not already there. We must have 100% attendance, the only exceptions being a medical or family emergency. Please contact Nancy Sloane at ext. 544 by this Friday to arrange carpool and rooming preferences. Again, we will be staying at the Summerset Lodge and Spa in Andover from Friday at 5:00 p.m. until Sunday at 1:00 p.m. Please also let Nancy know if you have any dietary restrictions or allergies.

Thank you,
Laura Collins

Vivian could hear the kids running into the house with the babysitter running after them and reminding them to dry off before jumping on the couch. Eager for a distraction again after reading the reports, Vivian went down to the living room, where Millie and Cassie were running and laughing hysterically as their babysitter chased them with a towel. Her face was red and flushed, and Vivian could see that she needed some help.

"Millie," Vivian said in her stern voice. "Millie. Stop."

Millie looked over at her and jumped from chair to chair to see if she was really serious. Cassie squealed with laughter. Millie said, "Come on, Vivi. We're just playing."

"I understand that but when Abby tells you something you need to listen."

Abby silently mouthed 'thank you' to Vivian and went to work drying off the girls.

"Your name is Vivi?" asked Cassie, Abby wrapping a towel around her. "That's a strange name. I never heard it before."

"It's short for Vivian. Like I'm guessing that Cassie is short for Cassandra, right?"

Cassie narrowed her eyes at Vivian, ignoring her question. "Wait, so your name is Vivian Sharpe?"

"That's right."

A smile spread across Cassie's face. "I heard that you chase squirrels," she giggled. "You just run after them for no reason."

Vivian's face flushed as Millie jumped to her defense. "No, she doesn't chase squirrels. Why would she do that? Chase squirrels? I've never seen her chase a squirrel in my whole life."

Cassie shrugged. "My sister and her friends were laughing about it on the phone. My oldest sister goes to school with you. Her name's Becky. She said her friend saw you chase a squirrel in the park and that your best friend is a witch."

Vivian had to think for a moment. Becky Newmark was a friend of Kendra's.

Abby, clearly embarrassed, went upstairs to get a change of clothes for the girls.

"That's not true," Millie said, stomping her foot. "Don't tell lies about my sister."

"They're not lies."

"They *are* lies."

"No, they're not. I just want to know why your sister acts so weird so I can tell my sister."

"You know, Cassie, that's very rude." Vivian finally spoke. "To call someone weird in her own home. To call someone weird any place, really. I don't think that your parents would be very happy to hear this."

Cassie shrugged again, her chin stuck out and a defiant look on her face, daring her.

Vivian, flustered, struggled for something to say, anything to get the focus off her. "Why don't you girls go downstairs and play dolls after you change?"

Cassie raced ahead of Millie to the basement. Millie, still shaken, walked over to Vivian and whispered in her ear, "You don't really chase squirrels, do you?"

Vivian looked into Millie's guileless blue eyes. She smiled and whispered back. "Not often."

Millie grinned triumphantly. "See? I knew you didn't." She started skipping off when she abruptly stopped. "And you're not really friends with witches, right?"

"Right."

"Good. I knew it."

Great, Vivian thought to herself as she climbed the stairs back to her room, shaken to her core by a child who couldn't weigh more than 45 pounds, *now I'm being openly mocked by six-year-olds*. Vivian remembered with an enormous sense of relief that she was out of school for the summer.

A BIRD WITH A SCHEDULE

That night, Vivian dreamed about sharks. Everywhere she looked, there were miniature sharks. There was a shark swimming in a plugged-up sink in a Gordenner bathroom and one in a fish bowl on Ms. Collins' desk. There was a giant aquarium spread across a wall next to the cafeteria, and a woman in a hairnet was standing on a chair and reaching into the top, catching wriggling miniature sharks with a net and dropping them with a splash into a giant pan of water on the floor. Vivian didn't know what they were there for, if they were going to end up in the cafeteria buffet line; as she watched the scene, another cafeteria worker approached with a big plastic bag of smaller fish in water and poured it into the pan with the sharks. In the break room, she saw sharks circling in the coffee pot and, in the cups of two people eating lunch and drinking coffee together around a little square table, she saw sharks. Then Vivian noticed Kyle walking by in the hallway. She said hello and he called over his shoulder to follow him because he was in a hurry, but he wanted to show her something. Vivian hadn't noticed before that he was pushing a cart, filled with little clanking fish bowls of circling, miniature sharks.

They walked to the mail slots. "I've got to show you how to do this because this is going to be your job next week."

He started picking up the bowls one by one and putting them in the slots.

"What is it you're doing?"

He looked at her as though that were a silly question. "You need to look it up in your employee manual. We're not supposed to talk about it. Could you start putting those out?" he said hurriedly as he jerked his head to the slots near Vivian, his rubber gloved hands full.

Dutifully, Vivian started grabbing bowls.

"Honey, let me give you some advice," Kyle said quietly, not looking at her. "Hold the bowl around the side, not up on top. Those suckers will bite if they get the chance." He rolled down his glove to expose his bandaged palm and kept working, putting bowl after bowl in each slot. "Don't forget to put one in your own slot."

She looked at her empty slot and placed a bowl with an angry looking shark in it. "What do we do with them once they're in our slots?" she asked.

"Feed them, of course," he said with a wink. "What do you else would you do? Let them starve?"

Kevin Newell walked into the room and muttered a perfunctory hello to Kyle and Vivian as he picked up his bowl and mail from his slot. He walked out just as quickly; Vivian got colder and colder until she finally woke up to find herself in her dark bedroom, bed sheets kicked off her, just after midnight.

Then she heard a sound like the clearing of a throat or a stifled cough and she jumped up, gasping, her first thought being that the Lynx was in her room. Her heart raced as she scanned the room frantically and then, finally, noticed Tolstoy sitting at her desk chair.

She clutched her blanket reflexively at her chest. "Tolstoy," she half-whispered, half-gasped, closing her eyes as she tried to steady her breathing.

Tolstoy smiled, a look of sympathy on his face. "I knew that would happen. I wish I could find a more gentle way to traverse. I try to be as subtle as possible," he said, his form glinting, "but it's not enough, I'm afraid."

Vivian gave one last deep inhale, and, now mostly recovered, could smile at Tolstoy, appreciating his presence, basking in it like the warmth she sought. He smiled back, a look of gratitude on his face. He floated over to her.

"Hello, Viv. I don't think that I said hello yet. How are you?"

"Oh, pretty good."

"Really?" He looked doubtful.

"I'm just a little stressed, you know. New job, getting threatening letters from this terrorist guy…"

"Not easy."

Vivian sighed. "I'm not one to complain, but, no, not at all easy."

"Exposing a massive corporate cover-up, too," Tolstoy added helpfully. "And not even knowing the full extent of what you're exposing."

"Thanks for reminding me. Yes, that too."

"That all adds up, doesn't it?"

"And you know that I'm, like, grounded and I can't talk to Wren on top of all that."

Tolstoy nodded. "It's certainly understandable that you would be under a lot of stress given all that. Given any one of those factors, in fact. I should think that you're holding up quite well given everything."

Vivian realized that this was the first time in weeks that she'd felt anyone had come close to truly understanding what she was experiencing and it came as a tremendous, unexpected relief. The more she tried to hold the tears back, the more they pooled and stung behind her lids; she grabbed some tissues from the box on her nightstand.

"I'm sorry," she said, burying her face in the tissues as the tears clouded her vision. "I didn't want to cry." She sniffed. "I'm not really sad. I'm just…I'm sorry."

Very gently Tolstoy said, "No need to be sorry, Viv. Let the tears out. Take your time."

Vivian hiccupped, her face wet and hot, trying to talk through the tears. "I just…"

"You don't need to talk on my behalf. I'm not in a hurry."

Vivian glanced over at Tolstoy and as she did, she felt that warmth filling up her chest, as she did the last time he visited. As her chest filled with that lovely warmth, it was almost as if she could feel her tears evaporate from the inside out.

Quietly, Tolstoy said, "That's a lot to carry, Viv, all those worries every day."

Looking at Tolstoy, Vivian suddenly felt a sense of peace she hadn't felt in weeks. "It is. But I don't want to dwell on it any more. I want to talk about other things."

Tolstoy smiled broadly. "I'm game," he said, slapping his hooves on his thighs; Vivian half-expected to hear a little clap. "What should we talk about?"

"Okay," Vivian said, trying to organize a list in her mind, then seeing it all dissolve. "Um. My life is a mess. Should I start there?"

"Oh, certainly. Messes don't scare me."

"That's good. I've got stuff coming at me from all directions and I've got the additional pressure of needing to get something done quickly, you know?"

Tolstoy nodded.

"And I know that if I talk to you about it, about the specifics, you're not going to be able to be more than a sounding board, right? You're going to be all vague and, you know, poetic with your response, I'm going to guess based on the past."

"Poetic? You are generous, Viv. It is true enough, though," he said. "I cannot be directive and specific. At the same time, this doesn't mean that we can't discuss things and possibly come to some place of benefit to you."

"I'm just wondering if I should I just keep working with my intuition."

"One doesn't want to overanalyze, not in this kind of situation."

"But at the same time, I need to be thoughtful and, you know, disciplined. I can't just run around like a crazy person, shouting at the top of my lungs," she said, pantomiming as she waved her arms.

Tolstoy pondered what she said. "It is a delicate dance between instinct and discipline. You just have to know when the time is right to observe more and when the time is right to take action."

"But how do I know that, Tolstoy? That's the part I don't get. How do I not royally screw up?"

Tolstoy started to talk, then stopped himself, his eyes twinkling impishly. "You're going to be irritated by what I say, I'm afraid."

"I promise that I won't be irritated."

"You asked, *How do you know when the time is right?* By using your discipline and intuition."

Vivian thought for a moment. "Okay, I know that I promised that I wouldn't be irritated, but now it's really hard for me not to be. Irritated. Like how do I know that magic moment when I have the right amount of discipline and the right amount of intuition? Will I hear a bell or something? Ding ding ding?"

Tolstoy took a deep breath and for the first time, Vivian worried that he might be annoyed with her. She wondered when he was just going to lose patience with her and find someone new to work with. Instead, though, he looked at her again with an expression of complete peace and understanding. "Viv, how did you know that you were doing the right thing when you found the birds and ran into town? When you accepted the internship at Gordenner? If you actually heard a bell, then this is something new that we haven't discussed before."

Vivian was relieved that he hadn't given up on her, at least not yet. "No. It just felt right. In those situations, I did what felt like the right thing to do."

"Well…" Tolstoy smiled a coy little grin at her.

"Oh, I see what you had me do there, Tolstoy. I just answered my own question, didn't I? You're a sneaky one…"

"But it's *true*," he said emphatically. "You feel it when you're moving forward on the right path. I don't think you need to worry about this any more because you have everything you need right here. And this," he said, hoof on his chest, "guides this," he said, a hoof to his head. "I'm sorry if it's vague but it's true."

"Okay, so then I should just accept that I will always do the right thing?"

Tolstoy squinted, choosing his words carefully after a brief pause. "Oh, that's not exactly what I meant because one can't be certain of that. That would get into this questionable, relativist area. For example, if you'd punched the man with the puppies in the box, would that be the right thing to have done just because you felt like it? But maybe that would mean that you wouldn't have gotten the dogs away from him. Or if you decided to ignore the ducks, would that have been right because that was what you wanted to do? If your values are in alignment with your actions, then, yes, I would say that you have done the right thing."

"Values and actions in alignment," she repeated dreamily. "That reminds me of something the Lynx wrote: 'Choice plus action equals consequence'. What do you think about that?"

"Do you want to talk about him, Viv?"

Vivian was so taken aback by the directness of his last question that she just blinked at Tolstoy a few times before responding. "Oh, my goodness. I didn't think that we could. Yes, let's talk about him. Should I be worried about him?"

Tolstoy thought before speaking. "Worried, no. Cautious, yes."

"What does he want with me, Tolstoy? Of all people, why me? God," she said, shaking her head, "why do I suddenly sound like a bad actress on a stupid soap opera? Never mind. What is going on with the Lynx? Inside his mind?"

Tolstoy looked like he was going to shrug, then thought better of it; he cocked his head to the side instead. "I cannot be inside this man's head. I cannot know his motivations any more than you or anyone else could. That said, he does seem to be following the warrior model in pursuing what he feels to be justice."

"But why is he doing that? Wouldn't he get farther if he were more reasonable?"

"These are age-old questions, Vivian. Every person has to decide for him- or herself how they will address injustice."

"Meaning?"

"Some people are methodical and measured. Some people are apathetic and indifferent. Some people become enraged and aggressive. Most people change depending on the circumstances. It seems to me that this individual is frustrated at seeing something very clearly that others either do not see or choose to ignore."

"You mean the pipe behind Gordenner? Most people don't know about that because it's hidden."

"I was speaking more generally. This man, the Lynx, he sees no distinction between human animals and other animals, that it's nothing more than sheer chance what form one takes at birth. It seems that the Lynx sees this – this placing humans above other animals, and then some animals above others again – as irrational and arbitrary and self-deceiving."

"See, I agree with that." Vivian sighed. "Should I feel scared about agreeing with the Lynx? Am I going to end up like him? A fugitive? A terrorist?"

Tolstoy chuckled a little, a bubbling stream. "I don't see that as a likelihood, Viv."

"But why not? He probably started out like me and just became more and more…" she searched for the right word.

"Alienated?"

"Yes, alienated. I'm sure that he didn't start out as angry as he is now or how he was 20 years ago. He grew that way over time, don't you think?"

"I do not know his personal evolution, Viv. But you cannot live your life worrying about being like other people. You can only live your life in accordance with the truth that resonates within you, guiding you to right action."

"But is there always going to be this 'truth within me' that tells me not to send bombs to people, not to threaten people? What if my version of 'truth' changes and then my actions are different? Like, this is something that Will and Mrs. Summer argue about: what is okay when we believe we are right? Where do we draw the line?"

"And what are your thoughts on that?" he asked.

"Well, I'm sort of new to this whole thing, so they're not fully formed..."

"Those are my favorite kinds of thoughts."

"I suppose," Vivian sighed. "I can say that as soon as I think that being violent is the wrong way to go about things, then I think that we should do anything possible to end suffering and abuse. And then I'm ashamed that I ever felt differently."

"It *is* complex, Viv. No doubt about that. This is why being true to your highest self gives you the very best ground to stand on."

Vivian sighed. "I just hope that that is always clear, my highest self."

"It won't be. You sometimes have to work at it."

"But then what?"

"Viv, you cannot control the future. All you can do is try to do your best every moment."

"That's all? Can I ever catch a break?"

"Certainly. You have to know when to charge forward and when to pull back."

"That's all?" She said this with a brittle laugh.

"That's it," he said, either not noticing or acknowledging her sarcasm. "It's no harder than living in an inauthentic way," he offered cheerfully.

Vivian thought about this for a moment, then shook off her blanket impatiently. "You've got to be the most frustrating pig spirit I've ever met, Tolstoy."

"I try my best. I have to be a good example for all the other fledgling pig spirits. I don't want them to take their work for granted. So what's next?" he asked, changing the tone brightly. "You have another research session and you have to figure out how to end this poisoning of the river water. You have to decide how to deal with this new product of theirs, this seed and spray."

"Yep. Just that. Listen, Tolstoy, it's hard for me to decide what to wear in the morning. How am I going to devise a plan like this?"

Tolstoy was radiant. "You really don't have to have a plan already. You don't have to have a plan at all. These are just things that are on the plate, so to speak."

"So I can just face it all as it becomes apparent what to do, right? We've already covered this. Trying to plan it out in advance just makes me want to go to sleep."

Tolstoy nodded. "I can see that. I think you should just work in the way that feels best to you. In the meantime, is there anything else?"

Vivian thought for a few moments. "Um, yes. Can we talk about you? I was wondering about how you move around and stuff. Like how do you get here and everywhere else from where you live? Do you live in the clouds? That's sort of where I imagine you."

"Ah, yes," Tolstoy smiled. "You humans have this image of angels lounging around the clouds, I understand. Well, I am not an angel, so I cannot speak for where they reside, if they reside anywhere. They may be in the clouds for all I know."

"Right. You're a spirit, which is different from an angel. Silly me. But where do you live?"

Tolstoy rested his head on his hoof. "Humans have a different view of space, of place. It would not be recognizable or identifiable to you where I reside if I describe it. It's not like I can point to the sky and say, 'I live there.' A complex transformation occurs when the spirit is set free, Viv. Your context simply is not sufficient for understanding the post-mortal existence. It is quite…" he searched for the right word, "exquisite, though, I'll tell you that."

"So is it like heaven?"

"Like heaven? I don't believe so. No," he shook his head thoughtfully. "Though I haven't been there myself, to this place called heaven. Where I live, it's more like a space than anything, and more than being like a space, really, it's a feeling and a tone, like the tone of an instrument, but not quite, and always shifting in harmony with one's resonance. Does that make sense to you?"

"Um, no. But that's fine."

"I'm afraid that my attempts to clear things up only serve to muddy them more. The senses that we are born with – sight, hearing, smell, you know – the ones that we would rely on to comprehend another world, they are what you think that you need to understand it, but once you pass, you'll see that they are so minor in comparison to your new adaptations. These new abilities are beyond the scope of mortal experience but I will try. You know your feelings? Love, sadness, eagerness…"

"Yes."

"Well, these emotions you have now, you will still have. But they become full sensory experiences. Even sadness becomes beautiful to feel. It's as if a concert were playing inside you and there is nothing you want to run and hide from anymore. It is all different and unique and exquisite. They roll through you like a wave and then you feel deeply serene. Do you understand that?"

"Kind of, I think. But I have to know, is there a guy sitting at the gates when you come in? St. Peter?"

Tolstoy tilted his head, thinking. "Gate? I didn't see any gates. Or this Peter fellow."

"So it's not like a club and you only know the secret handshake once you are there?"

Tolstoy considered this. "No, not really. It is hard to convey to a mortal, though. Your language and experiences and comprehension cannot approximate it. It is much more expansive than what the mind could conjure. It is not your fault. It just is what it is."

"But you're happy there? In this 'space'?"

Tolstoy beamed. "Oh, perfectly, blissfully, yes, so happy. Similar to how you are unable to comprehend where I reside, I am no longer able to comprehend dwelling anywhere else."

"Are there others there? Others like you? Spirits?"

Tolstoy nodded and answered obliquely, "Yes. But I can only speak for myself."

"So there's no use in asking you to look in on my mother's mother, right? To find out if she's there."

"No, no use in that. It would violate the terms of my visiting with you."

"And you can't have that."

"No," he said gently. "I can't."

They looked at each other for a few moments, then Vivian looked away. Finally, she started picking at imaginary threads on her sheet and said. "I love it when you visit, Tolstoy. Despite the initial heart attack and lingering confusion, I love your visits."

"And I love to visit you."

She thought that she would have died if he hadn't said that, just dissolve into a fatally embarrassed puddle right there on the bed. Her relief was brief, though, before she felt she had to continue. "Tolstoy, I…" Vivian stammered, clearly embarrassed but wanting to say something. "I don't want you to take this the wrong way. But…"

"I know, Vivian."

"What? What was I going to say?" Vivian blushed despite herself.

"That you love me. I can feel the vibration in you. I don't know the wrong way to take that one is loved, though," he smiled softly.

Vivian's desire to explain herself took precedence over her natural shyness. "I just meant, like, in the human world, saying that often means 'in love' like wanting to get married and have babies together."

"Well, I'm not afraid to say that I am in love with you, in that it's an active state of being. I am *in* love. What a beautiful place to be, and, if I have to say so, that comes the closest to describing where I live. That doesn't mean that I want to get married and have babies together, even if that were possible."

"Good. `Cause I am sort of at the edge of what I can handle socially. These kids who think that they're living on the edge because they, like, dye their hair pink or pierce their nostrils, they have nothing on me." Vivian giggled. "So there are no pig-human-spirit babies in the immediate future?"

Tolstoy shook his head, his eyes twinkling. "Not even in the distant future."

Vivian sighed with relief. "See, even though you are a pig spirit and I am a girl human mortal, the fact that you are a male factors into things. Like I'm going to be weird about being misunderstood. I just wouldn't want you to think that I was 'making any moves' on you, Tolstoy."

"Oh, nothing of the sort," he snorted, dismissing the thought with a wave of his hoof. "I know nothing of that sort of thing. I do know about love, though, and I gratefully reciprocate."

"So, T – can I call you T? You know, a kind of nickname? Like Viv?"

He nodded.

"Well, T, I'm going to get back to bed. I've got a lot of work ahead of me with all this…"

"All this corporate crime and intrigue?"

"Yes, all that. But I'm going to make you proud of me. No matter what happens, I'm going to make you proud of me."

Tolstoy smiled. His glow seemed to magnify, casting off a soft light in the dark bedroom. "I know you will, Viv. I already am so proud of you, so happy to know you. More than anything, you're going to be proud of yourself."

Vivian found herself getting a little choked up. "You'll come back soon?"

"As soon as I can," he said earnestly.

Vivian didn't know what to say so, quietly, she put her hand to her chest where she felt the radiant warmth. Tolstoy did the same, a gentle smile on his face, and then he slowly started dissolving in wavy lines, the sparks glinting and popping in the air like the ghost images of fireworks on the fourth of July. Eventually every trace of him was gone. She went back to sleep with that warmth filling up her chest like a contented cat in the afternoon sun, the thought of her work ahead fading into a distant, almost invisible, worry.

The next morning, Vivian was awakened by the phone ringing. After several rings, she remembered that her mother was at the gym, and her father was on his way to attend a daylong seminar on historical societies in New Dublin. She grabbed the phone on the final ring.

"Hello? Vivian, is that you? It's Will."

She must have made some sort of groggy grunt or another, because then he said, "Listen, I'm sorry for calling so early, I'm sorry if I woke you, but I wasn't sure if you went to Gordenner this morning and I didn't want to miss you."

Vivian blinked at the clock on her nightstand, clearing her eyes. It was 6:47. "I don't work today."

"Oh, I'm sorry," he said distractedly. "Do you have a minute to talk anyway? I've got a really busy day but there's some information I wanted to share with you. Do you want to call me back when you're ready to talk?"

"No," Vivian said, stifling the yawn that tried to contradict her. "I'm ready now. I'm fine." She sat up in bed.

"Cool. Anyway, I'm just going to get into it, if you don't mind."

"Go ahead."

"Good." Vivian heard Will shuffle some papers. "So you might already know that when Robert Fontaine came on board at the plant, he started shaking things up from the get-go. The only thing he wanted to do was get them immersed in some pretty intense genetic engineering projects, like what they dabbled in before but had gotten derailed. Are you with me, Vivian?"

"Hmm? Yes."

"Anyway, you'll recall that I told you about the Miracle Seeds and Spray; this was in the early, early days of genetic engineering. This was before Fontaine was there. They dropped it because it was such a nightmare in terms of getting the FDA approval, letting their internal documents be available for government oversight. It was that bad," he said. "It was such a hot potato that the FDA wouldn't ever approve it. Imagine that. When they were working on the development, though, it was a big deal because of all the patents they were applying for, and they were making the competition very nervous."

"Really?"

"Yeah, no one knew what they were up to, but it was clear something was happening."

"And that was Bountiful?"

"Yeah, actually, the precursor to it. It changes the nature of the soil over time so that test fields would only be able to grow more Miracle Wheat and pretty much nothing else. This was recorded in their in-house documents that were eventually made public through the Freedom of Information Act. And in order to make this stuff, they relied on a bacterium that they genetically engineered into the seed."

"Gross."

"Totally common in the manipulation of plants. Anyway, this stuff produced a horrible byproduct, though, and it was totally necessary to the production of the seeds. You couldn't have the seeds without the byproduct. That is what we found in Colman's Creek, and what you found when you discovered those ducks, that's what they're pumping out of that underground pipe: the byproduct of the seeds."

"And Bountiful is just Miracle Wheat being repackaged, right?"

"Right. They found markets overseas with more lax standards than our own and a more desperate population. That was the point of Fontaine's trip to Southeast Asia, to help drum up support, which it seems was successful for Gordenner. This seed is enhanced – that's their word: *enhanced* rather than engineered – with folic acid, and that, besides its initial hyper-fertility, is what they're playing up. They don't let on that this folic acid is virtually unusable unless one consumes humanly impossible quantities of the product..."

"I think I remember you saying thirteen loaves of bread a day."

"Thirteen," he said, sounding uncharacteristically sunny. "You'd need 13 loaves a day. Now how is that even possible? If you were even able to eat that many loaves of bread a day, you wouldn't be able to eat anything else, which would lead to other nutritional deficiencies."

"That makes sense."

"Okay, but here is the real reason why I called. Are you going to be at the press conference Thursday?"

"I don't think so. They haven't asked me. Honestly, I'm not sure how things are going to work but it will somehow."

"Good. There's a guy coming in, this former ambassador to Laos who now does contract work with various Asian governments to cut through the red tape and bring U.S. agricultural products there. Funny how that works out, huh? He's also a good buddy of the big guy, Fontaine. Small world. His name is Helmut Burr. Anyway, he's coming in and he's going to be meeting with Fontaine and your boss..."

"Ms. Collins."

"...Right, Laura Collins – about finally green-lighting the deal altogether. They're signing contracts and final details and all that jazz. He'll probably be there through early next week with everything they've got to go over, from what I understand."

"That's why they're having the press conference? How did you know? I hadn't even heard anything about this guy."

Will snorted. "You wouldn't have. It's a bigwig sort of thing. I know about it because I managed to get myself on the mailing list for the Citizens United to Feed a Hungry World, which is basically a sleazy front group created by Gordenner and other big agribusiness interests. It's to support their efforts abroad. The newsletter is great, a really sickening read. I can show it to you if you want. Fascinating stuff. I saw that Burr would be traveling here and then I was able to make a few phone calls, assume a few accents and new identities for myself and pieced it all together. As secretive as Gordenner is as a company, some of their switchboard operators and secretaries are downright gullible. People in Center City are intimidated by a lousy phony accent, apparently," he laughed.

"But where does this leave me? What am I supposed to do with this information?" Vivian looked at the clock again. It was not even 7:00 and she was already fatigued.

"The thing is that I think we need to move quickly, quicker than I thought. We've got to figure out a way to intervene and expose what they're doing. Let the media know about these products. Honestly, if this spray is released, it will probably horribly pollute the groundwater anywhere it's used. I could see them being in cahoots with another company, like a water purification company, and getting huge kickbacks for getting them set up. Or maybe they'll just create their own. I wouldn't put anything past them, not a thing."

"And this guy? What was his name again?"

"Helmut Burr. Just the name makes me feel all warm and tingly," he laughed. This was Will in a good mood, Vivian thought. His good moods had a way of making her become a little nervous.

"But how does his coming in affect me?"

"Well, I just thought that now the media will be there for their press conference so we should move. Like, if it's publicly revealed what's going on in front of Burr and reporters at their press conference, it could make the whole thing blow up in Gordenner's face, in Fontaine's face, in Laura Collins' face."

Vivian winced and felt her stomach dive a little. "How am I going to do that to her?" She hadn't meant to say this out loud but she did and immediately regretted it.

"Do *what* to her?" Will said, unable to conceal his irritation and impatience. "Bring her some reckoning with what she has created? Hold her feet to the fire? Vivian, don't tell me that you're wimping out."

"I'm not," she said so forcefully she surprised herself. "I'm not wimping out. I'm just, you know, human."

He didn't say anything.

"Are you still there?"

He sighed. "I'm still here. I'm just afraid that this is all going to be a waste of our time if you can't follow through with what you started."

"I can, Will. I'm going to follow through. I'm still going to be human, though."

"You can't afford to be human, Vivian," he said.

"Okay," she said, nearly laughing. "Can you give me some advice on how to avoid that whole being human thing?"

Will charged ahead undeterred. "Just think of all you're going to do to benefit the world. Think of all those animals that won't get that toxic sludge spewed all over them; think of the water that's not going to be polluted. Think of the people who won't be exploited and poisoned, all the children who won't drink that polluted water, the fact that if you are successful in stopping Bountiful, you'll be a hero."

Vivian imagined herself accepting an honor to a standing ovation. When she looked in the crowd, though, all she could focus on was Ms. Collins, looking at her with a look of utter contempt in the center of the front row. She changed the subject abruptly. "I will do everything I can to make something positive come out of this, Will. That's all I can say for now. I will try my hardest."

"You have to. Harder than your hardest. This is serious business."

"I understand."

"I don't know if this will inspire you, but I just read this report on a test field of Bountiful in Sri Lanka." She could hear paper crinkling on the line. "It's from the environmental council there. Apparently in a nearby stream, directly downstream from the field and seed production laboratory, the fish kills have been enormous, unprecedented. Something like a 30% reduction in aquatic life. Can you imagine that? They're seeing massive bird die-offs, water that's unable to sustain living organisms. This is *just* the water, too. Who knows its long-term affect on human health yet? Sadly, the Sri Lankan government has totally squashed this group's ability to have their voices heard there, but the information is coming to U.S. activist communities. You're the missing link here, Vivian. I'm convinced of it."

"Somewhere between human and ape?" she said light-heartedly, despite her increasing desire to run somewhere – anywhere – and go into hiding.

Will chuckled in a distracted sort of way, like he felt he needed to in order to seem good humored, at least that was how Vivian saw it. "Listen, I've got some lab work to do, so I'd better get going. Okay?" He paused. "I don't know what else to say."

"That's enough."

Vivian went down the hall to take a shower, and on the way there, she stopped to glance in Millie's bedroom. She was still asleep, one silky arm slung around the stuffed lion, Leo, Vivian had gotten at around Millie's age and passed down to her. Leo had little red ink stained blotches around his muzzle, sympathetic chicken pox Millie had drawn on him last year, but otherwise looked much the same. Her little sister was much more of a traditional girl than Vivian was at that age, she observed, looking around her orderly room, with her doll collection and teapots and pink-hued wardrobe. Trying to imagine Millie at Vivian's age, in nine years, she couldn't imagine Millie ever getting into this type of situation: she'll be one of the popular, breezy, chatty girls, Vivian guessed, rushing into class after the final bell with a giggle (never getting more than a slight reprimand) and pressed close together with her friends sipping cocoa at chilly football games. She'll never have a worry. Millie started to rustle in bed, forcing Vivian out of her reverie and to the bathroom to start her shower.

As Vivian was reaching to turn off the shower, something blurry caught her eye. The glass block window above the bathtub was foggy, but she could see something in their back yard that wasn't normally there: some kind of small, dark shape moving on their tree. She wiped the window but it was still inscrutable. It almost looked like there was also something fluttering against one of the branches. A bird?

She got dressed quickly and peeked in on Millie, still asleep, as she went downstairs to glance outside. A towel was still wrapped around her head like a turban, which she had forgotten. She looked out the back window in the kitchen and saw a robin and a squirrel, possibly Billy, from that day by the river, sitting on a branch together in a very peculiar way, just sitting side-by-side and watching her house, as if they were waiting for her. The squirrel's tail twitched enthusiastically as he noticed Vivian's head peeking out the window. Below the branch where they sat, a piece of paper flapped in the breeze, impaled on a twig of the branch below them. Vivian knew at once that it was not a piece of garbage that had blown over to their yard and gotten itself stuck: it was intentionally placed there for her to find.

As she opened the door, the bird flew off immediately and the squirrel scurried up the tree to a higher branch, disappearing in the leaves above. Vivian guessed that from the way that her pulse and anxiety level remained neutral, it was not a message to her from the Lynx. It was definitely left there for her to read, though.

It was a small white piece of paper from a spiral calendar of some sort, a page from a daily planner, with neat blue pen ink nearly filling the page. It was clawed in places, with several small holes puncturing it, clearly transported to the tree by an animal or two, but it was easily readable. Vivian sat down on her mother's wooden Adirondack chair and squinted at the paper. The other side was also filled with handwritten words on every line, organized by the hour. When she removed the paper from the branch, the date that was facing her was the next day's date.

9:00 a.m. Phone with Julie in legal. Ext. 335.
10:00 a.m.
11:00 a.m. Last drafts due. Have K. get sign-offs.
11:15 a.m. Pick up H.B. at Victoria Inn. 1408 Roosevelt W.

11:30 a.m. Lunch at Cipriani's.
12:00 – 1:00 p.m.
1:30 p.m. Something had been written here and crossed off. On the rest of the line, it read, *"Market research."*
3:00 p.m. Meeting with Neil – his office.
4:00 p.m. Collect contracts/conference call Martin and Robert.
Nothing was written again until 6:00 p.m. *Go over results/game plan action list at Robert's.*

Vivian squinted at the sheet for several minutes, trying to decipher it, as if the more she narrowed her eyes, the more likely it would make sense. As soon as she had the thought that this might have been just a piece of litter that got stuck in the tree, the squirrel above her started chattering angrily, making her feel that he was reading her mind. She leaned back on the Adirondack and pulled at the loose pieces of paper from where it had been torn, reading the words one after the next, trying to make sense of them.

As she clutched the paper, she became aware of suddenly getting very cold. Vivian knew that the air was still, and that it was technically warm out that morning; she deduced that the cold was inside her, not because of anything happening outside of her body. At the moment that she had that thought, she realized that the sensation was identical to how she felt whenever Kevin Newell was near her. She looked around her yard nervously for a moment or two when it occurred to her in a sudden flash that the paper she held was from his date book. With this realization, the squirrel, hidden between and behind the leaves of the giant elm tree in her backyard, resumed his manic chattering, distinctly different – though she'd have had a hard time describing how –from his earlier vocalizing. This time, it was as though he were saying, exasperated but grateful, "Yes, yes, yes!"

LAST DAY

Mrs. Sharpe called out to Vivian as she was leaving for Gordenner the next morning.

"Vivian? Hold on." She hurried down the steps, brushing and shaking out her hair as she walked. "I noticed on the phone that you received a call from your friend William Carson yesterday. Can you explain this?"

Vivian had forgotten that their phone could display all incoming and outgoing calls. "I'm sorry. I didn't tell him that I wasn't allowed to talk, just Wren."

"Why was he calling you?"

She shrugged, trying to seem blasé, though her pulse quickened. "He didn't realize that I was in trouble and called."

"So I gathered," Mrs. Sharpe said, a sardonic tone in her voice.

"We didn't talk long," Vivian said quietly, realizing the futility of this tact of argument immediately. As anticipated, her mother dismissed it with a quick shake of her head.

"Doesn't matter. Just to clarify, Vivian, he is also on your forbidden list this month. Understand?"

"Yes."

They regarded at each other awkwardly for a moment. "Good."

"Mom?"

"Hmm?"

"Can I leave now? I'm going to miss the bus otherwise."

Mrs. Sharpe, a little startled, said, "Oh, yes, yes. Wouldn't want to make you late. See you at dinner." She kissed Vivian on the cheek.

"Okay. Bye, Dad," she called into the kitchen.

Her father, a little embarrassed at listening in, coughed a little, with a splash of something, presumably coffee, on the kitchen counter. "Oops. Shoot. Have a nice day, honey."

After her conversation with Will, she realized that somehow, she would have to make it back to Gordenner the evening before the press conference. Even though she was on a serious lockdown at

275

home, even though she didn't have a key to get in and there was a security guard as well as high-tech cameras, she had to get in. She would worry about the details later, she told herself as she noticed the bus turn down the road toward Gordenner and pulled the cord; for now, she would try to get through the day.

As Vivian walked down the street to the gate that led to the parking lot, she was very aware that the security guard – she tried to remember his name…Was it Lenny? Larry? – was watching her from his booth. He always made her so nervous, and the best she could do under the circumstances was try to smile and act nonchalant. The more she tried, though, the more she felt sure that there was a physical manifestation of her guilt that he could somehow see; a change in her expression or demeanor that signaled to him that she wasn't as she appeared.

As she neared his booth, he pushed the button to raise the gate. Nothing happened, and he pressed it again. It remained shut. With a shake of his head, he left the booth and pushed the gate open with his hands.

"Not working today?" Vivian asked, thinking that people with guilty consciences do not make idle conversation.

He didn't look at her. "No. There must have been an electrical short. It looks like it won't be fixed until Friday."

"That's too bad."

He looked at her in a quizzical way – at least she thought he did – behind his mirrored sunglasses.

"I just mean that that's a pain for you to have to keep opening and shutting the gate until then."

"I suppose. Anyone can just push it open, though." Without another word, he headed back to his booth.

At the front door, Vivian pressed on the doorbell until Betty at the front desk walked over and manually unlocked the door.

"The electrical system seems to be dysfunctional today. I've gotten more exercise this morning than all last year combined, I think," she laughed.

"Oh. The security guard – I'm sorry – what is his name again?"

"Larry."

"Larry mentioned that there was some kind of short. The gate wasn't working."

"I guess they're all connected," Betty said, holding the door open for some people who were hurrying down the sidewalk. "The doorbell, the alarm system, the locks. What do I know about that, though?"

"That's true. So the system won't be fixed until Friday? That was what Larry said."

"At the earliest," Betty said, her eyes sparkling with excitement. "There was a missing part or something that needs to be sent here from New Jersey. Until then, everything will be done the old-fashioned way: with keys," she playfully gasped. "Whatever will we do?"

Walking to the elevator, Vivian made a mental note that she would have to get her hands on some keys that day. With no alarm system or locking gates, this was her chance.

Some of the faces Vivian passed in the hallways on her way to her office were beginning to look familiar, like the woman with the short brown bangs and pointy eyebrows who reminded her of an elf and the serious-looking man who always seemed to be racing past her with a clipboard. Vivian noticed keys casually flung on desks, keys hanging from hooks on bags, keys cupped in hands and tossed from one to the other, hands totally without any awareness that she was observing. The realization that before the end of the day she would be a premeditated thief, and, by that evening, a burglar, struck Vivian as so sad, the only thing left for her to do was laugh aloud. A woman passing her in the hallway smiled at her, Vivian noticed, probably thinking that she was just a free-spirited teenager having some random, silly thought. Wren would understand, Vivian comforted herself, as she started down the hallway to her office, and she made a mental note of calling her later that morning when she noticed Ms. Collins standing in front of her desk, scribbling something on a yellow note pad.

"Oh, hello, Vivian," she said, barely looking up at the clock. "I was just on my way to a meeting but I wanted to give you some instructions for the morning. Give me just a minute." She turned back to her note, wrote some more, and then sighed, running a hand through her hair, making it stand up even more. "Why am I still writing this when you're standing right here? Someone's going to need a little week at a Costa Rican spa once next week is over. If I survive that long." She grinned and put down her pen, tapping her foot. "And how are you?"

"I'm fine..."

"Good, Vivian. Listen, today is going to be insane for me. Insane. I'm going to be running around and in meetings all day –

and you haven't forgotten the market research at 1:30, right? I saw it on your calendar."

Vivian nodded. "Right."

"We just need to work out the kinks in that. So if you don't mind, I'm just going to leave you some instructions and work to get done and if you need me, you can just page me, okay?"

"Got it." Ms. Collins was talking faster than Vivian had ever heard her speak yet, but she was able to keep up. It was good, she realized, that she'd had a little time to train for this.

"Good. First off, copies: I'm going to need twenty-five copies each of these reports by 11:15 at the latest. If Nadine gives you a hard time, you're just going to have to tell her that I said it was executive privilege and I'll make it up to her some other time. I'll buy her a latté every day for a month. Just tell her I need them by 11:15, my apologies but were late coming to me. If she has issues, she can take them up with me later. Non-negotiable." She handed Vivian a large stack of papers. "Second, all calls, unless they're from Mr. Fontaine's office or a man named Helmut Burr, must go directly into voicemail, okay? I'm sorry if people have their *widdew feewings* hurt, but I can't be disturbed today. If Mr. Fontaine or Mr. Burr does call, though, they should know to reach me on my direct line, but if they do call your line, page me immediately. Okay?"

Vivian nodded. Helmut Burr, she found herself repeating in her mind, Helmut Burr. She noticed Ms. Collins looking at her with her head tilted and a slight frown so she blinked and refocused her expression. "Mr. Fontaine or Mr. Burr," she said.

She regarded Vivian skeptically. "I'm going to write that down for you." She tore a sheet off the pad and whipped off the names with an impossible speed, slapping it on Vivian's desk. She went back into her office and came out carrying a large box of files. "Okay, these will need to be filed chronologically. You don't have to finish that by lunch or anything. Okay," she sighed, "this really was not in your internship description, but I was asked if you could make sure that the first floor big conference room is stocked with coffee, filters, cups, plates and napkins by the time you leave today. You can get them in the supply room. The big conference room is number 103, I think, right down the hall from the main elevators. You can't miss it. If you manage to, ask someone. Anyway, we need that stocked tonight for tomorrow morning's press conference. We'll need a couple of sleeves of cups. Could you also call the cafeteria and ask to speak to Jean there? You need to confirm with her that tomorrow we're going need orange juice and an assortment of sweet rolls and fruit for 25 by no later than 8:45 in the morning – no, make that 8:30. Better be safe. Jean's extension is in the directory in your top drawer. 1107, 1117, something like that."

Vivian nodded.

Ms. Collins picked up some notes that were on top of Vivian's desk. "Okay. Could you call back this one – the printer – and tell him that we need our order a little earlier, if possible – Monday instead of Tuesday? End of the day is fine. Ask to talk to Bob. He'll know what you mean." She wrote '*Bob – printer*' on it and slapped that note on the table. "This one, could you reschedule for next weekend? I just need color, no cut, if they ask. Morning is best." Vivian nodded and Ms. Collins slapped that note on top of the previous one. "Could you call back this *Atlanta Journal* reporter," she glanced at the note, "Andrea Waldrum and reschedule for next Wednesday? I can talk at 10:00 until 10:35 or 1:30 until 2:30." She put the final note on top of the stack and took a breath of relief. "I'm so glad that I can just scratch these things off my list. What a relief. After tomorrow, things will slow down a little for a while." She went to her office, grabbed her briefcase, pulling the door shut behind her as she walked out. "So you might not see me until 1:30. I trust that you'll be fine?"

"Yes, absolutely. I'll let you know if anything comes up, but I should be fine."

"Thanks, Vivian. After the research, I'll need you to make some press kits. I'll get that to you when you need it, okay? It'll come together lickety-split. You're a dream." She started to walk out of the office when she stopped. "Oh – don't forget – take your lunch break at 12:30. And remember to take your," she pointed at Vivian's purse.

"I will." Vivian was very eager to call Wren but trying not to seem preoccupied.

Ms. Collins was walking by the window down the hall in front of the office when she held up a finger, reminding herself of something, and stuck her head back in the room. "Vivian, there was something in your mail slot this morning. I put it on your phone." Propped against her phone was a large envelope with her name typed across. Ms. Collins turned back down the hallway and Vivian listened to the sound of her clicking heels recede before she sat down and picked up the envelope.

She noticed that her last name was spelled incorrectly: "Sharp" the way the Lynx wrote it. Her fingers started shaking, and, just as she was about to open it, her phone rang – was it always that loud? – causing her to let out a small sound that was between a shriek and a gasp. Luckily, no one seemed to hear.

"Hello?" Vivian said, trying to keep her heart, beating as fast as she could imagine possible, from pounding straight out of her chest with her hand pressed against it. "This is Vivian. Thank you for calling Gordenner; have a nice day." She slapped her hand against her forehead, gasping. "I mean, Ms. Collins' office. How may I help you?"

A familiar voice giggled on the other end. "Rough morning, Viv?" After a few moments without a response, she said, "This is Wren, goofball."

Vivian sighed with relief and lowered her voice. Her hand was shaking. "Oh, thank goodness. I'm a basket case, girl. Truly." Another call tried to come through; she ignored it.

"Your phone just beeped."

"I know. Someone's trying to call and I'm intentionally ignoring it. The first of my crimes of the day."

"What's going on? Oh, silly question. That whole espionage thing, right?"

"Yep. That."

"Anything else? You seem pretty frazzled."

"Hmm…I talked to Will yesterday."

"That would do it," Wren laughed. "I know he called; he told me."

"And I saw Tolstoy since we talked. You know? My pig friend."

"Pig friend, spirit guide. Whatever. That's great. How is he?"

"Good. And it was good to see him, even if he may be just a really vivid figment of my imagination, an example of my emotional breakdown. "

"He's not."

"Whether he is or not, really, right now the sad thing is how much I need those interactions with him for the sake of my mental health," Vivian laughed with a bitterness she hadn't known before. "Talking to a possibly imaginary pig is the only thing that makes me feel sane right now, crazily enough. He's also my main social connection at the moment."

"I know, but that's only temporary."

"Okay, and so I talked to Will and Tolstoy and it looks like I'm about to hear from the Lynx again."

"What?" Wren sounded alarmed. "What do you mean? Is that the Lynx calling you?"

Vivian rubbed her thumb over her name on the envelope, smudging it. "No. I got a letter from him. It's in my hands right now, still in the envelope."

"So you haven't read it."

"Not yet. Want me to?"

"Of course."

Vivian was glad to have Wren on the line with her when she opened the envelope. She slowly unfolded the paper inside. There was a letter folded into another set of papers, which were stapled together. "Now remember that I'm going to have to do this quietly, okay? And I may have to stop suddenly." She could hear that another call was trying to get through again and she continued to ignore it again. Recognizing the typewritten letters and seeing his signature right away, Vivian said, "Yep. It's from him."

"What does it say?" Wren whispered, a little breathlessly.

"Let's see." Vivian briefly considered shutting the door to her office but dismissed the idea, realizing that would make her more conspicuous. She swiveled in her chair so that she wasn't facing the window and the hall, but she had to also keep an eye on it in case anyone walked into her office. "Let's see…

"Vivian, I received your note. I understand your motivations now. Be aware that the Factory is going to have "research" presented tonight to finalize the business agreement for invading other countries with their Bioengineered Biohazard, 'Bountiful.' The research submitted is pure folly and fiction: the real report is included here. They have doctored the new research report to the point where it does not resemble truth to an even slight extent, which is what the Factory does, to try to make it presentable. I recommend making copies of this report. This is highly confidential. Do not let anyone see you with this document. Second, I recommend getting the true document in the hands of truth-telling journalists. Good luck with that one. There will be a press conference tomorrow morning at 9:30. They are probably all hacks, crooks, and professional prostitutes but it wouldn't hurt to get this report to them. The worst they will do is ignore it; the best they will do is their job.
The Lynx"

Neither said anything until Wren muttered a quiet, "Huh."

Vivian read it over again. "Well, at least there were no threats in this one."

"I know. It's almost as if he's working with you."

"Yeah. I don't know what is scarier, him wanting to destroy me or work with me. So," Vivian said, refolding the letter and sticking it and the envelope into her bag, "I don't know what I'm supposed to do with this now."

"Find a journalist who will help?"

"Yes, but..." Vivian stopped speaking as the answer flooded into her mind.

"What?"

Vivian was silent and Wren repeated herself, louder. "What?"

"I think I have a solution. I know what to do."

"What's that?" Wren said excitedly.

"Well, I need to get copies of the real report to the media who are at the press conference tomorrow."

"Right, great idea, but how do you get it to them?"

"That's just it. Ms. Collins said something about me stuffing press packets later today. All I would need to do is stick this in. But I'd need copies somehow."

"Don't you have a copier there?"

"Not in my office, no. I'd have to get copies in the main copier room, and someone else does that. I'm not allowed to copy them myself. I just wouldn't feel safe handing these off to the woman in charge there."

"I can see that."

"And Kyle – I could get copies in his office – but there are too many to make. I can only do one or two there. Plus I wouldn't want him to see what I have. It's too risky."

"Of course. So...?"

"So, this is what I think I have to do," Vivian said as the plan crystallized in her mind. "When I leave here, I'm going to go home like I always do with the report in my bag. I'm going to have to sneak out of the house and make copies at Copy Queen or something."

"Then what? Wait," she shouted. "You're going to sneak out of the house?"

"That's the only way I can get out," Vivian said matter-of-factly. "I'll have to go to bed early, quote unquote, pray mightily that no one comes to my room, and then hustle to make copies and get back here tonight to add these reports into the press kit folders and sneak back into the house."

"Oh, that's all. Go back to Gordenner at night on your bike? Are you serious? I mean, they have that scary security guard who's got it out for you."

"Actually, he was kind of human today," Vivian said offhandedly. "This is not something I want to do either, though. It just seems like the only way. Then there is that small matter of keys."

"What do you mean?"

"I'll need keys to get in and..."

"Wait, wait, wait. What about the security guard? What about an alarm system?"

"Well, with the guard, I'm just going to have to watch him and wait until he leaves his booth. He has to take a break sometimes and he's not always in there anyway. He has to walk around the grounds..."

"Vivian, you can't..."

"Wren, listen to me, I have to." Vivian sounded more emphatic than she meant to, but she couldn't help it. "Do you know what this company is planning to do with this Bountiful product? Everyone it's going to poison? Anyway, I'll get past Larry..."

"Who's he?"

"The security guard. I'll get past him and then I'll just slip in with some keys." Someone tried to call again, making Vivian anxious. She let the call go into voicemail.

"What keys? Whose keys?"

"That remains unknown at this point."

"Who are you? Catwoman?"

Vivian continued undaunted, "By the end of the day, I'll be in possession of a set of keys. Considering everything, this will probably be the easiest of what I've got to pull off today."

"You're right," Wren said.

"And the security alarm is down right now so I don't have to worry about that. Then I just switch the reports and I'm in the clear."

Wren sighed in frustration. "But how are you going to get there and home? The bus doesn't run at night."

"I'll ride my bike. I'll leave it in the bushes when I get home and just take off as soon as I can."

Wren was silent for a few moments, until she said, very simply, "I'm coming with you."

"Wren, you can't," Vivian looked out into the hallway. People hurriedly walked past, no one lingered. "You really can't. This is serious stuff."

"You think that I don't know that? That's why I need to be there. You think I'm not serious?"

"That's not..."

"Well, good, because I'm coming along. You need an assistant – no, what's the word?"

"In this case, it would be accomplice, I think. But, still, it's just that you can't..."

"Why not? Listen, your plan is good but not perfect. You need quick and easy transportation to and from: I've got that. You need someone to be on lookout when you're switching the report: I can do that. You need someone to call your parents when you get arrested: I can do that, too."

Vivian had to smile despite herself. As if Wren could sense Vivian's mood changing, she said in a playful tone, "Come on. You need me. Don't act coy. You know you do. I'll pick you up..."

"But it can't be at my house `cause..."

"So what? I'll pick you up at the end of the block or whatever, and we'll get copies and go to Gordenner. Wait. Can't you just tell the security guard that you're there to do some work?"

"Nope. He could call Ms. Collins and find out it wasn't true. I'll have to sneak in. No one but us can know."

"Okay, so that's what it is. Let's both wear dark clothing. I've got some of that green stage make-up we can smudge on our faces to blend in better."

Vivian briefly entertained the image of the two of them crawling into the building on their elbows and knees like in a military recruitment commercial. "I don't think we'll need it. But I'll be by my house, by the cul-de-sac at the end. There's a little space inside the bushes where I can hide until you show up. Okay?" This was a place where Vivian used to play with her friends when she was a child; when she was growing up, it was also where the teenagers would sneak off to smoke cigarettes.

"Yes, fine. What time?"

"I think be there at eight o'clock. I don't think anyone should be in my part of Gordenner then."

"What if someone is? What's our explanation?"

"We need one of those, don't we?" Vivian said, feeling her energy drain.

"Really, to be safe, we do."

They were both silent on their ends of the phone until Vivian blurted out, "I know."

"Oh, goody. What?"

"I'll forget to do something – to get the cups and coffee set up..."

"Cups and coffee?"

"It's one of my jobs for the press conference," she said distractedly. "Anyway, I'll forget that on purpose and so we'll be forced to return. I'll say that someone let me in, I don't know anyone at Gordenner so I won't know any names."

"You're brilliant," Wren gushed. "I think you have a mind for this misdemeanors."

"Oh, I don't know. This might very well be a felony I'm talking about."

"One has to aim high," Wren laughed. "I would expect no less from you."

"You sure know how to flatter a girl. So we'll say that we ran into someone and he let us in."

"And why am I there?"

"You were my ride."

"Which will be the only truthful thing we'll have said at the point."

"We can't become total liars overnight. We've got to ease into it."

"True." Wren thought out Vivian's scenario. "Okay, that works. I think. I'll let you know if I come up with anything better."

"You do that. Listen. I've got to run."

"I know. I'll see you tonight at eight at the cul-de-sac on the end of your block."

"Yes. See you then."

After a pause, Wren said, "Viv?"

"Yes?"

"Should I feel all James Bond-y right now?"

"Not until we get out safely. Then you can feel like James Bond."

Wren thought about this for a moment. "Anyways, he's all sexist and violent, right? I don't like him. I don't want to be James Bond. I'll just be myself, like, only tougher."

"Perfect." Vivian swiveled to glance at the clock. "Okay, I've *really* got to run."

"See you at eight."

Vivian took a few breaths and checked her messages. There were three from the previous evening – two reporters and Mr. Newell's secretary asking for a returned call – and more from that morning – another reporter, one hang-up, and a message from Will. Upon hearing his voice, Vivian felt her shoulder muscles immediately tense up. He spoke quickly.

"Vivian, this is Will. Don't listen to this on speakerphone, okay? Listen, I'm going to need to get a press badge for tomorrow, for the press conference. Can you get me one? I need to be there: some national media is going to be there in addition to local press. Call me back, okay? I'll be home for another ten minutes. It's 9:15 now."

Vivian was trying to wrap her brain around that message and was annoyed that Will hadn't even left her his phone number, when she heard his voice again on the next one.

"Vivian, this is Will again," he paused for a moment. "Listen, just so you know, I managed to talk to some woman and I got myself a press badge through my college paper. I know you're going to be at the press conference tomorrow so I just wanted you to know to act like you don't know me. We've got to play things really cool. I didn't want to leave you a message there at work but I needed to make sure that I reached you. Okay. Later." Vivian deleted the message immediately. *So Will is going to be there*, she thought and immediately moved on mentally. She had no room in her mind to think about the next day so she pushed it aside.

She refolded the report and the letter from the Lynx and put it in her purse, which she then placed on her lap, but, feeling awkward, she placed it the bottom drawer of her desk; she stared at the drawer for a few moments before she put her purse back on her lap. She glanced back at the notes from Ms. Collins and started making the phone calls she had asked of her. Again, it gave Vivian a small feeling of security, as she checked items off her list and did at least some of what was expected of her. One by one, she crossed the messages off and tossed them out. Finally, she noticed the piece of paper with the name Helmut Burr written on it. As she looked at it, the letters *HB* appeared in her mind: of course, this was whom Mr. Newell had referred to on the page torn from his day planner, the man Will had mentioned. Helmut Burr. Of course he was *HB*.

Vivian shrugged it off and called Jean in the cafeteria to arrange for the food Ms. Collins had requested.

Then Vivian started down the hall with the report to make copies. Along the way, she made a mental note of every set of keys she noticed unattached to a person. There was a set on a desk in a large office down the hall, but there were dozens of people in that room and no reason for her to be there, not even for a moment; there was also a set of keys attached to a purse by a keychain next to a phone that would be easy enough to unclip if it were not in another office with filled with activity. Other than that, she did not notice any other keys randomly loose without a person nearby. Vivian resolved to make the acquiring of a set of keys her lunch-hour project.

In Vivian's favorite restroom, the one on the second floor near the stairwell (people rarely took the stairs, she noticed) with the extra roomy stalls, she quickly glanced at the report Ms. Collins gave her to copy. She heard the door to the restroom swoosh open, so she waited until the next stall was occupied before she hurried out, clutching the report in her hand.

Vivian was nearly at the copier room when she realized with a start that her purse strap was no longer hanging from her shoulder. She had left it in the bathroom, on the chair next to the sink. Her heart raced, and it was impossible for her not to look mortified as she hurried back there, imagining the letter from the Lynx inside and her Center City High School I.D. card in her wallet. As Vivian opened the bathroom door, she gasped as she saw a woman standing by the sink, sticking her hand in its unzipped pouch, feeling around for a wallet, presumably.

Vivian startled the woman as she burst in the room.

"Oh, hi," Vivian said, quite loudly, surprising herself. "That's my purse. I just forgot it."

The woman, startled, said, "I was just looking for your wallet to find where it belonged." She handed it to Vivian.

"I know," Vivian said, zipping the pouch. "I'm not in the habit of carrying my purse around with me yet, I guess."

The woman looked at her coolly and turned back to the sink, checking her teeth in the mirror. "You've got to be careful with personal belongings here."

"I know," she said, starting for the door. "Thanks."

"Stupid, stupid, stupid," Vivian muttered to herself, relieved but disappointed with her carelessness, as she headed back to the copier room. Her face, she was sure, was bright pink. She was going to have to be more thorough, she told herself as she grabbed a pen and the order form for copies. She was not going to be able to just traipse into Gordenner after hours and hope for the best; she was going to have to be focused. She filled out the form and clipped it to the report in the basket. Before she could leave the room, though, Vivian heard a voice above the whirring motors and machines. "Excuse me. You can't be serious about needing these by 11:15." Nadine was standing behind the counter, clutching her order form, and she gestured widely to the copiers, all shooting out papers and flashing brightly under the tops. "That's simply not possible. There are dozens of orders in front of yours and they're all behind schedule as is."

Vivian felt her hands shake as she spoke. "I'm sorry. Ms. Collins..."

"Listen," Nadine said, folding her arms across her chest, "I don't care what Ms. Collins says. What about the others who were in line before her? What am I supposed to tell them as to why their copies are even further delayed? Does Ms. Collins want to handle that for me? Do a little PR on my behalf?" She made a brittle little sound Vivian could only interpret as something approximating laughter.

"I think that she got the report late to her..."

"You see, that's the problem," she drummed her fingers on the counter impatiently. "Everyone wants to pass the buck and everyone also wants special privileges. Does anybody see how busy I am? It's because seventy-five percent of the orders I get are at the eleventh hour like this, forcing me to squeeze an impossible amount of work into a tiny bit of time."

Vivian realized that sympathy was the only approach she could take to end this exchange quickly. "I'm really sorry..."

Nadine sighed loudly, the sound like a tire slowly deflating, and smoothed her hair back with one hand. She chewed on her lip and glanced at the clock furtively. "It's not your fault. Okay, I'll get it to you as soon as I can. This is extraordinary, super, deluxe priority like everything else from Ms. Collins, right? Stop the presses!"

This was Nadine joking, Vivian realized, so she laughed as she knew she should. "Thank you."

Nadine, softened, took the work order and report from the bin and glanced over the work order. "Okay, this isn't so bad," she said grudgingly. "It'll be in her mail bin by 11:15, I suppose."

"Thank you so much," Vivian said as she watched her briefly glance over the report. "I appreciate it."

Nadine mumbled something inaudibly as she turned back to the copiers and Vivian hurried out of the copier room, a little punch-drunk. She began to feel the sensation of being unattached to her body, as she passed the office workers and executives in the hallway back to her office. Her head felt like a helium balloon floating in the general area above her body and her legs were wound-up, mechanical toy legs that delivered her where she needed to go. Taking a few breaths after she fell into her chair behind her desk, she felt a little better and put her purse back in the drawer. She felt nervous almost immediately, however, and returned it to her lap. It would have to stay there, she realized.

She spent the rest of the morning filing papers and taking messages for Ms. Collins. It seemed that as soon as she hung up with one call, took a deep breath and got back to her stack of papers, the phone rang again, with another person who was irritated at having to leave a message rather than speak to Ms. Collins directly. Her increasing ability to not be bothered by the string of inpatient callers on the other line brought her hope for the days ahead.

That morning went by quickly for her, which was surprising, given how much she was dreading her lunch-hour project of securing keys for that evening. In the crowded cafeteria, as she was bent down, unpacking her lunch from her bag, she was jolted upright as a tray dropped down on the empty table she had found in the corner. It was Kyle, grinning his wry smile in what seemed to be perpetual amusement at how easy it was to startle Vivian. On his tray he had a sandwich wrapped in plastic and a couple of apples rolling around.

"How are you, missy? Got an empty seat?" he said, as he sat in one. He looked happy to see her, the realization of which nearly made Vivian feel guilty and briefly want to disappear.

"Sure," she said. "How are you?"

"Oh, things are a little hectic right now." He took a bite out of his sandwich and Vivian tried to keep focusing on his eyes or her own lunch so she wouldn't have to look at his sandwich. "There's a big meeting tonight and a big to-do tomorrow with all the Bountiful Wheat stuff that's going to be released, so things are a little on edge in my part of the building. I imagine it's the same where you're at."

She nodded. "Ms. Collins has refused all phone calls today and is basically in meetings the whole day. I mean, she's usually pretty – you know..."

"Type A?" he offered.

"I guess you could say that," Vivian laughed, "but today is even more so."

"All that wheeling and dealing," Kyle shrugged. "Life's too short to spend it on this stuff, you know? I'd rather hang out with my animals and putter around the house, frankly. Or have a great meal and bottle of wine with friends. I have no interest in living that stressful a life." He was in a talkative mood, even more so than usual. "How about you?"

"What do you mean?"

"I mean, is that the sort of thing you think you want with your life: going from high-pressured meeting to phone call to business trip?"

Vivian was a little discombobulated at being asked such a question by an adult, someone who clearly was interested in her thoughts. She wasn't sure if she'd ever experienced this type of interaction with an adult before, except perhaps her father. "Um, I don't think it would be so bad, not if you believe in what you're doing."

"What do you mean, *believe in what you're doing?*" he asked, putting his sandwich down and taking a loud, crunchy bite out of his apple.

"I mean, if what you do is important to you, meaningful. Otherwise, it would seem like a waste of time and energy, I think."

Kyle's eyes sparkled. Vivian was becoming convinced that he could do that at will. "Hmm. Maybe I don't relate to all busyness because I haven't found my passion yet. Food for thought."

Vivian looked back down at her tray, embarrassed. "I didn't mean that you don't..."

He waved his hand good-naturedly. "No, no, I didn't take it wrong. You're right, I think. I think that if you really care about what you're doing, you might never run out of excitement about it. My housemate's like that. He's a doctor, an oncologist."

"What's that? An onc..?"

"Oncologist. A cancer doctor. He works crazy, long hours but he never seems to resent going in to work. He might sleep three, four hours a night, but he always wakes up bright-eyed and bushy-tailed. He loves what he does, though. Anyway," Kyle said, in such a way that it was clear he had something else he wanted to talk about. "Your friend I met that one day. What was her name?"

"Wren."

"Wren. That's right. How could I forget? Does she go to Center City High with you?"

Vivian nodded. "I just met her this year, though. This was her first year there."

"Oh?"

"Yeah. She was home-schooled before that."

"I could imagine Wren being a very popular girl at school. She's so pretty and warm and interesting. Like you, of course," he winked.

Vivian smiled a little. "Yeah, well, aside from the pretty thing, that's not really what makes someone popular at our school. She sort of lacks exactly what makes a girl popular at Center City."

"So what makes someone popular at your school?"

"Following the trends. A sort of snobby attitude. Superficiality. You know," she shrugged, "stupid things."

Kyle cocked his head sympathetically, his eyes bright-blue lasers. "I'm sorry to hear that. I guess the high school experience isn't much different than when I went."

"Besides, "Vivian added, "*we* might think that Wren is beautiful, but I don't think the people at my school do."

"This is a pretty white-bread, cookie-cutter town. I hope you know that there is a lot to life outside of that school and this town. If the people here don't appreciate you, don't think that it's any liability in the real world. There's a lot more to life out there."

"Oh, I know."

"I'm sure you do. Center City has got to be the most boring place on earth," he said, an unfamiliar, contemptuous look on his perfect features. "Speaking of white bread, is that another peanut butter and jelly sandwich?"

"It is," Vivian said, looking at the sandwich in her hands. "I'm not much of a cook yet, I'm afraid."

"You'll learn, probably when you go away to college. I assume that you're going to college."

Vivian nodded absent-mindedly. "Next year is when I have to start putting more thought into it, but, yes, definitely."

"I might go back to college."

"Oh, really? What do you want to study?"

"Well, I got a journalism degree a while back I'm not doing anything with, but I'm thinking interior design. That may be what my passion is."

As they talked, Vivian started getting anxious, aware of the minutes ticking by and closing in on her lunch-hour project: the acquisition of keys. She began casting furtive glances throughout about the cafeteria, looking for a stray set of keys amid the trays, bags of chips and water bottles. Unlike in the offices she passed, sets of keys were splayed across tables everywhere in the cafeteria like silver sea anemones. It was the equivalent of a bonanza to her, and she tried not to become overwhelmed with the surfeit of possibilities; she decided instead to hone in on the most accessible set.

Kyle told her about his plans for a remodeling of his kitchen and sunroom, allowing her little more to do than nod and say "Oh?" and "Wow" at appropriate junctures and keep scanning the area for the closest keys.

Before long, Vivian noticed one set on the floor next to a purse that was beside an empty chair of the table behind hers. It was close enough that Vivian could see that it wouldn't take much effort to secure them. The owner, a woman with bright yellow hair and equally bright pink lipstick, had gone to talk to someone at a table a good distance away; the table was empty, though there was untouched food on her tray. Vivian, nodding and maintaining eye contact with Kyle as he talked, shifted to the side and subtly put the toe of her shoe over the keys, slowly dragging them over to where she sat.

"What do you think you'll major in?" Kyle asked.

"Hmm?" The woman looked up and locked eyes with Vivian for a second. The next thing Vivian knew, she was walking over toward her, an indecipherable expression on her face. Vivian would tell her it was an accident, the keys getting caught under her foot. She would giggle, rolling her eyes at herself. Instead, the woman walked over to the table and grabbed her purse, not looking for a moment for keys, and picked up her tray. She walked back to the table she had been visiting and set her tray down there. It took all of Vivian's willpower not to react visibly. She felt her heart beating again.

"In college. What do you think you'll major in? I guess you have some time to think about it."

"Yeah, right," Vivian said. "I have no idea right now." Vivian was done eating and wanted to get out of there. She took her purse off the table and put it in her lap, looking through it for something, anything to give her an excuse for opening it. She found some lip balm and placed her purse down by her feet.

"I should get going." She looked over at the clock and put on some lip balm distractedly. "I'll see you later, Kyle," Vivian said as she organized her tray. As she reached down to pick up her purse again, she scooped up the keys in the palm of her hand. Luckily, this was not a very big set. Pushed up against the soft pads of her fingers, they didn't make a sound. Just two regular door keys, a car key and a large one.

"Have a good afternoon," he said. "I hope I wasn't talking too much."

"No, not at all. I love talking to you. I've just got…stuff to do." Vivian smiled at him, she hoped not too overbearingly. Although she was adding the act of stealing to her internal list of immoral acts during their conversation, Kyle comforted her, almost made her feel like she was normal again. She opened her purse, hands still cupped around the keys, and dropped them inside in one movement. A fleeting glance at the woman with the yellow hair showed Vivian that she was still engrossed in her conversation.

As Vivian walked to the conveyer belt and loaded her tray, she half-expected a rough hand on her shoulder, perhaps the hand of the woman whose keys she stole, perhaps the hand of a security guard, but it never happened. She felt relief wash over her as she walked out of the cafeteria doors, as if she had somehow made it out of the danger zone. The feeling didn't last for long before it hit her that it was just the first challenge of an obstacle course – the easy ones were always at the beginning. She went to the bathroom to study the set and make sure they included the front door key for Gordenner. They did, in addition to a car key and two others. Vivian shook off as best she could the mental image of the poor woman standing outside her car, fumbling around for her keys futilely, patting her pockets. She hoped she had someone who would pick her up without too much trouble and let her into her home, and that she would not be made to feel like she was stupid or unorganized. Didn't adults always give spare sets of keys to at least one other person? Vivian clasped her hands together, in the only gesture that made sense to her, and asked for forgiveness, hoping that this was so.

In the twenty minutes she had before her market research session, Vivian paced the halls for a while then stopped to glance out of the giant bay window in the atrium, overlooking the river. Staring at it, she saw dead, poisoned fish and birds pouring out of the pipes with inky black water. She blinked, and it was back to normal. She had no idea how long she stood there at the window letting this fantasy unspool before she heard someone call her name. Whirling around, a series of lies already on her tongue, she saw Ms. Collins and Mr. Newell standing about a foot from her. Ms. Collins looked at her in a way Vivian recognized from her mother; she was obviously irritated by her appearance of daydreaming. Mr. Newell looked a little more well-rested than usual, a little color on his cheeks, but his face still looked as if it just naturally wanted to be in a grimace.

"Oh, hi," Vivian said, nonchalantly, trying to not rub her arms from the sudden burst of cold. "I was just looking outside."

"I noticed," Ms. Collins said dryly, pausing to look at her watch. "If you're ready to start the meeting, we'll be a little early, but we're pressed for time all day so it would be good for us. Nothing you need to do, right? No urgent matters?" Ms. Collins was being sarcastic – she seemed a little angry about something – but Vivian acted as if she hadn't noticed.

"No, I'm fine with getting started now."

They walked together to the market research room, and Mr. Newell stopped to use the restroom. Ms. Collins and Vivian went into the room together. Ms. Collins poured herself a cup of coffee. "Tea again, Vivian?" she asked.

"Oh, please. Thank you."

Bringing the two cups over, Ms. Collins sat across from Vivian. "How has your morning been going?"

"Fine. I made the phone calls you asked and put in the order in the copier room. You should have the copies in your mail slot now. I wrote some messages."

Ms. Collins raised an eyebrow. "Interesting. I tried to call a couple of times and didn't get through to you. I could tell from the sound of the beep that you were on the other line."

"Oh, was that you? Yes, I was taking calls when you tried to call through, I'm guessing. The phone was ringing all morning."

"You do know that your job is to make sure that *all* my calls are answered if you're in the office, right, not just when it's convenient for you. All you have to do if you can see that someone is trying to get through on the other line is put the one you're talking to on hold and pick up. It's simple. It explains how to do it in your manual."

"I'm sorry. I guess I got flustered."

"There's nothing to get flustered about, Vivian. Just learn how to do it, okay? It's not hard. I need to know that I can count on you, especially on a day like today when I've got ten million plates in the air."

"I'm sorry. I'll read the manual again when we are done here."

"You've got to fill folders when we're done here. Remember? That's the priority."

"Okay, I'll do that first and then the manual."

Ms. Collins flashed a brief smile. It was amazing how the smallest show of warmth could brighten up her face. "I don't mean to be grouchy. I've just got a lot of stresses right now."

"I know. I'll try to make things easier for you." Mr. Newell walked in and with him came a bracing cold breeze. Vivian wrapped her fingers around her cup for warmth and took a big sip.

"Thanks, Vivian." Ms. Collins said.

Mr. Newell looked at them both, realizing that they were discussing something that didn't involve him, sat across from Ms. Collins and took out a notebook and pen from a big binder.

Ms. Collins did the same and put on her glasses. "We're going to do things a little different this time, Vivian. Rather than a full-blown research session, it's going to be a little more casual. Just a kind of interview without a presentation because you already know about Bountiful. This will help us learn better how to phrase and frame the issues, okay?"

Vivian nodded. As her hands reached for her arms, she realized with annoyance that she had forgotten her sweater back at the office. She'd just have to accept the cold.

Mr. Newell thumbed through his notebook and pulled two sheets from it, giving one copy to Ms. Collins. He read from this, woodenly as usual, but with an added air of something else. It took Vivian a few moments to identify that other quality: it was nervousness.

Mr. Newell cleared his throat. "Okay, first, we need to talk about starvation more."

"Okay."

"Are you aware that people in many other countries often do not have access to adequate nutrition and calories?"

"Yes."

"Is this troubling to you?"

"Yes."

"What do you think would influence your emotions most on the topic of starvation? For example, images of starving people in film or photographs? Information and education? Something else?"

"I'd say information and education."

He and Ms. Collins both jotted down some notes. He continued. "Is it hard to imagine starvation, and, if so, does this influence your feelings about it?"

"Um, I imagine how I think it would be but I don't know how close or far off I am from it."

"What would it take for you to be able to imagine starvation? Would the images or testimony of starving people help you to understand it on a deeper level? If you talked to someone whose child had starved, would that add to your ability to understand what it might feel like?"

"Probably."

"Good. What do you feel about people who protest?"

Vivian was jarred a little from the abrupt change of direction. "Protest what?"

"Protest anything," he said impatiently. "Protest the government. Protest corporations. Protest products."

"I don't think negatively about them, in general, but I guess it depends on what is being protested."

"So you don't have a general pro or con feeling about protesters?"

"No. I mean, I don't really know any. And it would have to be based on the..."

"Circumstances."

"Right."

Mr. Newell looked at Ms. Collins. She nodded at him ever so slightly. "How would you feel about people who might protest a Gordenner product?"

Her face started to get warm despite the goosebumps on her arms. "It would depend on the situation."

"Well, I'm going to cut to the chase here because obviously this marketing session is about Bountiful so that is what I am referring to. We have a good guess that there will be protests when Bountiful comes out and we..."

Ms. Collins shook her head a little and jumped in. "Vivian, you're probably wondering why on such a busy day we are taking the time out to interview you yet again on Bountiful."

Vivian nodded. "I am."

"Here's the deal: we were a little shaken by your responses at our last session and it led us to think that there are still some kinks we need to work out. Tomorrow is a huge day: we're having a press conference in the morning with big, national news outlets there. We've worked very hard for this to happen. We need to make sure that there is no chance of any of us being caught off guard by a question or an implication of some sort we hadn't anticipated. This is why we're spending extra time – time we really don't have – working out every conceivable snag. Tomorrow morning must be flawless."

"Okay. But what does that have to do with what Mr. Newell was asking about protests?"

Mr. Newell leaned forward in his seat until it squeaked. "There is a segment of the population that is going to be negative about our new product line no matter what, no matter how positive and revolutionary it is. We need to be preemptive about that."

"Why would they be negative, though?" Vivian asked. She couldn't stop herself. "If it's all so positive, does it matter what this little segment of the population says? I mean, if what you're saying is true, if it is such an amazingly positive product?"

"Vivian," Ms. Collins jumped in, "if it were just a few isolated wackos and crazies, we wouldn't bother with that. You're right. But there is a very small percentage – okay, maybe a little bigger than that – about eight percent of people polled who don't trust our technology, who believe food should be grown in an old-fashioned, idealized way, and that just doesn't reflect reality when it comes to the millions of people who are in dire straits. It is a pleasant fantasy, but it doesn't reflect reality. And these people want to impose their ideals on the rest of us, make everyone live the same way, their way, regardless of need."

"Well said," Mr. Newell said.

"But what is it about the technology that is so upsetting to people?" Vivian pressed.

Ms. Collins sighed. Vivian braced herself, expecting to be yelled at, but it didn't happen. "As I said, regardless of the details, these people – about one to two percent of the eight percent or so – are going to be on the offensive. They are relatively small in number, but they make up for it in terms of influence: they are very loud and aggressive about getting their message out. The last thing that we need is for this revolutionary new product be given a black eye before it's even out of the gate, before we can let the world see the positive impact of it on developing nations. Do you understand what I'm saying?"

Vivian nodded. Her pulse was racing but she tried to stay calm. "I do, but I still don't see how you're going to be able to avoid talking about the technology."

At this, Ms. Collins stared at Vivian momentarily as if she were some strange and unsavory oddity she'd awoken to find on her lawn one morning; its effect had Vivian feeling for the first time like one of the microscope slides from her science class. Finally, Ms. Collins turned to Mr. Newell. "This is your domain, Kevin. You're going to be the one up there tomorrow."

"The technology, Vivian," he said, "is complicated, but it's also very simple. It has to do with engineering plants to both be able to withstand the harshest conditions and to be able to provide a maximum of nutrients that might otherwise be hard to access in a third world environ..."

"You want to say *developing nations*, Kevin. Remember?" Ms. Collins sighed, sounding exasperated. "Developing nations is what we settled on. That's what people say these days. It's more considerate, more polite."

He rolled his eyes and continued. "In developing nations. So it is no different from what farmers have done for generations – breeding seeds for the best characteristics – but in a more suitable environment, one where we can carefully observe and control its progress from a laboratory and test fields, where we can separate out what we really want."

"Are you controlling it, though?"

Ms. Collins raised an eyebrow. "What do you mean?"

"I mean, once Bountiful is released, how can it be controlled? The seeds will be spread through pollination like any other seeds, right?"

They both begrudgingly nodded at Vivian, looking at her suspiciously, not sure where she was going.

"And if this technology is flawed in any way..."

"What makes you think that the technology is flawed, Vivian? I don't understand this." Ms. Collins sat ramrod straight in her chair, steam from her coffee still rising, creating a weird effect around her.

"We're talking about feeding starving people here. That's what the story is about: not the technology. Why do you insist on bringing it back to that? Frankly, I don't understand your preoccupation with the technology. It's a *human interest* story," she said, punctuating the words with slaps on the table. "How can I get you to see that?"

Vivian was shaken but she continued. "I agree, it's a human interest story, because what if the local water is ruined as a result of the technology? How is that helping starving people? So then they will die of dehydration or poisoning instead? If the water in Sri Lanka is totally polluted, killing fish and birds, how is that helping?"

The room was silent. "Vivian," Mr. Newell finally said quietly, tapping his pen on the table, "what do you know?"

Ms. Collins looked at him and shook her head in disbelief.

At this point, Vivian realized that she was no longer cold. Her shoulders and arms had warmed up considerably and her chest was starting to radiate heat. She felt that this must be a good sign; she was no longer scared. "Nothing. I know nothing except..."

"I mean, what made you pull Sri Lanka out of thin air like that? This is all very strange."

"All I know is that this technology – whatever it is – will need to be addressed."

"It has been," Ms. Collins said sharply, slamming her open palm down on her leg. "It *has* been addressed over and over." She looked at Mr. Newell, shaking her head incredulously again. "I don't understand this at all."

"Have you been reading confidential papers, Vivian?" Mr. Newell said, nodding his head at her. "Have you?"

"No," Vivian said, emphatically.

He directed his eyes at Ms. Collins, ignoring Vivian. "What kind of paperwork is she doing? What is she doing in your office?"

Vivian, her face getting hot, started to talk but Ms. Collins cut her off. "Filing, answering phones. You know." Ms. Collins stared at Vivian as though she were an inscrutable puzzle, but added, "I haven't seen anything weird."

Mr. Newell turned back to Vivian. "I mean, didn't you get this job after you'd been found sneaking around the property with your friend?" he said, not looking away from her for a moment.

"I wasn't sneaking. I came here looking for a job."

He snorted and looked back down to his paper, jotting something down. "Whatever you want us to believe, Vivian. Have you even done a background check on her?" he said, gesturing at Vivian with a pen as he turned to Ms. Collins. "Do we even know for a fact that she is who she says she is?"

Ms. Collins started to say something when Vivian said, reaching for her purse, "Do you want to see my school ID? I don't have a driver's license yet, but I have a school ID and a library card you can check it against."

Ms. Collins smiled wanly, still looking bewildered and stunned from the whole exchange. "We don't need that. Let's not blow things out of proportion, Kevin. Let's not be paranoid. I did talk to her mother – she owns *Look Sharpe!* on Washington..."

"This means?" he said.

"...and I believe she is who she says she is. I just think that we're a little on edge from everything."

Mr. Newell didn't say anything, didn't acknowledge in any way what Ms. Collins had said; he just looked back down to the sheet he'd been reading from and made some notes in the margins.

"I am Vivian Sharpe," Vivian said forcefully, throwing her identification cards onto the table, her voice cracking with emotion. "I am who I say I am. I go to Center City High School and I came here looking for a job. That is the truth." Her chest tingled a little with this. "I'm sorry that my questions have made you suspicious of me, Mr. Newell, but if I understand my role here in this market research, I'm doing what I am supposed to be doing."

Ms. Collins looked at him. He kept his gaze downward, seemingly occupied with his sheet, and gave the slightest of shrugs, a dismissive grunt. Ms. Collins was invisible to him now.

The room was uncomfortably silent for a minute as he continued jotting down notes in his notebook, and Ms. Collins excused herself to use the restroom. Vivian, by this point, was too warm to drink any tea, so she occupied herself drumming her fingers on the table until Mr. Newell glanced over disapprovingly. She drew her fingers back immediately, as though she'd been hissed at by a rattlesnake. She would be fine with just sitting still, she told herself.

When Ms. Collins returned, Vivian's relief was palpable. Mr. Newell looked up from his sheet, cleared his throat again and said, "You know what?" he capped his pen and put it back down on the table, turning to Ms. Collins. "I feel confident that we've exhausted this. I know everything I need to know. Tomorrow's going to be fine. We've already submitted the list of questions to the journalists and their deadline for submitting any new questions is today at 4:00. If there's anything new, we'll work it out before the news conference. This is a waste of our time."

Ms. Collins was silent for a few moments and then she nodded with a reluctant air. "Okay. Heaven knows we've got a lot to do before tomorrow." She gathered her belongings with a big sweep of her arm.

Walking down the hall together, Vivian was uncomfortable with the silence between them. "I'm sorry, Ms. Collins."

"Sorry for what?" she asked brusquely.

"I'm sorry if you're angry with me."

Ms. Collins looked at her with a little crinkling of her forehead that made Vivian feel guilty. "I'm not angry. I'm disappointed that things still did not go better. I wish I knew how to get through to you in a way that is effective. I wasn't expecting this to be so difficult. That's all. I'm starting to doubt myself. I'm not used to this sort of challenge."

"I can see that."

"You're a tough cookie, you know," Ms. Collins said, an approving tone in her voice. "I respect that. I mean, you come off as so…well, not weak, but kind of passive, easy-going."

Vivian nodded. She whipped around the corner with Ms. Collins.

"I had no idea when we met that you'd have this fighter inside you. I'd like to think that if I had a daughter, she'd be a little like you. I was like you at your age."

"How so?"

"I voiced my opinions. I wasn't afraid of anyone. I was ambitious. None of that has changed, mind you," she said with a chuckle. "Now I'm just a tough old broad rather than a young lady."

"I'm not all that brave, Ms. Collins, and you're not old."

Ms. Collins pressed the button for the elevator. "Maybe not in the grand scheme of things, but in terms of what society thinks of women. We women have a very short shelf life in terms of our value."

"Really? You're still out there doing what you do."

"Listen, this is not a complaint," she said a little sharply. "It's very liberating as a woman to not have your youth hanging all over you like a bunch of shiny wrapping paper and ribbons. You'll see when you get older. I wouldn't be your age again for anything.

Believe me, I had fun, but I feel so much more comfortable in my skin now. I wouldn't change a thing. Not a thing. I have freedom and the life I want. Hi, Annie," she said to a woman who had just joined them in waiting for the elevator. "This is my intern, Vivian. Vivian, Ms. Callahan is in sales. Head of the department, in fact."

"Nice to meet you, Ms. Callahan," Vivian said.

"So you're the one I heard of," Ms. Callahan said with a friendly dryness, "keeping this nutty lady sane. Or at least preventing her from absolute madness."

"Vivian's doing her best but it's a losing battle."

They walked on to the elevator together as a half-dozen hurried off. Pressing their floor, Ms. Collins turned to Ms. Callahan and said with a wink, "You mark my words: in twenty years or less, this girl is going to be CEO."

COPIES ARE MADE

Back at their office, Ms. Collins dropped a box of materials with a stack of folders piled high into Vivian's hands and excused herself.

"Could you just get these together? There are four separate pieces to go into twenty-five folders. You can stack them here when you're done," she said, indicating a spot outside the office door with a plastic crate. "I'm going to be occupied for the rest of the day, so if you wouldn't mind just leaving when it's time, that would be great. One of the guys will come by tomorrow morning to pick up the box. No need to notify me when you leave or anything, 'kay?"

"Okay," she said. "I'll see you Friday."

Ms. Collins blinked at her uncomprehendingly for a moment before she shook her head, her face clouding over. "Oh, no, Vivian. I'm going to need you for tomorrow. Didn't I already ask that?" She frowned.

"I don't remember that…"

"Oh, it must have slipped my mind," she said quickly. "I'm definitely going to need you tomorrow to help check in people and hand out press packets. Be my right hand girl. Okay? It'll just be for an hour or two."

Vivian nodded. This was the opportunity that she needed, she realized with a mixture of excitement and dread. "What time?"

"Just get here before 9:00 – like 8:45 or so. The conference starts at 9:30. I'm not sure how early people will show up here, but I think if you got here at 8:45 that should be good."

"That's fine."

"Great." She hurried off, her heels clicking lighter as she disappeared.

Vivian spent the rest of the afternoon filling folders with the materials Ms. Collins had given her. She organized them into neat stacks on some empty desks in the hallway outside their office and, one by one, stuffed each folder. In addition to the report Ms. Collins had given her to make copies of that morning, there were glossy pamphlets describing Gordenner and Bountiful and a heavy, vibrantly photographed brochure that looked like a travel magazine but was an advertisement for their overseas adventures, featuring brown-skinned people with bright garments and broad smiles. Flipping through it quickly, Vivian noticed a picture of Robert Fontaine, a lone, pale figure in an improbably crisp white oxford, surrounded conspicuously by an arc of colorfully attired villagers and several oxen in a dry, empty field. "A village has hope again, thanks to the Promise of Bountiful," the text read in flowing typography.

Back at the office, Vivian remembered to put her sweater on top of her purse. This would be her last day here, she was certain. For the last ten minutes, she organized the folders alphabetically, her mind eased by such tasks.

On her way out the door, she found herself walking by her mail slot, pulled like a magnet by an unavoidable urge to look inside. There was a letter inside with her name typed incorrectly across it: another note from the Lynx. A few people passed as she stood there considering the envelope; two women in high heels who cruised by at a pace Ms. Collins would admire while managing to maintain a conversation and hold their cups of coffee steady. The delivery person Vivian recognized from the elevator with Kyle the other day. He whizzed by as well, scarcely glancing up as he rounded the corner.

Vivian took the letter into a nearby restroom stall.

Vivian,
Tonight the door in the back on the south (right) side of the building (next to the pipes) will be the best door for avoiding detection. The security camera will be disabled. You will be safe.

Vivian grimly noted that this was near where the security guard had found her and Wren two weeks before. She couldn't begin to know how he knew that she was coming back and briefly considered that her phone was tapped. At this point, it was just another bizarre development. Into her purse went the note, along with the Lynx's letter from earlier in the day and the original report she would need copies of when she returned that evening.

She decided to stop by Kyle's office on the way out. She wanted to leave Kyle with one last good impression, Vivian thought to herself, before she destroyed the whole façade the next morning, and perhaps he would say, if not kind, then not overly harsh words about her if he were interviewed about her. She would really miss him.

When she saw Kyle sitting at his desk, it was as though he had a shroud of innocence surrounding him. Looking at him, Vivian felt such a wave of envy – envy of the innocence that came with not knowing, the sort of envy she felt for her sister – that she almost turned around and walked away. He noticed her before she had the chance, though.

"You on your way out, sunshine?" he asked, not glancing down as he typed.

"Yep. I just wanted to tell you that I would love to talk to you some day about being an interior designer. You becoming one, I mean." She sounded rushed and unnatural. She knew that.

"Oh, Vivian," he said with a small laugh, "you don't feel bad about having to rush out earlier today, do you? I understood."

"I do feel bad because I'm interested. Anyway, I just wanted you to know that. I think you're a great guy and I hope you do decide to go back to school."

Kyle looked bemused. *"Oookay…"* he drawled, a tilt of his head. "I appreciate it, Vivian." He had stopped typing, fingers still poised over the keyboard.

"Okay, so I guess that's it," she said, embarrassed. She reached in her purse for bus fare, for anything. "I'll see you soon."

"See you soon, missy."

She had started to walk away when she heard him call after her.

"Oh, hey, Vivian," he said. She whipped around. "Thank you. You're sweet."

As she left the building, she noticed the security guard watching her from behind his sunglasses in his booth by the parking lot. As she got closer, he left the booth and swung the gate open for her with his hands. Her mind instantly turned to the stolen keys in her purse and she clutched it closer.

"The system is still down," he said to her in something of a monotone. She could see the concrete parking lot in his mirrored sunglasses but nothing else. "Won't be fixed until next week. In the meantime, employees can use their keys. You need a set, don't you?"

"Of keys?" Vivian was baffled by this exchange, uncertain as to whether he really did just offer her a set of keys.

He nodded.

"Um, I'm not supposed to get any until I've been here three weeks," she said. She thought of her foot over the keys in the cafeteria and tried to remain calm. "I should be fine without any."

"You sure?" he asked, heading back to the booth.

"No. I'm fine."

After shutting the gate, Vivian thanked him. Even though she didn't turn around, she knew that he was watching her and so she hurried to the bus stop. Vivian had the unsettling feeling about the security guard: he knew something, but she didn't know what. Did he know that she stole those keys? If so, why would he offer her some new ones? Why was a company so nervous about security offering keys to people still on their probationary period? Could he have been baiting her in some way? The bus finally pulled up with a belch of exhaust and Vivian climbed on, instantly filing away the weird exchange with the security guard. She had other things to worry about.

For the next few hours, Vivian laid the groundwork with her family for going to bed early. She complained of a stomachache, or a vague malaise, perhaps the flu, and emphasized that she was really tired, too tired if anyone should call. Her parents glanced at each other briefly, a look that said what everyone already knew: Wren was the only one who called her anymore and Vivian was forbidden from talking to her. They agreed all the same. She ate dinner quickly; she just cut up a sweet potato and moved the pieces around on her plate and excused herself to go to bed. To add a level of authenticity to this, she filled a glass of ice water to bring upstairs, coughed a few times, and doubled back, returning to borrow one of her mother's magazines that was in the guest room, one that made her eyes water with all the perfume inserts, *Stylistica*.

She cleared out her purse of all unnecessary items, then decided against a purse and put everything she needed – the report, the keys, a flashlight, her wallet with ten dollars – in her backpack so her hands would be free. She remembered with a small amount of dread that she hadn't read the report yet. She figured that she should probably know what it said since she was going to put it in peoples' folders. She sat on the edge of her bed and read it. It was actually a combination of reports copied and stapled together, the first one from a year ago.

Internal Document

April 18

Restricted Access (limited to key Marketing, Sales and Executive Bountiful team)

Re: Preliminary Audit, April

Per the agreement to report findings by this date, the Environmental team reports that results of the application of Bountiful Spray are inconclusive at present date and further testing is necessary.

Laboratory results and field results are concerning. The internal audit suggests that more extensive tests out of laboratory are needed than we see planned in order to make safe environmental claims. Given laboratory results, the product(s) would not pass FDA guidelines at this juncture.

In seven laboratory experiments, Bountiful Spray did indeed kill over 60% of potential plant competitors as is claimed. Up to 35% of non-direct competitor plants (non-invasive/not weeds) were also killed when spray was applied even hundreds of yards away. Concerns are raised about the ability of Bountiful Wheat to be grown in concert with other plants. The key Bountiful team was instructed of this in the March 26 report (Subject line: "Poisonous capabilities widespread.")

In over two years of field study at the Gordenner facility in Compton, the Environmental Consultants and their team noted not only the killing of competitor and non-competitor plants, but a degradation of soil to such a degree that more than two seasons of spray application could not be advised without a reformulation. Groundwater and local fresh water also are degraded to the point that high native fish (up to 25 percent) and aquatic bird (more than 20 percent) die-offs were noted, though the direct link is not established at this point. It is a distinct possibility that water consumption would not be advisable without treatment facilities in all communities — and indeterminate downstream communities — where Bountiful is grown and sprayed. The effect on humans is unknown at this point.

In the laboratory, mortality rates on mice and rats (direct application of the spray) are more than 70 percent and almost 40 percent mortality when consuming water mixed with a small percentage (precisely 1/66 the amount) of Bountiful spray (see March 22 laboratory results memo per mortality). The key Bountiful team was also instructed of this in the March 13 confidential memo.

At this time, the Environmental team recommends halting all production of Bountiful until these concerns are addressed.

Sincerely,

B. Beard and H. Cunningham

Senior Internal Environmental Auditors

Internal Document

April 18
Restricted Access (limited to key Marketing, Sales and Executive Bountiful team)
Re: Preliminary Audit, June and Moving Forward
Folks,
Do not take this as bad news. This is not unexpected. We have created a revolutionary product; the Environmental Auditors always err on the side of caution, as they should. Our job, however, is to champion Bountiful until it can stand on its own legs. The world needs us to stand unfalteringly behind this product until and after it is released. This is a temporary setback. We all know, however, that by this time next year we will begin the targeted marketing phase of Bountiful, and, six months later, it be on the market. We are already in negotiations in key overseas markets; this is all window dressing at this point. Let's not get thrown off course.
    Robert Fontaine
    CEO

April 27
Internal Document
Restricted Access (limited to key Marketing, Sales and Executive Bountiful team)
Re: Integrity of Test Concerns
The Internal Environmental Audit team is concerned about our ability to test Gordenner products, specifically the Bountiful line, with integrity given recent improprieties. They have been detailed in several recent memos (Jan. 27, March 13 and April 18), and, though we have been assured repeatedly that the integrity will be maintained, it is becoming clear that we need much more of a commitment toward this end due to more transgressions, ranging from the minor to much more egregious violations of conduct. Some of these are:
    Intentionally misleading and inappropriate rewording of status reports to the Board of Directors. This occurred four separate times (December, January, February, and April in the last several months [there was no status report in March]). We did not know that these documents had been revised and reworded until a Board member approached one of our scientists with specific questions. Going against company policy, this was printed on paper with the Internal Audit department's official letterhead, giving the impression that the document came from this department. Despite our frequently stated desires for an internal investigation, it seems that no one has pursued the parties responsible for these revised reports, and certainly no one has stepped forward and claimed responsibility.

On numerous occasions, members of the Environmental Internal Audit team have been approached by the Director of New Product Development, Kevin Newell, and asked to "reframe" our scientific direction. In addition to being unaware of how to "reframe" legitimate scientific inquiry, members of our team have felt threatened and intimidated by this inappropriate interference and we find it to be unacceptable and highly unprofessional. We have asked for Mr. Newell to put all further communication to our team in writing that is CC'd to Robert Fontaine and Laura Collins (memo of March 13). After last week's unscheduled visit to our labs by Mr. Newell, we are asking it again.

Serious concerns about the safety of our team while working with the new technology we are testing have been consistently brushed aside or ignored. Improved measures such as up-to-date protective gear (puncture-resistant gloves, mask respirators and newer-model safety glasses in particular) do not seem to be part of the budgetary plan. Several members of our team have inquired as to purchasing these items on their own and being reimbursed upon submission of receipts. We have not gotten word back from HR as to how to proceed, and team members are concerned about their short-term and long-term well-being. Specific health concerns, especially regarding an increased frequency of headaches among lab workers reported, have also been ignored.

In addition to concerns over our safety, we also ask that members of the Board who are touring the labs please adhere to protocol outlined in our Lab Safety Manual. We have seen people escorted through who have no protective gear on whatsoever. We also ask that we be informed of any visitors 24 hours in advance to minimize disruption.

We trust that our requests are reasonable, and we hope that it is understood that they are made only with maintaining the integrity of our scientific exploration as our driving motivation. Please contact us with any concerns or questions.

Sincerely,

B. Beard and H. Cunningham
Senior Internal Environmental Auditors

April 28

Restricted Access (limited to Environmental Audit Team and key Marketing, Sales and Executive Bountiful Team)

Re: B. Beard and H. Cunningham Resignation Effective Immediately and Mandatory Meeting.

Bradley Beard and Hayford Cunningham have submitted formal resignation documents effective immediately. All questions regarding their resignation must be directed specifically to HR liaison Helen Shruske. As always and in keeping with company policy, speculation will be considered gossip, which is against company policy. The appropriate disciplinary actions will be taken against employees engaging in this activity. There will be a mandatory Environmental Audit meeting at 3:00 p.m. in the Green Room. All employees in EA are required to attend.

Stephen Gallbright
Environmental Audit Manager

May 5
Restricted Access (limited to Environmental Audit Team and key Marketing, Sales and Executive Bountiful Team)
Re: Folding of Environmental Audit Team into Laboratory Sciences Department

It has come to my attention that despite the stated company policy forbidding such behavior, speculation is affecting productivity. The rumor mill is working overtime! In an effort to get us back on track, today's 3:00 meeting will address the merger of the EA Team into Laboratory Services. No lay-offs are anticipated. Laboratory Services will now conduct any and all auditing as well as research following new guidelines and protocol, which will available by April 23. Again, all in the department are required to attend today's meeting.

Although essential details will be shared at today's meeting, please note that from this point on, Kevin Newell will now co-manage the department in addition to New Product Development; I will now also co-manage Laboratory Services. Please include both of us on all questions and communications regarding this merger. He can be reached at Ext. 4.

Stephen Gallbright
Laboratory Services Co-Manager

London World News
Date: December 15
Jakarta, Indonesia
A summit of international biotechnology business leaders was disrupted today by thousands of angry protestors, when dozens broke through police barricades to disrupt the closed-door meeting. Police deployed pepper spray and rubber bullets to disperse the unruly crowd; several injuries were reported, including a police officer whose collarbone was broken during a scuffle. Several cars were set on fire and two windows were broken at Jakarta's Plaza Centre Tower, where the meeting was taking place. There were 17 arrests reported, although some activists claimed that the actual arrest count is higher.

Merpati Salimputri, director of Indonesians Together for a Local Economy (ITLE), said, "The Indonesian government is clearly in the pocket of the Western biotech industry. We are demanding that our indigenous farmers and traditional farming practices be protected and respected by our government."

She added, "This way of life will disappear if we don't stand in opposition to these modern-day corporate imperialists."

Attending the summit were leaders of Gordenner, U.S.A., NatureLife, and Gemini Laboratories, the top three biotechnology companies in the United States, along with former U.S. senator Charles Cahill, representing Food for the Future, a consortium of international biotech interests. They were meeting with representatives of the Indonesian government as well as those of other South Asian countries. A representative from the Indonesian Department of Agriculture refused to confirm which countries were in attendance. The purpose of the meeting was to discuss new innovations in the burgeoning field of biotechnology and preparing the South Asian market for distribution.

Indonesia's Minister of Agriculture, Ramelan Malik, said, "We are a population of well over 200 million in this country alone and these protestors want to take us back to the Stone Age. We are interested in becoming a modern country, one where every child can be fed. The old methods are not enough. This is why we are looking to biotechnology."

According to protestors, the Indonesian government is already implementing biotechnology, looked upon with suspicion outside of most Western nations, in its agricultural programs. Ms. Salimputri of ITLE claims that Gordenner, U.S.A. has already begun planting biotech test fields throughout Indonesia.

"They are preying on the indigent farmers, distributing this free seed and paying them to maintain the plants. We don't even know what this genetically engineered stuff does yet. What we do know is that the fish and birds are dying wherever this product is used."

Ms. Salimputri contends that there have been massive fish and bird die-offs since the seed was introduced six months ago, mostly concentrated in rural communities; she also claims that there has been an increase in the rate of miscarriage. She could not supply any data to support these claims. The Ministries of the Environment and Health do not have current statistics publicly available.

"What [Merpati Salimputri] says is an obvious lie. She maintains an organization that uses terrorist methods to achieve their goals," said Minister Malik. "What do you expect?"

London World News
Date: February 26

A report smuggled from the Indonesian Ministry of the Environment details a previously unheard-of mortality rate among birds and fish last year. Millions of birds, including many endangered and rare varieties, have been found dead throughout Indonesia without a known cause. Some scientists have hypothesized that the birds may have eaten diseased fish, but there is also a growing concern that it is linked to novel forms of agriculture being introduced to Indonesia, though a direct link has not been established yet. According to the leaked report, nearly 25 percent of the nation's fish population has perished since the start of the year. Many varieties of indigenous birds, such as great-billed parrots and rainbow lories, have seen dramatic population decreases, especially in rural areas.

Jakarta News
Date: March 8
Merpati Salimputri, 27, was found shot to death this morning outside her apartment in Jakarta. Ms. Salimputri was a longtime activist who frequently criticised the Indonesian government in its promotion of Western agricultural and economic practices. She founded Indonesians Together for a Local Economy, a non-profit that was critical of globalism and free trade, while in college.

Police have ruled out robbery as a motive behind her shooting and there are currently no suspects. There were no witnesses at the scene, but neighbors reported hearing a scream followed by gunshots and a car speeding away at 6:30 a.m.

She is survived by her parents, two sisters and a brother. Ms. Salimputri was engaged to be married in June.

Vivian's head was spinning and she'd curled up in a ball on her bed. She took out the sheet she'd copied for Ms. Collins earlier, the one she'd put in all the press packets.

Welcome!
At Gordenner, we have nearly 60 years of dedicated hard work and experience with helping food growers bring the highest quality food possible to the American table. Every significant technological breakthrough in modern agriculture has been explored and innovated at our Center City facility, each with the goal of bringing the best quality plants and highest level of productivity to the hundreds of thousands of farmers who rely on us growing season after growing season. We are excited to share with the assembled media today our latest, and, we believe, most exciting innovation to date.

Seeds, without which we would not survive, have been cultivated to produce the maximum yield for thousands of years. For generations, farmers would breed high-performing plants together for the purpose of bringing together desirable characteristics (such as drought-resistance and high fertility) into a single plant. At Gordenner, we have built on this tradition, developing seeds that not only have the highest yield but are also designed to bring the best nutritional profile possible to a single plant. Imagine corn with high levels of beta-carotene or russet potatoes with omega 3 fatty acids. Imagine the sort of health benefits this could bring to consumers. This is the sort of innovation we are actively creating in our laboratories.

The Promise of Bountiful.

We are proud to introduce to the world our latest innovation, the Bountiful product line. Our first two items, Bountiful Wheat and Bountiful Spray, have truly staggering possibilities. Wheat is a significant, important crop. Every culture across the world has some variety of bread, grain, porridge or pasta as part of its cultural heritage and as an inexpensive food source. Bountiful Wheat seeds have been developed to grow in virtually all climates and conditions. Our technology team has spent the better part of a decade refining and developing these seeds so they have the maximum nutritional punch: they are rich in Vitamin A and folic acid. Vitamin A is critical for immunity strength and eyesight; Folic Acid is critical for fetal brain and spinal-cord development.

The Bountiful Spray has been produced to maximize the seeds' chances of surviving in various conditions: it is both a potent herbicide and a pesticide. Farmers would have a reliable cash crop and a reliable food source for their own families. Using these two products side-by-side, we can have a profound one-two punch for ending world poverty, birth defects, malnutrition, and starvation.

The precise productivity rates are still being measured, but trials in Indonesian test fields showed a 35% yield increase in the first year. We predict similar results throughout South Asia and Africa – very populous, impoverished parts of the globe that could most benefit from a consistent, high-yield food source.

We thank you for sharing in our excitement over our new product line, Bountiful. There is no doubt that we at Gordenner are forging a new path in world agricultural systems, one that will lead to health and prosperity, for today and for future generations.

We take our role as innovators in the field of agriculture seriously, but being citizens of the world is equally important. We all hope for a world in which no child should ever go hungry again. Now, thanks to Bountiful Wheat and Bountiful Spray, we are one step closer to that dream becoming a reality.

Please send any media inquiries to Laura Collins at 492-8000, Ext. 5.
Sincerely,
Robert Fontaine, CEO
Gordenner, USA

Vivian kneeled by her bed and tried to pray, but her family never really went to church, so she didn't know how: what to ask for, how to word it. She remembered Wren telling her once about creating a circle of light around oneself for protection, but didn't know how to visualize it; she got nervous about doing it wrong, so she gave up on that, too. Finally, she found that if she closed her eyes and breathed deeply, she could feel the warmth in her chest again that she had had with Tolstoy that day. At 7:54, she got up, turned off all the lights in her room, massed her pillows together in the shape of a body under her covers and opened the window leading out to the side of the house.

As she stuck the balls of her feet between twisted ropes of ivy, Vivian remembered doing this once before, when she sneaked out in sixth grade to meet her best friend of that year, a mischievous girl named Kate. Kate had dared her to do it, to meet her by the skating rink on a Friday night after 10:00, and so she did. The purpose of this was sort of lost on Vivian; the rink was closed at 10:00, but she couldn't resist the dare. She met Kate, they laughed as they ran around the small hill behind the rink, delirious with their act of rebellion, and then she returned home within twenty minutes, still undetected. On this night, Vivian was relieved to find that the ivy was still snug like netting against the house, just as she'd remembered, and it supported her weight just fine. *Leg, leg, arm, arm,* she thought to herself on the way down.

It was still light out as she bent down in front of the bushes at her house and glanced in the windows. The sheer curtains were drawn on the main floor but she could see a form – her father's, she thought – cross past the doorway in the kitchen. She caught her breath and hurried past. Thankfully, she didn't see many people, other than a couple of small children down the block chasing after early fireflies across a few front yards.

She went to the cul-de-sac, took a glance around, and, seeing no one, ducked between the bushes. Vivian hadn't been there in years, but she remembered all the summer days spent back here in the secret hiding space of her block, and the rich, moist smell of the dirt. There were tennis balls back there and some stubbed-out cigarettes. It wasn't long before Vivian heard the rumble of a car and headlights blaring through the leaves. She squinted through some branches, only to be blinded by the headlights. "Viv?" She heard a hoarse whisper. Her heart jumped as she ducked through the bushes again and hurried into Wren's car.

"I had no idea where you were going to be," Wren laughed with relief. "I wasn't thinking behind the bushes. I almost jumped when you came out of there."

It was so reassuring for Vivian to see her again, to see someone familiar and friendly.

"Yes, I know. Old hiding place. So, you ready?"

"Off to…?"

"Make copies first. Let's go to Copy Queen; it's by the Loco Taco on Fifth. On the right side of the street. It's on the way."

"Loco Taco has lard in their beans," Wren said as they drove past Vivian's house. Vivian ducked down in her seat and looked out the back to check if she had remembered to leave her bedroom window open a crack for re-entry. She had. The light in her father's study was also on.

"What's that?" she said distractedly.

"Loco Taco: their vegetarian burritos aren't vegetarian. Lard." She turned off of her street to Vivian's great relief.

"I'll remember not to go there."

"Do," Wren said. "Fast food is bleh anyway, but I thought you'd like to know just in case. The one time I went there, they looked at me like I was from some other planet when I asked for the burrito without cheese or sour cream. I didn't know about the lard then, it was a few years ago. Anyway, I got really sick. We found out later there is lard in the beans."

"Yikes. What is lard anyway?" Vivian was grateful to talk about something off-topic. She sensed that Wren was, too.

"I think it's, like, congealed animal fat or something. My grandma on my dad's side keeps a big ol' jar of it on her kitchen counter, just sitting there all gross."

They didn't say anything for a minute.

"So," Wren asked, "are you nervous?"

"A little, yeah. My heart's kind of fluttery and all that. I'm trying to manage it."

"Do you know what happens after these copies go into the folders, assuming we pull it off? What happens then?"

Vivian shook her head, marveling at the absurdity. "Then? I have no idea. We take off for the tropics? Enter the Witness Protection Program? I'm sort of trusting that everything with Tolstoy would not lead me here just to have me fail. But what those next steps are, I have no idea."

After a moment, Wren nodded. "Cool."

They pulled in front of the copy shop. "Maybe I should go in," Wren suggested. "Just an added level of security in case you might see someone from Gordenner or something."

"Good idea." Vivian grabbed her wallet out of her bag and handed Wren a ten-dollar bill. "Could you make the copies yourself, rather than hand it to someone behind the counter? Another added level of security."

"Sure." Wren put the money in her pocket. "We were born to do this." She was almost at the door of the copy shop when Vivian called out after her.

"Hey, Wren – 25 copies, okay."

"Right," Wren said, a look embarrassment flashing across her face. "I should have known to ask that. Duh."

From the car, Vivian watched Wren make copies in a window that faced her. The words "the point of no return" kept repeating in her head until she was finally aware of it and forced herself to think of something else. Her thoughts settled on Ms. Collins. She would be furious with Vivian. She would be filled with disappointment and bitterness at just the thought of her for the rest of her life. Feeling lightheaded from too many shallow breaths, she thought of what she'd read from the Lynx earlier, and she knew that she had to do it. When she looked in the window again, she noticed an employee in a red shirt coming over to talk to Wren and look at her copier. Vivian felt her throat constricting and was ready to jump out of the car when he knelt by the side of the machine and put something into the side of it. A few minutes later, Wren stapled the copies together, paid and returned to the car.

"Stupid copier," she exhaled as if she'd been holding her breath. "It was out of ink. Well, at least they're all done." She handed the copies to Vivian and started the car back up. Vivian flipped through them.

"They look good. This information about Bountiful is scarier than I ever imagined." She thought of the Indonesian woman shot outside her apartment, ready to start her day, and planning to get married.

"That's the stuff from the Lynx?"

"Right. But it's actually from them mostly. Internal documents. Bountiful is really a disaster." Vivian rolled down the passenger window despite concerns about being seen. She needed some fresh air.

"I'll take your word for it."

"Birds are dying; fish are dying. People are eating the fish. Wherever it's planted and sprayed the groundwater is polluted. They just want to get this stuff out and make a ton of money."

Wren didn't say anything, just nodded solemnly.

"Ms. Collins is going to be royally pissed at me. By the time all this is done, she's going to know I was the one who gave the media this information, you know? They're going to piece it together and she's going to hate me."

"You don't know that…"

"I do, Wren," she said emphatically. "I do. I know that. And, of course my whole purpose was to do this, I'm guessing, to insert these papers in the folders for the press. Apparently that's why I pursued an internship."

"I'm getting the chills," Wren said quietly, her knuckles jutting out as her hands gripped the steering wheel.

"I'm accepting that she's going to hate me, and you know, I've really come to like her. I know that sounds idiotic. I don't know how much she knows about all this stuff about Bountiful, though," Vivian said, thumping her thumb on the papers.

"How could she not know?"

"I don't know. I just think that she sticks with PR and marketing and doesn't look into the specifics of it. It was clear during the market research sessions that she has no interest in anything related to questioning the science."

"Ah."

Vivian sighed, looking out the window. "The point of all this is that I just want to make sure that this is the right thing to do. It is, isn't it?"

"Yes. I..."

"Do you know that I stole someone's keys today? Just right out there in the daylight like some common criminal?"

"I didn't. So we could get into the building?"

Vivian nodded. "I feel so terrible about that. Her night was probably totally ruined. She's probably at the hardware store right now getting new keys made instead of, like, playing with her dog or having dinner with her son. What if she's a single mom and I just made her life that much more difficult?"

"What if she's not? What if she was looking for a chance to, you know, go to the hardware store so she could flirt with the cute clerk and he'll ask her out and they'll be happily-ever-after? You could have brought that whole thing into being."

Vivian laughed. "I guess."

"The point is that you can't speculate, 'cause you don't know. You *can't* know. You just have to ask for forgiveness and hope that the ends justify the means."

"I hope you're right," Vivian said quietly.

Neither one said anything, then Wren looked at her friend. "To Gordenner, Batman?"

"To Gordenner."

VIVIAN AND WREN DISCOVERED

Wren parked the car outside the gate to the Gordenner parking lot, back by some bushes. No one appeared to be in the attendant's booth.

Vivian had her keys in hand, her heart racing. "Okay, so first we'll just unlock the gate, then we'll run to the back. There's an unlocked door there, apparently."

"We should have a code word or something just to let one another know that everything's okay."

"Okay, how about 'Quick! Run, run, run!'"

"I was thinking more along the lines of, like, *blue sky*. Or *purple cow* or something."

"Blue sky, okay?" Vivian said. "I like blue sky."

"We'll need another word for it not being safe. Like…"

"Storms ahead?"

"That sounds good. Blue sky and storms ahead. Blue sky good, storms ahead bad."

Her keys grasped tight in her hand, the ridges cutting into her palm, Vivian immediately noticed that something was off about the gate: it was ajar. She slowly pushed it open and peered inside. The lot, other than a couple of cars, was empty, with lights throwing bright pools onto the concrete. "Blue sky," she whispered to Wren, and she ran ahead, ducking, remaining outside the light as much as she could. She focused on the sound of Wren's feet hitting the concrete of the parking lot behind her and the sense of security that gave her.

In the back, they leaned against the building, wordlessly panting, and caught their breath for a moment. They glanced at each other and Vivian nodded. She put the key in and felt immense relief as it easily turned and clicked open. Here they were, going back in the entrance they originally went through together the day they were found by the security guard by the pipes. The buzzing sound of the building gave way as they carefully shut the door to the stairwell behind them, Vivian having motioned to Wren not to

319

press the elevator button. Taking the steps seemed safer and quieter to her: at least no bell would signal their arrival.

At the second floor, Vivian slowly pushed the door open and peered out.

"Blue sky."

She took out her flashlight and Wren did the same. They hurried down hallways that seemed ghostly without the rush of people and activity, pausing at every doorway to determine that the room was empty. "Blue sky," Vivian would whisper, grateful for this little gesture that made her feel so much more in control.

Finally, they rounded the corner to her office, where the folders were in the crate outside her office door. She pointed her flashlight on them and Wren nodded.

"I'm going to go check out the other end of the hall and make sure that no one's coming," Wren said.

"Okay." Vivian quietly unzipped her backpack as Wren dashed off. Vivian could feel her right temple pulsing as she took the papers out, sweat beading on her neck, her fingers slippery; she had to concentrate not to drop the new papers all over the floor. Rather than stoop over the folders on the floor and rush through it haphazardly, she took them out and placed them on an empty desk in the hallway. "This will take five minutes," she told herself, trying to sound reassuring. "We'll be out in five minutes."

She went through them one by one, replacing the letter from Gordenner with the articles given to her by the Lynx, and she made two piles, one with the new papers, one that hadn't been changed yet. Midway through, she got confused as to which pile was which, and she hurriedly flipped through them again. "Right is right," she told herself, a mnemonic meaning that the pile on the right was the one that was complete. Little things like this gave her a small measure of calm.

Vivian was so absorbed in doing this task quickly but correctly that, when a flashlight appeared from the other direction down the hall, she barely glanced at it, figuring that Wren had gone the other way when she wasn't paying attention. When another flashlight appeared, though, held at a lower level and shaking back and forth as the person, presumably Wren, reentered the room in a hurry, her breath gasping and sputtering in surprise, Vivian realized that there were now two people with flashlights pointed towards her.

"Blue sk – I mean, storms ahead," Wren whispered absurdly before her voice trailed off.

Vivian, frozen with the final folder in her hands, squinted at the beam pointed squarely at her face. She could see nothing else but a big burst of white-hot light in her eyes.

"Hello?" she said, trying not to sound startled. "I was just finishing up some work."

The light remained fixed on her. Wren started to say something, then stopped.

"I came back to finish something I'd forgotten," Vivian said to the blinding light, too scared to even cover her burning eyes. "A last-minute thing."

The light remained on her for a few moments – long enough for Vivian to realize that she had no real fear in her heart, which was disorienting in itself – until it was clicked off and she could hear footsteps. As soon as they stopped the overhead light came on. The security guard stood against the wall, his hand still on the light switch.

Instead of reaching for his walkie-talkie or handcuffs, his demeanor was eerily calm. "I was expecting to find you here," he said, his voice subdued. He was not wearing sunglasses, the first time Vivian had seen him without them, which made him look older and much less intimidating than usual.

"I know this looks weird," Vivian said, "but I had last minute work to do I forgot about earlier. And the cups downstairs," she said nonsensically, remembering her original alibi. She couldn't understand why her heart was not racing. Wren just stood in the doorway, her eyes wide and her flashlight still on, pointed toward the guard.

He glanced at the folders near Vivian, nodding at them. "Did you finish what you came here to do?"

"Yes. Yes. I can leave any time. I don't even need to do the cups. I'm sorry to have surprised you like this," she said, even as she noticed that he did not seem surprised at all. She took the pile of folders and dropped them back in the crate. "I just didn't want to screw up tomorrow."

"What about those?" he said, indicating the papers she'd removed. "Do you still need those?"

"No – I can just throw those away." Vivian folded them in half self-consciously and put them in the green recycling bin in the corner of the room.

They all stood there awkwardly while Vivian gathered together her backpack. It was as though they were all vacuum-packed in there, the air squeezed out of the room, and she found herself looking back at the security guard. He met her eyes directly as if he were waiting for her to say something. The next words tumbled out of her without her being able to stop them. "Are you really working security here?"

The slightest expression crossed his face, so fleetingly and subtly she couldn't interpret it, but it may have been surprise or maybe it was relief. "No, young lady, I'm not," he said. He made no attempt to say more, nor did he try to end the conversation.

"Well, that makes two of us," she said. "I'm not really an intern."

"Viv…" Wren said nervously. "We should get going."

The security guard held up his hand in a gesture of calm. "She's okay."

"Do you mind if I ask you why you're here, what you're doing?" Vivian asked. "Feel free to tell me that it's none of my business, but I was just wondering."

He walked over to where Vivian was standing and pulled out a chair, sitting down next to the table where she had been working. He nodded to Wren, and she joined them; Wren and Vivian sat down and finally turned off their flashlights. He pulled out his wallet, attached to a long key chain hooked around a belt loop. He unhooked it and opened it up to a photo.

He passed it over to Vivian. It was a portrait of a little girl, a class photo, smiling brightly, with dimples and long brown hair in braids. She looked like someone who would be friends with Millie.

"This is my granddaughter, Victoria. We call her Tori. My first grandchild."

A wave of something indescribably sad washed over Vivian as she held his wallet. She nodded and handed it to Wren.

"This was her four years ago, before she got sick." He was quiet for a few moments, his eyes seeming to search the ceiling for something. "She died last August. She was eight."

Vivian and Wren both gasped. "I am so sorry," Vivian said, clutching her heart.

"Brain cancer," he said, unprompted. He reached over and took the wallet from Wren, then he took out another photo, one that had been in front of the photo he showed them. He passed it to Vivian. It was of his granddaughter, several years older, with a shaved head sitting in a hospital bed with stuffed animals and an older woman, her arm around the girl's shoulder. The girl smiled broadly, seemingly in defiance of her shaved head and the dark circles under her eyes.

"That's my wife with Tori about three months before she passed away. The sparkle was still in her eyes, right up to the end," he said. "My wife and Tori were so close. Best friends, really."

"That poor woman…" Wren said, sounding like she hadn't meant to say it out loud.

"Her name was Nell. One month after Tori died, on that date in fact, I was at the cemetery and my wife walked into the garage, started the engine and sat in the car until she died, too. I can't say I blame her. I was thinking about doing the same thing myself," he said matter-of-factly, "but she beat me to the punch. She was always quicker than me."

"I'm so sorry," Vivian murmured.

He looked as if he were going to say something else, then he shook himself a little and blinked. A new expression was on his face, one that looked like the one she was familiar with, the steely look. "Which brings me to why I'm here…" He cleared his throat. "Do either of you know the brain cancer rate in Center City?"

They both shook their heads.

"It is twenty times higher here than the national average: that's just brain cancer. We're also higher in bladder cancer and breast cancer. There is no incidence of brain cancer on either side of Tori's family. No cancer at all, in fact. But just this year, five children in Tori's school have been diagnosed with brain cancer, a school of about 325 kids. *Just this year.* That's way higher than the national average. Did you know that?"

They both shook their heads again. "No, I didn't," Wren said, her face pale.

"I'm here because Gordenner is polluting the water of Center City, polluting it to the point that whatever it's producing – that Bountiful garbage – is poisoning our town. Gordenner poisoned and killed Tori. Every time her parents made her hot chocolate or heated her up some noodles, they were killing her, the light of their lives. This sweet girl who would never harm anyone…"

"How do you know this for sure?" Vivian asked gently. "That it was caused by Gordenner?"

"That's just it – I don't. I can't. For one, have you ever noticed the Center City Hospital's children's wing has the name Coleman Jenner attached to it? The Coleman Jenner Children's Hospital? He was one of the founders of Gordenner, along with Louis

Gordon. And who do you think sits on the board of directors of *The Patriot?* Robert Fontaine. So even if the hospital released the growing cancer rate, the newspaper wouldn't report on it. And I know that you saw the pipe out back, the one that flows out to the creek. You saw the untreated sewage Gordenner releases into our water supply through the creek. It's carcinogenic – cancer-causing. We know that from their own reports."

Vivian started to say something when he interrupted her.

"So, no, I can't prove to you without a shadow of a doubt that it was the muck from Gordenner that caused Tori's cancer or the cancer of all those other children, but I can prove that they intentionally and secretively are releasing toxins into the town's water supply and that those toxins are carcinogenic. That I can prove."

"How did you figure out that it was Gordenner in the first place, though?"

"There's someone who's been tracking them for a long time," he said obliquely. "And this someone got in contact with me."

"Are you talking about the Lynx?" Vivian asked.

"There's no point in being coy with you," he said with a slight smile. "We're on the same team. Yes, it was the Lynx. He sent me a letter after Tori passed away, letting me know everything he knew about this place. He knew about the pipeline and everything. He knew that a girl from the part of town closest to Gordenner and the river died."

"Have you met the Lynx?" Wren asked.

"No. To the best of my knowledge, no one has seen him for years, at least not while knowing who he was. The idea of me being wrapped up with this guy is kind of shocking given everything, but it's the best bet I have. And he hasn't steered me wrong yet. Everything he has claimed has been proven to be true."

Vivian and Wren were both silent, reeling.

The security guard looked at a spot on the ceiling for a few moments, then looked back down at them, his gaze misty but direct. "If you knew anything of my life before all this, you would be shocked. I had an auto body shop, just an ordinary, straight-arrow kind of guy. I've always believed everything 'authority figures' told me. I would never question anything – I was of a generation that believed that if something wasn't good for you, it wouldn't exist, that there were agencies in charge of things that looked out for us. I know that isn't true now. This has been a major loss of innocence, if you can believe that of someone in his sixties. So I'm here to try to bring these criminals to justice. One way or another. Lynx is the guy working on the outside; I'm the guy working on the inside."

"So every time there's a break-in…"

"It's me and the Lynx working together," he said simply. "We coordinate our schedules. There's also another guy working internally. That's all I can say on that. There's only so long that can continue, though, before people start asking questions as to why it's still happening with their ramped-up security."

"So what do you say?"

"Well," he said, "The Lynx is always able to stay a step or two ahead of their security measures. They have no idea how and neither does their security team."

"But what do you hope to do?" Wren asked. "What's your ultimate goal?"

"To amass enough evidence against them that they knew what they were doing and concealed the smoking guns. To make sure all the guilty parties go to prison for as long as possible," he said, his eyes blazing.

"Cool," Wren said.

"And why are you here?" he asked, looking at Vivian. "With all of the sleuthing I've been doing, I've not been able to figure that one out."

"Oh, jeez, it's long and complicated but…"

"Vivian is telepathic," Wren interjected, beaming with pride at her friend.

"Not exactly," she demurred.

"So exactly," Wren said, her eyes wide and dramatic. "Vivian followed this squirrel one day who was trying to communicate with her…"

"Wren, could we skip the whole 'Vivian is nuts' aspect of this story?"

"Why? You should be proud. I mean, not about being nuts, but you're not nuts. Anyway, blah blah blah, she found these ducks that were poisoned by the river, and working with Will was able…"

"Who's Will?"

"Oh, he's this awesomely intense environmentalist vegan friend of my mom's − he goes to college here. Anyway, he and Vivian and my mom were able to trace it back to Gordenner. So that was when you saw us sneaking around in back."

He leaned back in his chair, nodding his head. "I knew something was up," he said, "but I didn't know what. Neither did the Lynx."

"He almost scared me away with what he sent me," Vivian said.

"I guess he felt like if you could take that pressure, you would have resolve with whatever you were planning to do here. That was his way of testing and preparing you, I guess. I think that when he saw you guys coming around, he had a sort of hope that he hadn't had before, like this new generation was picking up where he'd left off."

Vivian felt strangely flattered that this man placed so much value on her. "I don't know what to say."

"Nothing needed," he said, waving a big mitt of a hand. "But, to quote your friend here, I'm interested to know what your ultimate goal is."

"That's the thing. I'm not really sure. I guess it's to expose to the public that Gordenner is poisoning the water and the wildlife. Now we also know about the people."

"Plus," Wren jumped in, looking at Vivian, "they're trying to sell this stuff exclusively in developing nations to get them dependent on this Bountiful junk and away from the way they've grown food for thousands of years. And we won't hear about the negative effects of it if it's, like, in Indonesia instead of in our own backyard here."

"So that's why we're here now," Vivian said, pointing at the folders. "We're here to throw a wrench into their press conference tomorrow."

"Vivian replaced this totally bogus PR thing from Gordenner with something that actually reflects what is happening. The reporters will see it when they first open their folders."

The security guard nodded again, eyes squinted at them. "Good. A chink in the armor. We'll see what the fall-out from that will be."

"Yes, we will," Vivian said. "One thing that I know is that I won't be here any longer."

"That's true," Wren said.

The security guard nodded solemnly and stood. "I'd better get going, but I want to thank you girls for what you're doing here. Something good will come of it."

"Thank you," Vivian said. As he started to walk away, she called out after him. "Excuse me?"

He turned around.

"I never did learn if your name was really Larry."

He shook his head. "It's not. It's Kurt."

"I'm sorry about your granddaughter and wife, Kurt. I can't tell you how sad that story is."

"I know how sad it is firsthand," he said, his voice cracking. He looked down and rubbed his eyes. After a few moments, he took a deep breath and looked at Vivian. "I'm not going to be able to bring them back, but I'm going to make damn well sure that Gordenner doesn't get away with it."

"I am too, sir," Vivian said, her voice also choking.

"Good luck, Kurt," Wren said solemnly as he turned to leave again.

"I don't need luck," he said with a small smile. "I need perseverance, same as you."

As he walked away, Vivian watched him through teary eyes. It was the first time she'd noticed that he had a slight limp. Wren must have had the same thoughts.

"He doesn't seem so intimidating any more," she said. "More like a child, that poor, sweet man."

Afterwards, they stacked the sleeves of cups neatly in the room where the press conference would be held in the morning, a big room with chairs already arranged in rows. Then they drove home in silence until they were a few blocks from Vivian's home. They'd only been inside Gordenner for about thirty minutes, but it felt like hours to Vivian. Finally she said, "I hope I don't disappoint anyone tomorrow."

"Like who?"

"Like Kurt, or Tori or Tolstoy or the Lynx…God, two beings who aren't even really here anymore, one who is considered an underground terrorist. I'm such a wacko."

"You know what, Viv?" Wren said, pulling over and putting her car in park with a flash of anger in her eyes, "Even if you are 'wacko', even if you are nuts, even if you have totally lost your mind, like cuckoo crazy, you are *still* doing the right thing. Who cares if Tolstoy isn't material? Who cares if he's a talking pig? Somehow, this has all led you here, where there is very much something that needs your attention, to a real situation. So at this point, I'd say that being crazy is irreverent."

"I think you mean *irrelevant*. Or maybe you were right."

"Oh, you know what I mean," she said with an unfamiliar frustrated tone in her voice. "It really doesn't matter. What matters is that you are doing something huge about this awful corporation that is totally poisoning our town and wants to do it to other towns. You know what I mean? It just doesn't matter who is communicating with you. A pink bird with polka dots and, I don't know, a purple beard could come up to your ear and whisper to you and it wouldn't matter."

"Point taken," Vivian said. "Thank you. But if a polka-dotted bird shows up at my window tonight, I'm totally telling him that I'm busy."

"Overextended. Send him my way."

"Will do."

"That's your prerogative, Viv. Hey, a rhyme," the familiar whimsical tone back in Wren's voice. She pulled back out onto the street and finally stopped a block away from Vivian's home. "I should probably let you out here."

Vivian nodded.

"I keep thinking about that little girl and her grandmother," Wren said.

Vivian knew that Wren was crying so she didn't look at her. "Me, too."

"I can't get her face out of my mind."

"Me, neither."

Wren took a long sigh, then shook her head. "Are you prepared for tomorrow?"

Vivian guffawed bitterly. "Not one bit. I mean, it is what it is. What am I supposed to do? I'll be there and my hope is that the right actions will just happen."

"They will," Wren said, reaching over to squeeze Vivian's hand. "They will. Let's talk tomorrow."

"I'll call you. Ideally not from jail."

"Ideally not. You're going to do great tomorrow. Just keep thinking about Tori and her grandmother and all the other kids with brain cancer and the ducks and all the other beings who could be poisoned by Gordenner."

"I will. I will. Somehow, it's all going to come together."

"Not somehow. Because of you. Y-O-U. Vivian Sharpe. As my mom would say, you have to own it. *Own it.* Now get out of here and get some sleep."

"Okay."

Walking down the sidewalk back to her home, Vivian was so preoccupied with other worries that she almost forgot that she'd sneaked out of the window earlier that evening and quite nearly walked right back in through the front door. She took a breath of relief that she remembered before it became a serious mistake.

Climbing back up the ivy proved to be a bigger challenge than climbing down, but she managed fine and no vine did snap, as she was picturing in her mind, leaving her dangling by one hand and swinging by her parents' bedroom window like Tarzan. Pushing her window open with ease, Vivian was grateful that she hadn't been caught, and that her room looked undisturbed from when she left it, pillows still in place under the covers.

She changed into her pajamas and was ready to climb into bed when she felt like should go to the bathroom and see if everything else looked normal in the house. She could hear the evening news on in her parent's bedroom; the door was open, so she stuck her head in the room. They were bright blue from the television light and her mom jumped a little seeing Vivian.

"Sorry, Mom. I just wanted to let you know that I was feeling better."

Mrs. Sharpe looked at Vivian like she wasn't sure why she needed to announce that, looked at her husband with a small shrug, then said, "That's good to know, dear."

"Okay. Goodnight."

"Goodnight, Vivian," her parents replied in unison.

"Oh, I think that I forgot to mention that I have to go in to work tomorrow morning for a couple of hours."

"On your day off?" her mother asked, eyebrows knit.

"Just this once. It's not something regular."

Her mother looked at Mr. Sharpe, who shrugged, then back to Vivian. "Well, I hope they appreciate what they have in you, Vivian."

"They do. Or they will soon."

THE PRESS CONFERENCE

Vivian wasn't expecting that she would sleep well that night, but she slept soundly and woke up without a problem when her clock-radio blared on at 7:15. She jumped out of bed, showered, then grabbed her outfit for the day (a preplanned outfit of charcoal pinstriped trousers, an off-white, scoop-necked top, and the sparkly earrings her parents had given her for Christmas). She got dressed with a different feeling today, more like her normal self than someone taking part in a charade. Putting on her socks, she realized that her chest was warm in the area of her heart and had been since she woke up. She imagined Tolstoy floating over her, smiling at her all night. She wrapped her arms around herself. "Good morning, Tolstoy. Today's the day." The warmth burned brighter and felt like a pair of mittens on a radiator.

In the kitchen, Mr. Sharpe was drinking coffee at the table, an empty plate with a few pieces of bread crust pushed to the side.

"Good morning, Vivian," he said, looking up from the paper that was fanned out in front of him on the table. "You look rested."

"I am. I feel much better." She started some oatmeal on the stove.

"So you're going in today…"

"Yeah. There's a press conference."

"A press conference? About what?"

Vivian shrugged. "Some new product."

"Ah." He put down the paper. "How are you liking it there at Gordenner? I haven't heard much from you about it since you started."

"Uh, it's fine, I guess."

"Well, that sounds like a ringing endorsement," he said, laughing. "Not a terribly exciting place, I take it?"

"It's not that. I'm still waking up, I guess." The bell of the toaster rang to her great relief. She took that as an opportunity to loudly clang in the cupboard for a plate and swung the refrigerator door open dramatically. "Apricots, cherries, apricots…" she repeated aloud as she rifled through the shelves. "Ah. Here." She brought everything over to the table. "Sorry, dad. I just don't have that much to say about it this morning. Try me later."

"I understand." If her father had any indication how much his daughter really wanted to share what she knew with him, more than anyone else in her family, he did not let on. "You know, Vivian," he said, clearing his throat, "your mother and I have talked about it, and we think that we can ease up on some of the restrictions we've put on you this summer."

She looked up, surprised. "Oh?"

"Yes. We see that you're a responsible, level-headed young lady and you're not getting into any trouble. Other than that little, I don't know, period of strangeness last weekend, you've had an unblemished record of trustworthy behavior."

Vivian felt a little insulted but she thanked him.

"So this doesn't mean all restrictions will be lifted, but we're going to let you be in contact with Wren again. Of course, no one can come to our house without our consent, and if we see you sliding into some strange behaviors again..."

"Dad..." Vivian wanted to hide under the table, she was so embarrassed.

"Okay, but you know what I mean. As long as everything's aboveboard, we see no harm in you enjoying summer with your friend."

Vivian nodded, feeling a slight flush of guilt as she thought of running into Wren's car the night before. "Thanks, Dad. I appreciate it."

Her father, perhaps feeling a little embarrassed as well, chattered on about a new diary found in someone's attic written by a Center City teenager in the 1960s, and how this might form the basis of a new book of his, charting Center City through periods of social change over 150 years. Vivian nodded and was grateful for a chance to not think about the future, not think about Gordenner and underground pipes and poisoned ducks and children. It wasn't long before she looked up at the clock on the wall and saw that it was time to catch the bus.

"Got to catch the 8:21, Dad," she said with a final few bites of her oatmeal. "See you later."

As she was leaving the kitchen, she was aware of the heat in her chest again, and the vision of Kurt and his granddaughter flashed in her mind. She stopped in the doorway.

"Oh, Dad?"

He looked up from his paper, a little taken aback. "Hmm?"

"I love you, Dad."

Neither Vivian nor her father were very demonstrative people, but this unexpected sentiment from her made Mr. Sharpe smile in such a way that he looked twenty years younger, like how she imagined he looked when he first met her mother.

"I love you too, daughter of mine."

Vivian would have preferred to have stared out the window of the 8:21 bus and focused on finding a place of peace inside herself, but the friendly bus driver greeted her that morning, and he was in an especially talkative mood. He talked about his dog, his neighbor's dog, how they growled at each other, the new fence he was installing, how it wasn't really on his property line but he was going to install it anyway because it was clear that his neighbor wasn't going to spend a dime on anything. Vivian smiled and nodded and said the occasional "huh" and, before she knew it, they were at her stop.

At the parking lot, the gate was open and Kurt was wearing his sunglasses, talking to a driver of a car and pointing, giving directions. The reporters were arriving. As Vivian walked past, he looked up and gave her a small nod. She did the same. Her heart fluttered.

The front door to Gordenner was open and Ms. Collins was standing near the front desk, wearing a crisp champagne-colored dress with a brown belt, laughing and talking to a woman with glossy dark hair pulled up into an elegant chignon. Vivian instantly recognized her as Maribeth Applebee, the lead reporter of Channel 4 News. This was as close to a celebrity sighting as Vivian had ever experienced, other than seeing Governor Driscoll's wife at *Look Sharpe!* the previous summer.

As soon as she noticed Vivian, Ms. Collins put her hand on the reporter's arm and said, "Excuse me, Maribeth. Vivian. Hello, dear. Could you go into room 103 – it's down the hall, to the right, by the elevators – and start greeting people? I have the guest list on the front table. Just check off names as people come in and hand them a packet. Can you do that for me?"

"Sure."

Before Vivian even responded, Ms. Collins was back in an animated conversation with Maribeth Applebee, pausing occasionally to put her hand on her friend's arm, smile and wave at new arrivals. Ms. Collins was in her element, Vivian observed to herself. Vivian couldn't help staring at her: Ms. Collins seemed to glow from some internal source, her spiky white-blonde hair even seemed to be vibrating with energy.

In the conference room, reporters were starting to file in and noisily set up cameras and microphones. Kevin Newell was standing behind the front desk, a slight scowl on his face as he handed new arrivals packets and tried to cross names off the guest list with one hand.

"I'm here now, Mr. Newell," Vivian said. "I can take over for you."

His face was a mixture of anger and relief. "You're late," he muttered when she stood beside him behind the desk.

"Actually this was when Ms. Collins told me to come in," she said, looking at the clock. "Eight forty-five."

"Then she messed up," he responded, not looking up. He patted the folders together loudly on the table. "Hello, Burt," he said, as he walked off with his hand extended to greet a newcomer in a grey jacket. Vivian realized that she did not feel chilled when she stood next to him, and she took that to be a good sign.

Reporters walked in, chatting with each other; camera crews came in, giant packs slung around their shoulders. Vivian checked their names off the list and handed them folders. She could see a few who weren't socializing or at the snack table sitting in their chairs, leafing through the packets. A few more were setting up tripods and cameras. Two reporters sat next to each other and one pointed something out inside the packet to the other, but Vivian couldn't see if it was something on the packet she'd inserted or not. Most were standing together in groups of three or four, eating mini-bagels on small plastic plates. Vivian turned back to the door and greeted more reporters.

Within a few minutes after she arrived, Robert Fontaine breezed into the room, a slender man of medium height with thick, dark eyebrows and a serious demeanor, with Ms. Collins by his side; on her other side was a tall man in an elegant grey suit, with salt-and-pepper hair. He looked like a character actor playing an ambassador and when a couple of photographers snapped pictures, Vivian knew instantly that the man in the grey suit was Helmut Burr.

Mr. Fontaine greeted Mr. Newell absentmindedly, stepping in to ask him something in a lowered voice, and looked around the room as he responded. Ms. Collins called a reporter over and introduced her to Mr. Fontaine and Ambassador Burr. After a few minutes, Ms. Collins put her hand on Mr. Fontaine's elbow and steered the group toward someone else when she noticed Vivian behind the table and detoured to her.

"Robert, Ambassador Burr, I want you to meet my intern, Vivian Sharpe. She's been with me for the past couple of weeks and has been so helpful."

Robert Fontaine extended a hand to her. To Vivian, it felt like they were both in slow motion.

"Nice to meet you, Vivian."

Vivian didn't know what to say, so the most honest response she could come up was a meek, "Thank you." Mr. Fontaine shook her hand, his eyes scanning the room briefly while he said hello.

"Vivian's a little shy at first," Ms. Collins remarked, like the proud mother of a diffident five-year-old, "but don't be fooled. She's a tough cookie."

Mr. Fontaine looked at her face briefly – he seemed to be searching for evidence of this toughness Ms. Collins spoke of – and nodded discreetly. "It's a pleasure."

Ms. Collins suddenly called out, "Maribeth," and began steering them toward the Channel 4 reporter while Vivian, feeling flustered and a little flushed at meeting Robert Fontaine face-to-face, was glad that she was socially awkward enough for them to not want to linger long. Then she saw Will, with a briefcase gripped tightly under white knuckles and an expression Vivian interpreted as nervous, come into the room. He paused at the doorway, scanning the room, and his eyes settled on her, to his obvious relief.

"Welcome," she said, looking down at her guest list. "Could I get your name, please?"

"Will Carson."

"Carson, Carson – ah," she said, tapping her pen on the desk. She scratched his name off the list. She scrupulously avoided eye contact with him. "Got it. Please take a folder and read the first packet," Vivian said, handing it to him. "There's coffee over there," she said, indicating the refreshment table. "We should be getting started in a few minutes."

He nodded indistinctly and opened his folder immediately; he started looking through it, slowly walking to a seat, As soon as he sat, he pulled out the papers Vivian had inserted and slouched down in his seat, reading. The next time Vivian glanced back, all but a few chairs were filled up and the last name was crossed off the guest list.

Ms. Collins walked to the microphone the podium, and cleared her throat. Mr. Fontaine and Mr. Newell were seated on the small stage behind Ms. Collins. Ambassador Burr was seated in the front row. Ms. Collins had a pleasant, relaxed smile on her face. Reporters who were lingering by the snack table hurried to their seats; photographers and camera people unzipped their bags. Vivian swiveled around in her chair to face Ms. Collins. They may have had a moment of eye contact, but Vivian wasn't sure.

"Good morning, everyone. Wow, quite a turnout. I think everyone is here." Cameras clicked and flashed against her, making her hair look even more stark white in the light. Photographers crouched and scooted closer. The company name and logo appeared on the screen behind her in vivid green letters. "Welcome. My name is Laura Collins and I am the marketing and PR director of Gordenner, U.S.A. I want to thank you all for being here this morning. As many of you know, Gordenner has had a long and rich history here in Center City. When Louis Gordon and Coleman Jenner founded this company in 1938, it was all about the seeds, using the best way they knew how to help farmers, and this country, recover from the Great Depression and the Dustbowl." Ms. Collins paused briefly to glance at a sheet on her podium. "Today, we're blessed to be living in a country where all of our basic needs are met. Even the poorest in this nation have easy access to affordable food. This is not so in developing nations, where millions still die of malnutrition and starvation. It was this knowledge that served as the impetus behind the line of products we're holding this press conference for this morning. We will be introducing our new product line, Bountiful, within the next few months in the most undernourished, impoverished nations across the world, with the goal of helping communities find nutritional sustenance and financial security.

"When I first took this position with Gordenner, my friends in New Dublin were shocked: I was giving up a job I loved in a modern building downtown to go work for an agricultural business in Center City. I'm someone, as my friends would testify, who loves urban living with all the trappings: the restaurants, the shopping, the culture. Why would I give that up to move to Center City? Because I am passionate about changing the world for the better, and I believe that Bountiful is the path to it.

"I would like to introduce Robert Fontaine, CEO of Gordenner. He has traveled abroad, most recently in Southeast Asia, where he has seen directly the benefit Bountiful could have to communities and individuals. We are truly excited to be able to share with the public our enthusiasm for the Bountiful product line, and the potential it has for reversing the rate of starvation and early death seen in impoverished nations. We believe that the innovation of Bountiful will help save the world. Please welcome Robert Fontaine."

After a polite applause, Mr. Fontaine walked to the podium and Ms. Collins took a seat behind him, next to Mr. Newell.

"Thanks, Laura. Good morning." Cameras clicked. "As Laura said, we are truly excited about our new product line, beginning with Bountiful Wheat and Bountiful Spray, which we think will be seen as the biggest innovation in agriculture in fifty years. I've been fortunate enough to be able to travel through Southeast Asia recently, as Laura said, and I saw firsthand the effect that our test fields are beginning to have on communities there just at the very beginning stages of what is possible."

Vivian could see Will turning around to look at her from the corner of her eye but she didn't dare meet his glance.

"I could see with my own eyes communities and families that were once on the brink of desperation turn their lives around with a reliable and nutritious food source. What we're talking about here with Bountiful is nothing short of a revolutionary, life-altering innovation that will have very far-ranging implications."

He cleared his throat. "The Bountiful Wheat seeds have the ability to grow in the harshest climates, drought conditions or difficult terrain. Not only is the wheat then available for harvest, but it has been enriched through a cutting-edge technology we developed to have the full RDA of folic acid – necessary for fetal development – and other necessary B vitamins. The positive impact this will have on birth defects alone will be staggering. The Bountiful Spray ensures that the Bountiful Wheat crop will be able to grow without threat from invasive species. What all this boils down to is the fact that we have a life-saving, quality-of-life-enriching product on our hands, created exclusively for the parts of the world hardest hit by starvation and poverty." Cameras flashed on him. "At Gordenner, our priority has always been to help farmers bring quality food to the table; now, with our Bountiful products, we will be doing this on the world stage, helping the world's most needy find something even more helpful than hope: we are helping them change the quality of their lives for the better. I am proud to be a part of the Gordenner team who is bringing the Bountiful products to the public. I would now like to introduce one of my colleagues, Kevin Newell, who has been with this project from its inception. Kevin?"

Mr. Newell took his place at the podium while Mr. Fontaine sat. He cleared his throat and smiled, producing something that looked remarkably out of place on his face.

"Good morning." He shuffled some papers and looked down for a moment at what he'd written. He coughed. "I have to speak honestly: public speaking is not my forte. Given the choice between public speaking and getting a root canal, I'd have to say, 'get that little plastic bib ready.'" A few in the audience tittered. He waited a few beats too long, having timed in a more boisterous response. "Really, though, the fact that I'm here to speak on a topic such as Bountiful, this revolutionary brand of nutritionally enhanced seeds and spray we have innovated right here in Center City at Gordenner's state-of-the-art laboratories, makes all the discomfort of public speaking disappear.

"Laura Collins, Robert Fontaine and myself – along with dozens of others – have worked very long hours in recent years creating, researching, and refining the Bountiful line with some of the brightest minds in the plant technology field. Our seeds, which are patented, grow wheat." The screen behind him faded from the Gordenner logo to a picture of a wheat field. He turned and looked at the screen briefly.

"This might not sound like much, but wheat is a staple plant pretty much across the globe. What you're eating this morning, bagels and muffins, of course, are created from wheat. Pasta is created from wheat. Dumplings. Almost every culture has some sort of bread, pasta or dumpling." The image switched to a screen divided into quarters, displaying different wheat products in every frame.

"Food is part of how cultures remain alive and connected. Recipes are passed down from grandmothers to their grandchildren standing in the kitchen with them no matter where people live, whether it be Iowa or Indonesia. Imagine, now, if this staple product, wheat, is enhanced with B-vitamins and folic acid. A deficiency of B-vitamins causes chronic fatigue and dangerous heart palpitations. A diet deficient in folic acid can cause the birth defect spina bifida as well as certain cancers. Now imagine that this product, which is enhanced with the RDA of B-vitamins and folic acid, is going to be widely available in developing nations, where populations struggle daily to keep their children alive and nourished. This is why we are gathered here today: to announce what we believe to be one of the most important innovations in plant technology, Bountiful Wheat and Spray." The screen behind him cut to an image of a brown hand, outstretched, holding small tan seeds. "We..."

Will's arm shot up; a few reporters seated near him gave Will a sideways glance. Kevin Newell looked momentarily startled. "Um, we'll have time for questions in a few minutes if you don't mind."

Vivian wasn't sure what Will would do, but his arm went down and he turned back to his folder where he was scribbling furiously on an inside pocket.

Mr. Newell coughed. "We are confident that Bountiful..." At this point, his words bled together into a sort of blur to Vivian's ears. He was speaking, she could hear the sound of his voice and see his mouth open and shut, see images of brown-skinned people in colorful, vibrant clothing – baking bread, harvesting wheat – change on the screen behind him. After a few moments of this, a new image came up, one of ducks at the river covered in slime, then of the dead duck with half-closed eyes in Vivian's palm. She looked around the room and she could see that no one was reacting, and Vivian knew at that moment that she was seeing images no one else could see. Her chest began to pulse with warmth again.

Mr. Newell's voice, still indistinct, droned on, and Vivian saw an image of the dead duckling turn into a river filled with sewage. She saw a pipe pumping out noxious chemicals. She saw a picture of Tori, Kurt's granddaughter, lying in a hospital bed with a shaved head and life-support machines plugged into her arms, and Vivian started shaking, her hands covering her mouth. Next, with the image of Tori still on the screen, she couldn't hear anything except two words. *Stand up.* She didn't know if it came from Mr. Newell or within herself or from Tolstoy, but she knew that was what she was supposed to do.

Vivian stood up, her heart beating like mad. She felt it viscerally for the first time as a muscle, blood flowing in and out with each pump, expanding and contracting.

When she first started walking toward the stage, no one seemed to notice. Once she walked past a few rows of reporters, though, heads turned and chairs creaked as people shifted and turned in their chairs. Time froze. At this point, Mr. Newell looked over at her, and he stopped in mid-sentence, his mouth frozen in a sideways oval as he stared at her, bewildered. He looked between her and Ms. Collins, a stricken, sick look on his face, as Vivian walked up the steps of the stage; Ms. Collins, her expression confused and uncomprehending, shook her head side to side. "Not now, Vivian," she said with a tight smile to the crowd, as if her silly young intern were interrupting her with a request to use the restroom.

As Vivian turned to face the room, reporters murmured back and forth, hands between faces, and a few giggled with embarrassment. She saw Will sitting on the edge of his chair, fingers gripped tight to the seat like he could barely restrain himself from jumping up as well.

"Vivian?" Now she could hear Mr. Newell's voice again. He was speaking into the microphone though she stood less than a foot away from him. "Vivian, would you mind taking a seat?"

She ignored him, her arms shaking with more energy than she could store in her body, so she steadied them, one hand clasped around the other forearm, pressed across her stomach. "I need to talk to everyone here today about Gordenner. I know more about this place than I ever knew in my whole lifetime of growing up here in Center City, and I think that you should know about it too."

"Vivian?" Vivian could hear Ms. Collins' voice behind her.

"I started here a little over two weeks ago, after I found some ducks in the Kickashaunee River that were covered in the most disgusting, nasty slime that you could imagine. Really, really gross stuff."

Now a few cameras began clicking at her. Mr. Newell tried to pull her by the elbow but she shook him off.

"Let her speak," Will shouted. "We deserve to hear her speak."

Ms. Collins was now at the podium. "Everyone. Really I'm sorry for this..."

"Once I found the ducks, I was able to discover that the Kickashaunee is being poisoned. What I found on them – this disgusting slime – is being pumped into our water supply by this place, by Gordenner. Not only that, but..."

"Really, Vivian. This is really enough. Everyone, we're going to take a five-minute break, please..." Ms. Collins spoke into the microphone. Now Mr. Fontaine was standing by her side.

"...but they are pumping this stuff – this toxic waste that's a byproduct of Bount..."

"What is she talking about?" she could hear someone say.

"Could somebody please call security?" Mr. Fontaine said, his voice eerily steady.

"Vivian, this is quite enough," Ms. Collins said.

"Toxic waste from Bountiful Wheat and Spray," she said louder, "is then being piped into the river through an underground pipe that feeds into a tributary."

"That's right," Will shouted. "Feeds right into Colman's Creek. I saw it myself." People whipped around in their chairs to stare at Will. Reporters were taking notes and pointing their small tape recorders between Vivian and Will.

"Who is he?" Mr. Fontaine said, turning to Ms. Collins who shook her head.

"Will Car..." he started to say.

"Young man, please identify yourself."

"I was saying: Will Carson, with the Center City College Beacon."

Mr. Fontaine charged off the stage.

Vivian kept talking. "So the thing is that they are destroying the wildlife and ecosystem in Center City with this chemical dumping, and they are doing it illegally, pretending that the water that flows out of here is safe - "

"Vivian, stop," a man's voice shouted.

"- but this is why it tests safe. The water that flows out of here *is* safe, because that's not from the underground pipe."

"Exactly," Will shouted.

"Now they are trying to export this product to other nations because it is not acceptable here."

"That is not true, Vivian." Ms. Collins said, her voice like a shard of ice. "Call security, Kevin. This is outrageous. This is slanderous."

"Yes, call security. Call the police. While you're at it, call the Environmental Protection Agency," Vivian responded, taken momentarily aback by the force of will behind her voice. For the first time, she faced Ms. Collins, who looked stark white. "Call them and tell them about the underground pipe, about the high rate of brain cancer in Center City, about the animals being -"

"Also, tell them about the giant vats of genetically engineered chemical byproduct that is illegally being pumped into this town's water supply," Will shouted, standing now.

" – poisoned."

"Lies," Ms. Collins spat out, shaking her head in disbelief. Looking at the crowd, she said louder, "All lies."

Mr. Fontaine was standing in the corner, talking with the ambassador; Kevin Newell joined them and they huddled together, watching Vivian and speaking in hushed tones even as they gestured wildly.

Vivian turned to Ms. Collins. "I didn't want to do this to you, but it had to be exposed..."

Ms. Collins turned off her microphone with the flick of a long red fingernail and turned to Vivian with another tight smile. "You are a two-faced little liar, Vivian Sharpe," Ms. Collins turned to the room, her face now flushed with anger. "Get that name right, reporters. Vivian Sharpe." She turned the microphone back on. "She told me she was here to become a marketing intern and I believed her."

"I am not a liar. Everyone here is free to see - "

"Not to mention their product is being marketed as this goodwill effort when all they are really doing is encouraging the monocropping of a genetically engineered, nutritionally suspect wheat. You'd need 13 loaves of bread a day to get the RDA they claim," Will said.

"I will not even dignify what that person said with a response. Please don't pay him any attention – he's obviously got his own agenda."

"Is that right?" a reporter turned toward Will asked, pen in hand. "Thirteen loaves a day?"

"It is. It's documented. I have printouts for everyone from their own lab." He held up his briefcase and a few reporters expressed interest.

"Kevin, how's it going with security?" Ms. Collins asked. "We have someone else here who is here under what I can only assume is a false identity. An imposter. He needs to be removed from the premises as well."

Mr. Newell held up a phone and threw his hands up in the air. "I can't get through. I'm getting the busy signal. Sounds like it's off the hook."

Ms. Collins walked over to Vivian, her back to the crowd, her arms folded across her chest. "Vivian, now is your chance. Leave. We won't press charges if you go now. I don't know what got into you, I have no idea what you're talking about, but it's in your best interest to leave while you have a chance. Leave. You're a little liar. Consider this the last bit of charity you'll get from me. Leave now and we'll just forget that you ever stepped foot in here. It's your call." Cameras flashed around them. Ms. Collins looked her straight in the eye, her arms crossed in front of her chest.

"I can't. I'm sorry, Ms. Collins," who set her jaw and shook her head disdainfully at Vivian, "but I came here to do this. To let the public know about what's happening so we can stop Bountiful..."

"Ms. Collins?" a young reporter asked, looking at the papers Vivian had inserted into the packet, "this says that there has been a 25% decrease in fish populations locally, 20% of birds. Is it fair to say that this is attributable to Bountiful?"

"Yes," Will called out from the back of the room.

"What? Where did you read that?"

"Right here," he said, waving the papers in front of her. "It also says that they've seen the same results in Indonesia where there are test fields."

"Nonsense. Where did you find that?"

"In my own folder, right here."

"I've got that, too," another reporter chimed in. "Can you also speak to how Gordenner is going to address the anti-Western sentiments that are building up in Southeast Asia?"

Ms. Collins was still looking at the first reporter, apparently stunned that these reports were inside the folders. She turned back to Vivian. "Did you insert some false information into our packets, Vivian?" she said, aghast but almost laughing at the absurdity. "I trusted you and look what happened. That is unforgivable. It's called tampering. You are going to be sued for that, too."

"It's all true, Ms. Collins. And you can't sue me without also dragging Gordenner through the mud. I mean, the minute you say this all is untrue, you're going to have to prove it and you're going to expose Gordenner..."

"Gordenner has done nothing wrong. We are trying to feed the world - "

"Excuse me, Ms. Collins, but Gordenner has done nothing wrong? I have to believe that you didn't know about this, but what about the underground pipe? What about that by-product getting into our water?" Vivian took a breath. "Did you know about that?"

"I don't believe you in the first place," Ms. Collins said, her voice rising. "You are a liar."

"Ms. Sharpe, is it S-h-a-r-p?" interrupted a reporter, his pen ready to write. Vivian hadn't noticed before, but a group of reporters was now massed by the stage, two feet from her and Ms. Collins.

"Sharpe with an 'e'," she said. There was a commotion over by Will, but she couldn't make out what was happening. She turned back to Ms. Collins when they were interrupted again.

"Aren't you related to Sally Sharpe of *Look Sharpe!* salon?" another asked.

"Yes, she is," Ms. Collins said.

"Laura Collins," a reporter with curly blonde hair asked, "are you prepared to make a statement? Is Mr. Fontaine?" She held out a recording device.

"No, I am not. Give me ten minutes. I'd like to have ten minutes to get some semblance of order."

She started to walk away when Vivian touched her arm. Ms. Collins flinched and drew away as if she had gotten an electric shock, but Vivian continued regardless. "Ms. Collins, I want to believe that you didn't know anything about this, about the deception of Gordenner. It really is just the tip of the iceberg here, what I'm talking about."

"Fft," Ms. Collins said dismissively but she didn't walk away.

"What I mean is that I think that you're an incredibly powerful woman, Ms. Collins, but I think that you've been duped just like this town has been duped by Gordenner."

She did a double-take. "Duped? Are you calling me stupid? Naïve? You?"

"No, I'm not. I'm saying that I think that you're a good person-"

"Oh, thank you very much. I don't need you to - "

"...who didn't mean for this to happen, who didn't sign off on this – that your intentions are good. Ms. Collins, you could do so much good in the world with all your talents. You really could."

By now, tape recorders were thrust in between them, as well as a couple of microphones from video cameras. Cameras flashed and the reporters moved in closer. The cameras were on Ms. Collins who stood as rigidly as a statue as reporters began shouting questions at her, one after the next. For the first time, Vivian saw her as vulnerable; she wanted to step in front of Ms. Collins and defend her, tell everyone that she was a good person, that she had a good heart, it wasn't her fault, but she couldn't make herself do it so she stood there, unable to move, as it felt like everything around her was collapsing in slow motion. *So this is how it happens*, Vivian thought to herself.

In the back of the room by Will, a couple of chairs fell to the ground and there was something happening, a sort of a scuffle. Vivian ran to him as the reporters surrounding Ms. Collins followed, fanning out around him. Mr. Fontaine and Mr. Newell had each grabbed one of Will's arms and were trying to pull him out of the room. They were pulling back but Will was straining against them, his legs locked and knocking against the chairs, refusing to go without a struggle. Vivian caught a glimpse of Ambassador Burr hurrying from the room.

"You're going to be next, Vivian," Will shouted. "Make sure you say everything you want to say." The cameras clicked and voices shouted again.

"Mr. Carson, who are you?" a reporter demanded. "A protester? A student?"

Will grimaced as he struggled against them. "I'm working with the student paper at..."

"He's a protester," Mr. Fontaine said, spitting out the word. "Nothing more productive to do with his time." He thrust with his shoulder and Will stumbled forward.

"Wait a minute," Vivian said. The cameras jerked toward her. "This man is being taken from the room because he's telling the truth. We are both telling the truth. If anyone wants, right now I can take you to the creek where the pipe we - "

"Young lady," Mr. Fontaine said, his face flushed as he stepped forward, letting go of Will's arm, which caused him to stumble back. "You had better start exercising a little more caution with your words. Your mother doesn't deserve to have her business ruined because of your behavior today."

"And you had better own up to what you have done," Vivian shouted, her heart racing as she pointed at him, feeling for the first time that this was the moment she had been working toward all along. "How many children are you responsible for killing, Mr.

Fontaine? How many birds? How much water is still drinkable in this town because of you and this company? How much more are you going to poison us before someone puts a stop to it? Are you really expecting that you can just do this without any consequences to you?"

He narrowed his eyes at her. "I am doing nothing wrong, Ms. Sharpe. None of us is. You are either insane or you have a hidden agenda."

"It's both," Mr. Newell said, sounding winded, and having let go of Will's other arm. "Everyone, this young lady has deceived us from the very beginning. I was suspicious from the start. We're going to press charges against her. As soon - "

"I'd like for everyone to take your seats, please," Mr. Fontaine said, his voice firm. "We will resume this press conference once these protesters are removed."

"Mr. Fontaine," a young woman with a microphone asked, raising her arm, "is there any truth to their allegation that there is an underground pipe leading to a creek behind the premises?"

"I refuse to address hearsay and propaganda. I would ask you to consider the source," he indicated Vivian with a flick of his head. "We caught this young woman trespassing on company property. The only thing that we are guilty of is being naïve and trusting her when she said that she wanted to work here."

"And what about - ?" the reporter continued.

"This young man – he could be a socialist, anti-progress, anti-corporation, anti-democracy for all we - "

Will laughed. "Anti-democracy? Oh, that's rich coming from a Gordenner official."

"As I said, I will not address charges levied by two protesters." He turned to face Vivian and Will, pointing to the door. "You can leave the premises of your own free will or you can be forcibly removed. What's your choice?"

Neither Vivian nor Will said anything.

"I'll assume that your silence means that you will not leave on your own. Is that a fair assumption?"

Again, silence.

"Okay. Kevin, did you call the police?"

He nodded, and Mr. Fontaine stormed away from the crowd with Kevin Newell close behind him.

The reporters closed in on Vivian and Will.

"I've got a sample right here of the byproduct Bountiful creates," Will said with all the bombast of a latter day carnival barker, reaching into his bag and pulling out a small vial. "I pulled this directly from Colman's creek behind Gordenner. That's also where you will find the underground pipe. You'll also find dozens of dead frogs, birds and fish out there." He held up the vial and took off the cap. People recoiled almost immediately at the odor; he replaced the cap. "This is the smallest of samples. Gallons and gallons of this stuff are going directly into our waterways every day."

"Ms. Sharpe," one of the reporters asked, "is it true that you took a job here under a false pretext as has been claimed?"

"I didn't see any other way of getting in here to expose what was happening."

"And what *is* happening?"

"Gordenner is poisoning our town with the byproduct of Bountiful and they plan to do it elsewhere as well."

"Ms. Sharpe," another reporter shouted, "do you live here in Center City?"

"Yes, I do."

"Then do you go to Center City High School?"

"Yes, I do."

"What year are you?"

"I'm going to be a junior in the fall. I'll be sixteen next month."

"Is your mother really the owner of *Look Sharpe*?"

Vivian tried not to visibly blanch. "Yes, she is."

"What do your parents think of your deception of Gordenner on your application?"

"Um, they didn't know."

"They will now," someone said and the reporters around her started laughing. "They will now."

"That's fine," she said.

"What was your goal here today?" a reporter asked. "Do you have a list of demands?"

"What? I'm not a terrorist," Vivian said. "No, I don't have a list of demands."

"Then what is it that you want?"

"The main thing is that they stop the production of the Bountiful products unless they can be produced without all the toxins. And that they don't dump into our town's water. Or any town's water."

"Also," Will added, "that they pay for the clean-up."

"Yes, that too."

"Were you two working together?" a reporter asked Vivian, pointing her pen at Will.

"In a way."

A voice called out, but Vivian was overwhelmed and blinded by the flashes of light in her face and she couldn't see who was speaking to her. "Vivian, Gordenner employs, I believe, two thousand people in Center City..."

"Actually, it's three thousand," Vivian said.

"Okay, three thousand: by far, the largest employer in Center City. Do you think that they should all quit their jobs? What would happen to all these people and their families if Gordenner closed down?"

"I'm not saying that they should close down. I'm talking about their products, that they are poisoning our water supply. Can't they make them in a non-toxic way?"

Vivian could finally see that the reporter she was talking to was Maribeth Applebee of Channel 4 News, which made her momentarily dumbstruck. She'd watched Channel 4 News with her father since as long ago as she could remember. "It seems that Gordenner has put a lot of time and energy into the development of Bountiful – what do you propose that they do instead of this?"

"I guess I would say that a lot of people put a lot of time and energy into raising healthy children – is it okay that Gordenner is poisoning them through our water supply?"

"So you don't care what happens to the people who work here, who trusted you?"

Vivian shook her head impatiently. "That's not true. I do care about the people who work here. I just don't think that it's okay to continue poisoning our town. Or any town. Whatever it takes for them to stop doing that, I'm willing to support."

"Even if it means the loss of thousands of jobs?"

"It shouldn't mean that, but yes."

More reporters shouted questions at her, and she was just answering one when another was lobbied at her, which made her feel like she was playing a new version of volleyball; meanwhile, Will was sequestered with three other reporters in the corner, animatedly answering questions as they recorded his words. Vivian felt breathless and dizzy as she stood there, a microphone shoved in her face, cameras pointed at her, clicking, but she also felt very firmly rooted, like it would take a bulldozer to knock her over.

Without any warning, a sea change occurred in the room and the expressions on the reporters' faces turned to one of anticipation and perhaps nervousness; Vivian glanced over her shoulder to where they were looking and she saw two police officers enter the room flanked by Ms. Collins and Mr. Fontaine.

"I understand that there has been a disturbance of the peace," one police officer said. He was tall with thinning hair under his cap. His partner gestured to Will and Ms. Collins nodded. He crossed the room to where Will was talking. The other walked to Vivian.

"Miss, I understand that you were advised that you would have to leave the premises."

Vivian nodded. "Yes, sir."

"Do you understand that you are on private property and they have every right to ask you to vacate the facilities?"

"Yes, I do. But..."

He raised his voice. "Just answer my questions. You are being arrested for disturbing the peace: are you ready to leave peacefully or do I have to remove you with force?"

Cameras clicked, photographers crouched around them, the petite teenager and the police officer.

"I'm a peaceful person, officer. That's why I'm here."

He scowled a little at her, his patience already frayed. "What I'm asking is if you are going to leave with us peacefully or resist arrest."

"I'm a peaceful person who is resisting arrest peacefully," Vivian said, her chest warm. "What I want to know is if anyone is going to investigate the underground pipe we talked about. While all this is going on, Gordenner is polluting our water, killing the animals, the children."

"Vivian, really," Ms. Collins said, her face pale, clearly exasperated. She took Vivian's elbow and turned her around to face away from the crowd. "This is insane. Please do me a favor, do your family a favor, and don't be taken away like this. Don't leave here in handcuffs. Think of the pictures in the paper. Think of college. Your mother will be humiliated. Your father. Think of others, Vivian. You have to think of others."

"I am, Ms. Collins. That's what makes this decision so easy."

"Vivian..."

"Vivian, have you ever been arrested before?" a reporter shouted.

"Please," she laughed and turned back to Ms. Collins. "I'm really sorry for disappointing you. I'm truly sorry for deceiving you, but it was necessary. I don't know what you know about Gordenner, Ms. Collins, but I hope for the sake of your conscience that you don't know about the pipe ..."

Ms. Collins put her hands to her ears. "Here you go again. I am done with this, Vivian. Done. I am asking you to think a little about your future, about your family..."

"I am, Ms. Collins."

Ms. Collins looked up to the ceiling and shook her head. "Vivian, these police officers are going to take you to jail. In handcuffs - "

"Laura Collins," another reporter spoke, "is Gordenner going to press charges?"

She dismissed this with an imperial wave of her hand, "- with all the media around. You are aware of that right? This isn't a movie. This isn't a TV show. This is real life. You understand that, right?"

"Of course I do."

"Then being taken away to jail in handcuffs while reporters take your picture is your choice."

Vivian turned to the police officer and held out her wrists as the pictures were snapped. "Officer, I'm ready to be escorted from the building." This was her natural response, but also what would happen in a movie, it was strange for her to note.

The officer looked at her quizzically for a moment, shrugged slightly, then recited her Miranda rights, again, just like in a movie. Vivian nodded and smiled beatifically; he cuffed her behind her back as the cameras clicked. She was expecting them to feel constricting, but there was something about the way they finally snapped in place, locked around her wrists, the cold, hard metal against her soft skin, that made them feel real in a way she couldn't have imagined. They started to walk past the reporters when the other police officer approached them leading Will, who was also handcuffed.

"We are being arrested for disturbing the peace of Gordenner U.S.A. by informing the public that they are poisoning the town of Center City," Will yelled to the cameras, his expression very earnest and his face radiant. "This company has lied, stolen and cheated since it began in 1938: now we're talking about them actually changing the quality of life. How much are the people of Center City willing to put up with? When is Gordenner going to be held accountable for their crimes against our community and our planet?" He was still shouting as he was pulled from the room. Vivian calmly walked from the room with the police officer at her side.

"Vivian Sharpe, would you like to make a last statement as you're taken to jail?" a reporter standing next to a film camera shouted at her.

"We have to stop Bountiful," was all she said before being escorted from the room with reporters who bumped into one another as they trailed close behind, the camera people trying to squeeze through the doorway all at once.

EVERYTHING CHANGES

It was very surprising to Vivian that after what was the most dramatic morning of her life – which included not only confrontation, revealing her deception and causing disappointment, but also an arrest, seeing Center City from the inside of a squad car (alongside Will, who was as in his element in the back seat of a police car as Ms. Collins was socializing with reporters), being booked and fingerprinted and sitting in a cell until whatever happened next – that what she really wanted to do in her cell, when finally blissfully alone, was lie on the cot with the scratchy blanket and take a nap, but that is what she did. It was still early in the day, probably around the time she would have been heading home from the press conference if not for her having engineered its implosion, but she was suddenly very sleepy, as though her internal batteries just ran out, and sleep embraced her fully.

When she work up, Vivian had no idea how long she had slept – maybe twenty minutes, maybe two hours – and she had only the faintest recollections of a dream (Millie skipping on the sidewalk, perhaps jumping rope), but a police officer was standing outside her cell, rattling keys as she opened the door. Vivian sprang up in an instant, wiping saliva off her cheek.

"What time is it?" she said, still confused and jarred from waking up in jail.

The police officer, a petite woman with a serious face, looked at her watch. "Almost 1:00," she said in a matter-of-fact tone.

"My parents will be worried about me," Vivian said. "I should have been home by now. I'm still on a curfew. Can I call them? I get a phone call, right?"

The officer smirked a little as she unlocked the cell door. "Your parents are here, Miss Sharpe," she said, her tone unreadable. She slid the door open with a jarring clank. Vivian, unsure of the protocol, waited to be told what to do. The police officer motioned for her to come forward. "Anyway, at least they're no longer worried where you are."

Vivian felt a knot in her stomach finally, and as she walked down the white concrete hallway, having been told not to veer from a blue line that was taped to the floor, she passed other cells, filled with women in jail uniforms like orange hospital scrubs. They stared at her unabashedly as she passed, calling out, "Look at this one," and, "What are you in for, Cinderella?" and discussing her as though she wasn't really there. Someone said, "I bet it's shoplifting; the kids are always with the shoplifting," and another remarked that she looked like she was going to be sick. One last voice called out as she turned the corner, trying to sound reassuring despite the bitterness of her words, "Don't be scared, kid. You're white. No problem."

Vivian was instructed by the officer to wait on the blue line while she got her keys ready to unlock another door, this one leading to a messy but somehow ascetic-looking room with police officers sitting at desks, talking on phones or typing, just like at Gordenner. It was interesting to see how much police dramas actually succeeded in capturing the look of such places, Vivian thought to herself. It took a moment to see her parents, who were sitting close together on a bench in the corner of the room. Vivian noticed was how odd it was to see her parents holding hands: she didn't think that she had ever seen that.

Upon seeing her daughter, Sally Sharpe jumped up and rushed over to her with Mr. Sharpe close behind. "My baby," she cried, her eyes moist and nose red, hugging Vivian until she pulled back to look at her, her hands gripping Vivian's arms tightly. "Are you okay? Did anyone try to hurt you?"

"Hi, Mom. You mean at Gordenner? Did someone try to hurt me this morning?" Vivian was having a hard time with understanding the question.

"No, dear," Ms. Sharpe said in such a way that Vivian could see that she was trying very hard to be patient. "I mean..." She couldn't bring herself to say *jail*. "I mean here. Did anyone try to hurt you?"

Vivian shook her head. "No. Why?"

"Good. I was so worried, thinking of you sitting...here." Her mother started crying and stepped away.

"Mom, it's okay. Everything's going to be okay..."

The police officer who retrieved Vivian coughed a little awkwardly – they didn't realize that she was still standing there – and gestured to a large empty desk with a computer and four chairs around it. "Why don't you all have a seat? Officer Geary will be here as soon as he can."

As soon as they sat at the table, Mrs. Sharpe took her daughter's hand, looking at it. "Vivian, your father and I are just at a loss…"

Her father finally spoke, his voice quiet, a little hoarse. He looked strange. Vivian wondered if he had been crying as well. "We need some…some sort of explanation, Vivian. We need to know what is going on. We've heard a million different stories now – something about an underground pipe, a big confrontation at Gordenner. Our heads are spinning. You have to understand."

"I do," Vivian said, squeezing her mother's hand. "I understand. But it's so complicated."

"Life is complicated, Vivian," she said brusquely. "Your father and I are grown-ups. We can take it."

Vivian took a deep breath and told them everything, beginning with finding the ducks. She briefly considered telling them about Tolstoy but decided that it was wise to avoid the whole subject. They watched Vivian as she talked, a skeptical expression on her mother's face, the father looking flustered, and they let her talk without interruption, her mother still grasping her hand. It all spilled out of her in a way that was depleting but comforting. She felt herself feeling lighter and lighter, a hot air balloon when the weights are dropped, as she talked. When she finished the whole story, ending up with her arrest that morning, neither spoke for a few moments. Finally, Mrs. Sharpe let go of her daughter's hand, sat up straight and shook her head (with disgust? with disbelief? Vivian wasn't sure) and spoke.

"You did the right thing, Vivian," she said in a subdued way. "I wish that you had told us sooner – I really, really wish that – but I feel that you did the right thing." She glanced over at her husband.

Mr. Sharpe, looking stunned, stared at his daughter. "You mean, they're piping this by-product – this toxic by-product – into our water, and you saw the pipe?"

"I did. I touched it with my own hands."

"And it's definitely from Gordenner?"

"I can't say definitely. I strongly suspect it. What we need to do is get that investigated."

Mr. Sharpe looked at his wife. "Well, if that's true, it's unconscionable. That's... staggering. Especially if we don't know what that does to our health. I can't imagine that it's good for you."

"I know, Dad," Vivian said quietly. "That's why I had to do this."

Mrs. Sharpe frowned a little. "Wasn't there another way, Vivian? An easier way to get the word out without creating all this craziness, this pandemonium?"

"Maybe there was, Mom. But I didn't see what that was."

"I mean, couldn't you have simply talked to us? Are we that controlling? That difficult to talk to?"

"No, Mom, it's not that. It was just something that I..."

Mrs. Sharpe's eyes opened wide as she suddenly gasped. "That's why Wren and that boy were at our house, right? To help you with this. This was why you got in trouble, right? This was what you couldn't tell us. Is that right?"

Vivian nodded. "That's right."

"So you could have avoided this whole time of punishment if you'd simply talked to us?"

"I know, Mom, but in the end I felt that this was the right thing for me to do."

"I don't dispute that: I just think that you should have talked to us."

"Well," Mr. Sharpe jumped in, "what's done is done. Now we just need to face the rest together. A united front."

Mrs. Sharpe rubbed her forehead for a moment and said, "You're right. What's done is done." She turned to Vivian. "I don't want you to believe that I think that you did the wrong thing, because I don't. I just wish..."

"That I'd talked to you."

"Yes."

"But if I'd talked to you, would you have let me work at Gordenner? Would you have let me research things the way I needed to?"

"I don't know," Mrs. Sharpe said and paused for a moment before acknowledging this with a subtle shrug, "Probably not."

"Would you have let me handle things the way I wanted to?"

"Probably not, but, Vivian, we're your parents," she said, looking up to the ceiling for some guidance. "We have to do what we think is..."

A police officer, a stocky older man with salt-and-pepper hair and a kind face, joined them at the table. "I'm Officer Geary," he said in a disarmingly friendly way. He extended a hand to Vivian's parents. They both stood. "Sorry to interrupt. You are Roosevelt and Sally Sharpe I presume?"

"That's right," Mr. Sharpe said, standing and shaking his hand.

"You know," Officer Geary said with a playful smile, "I've always wondered about that name Roosevelt. Like the Roosevelt presidents. Why is it that the name is not pronounced *roo* like in kangaroo but like *ro* as in road? I would think that with the two o's, it would be *roo*. You know what I mean?"

Clearly, Mr. Sharpe was not expecting such an icebreaker and blinked a few times before responding. "I believe that it's because the Roosevelt family was of Dutch origin and the double o is pronounced with a hard 'o'."

Officer Geary nodded slowly. "Ah. Dutch. Now that makes sense. Thanks for clearing that up. I've been wondering about that since I was a kid. Anyway," he said, gesturing with a broad sweep of his arm to the rest of the room, "welcome to my humble home away from home."

"Nice to meet you," Mr. Sharpe said. "I mean, it could be under better circumstances, you know, our daughter being arrested and everything…"

Mrs. Sharpe smiled calmly at her husband. "You can stop talking now, Roosevelt." She turned to face Officer Geary. "Officer, I'm not trying to be rude..."

"But could I cut to the chase…?" he suggested in a good-natured tone.

"Exactly. We'd just like to know what the next steps are. We've never been through this sort of thing before. I'm sure you understand why I'm anxious."

"Of course." He typed on the keyboard for a few moments, then spent a little while muttering to himself while reading something on the computer. Mr. And Mrs. Sharpe shifted nervously; Vivian just thought of what a peaceful demeanor this police officer had.

"Okay," he said, clearing his throat. "It looks like it went through. A Laura Collins called about an hour ago and said that no charges would be filed against Vivian. She is forbidden to enter Gordenner property again – they haven't gone so far as to file a restraining order yet, but it is private property – and any of Vivian's personal effects will be delivered to your home by an employee. Anyway, no charges are filed against you or Mr. Carson, so that's where it stands…"

Mrs. Sharpe clapped her hands giddily. "That's wonderful. Did you hear that, darling?" she said, turning to Vivian. "No charges."

"The arresting officer, Officer Sullivan, said that he did have to use the `cuffs but that Vivian actually asked for them and went willingly." He chuckled. "This is quite an…well, let's say, it is an unusual approach. Anyway, Officer Sullivan didn't seem to think that she should be charged with resisting arrest either."

"So nothing?" Mrs. Sharpe said, barely able to conceal her glee.

Officer Geary gave her a friendly shrug. "I got nothin'."

As this all sank in, her mother became radiant with relief, but Vivian festered inside.

"Isn't that wonderful?" Sally Sharpe asked, a broad smile on her face, her eyebrows raised, like she was talking to a small child who'd just eaten all her spinach. "No charges."

Vivian got angry. "But what does this mean about Gordenner illegally dumping chemicals into our water? That's what I want to know. Are they just trying to sweep all this under the rug?"

"Vivian…" her mother said, her voice a warning.

"She's right," her father interrupted. Vivian was surprised by the adamant sound of his voice, the color in his cheeks. "She's right. This company has been skirting the environmental protection laws of this state since they started. They have been fined and sued and fined again and they just keep doing it. In 1947, they created a chemical spill that caused a bluish skin tone in the babies born that year," he thought for a moment, his eyes becoming blurry the way they did when he was trying to recall something, "in 1954, no, '55, they released a chemical cloud so big over their manufacturing plant, it could be seen for miles in every direction. They were fined in 1971 – they couldn't have been before that because the EPA was only created in 1970 – 1972, 1975, 1976 and on and on, usually without much more than a slap on the wrist. How do we know that our water is safe? Who is going to hold them accountable? They're not going to regulate themselves, that's for certain. They're laughing all the way to the bank."

"I didn't know you knew so much about Gordenner," Vivian said.

"I'm an historian," he said matter-of-factly.

"I know, but…"

"But what? You thought all my information was useless?"

She nodded, not sure if he was angry or not. Mr. Sharpe smiled at last. "Shows what you know, my child."

"But to your original question," Officer Geary said, nodding at Mr. Sharpe, "only time will tell. You have my assurance that we'll do our work and we'll see where it goes from there."

Mrs. Sharpe looked between her husband and Officer Geary, fatigue settling between her brows. She patted Mr. Sharpe's hand while looking at the officer. "This morning has put quite a strain on my husband and myself."

"And your daughter as well, I imagine."

"Oh, yes, her too, of course. What I'm saying is that none of us is actually behaving like ourselves..."

"But Vivian and Roosevelt – with the hard o – raise an important issue," Officer Geary said, nodding at Vivian. "It seems like you have upset the apple cart a little, Vivian. That's not a bad thing. It sounds like Gordenner headquarters is going to be very busy for the next few weeks with visits from various regulatory agencies. And answering questions from reporters."

"How do you know that?" she asked.

He smiled cryptically. "Your father is an historian – it's his job to know things. I'm a police officer – same thing. Anyway, this is all to say that if they have been indeed polluting the Kickashaunee, they're about to get caught."

"And what will happen to the people who work there?"

"What do you mean?"

"Will they go to prison?"

Officer Geary looked at Vivian thoughtfully. "It depends on what they knew, what they did. That sort of thing. There's no way of saying at this point. What I do know, though, is that there's going to be some serious inquiry. If things are like you claim, there are some serious penalties for what they've done. That's more for the lawyers and the judges to hash out, but..."

"So now what?" Mrs. Sharpe said, with a hint of an impatience creeping back into her voice. "Can we go yet?"

Officer Geary smiled at Mr. Sharpe, perhaps sympathetically. "I see no reason for holding you up any longer. It was nice to meet you all." He pushed away from the desk and stood up. He turned to Vivian, lowering his voice to talk privately. "Thanks for what you did, kid. It gives me some hope for the future."

On the ride home, with the window beside her wide open and the wind whipping her hair around, Vivian was so grateful for the sun on her face after having spent just a few hours in jail, she closed her eyes and hungrily lapped it up. Her mind turned to animals being trucked to slaughter, maybe glancing out a small hole in an unfamiliar, odious crowded metal contraption, and experiencing that little patch of blue sky, a bright spotlight of sun in the dead of winter. For many, this would be their first glimpse of the outside world. Was it scary to them, the light too blinding? Did it look like heaven to them because their lives had been so constrained, so miserable? Did they feel hope, or did they want to return to where they'd been, what they knew? Vivian, lost in thought alone in the back seat, didn't immediately register when her mother, who was driving, turned to talk to her until she saw her mother's weary dark blue eyes locking on hers with an irritated expression.

"Vivian? What do you think about that?"

"Oh. I didn't hear you." She rolled up her window a little and leaned forward. "I'm sorry. What were you saying?"

"I was asking if you were hungry. Do you want to get something to eat?"

"Oh. I'm okay. I'd rather go home. I'll grab something there."

At home, things were quiet – Millie had been whisked to a neighbor when her father received the call from Center City Jail – and Vivian sat at the kitchen table, a sesame bagel growing cool in front of her, feeling the way she often felt growing up: that she was in a strange sort of museum that she understood to be her home. It had been a while since she felt that way. At times, though, her mother's meticulous housekeeping and her father's background in maintaining historic homes commingled with Vivian's frequent sense of displacement, making her feel like she was temporarily inhabiting a well-done exhibit of a family's home, one in which she was supposed to have lived at some point. Her father came out from his study and pulled up a chair across from her; her mother thought it best return to work that afternoon to put to rest any rumors.

"Honey, I talked with Mark," he said with a serious look on his face. Mark Fergusson was Mr. Sharpe's friend who was a lawyer with the leading environmental agency of their county. "He said that things are shaken up at Gordenner, indeed. Once you spoke at that press conference, word got out quickly. It's gotten federal attention, national attention. I mean, it's all pretty recent, but…" Mr. Sharpe paused awkwardly, waiting for Vivian to say something but she remained silent. Finally, she nodded, helping him to realize that she'd heard what he had said. He continued, "Apparently, he's working with Will right now..."

"Will got out of jail?" She felt a pang of guilt, just now realizing that she'd forgotten about Will being there as well.

"Yes. Not long after you, as I understand it. Wren's family – maybe just her and her mother, from what I gather – picked him up. Anyway, Mark is working with Will to get to the bottom of the underground pipe. He was heading out to Gordenner in a few minutes."

"Great."

He looked at Vivian quizzically. "I would expect more enthusiasm. Isn't this what you wanted?"

Vivian sighed. He was right: this was what she had been working toward but now that it was here, she just felt sluggish and depressed, not triumphant, not like she was expecting. "Yeah, this was what I wanted. But I'm tired. And confused. I feel a little weird, like…" she shrugged. Words weren't coming to her easily. "I don't know." She rested on her folded arms on the tabletop. "Kind of sad, I guess."

"Honey, I understand. But you started something and now you've got to follow through."

"Follow through how? What am I supposed to do now?"

"Well, there are reporters who want to talk to you." He took a folded note from his pocket. "Every few minutes while I was on the phone with Mark, another reporter called. Apparently the story about this teenaged girl who is taking on a giant in agribusiness is rather compelling from a news angle."

Vivian glanced at the note, written in her father's scrawling penmanship. She folded it back up on the table. "Dad, I don't know. This is…I don't know."

"Vivian, you know that there's not much I pressure you into, right? Well, this is one of those cases where I'll have to insist. If…"

"Insist?" she said incredulously.

"Yes, insist," he said kindly but with a definite conviction. "In order for you to get the word out, you need to talk to the media. You are the only one who can give voice to what you know. If you don't talk to the media, they will only talk to Gordenner. I can guarantee that."

Vivian nodded, her head on her hand.

"In order for you to give the best picture of what happened – and represent yourself the best way possible – you're going to need to follow up on this. I'm more than happy to be in the room with you when you talk to..."

Vivian's eyes began to sting. "I don't see how you can force me to do something against my will, Dad."

"So it's against your will to bring what you started with Gordenner to a proper closure? You'd rather just throw a bomb in the room and run away? Hit and run? That's not my daughter."

"Dad... I'm scared."

Mr. Sharpe rubbed his forehead, a pained expression on his face. "I know this is difficult, Vivian. But think of the greater effect you will have if you see things through."

"You're right," she said quietly. "You're right."

Neither one spoke until Vivian finally looked up from the table. "I think that I just need to lie down for a little bit. Is that okay? Like twenty minutes? I'll talk to them but I just need to rest first."

Her father smiled, unable to conceal his pride in her. "That's just fine. It's understandable."

She stood up a little too quickly and got a head rush, leaving her legs wobbly. She steadied herself against the chair.

"You okay, honey? Do you need any help?"

Vivian waved her father off, embarrassed. "I'm fine."

A LAST VISIT

Vivian shut the shades, and crawled into her bed like she remembered doing when she was sick or lonely as a child, the sheets pulled up close under the chin. Her forehead felt feverish, her whole body pulsed with warmth, but she didn't have a headache, didn't really feel ill. An image of Ms. Collins looking at her with eyes glaring jumped into her mind, and she cried, muffling her quiet sobs with a pillow, creating small rivers in the folds. Before long, she had the familiar sensation of entering a tunnel or descending into a mine and she was content that she would be asleep soon, her second nap of this long day.

In her dream, she first became aware of a sound: a robin singing. She was lying on the grass in her backyard, and she heard the song from up above her somewhere. She sat up and shielded her eyes; the robin, plump with a proud chestnut breast, hopped across the lawn a little closer to her. As Vivian inched her fingers through the grass (to touch him? to feed him? She was unsure) she saw something blurry in the corner of her eye: it was Billy, the squirrel who led her to the ducks, high up in the majestic oak tree, jumping from branch to branch with the grace of a fearless acrobat, his tail twitching, and she was certain that he knew her eyes were on him. Ducks flew overhead, quacking, a mother with two babies not far behind, and Vivian felt a sense of peace and freedom settle deep within her, rooting her to the earth, while at the same time, she knew she could fly if she were so inclined.

Just as she was ready to try, she heard a low hum, coming from the sky. It seemed to be surrounding her. The tone went up the scale a little, down again, then back to the middle. It seemed to be coming from inside of her now, as well as outside; her body seemed to be imbued with it. Vivian felt as though she could be floating, she was so serene. As soon as she had that thought, she *was* floating on a gentle river, a light raft beneath her, and she lazily bumped and turned along with the current until she realized that she recognized where she was: the Kickashaunee River. She sat up and peered into the water and it was a clear, crystalline blue. Fish darted and swam in speckled, metallic packs, making the river seem more vibrant than Vivian had ever recalled. Finally, as she was skimming her hand through the cool water, the raft bumped to a stop. It was wedged in the side of the river, held in place by two giant roots on either side. She noticed a rope hanging down and she knew that this was hers to climb, so she did, up to the landing, and she walked through the bushes and roots until she saw Tolstoy in the meadow down the hill, with puppies running around him, jumping on the tall prairie grass, chasing dragonflies. Tolstoy looked up at Vivian and smiled, then spread his arms wide. The tone, which Vivian had stopped noticing, grew louder as his arms rose. Then, his arms now down at his side, he spoke: *Thank you*, his voice and the tone merging into one mesmerizing, complete sound.

Vivian felt an immediate and deep sense of anticipation as soon as she woke, and she bolted upright, scanning the room with eyes still adjusting to the light. Tolstoy was there, as he always was following a dream of him, floating by her desk as she had come to expect. He didn't appear much different than he had in the past, but because it was still daylight, Tolstoy was a little more transparent looking, a little more glinty in the light. Vivian was so happy to see him that for a few moments, she couldn't talk, she just wept. He remained where he was, a sweetly patient expression on his wide face.

"It's you," she finally choked out, her voice hoarse and dry. "It's finally you. I can't believe it. Finally."

"Finally," he concurred good-naturedly. "It must have seemed like a very long time to you."

"I was *in jail*, Tolstoy. Today. Me. Straight, boring as possible, never even been sent to the principal's office me. I was in a *police* car. I had *handcuffs* on me," she said, holding her wrists out dramatically. "I was cuffed, Tolstoy."

He nodded his head and said in an observational way, "I know. Jails are not a lot of fun, are they? It seemed a little like the Factory, but not as atrocious. The same basic concept, though."

"That makes sense."

Tolstoy exhaled, a long, slightly whistling breath. "But, my dear, you made it."

"Were you worried about me?"

He clicked his tongue in disbelief. "Not for a moment. Would I have approached you if I thought this was beyond your capabilities?"

Vivian smiled, a little embarrassed by her pride, but then she shrugged, accepting it. "I guess not."

"And this morning…" he started.

"I created quite a… hoopla, didn't I?"

"Oh yes," Tolstoy said, his eyes gleaming. "A hoopla, indeed. It was quite electrifying." He looked at the side of her bed.

Vivian read his thoughts. "Yes, Tolstoy, come closer. Come here." She patted the side of her bed.

"You know I like to be close to you when we are face-to-face."

"Of course," Vivian said, realizing that she was still under the covers. He floated over to her side. "So how did I do?"

Tolstoy smiled slyly, turning to look at her from the side. "How do you think you did?"

"I'm not exactly sure, but I think that I did a good job. I mean, reporters are calling and all that. That was one of the goals, right? I'm supposed to issue a statement or something pretty soon."

He nodded. "Now this is your real opportunity, Viv. The ball is truly rolling now. People want to hear what you have to say."

Vivian turned quiet. "I know that I should be happy – I feel like I should be celebrating or something – but for some reason I just feel sad about the whole thing. Depressed."

A thoughtful expression appeared on Tolstoy's face. "Depressed is kind of an interesting word, don't you think? *Depressed*. It's also the word used for pushing something in. We never feel that way where I live. Why do you feel pushed in?"

"I'm not sure, I mean, this was what I was working toward the whole time, right?"

"Does it feel anticlimactic? Like '*Now what?*'"

She considered this. "Sort of, but that's not all."

"What is it then?"

Vivian was silent for a few moments before she quietly said, "I guess I feel guilty."

"Why is that?"

Vivian shrugged.

Tolstoy looked at her in such a way that she knew he wasn't going to accept that.

"What, Tolstoy?" she said, throwing up her hands in irritation. "I don't know why I feel so bad. Is that so hard to understand?"

He absorbed this for a moment in a way that reminded Vivian of sucking on a hard candy, like he was trying to extract from what she said all that he could. "Vivian, you know that it doesn't make you a bad person to admit to what you feel less than great about. Humans seem to run and run and run from the things they can't face about themselves, but it's right there alongside them the whole time, breathing down their necks the whole time, affecting everything. You may as well face it so you can work with it."

Vivian didn't say anything, kept her eyes on the comforter she was kneading with her fingers.

"I'm in no hurry," he said gently, then turned to gaze out the window.

She didn't need much time. "I guess I feel terrible about Ms. Collins. She trusted me, Tolstoy, and I lied to her. How can I feel good about that? Lying? I'm not that kind of person."

Tolstoy was quiet for a while, contemplating her words. "Vivian, you are just going to have to find peace within yourself on this. There is nothing that I can say that would truly create this reconciliation with yourself. I could make you feel better for a moment by choosing the words you want to hear and saying them, but that would just be a temporary salve. This is between you and you," he said, thumping his chest. "You need to find the truth – the deep truth, not a superficial excuse – within yourself on this and accept whatever consequences."

"Like Ms. Collins hating me? Like the whole town thinking that I'm crazy?"

He nodded in the merest of ways. "If necessary. Every action has a consequence, as you know. People try to live their lives as if this were not so. It is a law of nature. So I don't think this is something you need to be scared of or anxious about: it's natural, pursuing this truth with yourself and accepting what arises. Remember that first night I was here, when you asked me if I were a ghost?

She nodded.

"Those who are running from their truth, they are the ghosts. You can only be partially present if you're hiding from something within you. The other part of you," he said, "is running in fear."

"Well, okay, then, I have a question, Tolstoy: how could I have been honest? Do you really think that I could have waltzed right into Gordenner, held out my hand and said, 'Hi! Nice to meet you. I'm Vivian Sharpe. I plan to infiltrate your company. Could I work with Ms. Collins, please?' I mean, honestly, do you think that I would have been offered a job there?"

Tolstoy chuckled, saying nothing.

"Well, then, what on earth was I supposed to do? I'm trying to find out what's going on with this horrible substance, and it seems to me the best place for me to be was inside. Everyone who knew counted on me to do it. Don't you agree?"

"I do."

"If I wasn't inside," she continued, "I wouldn't have been able to take over the press conference. I wouldn't have had their trust. But I had to lie to get it."

"And therein lies the rub," said Tolstoy. "You're likely not going to come to a reconciliation with yourself quickly because you need time to contemplate. In the meantime, you have created enormous good, I think, something that will reverberate throughout the community. You can't worry about the future right now: now is the time to keep putting one foot in front of the other, breathing, walking a path of integrity."

"But will people trust me, what I have to say?"

"Only time will tell. But I believe that people will understand your motivations once you've told your story."

"That I was visited by a pig from a different dimension after eating his remains – okay, I suddenly feel like throwing up – at a party?"

He chuckled again, which seemed odd to Vivian as he was the one consumed, but it also seemed in keeping with everything she'd come to expect from him. "Well, perhaps the public is not ready for the *whole* story yet, but…"

"I agree. No one is ready. Except Wren. If the world were made up of only people like Wren, I would have no problems."

"If the world were made up of only Wrens, *no one* would have any problems. But regarding whether people will trust you, you can't worry about that. As I said, one foot in front of the next," he said, miming with his front legs, "walking a path of integrity. You can't control how others will interpret that, but you *can* do your best."

For the first time, Vivian realized that her chest was warm again. She put her hand over her heart, and she remembered being in second grade, reciting the Pledge of Allegiance. Her skin felt warm to the touch. "You're right. I know you're right. How did you get to be so right all the time, Tolstoy?"

"I don't know if I am, but if so, it's merely one of the perks of the job," he said, winking.

"So where do I go from here? The statement and all that? The aftermath?"

Tolstoy smiled at her silently, a little nervously at first, then he spoke. "This is where I begin my departure."

Vivian scowled, suddenly anxious. "What do you mean *departure*? That sounds so final. You're coming back, right? I mean, this isn't over, is it, this thing with us working together?"

"Oh, no. It's not over. But my involvement in this particular assignment must conclude today."

Vivian felt her stomach drop, reaching out for him desperately like she could grab hold of him. "Why, Tolstoy? I still need your help."

"With what?"

She thought for a moment and said, "Well, for starters, I think that if I'm going to help bring this huge change about, I'm going to need a new name."

Tolstoy looked at her, his eyes curious, and saw that she was serious. "What's wrong with Vivian Sharpe? I like your name."

"Oh, it's okay I suppose, but it lacks a certain...zing." Vivian said. "A particular pizzazz."

"Well, what are you looking for in a name?"

"Something that describes who I am and what I do, but something simple, you know? Wait: you know about superheroes, right? What they do?"

"Would I be wrong in saying that they reach beyond the simply heroic to a level of accelerated heroism? They perform extraordinary feats?"

"That's not all, though. Superheroes have powers ordinary people don't, like they can fly or climb buildings or have X-ray vision."

Tolstoy nodded slowly. "How odd. Heh. Not really."

"Well, I'm just wondering, what's my superpower? Like, I would feel weird running around calling myself a superhero if I didn't at least have one special power all my own. Even just a simple one, like, I don't know, I could become invisible or something."

"Become invisible," Tolstoy repeated back without affectation. "Well, I don't think that you should do that one."

"It was just an example. Anyway, I'd want something unique. Like I could, I don't know, burrow into the ground or something, though I don't know why I'd want to do that. Sounds kind of gross. Oh, I know," she said brightly.

"What?"

"I could become like a chameleon and blend into my surroundings. That would be kind of neat and original. Like, 'Oh! I didn't notice you standing there while I was shredding these papers!'"

Tolstoy looked at her skeptically and shook his head. "The thing is, Viv, I think that you're already proving yourself to be a superhero with a special power. You don't need to become a chameleon."

"But what *do* I do?"

"You sense. You feel. You act. Isn't that enough?"

"But don't I need more? A little something extra. A little oomph? I just don't think people will be so impressed by my feelings."

Tolstoy laughed. "Is that what this is about? Impressing people?"

"Well, no," Vivian said, feeling a little embarrassed. "Of course not. But I've got to have people take me seriously as a superhero, right? If I had a superpower that just blew everyone away, that made them speechless, maybe they'd listen better to what I had to say."

Tolstoy pondered this for a moment, his head cocked on his shoulder. "Perhaps. But just as likely in that scenario, they'd be so dumbstruck by all the bells and whistles of your superpower, they wouldn't hear your words. And perhaps they'd think it was only possible for someone with your extraordinary abilities to make these changes. I think that you should strive to be the most like yourself as possible."

"Boring..." Vivian laughed. "People don't have the attention span for that."

Tolstoy continued, deep in thought. "It is an interesting proposition, Viv, really. Personally I think that the more subtle and discreet your abilities are, the more likely people will be able to hear what you have to say. I mean, if you're flying through the air and scaling buildings and disappearing, don't you think your message might be lost?"

Vivian burst out laughing. "Spoken as a reincarnated being who can materialize at will."

"Not to mention float. I can float, too."

Vivian covered her mouth, trying not to laugh too loud. "Yes, that too."

"Point taken," Tolstoy said, smiling at first, then looking thoughtful. "Perhaps something extreme is called for to be able to break through to people. We want people to take notice, and with so much competing for everyone's attention, will a simple, honest message be able to cut through all that?"

"And it all starts with a name."

"If you feel that you must, then, yes, I agree," Tolstoy said, forehead furrowed in thought.

"I'm kind of embarrassed to say this…"

"Just say it."

"V-Girl," Vivian shyly at first, then started laughing.

"V-Girl. I like it."

"I like it, too."

Tolstoy was silent for a few moments, then smiled at Vivian. "Well, V-Girl, you are entering a realm where only humans of this earth can dwell. This is not my place. This is not my realm. This is for you and the other humans now. This is your work."

"Well, then where are you going?" Vivian said, realizing before she said it that she would sound like an angry housewife again, but she couldn't stop herself.

"Back to my home," he said carefully. "I have other sorts of appointments I need to be present at, I've got so many things on my docket to learn and see and experience, which is very exciting, of course. Oh, and of course, I still get to see how things work themselves out here with this situation."

"So you're ditching me then."

"Ditching you?"

"Leaving. 'See ya later.' 'Catch you on the rebound.' 'Sayonara'."

Tolstoy looked nonplussed. "Well, I'll certainly be back. We've got a lot of work ahead."

Vivian caught sight of herself at the mirror over her vanity with her lower lip jutted out and her arms folded across her chest, like a child who couldn't get the toy she wanted. The absurdity of the situation struck her as suddenly very funny – being angry at this loopy pig spirit for leaving too soon and wanting to ask for more of a commitment from him – and she burst out laughing. Tolstoy looked at her quizzically at first, then laughed along with her heartily. They both laughed together, gales of laughter that continued long after she thought they would, the first big laugh Vivian had had in as long as she could remember. Finally, Vivian wiped her eyes and took two deep breaths to collect herself.

"So you're leaving…"

"I am. But I'll be back. You can be sure of that. And before I leave – well, it's kind of awkward because incarnates have physical expressions of feelings, hugs, pats, kisses – but it can't be the same between us because I'm…."

"Dead?"

"Dead? Oh, silly you," he laughed, dismissing the notion with a hoof. "I don't have the same means for expressing these feelings."

"I always have the warmth you gave me."

His face brightened. "Has that been helpful?"

She nodded. "I feel it now."

"You know what that is, right?"

"It's love," she said shyly.

"It's love," he nodded.

They looked at each other in silence until Vivian looked down, embarrassed with the intimacy. She hoped that she wasn't blushing.

"And I have a bit of you here with me, too," Tolstoy said, a front hoof on his chest. "That will tide me over until I see you again."

Vivian got choked up and swallowed hard, trying not to cry. "How soon?"

"As soon as possible."

"Well, what if I'm an old lady by then?"

"You won't be," he said simply.

"You promise?"

"You humans and your need for assurances," he laughed, then developed a serious expression when he noticed Vivian's solemn face. "I promise. You did good, kid."

"Thank you, Tolstoy. I think so, too." She looked up and put her hand on her heart. "I love you."

He lifted his hoof to his heart as well, keeping his eyes on Vivian as he began to fade away in ripples, a tender look on his face, one that made her cry. "I love you, too."

Vivian sat in her bed for a few moments and took a deep breath. She blew her nose and wiped her face. Then she stood up and opened her bedroom door.

"Dad?" she called out.

She heard the kitchen chair scrape against the kitchen floor and her father tell someone – perhaps someone on the phone – to hold on. "Yes, Vivian?"

"I'm ready to get to work."

THE CIRCUIT

The next few weeks were a blur for Vivian, reminiscent to her of a merry-go-round going a few speeds too fast, where she could see featureless faces as she passed for just a moment, but not make out features, hear voices as they spoke around her, but not distinguish the words, until the world around her finally blended into one spinning, whirling view that somehow did not leave her feeling queasy: this was her new world.

There were reporters calling from New Zealand to talk to over the phone, accents that were hard for her to understand (South African? Venezuelan?), oddly dissonant radio programs calling her live from Berkeley, news crews sent from New Dublin to Center City arriving to tape her for national news programs (riding her bike down the street, looking pensive as she sat on the Kickashaunee river bank) for supplemental footage. She tried to look "natural," as she was coached by the producer, and she tried to forget about the camera pointing at her a few feet away, but she felt awkward instead and hoped that her skin didn't turn bright pink as it often did when she felt embarrassed; Vivian was relieved when watching the final edited version on television that she did look natural somehow, her skin its familiar tone, and the footage they shot cut away easily to an interview.

Vivian was flown with her father to New York to be interviewed on the national daytime news program *This Morning*, and no sooner did she begin to adjust to the throngs of bodies on Madison Avenue quickly weaving between one another and somehow not colliding and the horns of the taxis constantly blaring then they were whisked off to another busy airport, which was buzzing with voices and babies crying and recorded announcements. Next they flew to yet another city, Los Angeles, to appear on *American Spotlight*, a legendary investigative news program that had been on television for thirty years.

Kurt Burroughs was a bulldog-faced man Vivian remembered from her earliest recollections of watching *American Spotlight* every

Friday evening with her father — one of the only programs he ever watched — and if she had been less sleep-deprived, she might have been more nervous about having him sitting there in person right across from her, her knees inches away from his knees, this man who made powerful executives run from him in fear and caused at least one former president to curse at him in a state of televised, apoplectic rage. As it was, though, Vivian was averaging about four hours of sleep a night, so seeing this renowned man with a mask of pancake make-up on struck her as grotesquely funny, and she felt very fortunate she didn't begin giggling uncontrollably in the middle of the interview. Instead, she found when she was almost fully drained, she could always dig into some inner reserve for what she needed in her interviews, managing to be, in turns, bright-eyed and engaged, solemn and circumspect. As she continued with the interviews, she found that she fell into a natural persona, one very close to her actual personality but boosted with a little self-assurance and maturity she hadn't had even a few months prior.

Vivian and her father fell into a comfortable rhythm and acceptance when they were traveling together, with her staying quiet and looking out windows to conserve her energy and Mr. Sharpe busying himself by keeping up-to-date with his reading. Occasionally, he would mutter "hmmph" to show interest, silently handing her an article in the *New York World Press* or *Calliope Magazine* and point a long tapered finger at a phrase or quotation he found particularly noteworthy for his daughter to see. Vivian was called a "teenaged crusader," a "breath of fresh air," a "naïf with a passion for animals," and a "Titian-haired firebrand." *New Youth Magazine* had Vivian on the cover, her arms folded across her chest in a stance of steely determination, and the words "Midwestern Messiah" as the headline. She barely recognized herself. Each time Vivian was confronted with her public image, as captured or manipulated or analyzed by a staggering array of media, she shook her head in amusement, finding it almost impossible to see herself in it.

Back home several weeks later, Vivian returned to find that Gordenner was on the defensive. She was labeled a liar, deceiving the very woman who eagerly took her under her wing. She was branded an opportunistic mudslinger. She was called heartless, a calculating, unscrupulous manipulator with a deceptively sweet exterior. Robert Fontaine himself was interviewed on *American Spotlight* and claimed that Vivian Sharpe would be personally responsible for the starvation of thousands, perhaps millions, in Southeast Asia. "Just because she and the other activists disapprove of Bountiful, as an entitled American who doesn't have to worry where her next meal is coming from, it doesn't mean that people should go to bed hungry at night," he told Kurt Burroughs. Mr. Burroughs squinted at him wordlessly, his trademark look, until Robert Fontaine, looking pale, ended the interview.

In Center City, no one at Gordenner would step forward and take responsibility for the underground pipe once it was determined that it did lead back to their factory. Mr. Fontaine claimed that it was there before his tenure at Gordenner and that he didn't even know of its existence until Vivian commandeered the press conference. All five prior living Gordenner presidents also claimed ignorance, though two workers did come forward and tell the press that they were on a team of eight who were instructed to dig the pipeline ditch six months after Mr. Fontaine was hired as president. No one else came forward, though, and any original documentation of communications from Mr. Fontaine's first year was lost to a recent computer virus. One of the two former Gordenner employees did produce an old memo from Mr. Fontaine issuing the directive to lay the pipeline in no uncertain terms, but his lawyer insisted that it was a doctored document, and his threats of a lawsuit made the two retreat into silence. Regardless, production on Bountiful was halted pending the completion of the investigations.

In Center City, Vivian was treated variously as both a celebrity and a pariah. She felt people staring at her, their eyes boring into her profile, whispering about her, unabashedly at times; people she had known since she was a child suddenly seemed unsure how to behave around her. They acted as though she were not quite human anymore, and although it made her feel self-conscious and irritable at first, she began to accept the role. Ironically, the degree of conspicuousness with which she was treated by most Center Citians gave her a little more distance, a little more of a private bubble around herself, something that she had been craving. Occasionally someone would break through the bubble to shake her hand and thank her or to berate her, like the man in the baseball cap on Main Street who sniped at her as he strode quickly past that she was a "good for nothing tree-hugger." After the first few times, these experiences no longer rattled her for the remainder of the day.

She was written about almost too many times for her to follow in *The Patriot*, which featured letters – about equally distributed in both camps – applauding or condemning her every day. The editorials in the local papers were, for the most part, impressed with her determination but equally critical of her methodology, generally seeming to reach a consensus that underground pipes of industrial by-product were undesirable, but that Gordenner created more good than harm, in terms of jobs, giving back to the Center City community and scientific innovations. Nationally and internationally, however, Vivian received much more of a consistently positive response, and she was called a folk hero and hope for the future.

After she returned from Los Angeles, Mrs. Sharpe had swiftly moved from wishing *the whole business*, as she called it, would go away, to an attitude of acceptance and even open excitement about it. She lost a few clients at *Look Sharpe!*, but acquired more. Business appeared to be better than ever, and the "old biddies and busy-bodies" who left were not the sort of core market she was trying to attract anyway, she said. As such, she figured there was no personal harm done, and when a big publishing house in Manhattan called to discuss the possibility of a book contract with her daughter, she couldn't help but see that Vivian's willful deception of her and Mr. Sharpe as well as key staffers of Gordenner could prove to be very lucrative. Most significantly, Sally Sharpe was no longer worried about Vivian's future: she was convinced that this modest little daughter of hers would *be something* one day, and that thought alone made her chest swell with pride.

The first time Vivian saw Wren after the night they broke into Gordenner was weeks later, when they decided to meet for a picnic – Wren was astonished that Vivian had never been to one – at Capital Park, not far from the Kickashaunee River where Vivian discovered the ducks on that day that seemed so very long ago. Wren insisted on bringing the lunch for them both if Vivian would bring the blanket. It had been a long time since they'd spent time together: even though the embargo on their communication had been lifted for a while, the conversations were stilted and rushed little moments on the phone, awkward and uncomfortable to both. She and Wren planned to meet by the giant elm tree, which was on the biggest hill in Center City (referred to as a mountain by the children of this decidedly horizontal town) near the middle of the park. The hill, which was known to Wren and her family as the

Fairy Mound, allowed a sweeping panoramic view of Capital Park and almost made this place seem like a majestic setting, as if it were in Switzerland or Bali or anywhere but Center City.

On the phone, Wren and Vivian had both been a little hesitant and prickly with one another, clearly trying to negotiate their friendship after all that had happened over the previous couple of weeks. Vivian seemed distant, Wren said, to which Vivian replied that Wren seemed different. Neither said anything for a few moments after that; when she did speak again, Vivian repeated their plans, knowing that when she saw Wren face-to-face, the wall of awkwardness that had come between them would crumble away. They would meet Saturday at noon on the Fairy Mound.

Vivian was the first to arrive, and as she left her bike at the bottom of the hill, she was grateful to have a few minutes to herself first. She laid the blanket out and, lying on her back, looked up at the sky, watching the clouds slowly pass, and she saw a flock of ducks in sharp relief flying past a cloud, their wings muscularly flapping, their bodies solid and sturdy against the wispy white. She wondered if one or more might be from the family she discovered, and she considered this for a few moments before her eyelids started to flutter and she drifted to sleep. More than anything, Vivian was what her father called "bone-weary" after these last few weeks, and as it became more evident that sleep would certainly be there for her if she would seek it, she gratefully succumbed to it. She dreamed of nothing, just felt the breeze and sun on her cheekbones and chest, and the sounds – of bees, of children shouting in the distance, of the distant river – washed around her like a warm tide.

Finally, she heard some rustling and she bolted upright to see Wren kneeling with her back to Vivian and unpacking her wicker picnic basket, her hair a force of nature, springing up in a halo of electric curls behind her purple scarf. At first glance, she looked like a goddess to Vivian, a benevolent Medusa, or an oil painting come to life, but as her eyes adjusted, Wren became more human. Wren was absorbed in unpacking her containers for a few more moments, humming to herself as she kneeled, when she noticed Vivian, sitting up now.

"Oh," she gasped, letting a container slip out of her hands, then she laughed. "You scared me. I didn't know you were awake."

"I wasn't," Vivian said, rubbing her eyes. "I am now."

"Sorry if I woke you."

"Oh, no. I needed to get up."

Wren smiled. "Yes, you did, unless I was to have a picnic by myself next to your sleeping body."

"And that wouldn't make much sense."

"Not much sense at all." She scrutinized Vivian's face for a moment. "You look tired."

"Thank you."

"No, I mean..."

"I know. I look tired because I *am* tired. Nice little cause-and-effect going on there."

Wren looked up at the sky, her expression a little defeated, then back to Vivian. "So maybe we should have rescheduled. Like after you got more rest or something. I hope you didn't feel pressured to meet me. You know, like, obligated."

"Heck, no. I wanted to be here."

"Good," Wren said, still unpacking, now slower.

After a minute of silence, Vivian said, "It's a beautiful day, isn't it?"

Wren barely acknowledged what she said, just shrugged her shoulders without looking up. "I suppose so."

"Wouldn't it be nice if it was always like this?"

Wren didn't respond, but Vivian thought she heard a sniffle.

"Is something the matter?"

Wren threw herself and her plates down on the ground so violently Vivian jumped back; Wren's eyes were wet and blazing. "Yes, something's the matter. We don't make small talk," she said, pointing back and forth between them, her words tumbling out in one breathless sentence. "We don't talk about the weather. I'm sorry. That's for the boring people."

"I didn't know you felt so strongly about the weather. I won't bring it up again."

"It's not that; it's just that I miss how we are. Were. I miss...us."

Vivian picked some grass, rubbed it between her fingers. She quietly said, "I do, too."

"So what do we do?"

"I think," Vivian said, "we just need to ignore all that other stuff that's been going on –"

"Like being on the covers of magazines?"

"– and focus on what we had before all that."

"And on the news? And the film crews following you around? I saw that in the paper, too."

Vivian became defensive. "I can't really help that. Am I supposed to not follow through? I hope you don't think I'm feeling like Miss Big Shot all of the..."

"No. I don't. It's just that it's a little phony to ignore all that other stuff."

"Why? When we first met, we didn't have any of that, so I think that we should just carry on as we were, before the three-ring circus came to town."

"Do you really think that's possible?'

Vivian paused for a moment to think, than responded assertively. "Yes, I do, if that's what we want. You've always been the believer, Wren, I'm the doubter. Yes, it's possible to ignore it."

Wren smiled a little. "I don't know if I can, but I'll try. I guess, if I can just put it out there, I've been feeling like you don't need me anymore. And I don't want to be another, you know, burden on your time."

"A burden on my time? How is that possible? I love spending time with you."

"Well, I know you used to," Wren said simply. "I just don't know if you've changed."

"Of course I've changed. So have you, right?"

Wren thought for a moment. "I suppose so,"

"I mean, I guess the thing is that we change together."

"Harmoniously."

"For the better."

"But how do we do that? Guarantee that we change in ways that are harmonious?"

Vivian shook her head, looking back down at the grass. Neither one said anything. After a few moments, Wren said, "I guess this is what we do: talk."

"Talking is good."

"And, oh," Wren said animatedly, "we need to *value* one another. If we don't value one another, what's the good in talking?"

"Hmm. You know what Tolstoy would say?"

Wren shook her head. "What?"

"Well, first he'd laugh at how silly this whole notion is, the two of us trying to figure out how to deal with this and then he'd say something kind of vague and I'd try to get him to be more specific and he'd challenge me to, like, answer the question myself, and I'd get all mad, but the thing is that I'd have had the answer all along. And so do you."

"So, what is the answer?" Wren asked. "How do we do this friendship thing with everything else that's going on?"

"Now is when Tolstoy would look at me like I should get the answer myself. So I'll ask you, just as Tolstoy would ask me: what's the answer?'

Wren smiled, then got teary. She looked up at the sky as she wiped her eyes. "We have to love each other."

Vivian nodded.

"I guess that was all I needed to hear," Wren said shyly. "And that there's still a place for me in your life."

"A place for you? Wren, I need you more than ever. I mean, I'm still going back to Center City High next year. I'm not going to Redheaded Whistleblowers School. I still need to face everyone else, and you know, like, ninety percent or more are of the jerk persuasion..."

"That low, huh? Just ninety percent?"

"Okay, I'm feeling generous. It's probably more like ninety-three percent."

"And the remaining seven to ten percent are totally boring to the point of..." Wren flung her hands up to the clouds, searching for an elusive word. Then she rolled her eyes and fell onto the grass, pretending to fall asleep from sheer boredom.

"Exactly. So that's what awaits us in the fall. And it's not like any of them are exactly ringing my phone off the hook to get some of my time, anyway. I'm fully expecting they'll be meaner than ever next year."

Wren sat back up. "They're ripening as we speak, like mean little turnips."

"You are so right."

"It'd be foolish to expect otherwise of them."

"And I'm many things, but I'm no fool," Vivian said, pointing an index finger with mock sincerity.

"And you could always use a friend," Wren said.

"And you could use one as well. We're in the same boat, girl. We need one another. And who knows? Maybe one them will see the error of their ways and join our side."

"Come toward the light," Wren said. "Step away from the darkness."

"And embrace the dork-ness." They squealed with laughter. "Like that will happen. But we'll have each other."

"And any foreign exchange students who cannot deal with this stupid town."

Vivian laughed. "I have to say, Wren, that's a nice thought, but I don't recall exchange students *ever* in Center City."

"Couldn't we just, like, get rid of two hundred of our worst – like the meanest, most petty and mindless – and send them off to, say, two hundred different countries..."

"Share the love around the globe a little instead of sending them all to one place? Two hundred points of light."

"...Exactly, and we get one of each of theirs in exchange. Is that so radical?"

"I don't think so," Vivian said, "but it might not improve our global image much, exporting these fine representatives of North American culture."

"That's true. At the very worst, it could instigate a war or something. A lot of these countries are just getting over, like, dictatorships and massive droughts and poverty, and then to send them one of our jerks..."

"That would just be cruel. So I think that we can handle it, right? Just two more years and we're done with all this nonsense."

"And next year, we'll be juniors, so we'll have a little more, you know, status."

Vivian just looked at Wren and they both broke out laughing. "Um, yeah. Right."

"See," Wren said, her eyes shining. "This is what I'm talking about. So we're friends again?"

"We never weren't," Vivian said, squeezing her friend's hand. "Thank goodness for us."

Wren squeezed back. "Yes, thank goodness." She reached for a container. "Falafel?"

The interest in Vivian and her role in nearly bringing a corporation to its knees continued, but it did begin to wane slightly but noticeably. Finally, one bright morning was the first time in three weeks her father was able to eat breakfast and read the paper without interruption. Vivian was grateful for this, and her family embraced getting back to "business as usual" as Mrs. Sharpe phrased it, though her father continued to stay awake long hours, researching any references he could find to Gordenner since its inception. They were still getting phone calls throughout the day and still fielding interview requests, but it was becoming more manageable and required fewer superhuman feats of organizational prowess and endurance. This gave Vivian a chance to catch up with the aftermath of what was happening at Gordenner.

According to *The Patriot*, Robert Fontaine had yet to be formally charged for his role in building the underground pipeline, but, according to Mr. Sharpe's friend at the Good Earth County environmental agency, it was just a matter of time before he would be charged. They were slowly unraveling a paper trail, and it was leading back to Mr. Fontaine. When it came to lying under oath, Mr. Fergusson told Vivian's father, taciturn people became much more willing to talk. Kevin Newell was not in much of a better position than his boss, and it was thought that it wouldn't take much for him to accept a plea bargain and cooperate with investigators.

On a drizzly Saturday morning, her parents were at work and Millie was home with Vivian. They were each busy at the kitchen table, Vivian leafing through the binder of news clippings her father had recently organized, and Millie painting a picture of a house and yard, when the doorbell rang. Millie jumped up, but Vivian beat her to the door. Looking through the peephole, she was surprised and excited to see Kyle on the other side of the door.

"Who is it?" Millie asked, grabbing the doorknob.

"Kyle," Vivian said, her hand over Millie's, swinging the door wide open. Kyle took a step back, as though he was not expecting that she would be there. He was holding a paper bag with the top folded over. "Hi, Kyle," Vivian said warmly. "I haven't seen you in forever."

Kyle smiled a little wanly, shifting his weight, as he looked down at the bag in his hands. He was wearing shorts and sandals, something it took Vivian a moment to adjust to seeing instead of his office clothes. "I, uh, brought you your stuff," he said, holding the bag out front.

Of course, Vivian thought to herself, of course this is awkward for him – while, in her mind, it was just like she was being reunited with a friend, as though all the drama of the past few weeks hadn't occurred. She found herself embarrassed suddenly, regretting her impulsive display of affection, not sure what to say. Before she had any time to linger on it much longer, she took the bag from his outstretched hand and Millie started shrieking.

"I know you! You're the handsome man. You drove Vivi home that night that my mommy got all upset."

"Millie," Vivian said a little more sharply than she'd meant, "could you go inside?"

Millie skipped out of the house, totally disregarding her sister, and stared up at Kyle. "You look like a movie star. Or a Ken doll."

"Millie…" Vivian said, her face hot, and she was certain it was bright pink as well. "Stop it. Now. Leave Kyle alone."

"Oh, it's okay," he laughed, brushing it off with a wave of his hand. "It's better than being called an ogre or something."

"What's an ogre? That's like a monster, right?" Millie said, still staring at him. "Like a troll. They're not real anyway. You're not that."

"Why, thank you," he said. He looked at Vivian and winked, making eye contact for the first time.

"Millie, really, this is grown-up time. Could you go inside? Or how about you play in the yard? I need to talk to Kyle alone."

Millie crossed her arms, her eyes finally turning away from Kyle and flashing at Vivian. "You're not a grown-up. You're a teenager."

"I don't care, Millie. I'm your babysitter."

"So?" Millie said defiantly, her feet firm on the wooden front porch. "You can't make me."

"Kyle," Vivian said, looking at him, "excuse me for a moment while I get the phone. You want me to call Mom, I suppo - "

"Fine," she said, her arms still crossed as she stomped down the steps, huffing. "But I don't like it and you're *not* a grownup."

"Whatever you say, Millie."

Millie muttered something inaudibly and grabbed a Hula Hoop by the side of the house, started rolling it down the driveway with a stick.

"So…" Kyle said, glancing at the bag, "That's just your stuff from the office. It should all be there."

"Thanks. I'd forgotten about that." Vivian couldn't have cared less.

"Sorry it took so long. Things have been a little…" he searched for a word.

"Chaotic?"

"Chaotic," he nodded and they both laughed a little uncomfortably. "I guess it was packed up in a box somewhere and it found its way to my desk…" he trailed off.

Vivian walked out of the doorway and sat on the top of the wide porch steps. "Sit with me for
a minute," she said. Then a little embarrassed by her show of boldness, until she softened it with, "okay?"

Kyle seemed grateful as he sat down on the step next to her; Vivian was relieved that he didn't refuse.

"So, I hope you don't think that I'm a bad person," she said, looking up at the sky, trying to sound nonchalant. "You know, with the whole thing. It's so weird…"

Kyle looked pained momentarily, as if he were not quite ready to talk about things, but then his face became neutral again. He scratched his leg. "It's hard to talk about, everything that happened."

She nodded. "I know."

"There were a lot of people who trusted you, Vivian. Myself included. Everything that happened," he looked over at Millie, now poking her stick in a puddle by the sidewalk, "It was pretty shocking."

"For everyone."

"But weren't you planning this all along? How could it have been shocking to you? I mean, the rest of us…"

Vivian scratched at some peeling white paint on the step with her thumb. "I wasn't really planning this. I didn't know what to expect or what was going to happen. But, it's weird. I can't expect you to understand. I barely do myself."

Kyle rubbed his chin on his shoulder and neither said anything for a minute. Finally, he said, "I guess I don't know the whole story. What I understand is that you made a… discovery… out behind the plant…"

"I did."

"… and that drove you to take a job with Gordenner. From there, it gets kind of sketchy up until the big press conference debacle, but I understand that there was some stealing of confidential materials."

She nodded. "That's right. But I had to, Kyle. Listen," Vivian said, turning to face him, "I know you don't really know me, but the thing is, I'm the most honest person in the world normally. You can ask anyone who knows me well. I wouldn't have done any of this if I didn't feel that I *had* to. I just had to do something."

Kyle was quiet, obviously thinking about what she said. "I can accept that," he said neutrally, his eyes watching a cloud.

Again, they fell into silence for a few moments, then Vivian spoke. "So, Ms. Collins. She must really hate me, huh?"

"We don't talk about that sort of thing."

"No?"

He shook his head. "Besides, she's leaving."

Vivian gasped, genuinely surprised. "Really? She's leaving?"

Kyle scanned the sidewalk. "I'm not supposed to be talking about any of this. It's going to be announced Monday, though. She's going back to New Dublin."

"Wow."

"She's taking some time off to figure out next steps, I think, but she never really liked it here. The only thing for her here was Bountiful, and, well…" his voice trailed off again.

"So she's not in trouble or anything?" Vivian could barely hide her relief at hearing this.

"I don't think so," he shook his head. "The investigators feel pretty certain that she didn't have much of a role in what they're looking into. She's free to go."

"That's good."

"You did Laura a favor, really, before she got too deeply into things. She's going to be subpoenaed, though. Probably will need to incriminate the others."

"And the others?"

Kyle grinned from one side of his mouth, a deep dimple appearing like a comma on his cheek. "I am not supposed to be talking about any of this, Vivian." He lowered his voice, his eyes on Millie. "It looks like Fontaine and Newell are going to be charged. It should happen next week, from what I hear."

"So what's going to happen to Gordenner?"

"No one knows," he shrugged, laughing. "My money's on a whole bunch of more board meetings and investigators swooping around."

"It's not going to close down, though, right?"

"No, no, I don't think so. They'll probably announce a new president, I'd guess, but first they have to sort out if Mr. Fontaine is resigning or being fired. But Bountiful is 'on indefinite hiatus', as they say."

Vivian took a deep breath. "That's a relief."

Kyle rubbed his hands over his legs, shaking off imaginary crumbs. "Yeah, my guess is that chapter is closed for good, I think.

Too much bad publicity now. " He added nonchalantly, "I don't imagine I'll be there much longer myself."

"Really? I hope you're not leaving town."

"Oh, no. I love the house too much. Not ready to say goodbye to it. But I'm thinking about the long term."

"Really?"

He nodded. "I think we talked about the interior design stuff, right? I'm dabbling into it a little more, helping some friends with a remodel. So that's exciting."

"Very cool, Kyle."

"So, like I said, just dabbling, but it's something. I'm enjoying it a lot, though."

"You've got to do what you love, right?"

"You know," he smiled as he stood, smoothing his pants, "in your own way, I think you taught me that. Follow what you love. Anyway…" he said, now sounding awkward.

"You're probably busy," Vivian said, standing.

"I'm on my way to the hardware store; got to look at some paint," he said, standing, "and be home in an hour for a delivery."

"It was so good to see you, Kyle."

"And you."

"So you don't think I'm evil anymore?"

"Never did," he smiled.

"Are you leaving now?" Millie called from the lawn, her hips shaking with the hoop spinning around, her arms straight up in the air.

He smiled. "Yep." Kyle turned back to Vivian. "Well…" He offered a hand and Vivian hugged him instead. He smelled like aftershave. "Stay safe," he said quietly.

"I will."

As soon as he started down the steps, Millie ran over to him and resumed talking as if nothing had happened. They walked to his car together. "Are you from here? What's your middle name? Mine is Suzanne. Do you know how to spell that? S-U -Z-A-N-N-E. There's a girl named Susan in my class. Know how to spell her name? S-U-S-A-N. Mine name has a 'z' and her name has an 's' in the middle − isn't that funny? Mine is the French version. How tall are you…?" Kyle tried his best to answer her questions, but as soon as he'd start talking, she'd ask another one.

They stood in front of his car, her asking what his favorite color was and if he knew how to ride a bike, when Vivian called out to her. "Millie, Kyle has to go now. You want to make a snack? A Popsicle?"

Millie whipped her head toward Vivian mid-sentence. "Do we have lime still?"

"I don't know. Maybe. Let's go see."

Just as suddenly, Millie skipped away from Kyle, down the sidewalk back to the house. Vivian smiled at him and they both waved.

Millie ran ahead to go wash her hands when Vivian saw something move from the corner of her eye, a flash of red. It was a cardinal, plump and bright, sitting near the bushes below their front porch, his body turned toward her.

"Hello, pretty bird," she said, and then she realized that he was there for a reason, that he had something for her. He was sitting on something grey, and he fluttered away singing as Vivian started down toward where he was. It was a small envelope on the ground, and as she got closer, she saw her name typed across the front, the last name misspelled.

She tore the envelope open, her heart racing. She could hear Millie in the kitchen, pulling a chair across the floor to reach the freezer. She closed her eyes briefly as she unfolded the page inside, a simple white sheet of Gordenner stationary, and she saw a familiar scribble of a cat and a few words. She took a deep breath and heard the freezer door shut.

Vivian, it read, *in case you were wondering, this is just the beginning.*

Vivian stared at the paper for a few moments longer, then refolded it, stuffed it back in its envelope and into her pocket. A neighbor from across the street nodded and waved to her as she swept her front sidewalk, saying something about Vivian looking good on the news earlier in the week. Vivian was only vaguely aware of what she was referring to, but she thanked her and turned back to her house, where she unwrapped a Popsicle and joined Millie at the kitchen table.

"Life is interesting, isn't it?"

Millie looked up, her mouth ringed in bright green juice, little brown eyebrows knit. "Huh? What are you talking about?"

Vivian smiled at her sister, took a bite, and savored the juice as the ice melted down her throat, which suddenly felt dry. "Nothing in particular, Millie. It's just interesting."

ABOUT THE AUTHOR

Marla Rose is a writer, activist and community builder actively involved in Chicago's flourishing vegan movement. In 1998, she and her husband created the pioneering vegan web magazine, *Vegan Street*. In 1999, at the request of the "Mad Cowboy" Howard Lyman, Marla co-founded and headed the Chicago chapter of EarthSave International, eventually producing an annual event called *The Conference for Conscious Living* that drew dozens of vegan leaders to Chicago over the next decade. This event ultimately grew into the innovative and popular festival, *Chicago VeganMania*, which has drawn thousands over the last three years. Meanwhile, Marla co-founded the Chicago Vegan Family Network, which has grown into a group of dozens of families all raising vegan children. In 2009, Marla and her husband were recognized by Mercy For Animals as Activists of the Year.

In 2004, Marla published her first book, *Marla's Vegan Guide to Chicago and the Universe*. Soon after, she began her blog, *Vegan Feminist Agitator*. She is a freelance feature writer and has had her work featured in *VegNews* magazine, *One Green Planet* and the *Advocacy for Animals* blog for *Encyclopaedia Britannica*, and she has an essay published in the collection, *This I Believe: On Motherhood*, which was published in May, 2012 . She also maintains two different columns for *Examiner.com*. Marla's work has been reprinted in the *Utne Reader*, and in 2010, she was nominated for a prestigious Maggie Award for best feature story.

The Adventures of Vivian Sharpe, Vegan Superhero
is Marla's first novel.

Follow the Adventures of Marla Rose at **marlarose.com**

Follow *The Adventures of Vivian Sharpe, Vegan Superhero*
at **viviansharpe.com**

Made in the USA
Middletown, DE
23 December 2018